Escape from Smyrna

An Historical Mystery Novel

Escape from Smyrna

An Historical Mystery Novel

Charles Gates

**TOP HAT
BOOKS**

Winchester, UK
Washington, USA

First published by Top Hat Books, 2013
Top Hat Books is an imprint of John Hunt Publishing Ltd., Laurel House, Station Approach,
Alresford, Hants, SO24 9JH, UK
office1@jhpbooks.net
www.johnhuntpublishing.com

For distributor details and how to order please visit the 'Ordering' section on our website.

Text copyright: Charles Gates 2012

ISBN: 978 1 78099 849 7

A CIP catalogue record for this book is available from the British Library.

Design: Stuart Davies

Printed and bound by CPI Group (UK) Ltd, Croydon, CR0 4YY

We operate a distinctive and ethical publishing philosophy in all
areas of our business, from our global network of authors to
production and worldwide distribution.

For

Laurel Goldman

PART ONE

Prologue

November, 1522. The Island of Rhodes.

Yusuf had discovered a small clearing concealed among the trees, a ledge accessible only from the steep wooded slopes of the butte. This was his secret retreat, and he came as often as he could to get away from the madness. He liked to gaze out over the wild undergrowth of grasses and prickly weeds toward the plowed fields along the seacoast below. He stroked his beard with bony, calloused fingers, listening to the birds and the cicadas, inhaling the rich odor of the damp earth. It calmed him, sitting by himself among the trees. It gave him strength to return to the interminable battle.

Yusuf and the other Ottoman soldiers were desperate to get home before the late autumn rains turned the roads to mud, but the Christian knights were not yielding to the Ottoman siege. The thick walls of Rhodes held firm. Still Suleyman, the young sultan, was determined to seize this fortress, the prize that had escaped even his mighty great-grandfather, the conqueror Mehmet.

One day in November, on the way to his clearing, Yusuf heard footsteps. He hid himself well above the sheep trail. A burly man with a sack over his shoulder pushed his way through the scrub pines toward Yusuf's secret place. A Greek Christian farmer, Yusuf thought, with those baggy black pants and the jacket of stiffened sheepskin. He had never seen another human being out here, only stray sheep and goats. Why had the man come to this remote spot? What could be in the sack? He would follow him. But it wouldn't do to get too close. Yusuf was nimble, but he was skin and bones. The farmer could pound him to a bloody pulp. Yusuf touched the amulets he wore around his neck and set out after the man, tracking him as silently as possible. When they reached the ledge, Yusuf hid flat on the ground behind some low bushes. The man was digging a hole with a small pickaxe. Beside him lay his sack and, on top of it, a small metal box.

The farmer looked around. He had a bushy black beard and rough red cheeks. When he turned, Yusuf saw he had a bad eye, the lid twisted and nearly shut. He prayed the man wouldn't spot him.

The farmer picked up the box and opened it. Yusuf strained to see what was inside, but the man quickly snapped the box shut and placed it in the hole. After shoving back the dirt, he tamped it down with his boot, swept the area with a pine branch, and strewed pebbles over it.

A crow alighted on a tree at the edge of the precipice. As soon as it saw the farmer, it cawed and flew off.

The damp and cold rising from the earth penetrated Yusuf's bones, but he lay still even after the man left. His mind was racing. A treasure lay in that box. That was the only possible explanation. Why else would the farmer bring it way up here? Why else did he keep looking around so anxiously, like a bear guarding a freshly killed carcass? Gold, silver, so close! He would get up now and find out. No! The man might be waiting nearby.

With the treasure in that box everything could be his, all that he wished for each time he came to this ledge and looked down at the farmlands on the seacoast. Plowed fields, tall wheat, a house by a poplar-lined stream.

The afternoon was passing. He got up on one knee. All was still. Even the cicadas had fallen silent. He ran to the place where the box lay buried and loosened the moist, gritty soil with his dagger, scooping it out with his free hand. Soon he felt the top of the box. He dug around the sides, stabbing in deep with his dagger, then twisting. Please God, let it be gold. Heavy, solid, thick gold.

At last he freed the box from the soil and pulled it out. He opened the catch and lifted the lid. Inside lay a golden necklace of oval lockets and a larger gold star. God be praised! It was the most beautiful thing he had ever seen. He picked it up with his rough, dirt-stained fingers, kissed it, and held it in the sunlight to see the gold and jewels gleam and sparkle. Tears came to his eyes. "God is great. Truly, God is great!"

He draped the necklace over his fingers. Each of the four lockets was decorated with a deep green stone surrounded by tiny red ones, all set in flower-shaped gold mountings. Each locket had writing on it, as did the star-shaped plaque. Although he couldn't read, he recognized the Arabic script.

He tried to open one of the lockets, but it was sealed.

Touching the necklace to his lips one last time, he slipped it into his thick sash, dropped the box back into the hole, and began to kick dirt over it.

Suddenly he heard steps. He whipped around. The one-eyed farmer brandished his pickaxe. "Come on, let's have it."

"You're speaking Turkish," Yusuf blurted out, astonished.

The farmer threw out his chest ever so slightly. "I marched with the Sultan Selim from Istanbul to Jerusalem!"

"How could you? Christians aren't soldiers."

"I became a Muslim. At least I pretended to. But I got my reward." The farmer gestured with his axe at the necklace in Yusuf's sash. "Relics from the Holy Places. Jerusalem. Mecca and Medina."

"Muslim relics?" Yusuf was only half listening, waiting for his chance.

"Muslim or Christian, it doesn't matter. When I had the fever, they kept me alive."

"You could have sold them. You could have bought land."

"More land?" The farmer sneered. "That's what my brother wants. That's why I have to hide them." He raised his axe and stepped forward. His good eye burned.

Yusuf darted out of reach. But he was cornered at the edge of the bluff. The farmer was going to kill him. He pulled the necklace out of his sash. "Let God decide!" he shouted, and flung the necklace into the air.

The farmer sprang forward. "You son of a whore!"

Yusuf drew his dagger from his sash. The farmer charged, his axe ready to strike. Grunting with rage, he hurled himself at Yusuf, but he slipped on a patch of gravel and lost his grip on his axe. He cried out when it fell to the ground and Yusuf kicked it to the brink of the clearing. The farmer rushed forward; just as he grabbed the axe, the earth gave way beneath his weight. He screamed, clawing for a hold. But there was nothing to support him, only crumbling soil and small clumps of grass.

Yusuf leaned over the edge of the cliff. He could see cactus and sharp rocks and shadows, but the farmer had vanished. Slowly Yusuf stood up. He heard a creaking noise.

Nothing. Only wind rushing through the pine trees, pushing their branches.

Yusuf touched the amulets around his neck. *He attacked me, and now he is dead. But I took his gold, like a thief. I caused him to die.*

He shivered. The frail light of the late autumn sun would shortly give way to cold darkness. In the distance, whitecaps formed patterns upon the sea. He pulled his thick cloak tight, but it could never keep him warm enough.

Where was the necklace of holy lockets? His eyes searched the valley for the flash of gold, but he could see nothing. The shadows were too deep.

He found his dagger and started back to camp. *I've lost the treasure,* he thought. *But it brought death. Let its bad luck fall on somebody else.*

* * *

Yusuf hadn't been able to get the necklace out of his mind. Maybe the relics were meant to be his. Two days later, when he could slip away from camp, he went further down the sloping hillside and made his way to the rocks below to search for the relics. He found the farmer, sprawled on his back in the shadow of two jagged boulders. Animals had ripped into him. His face was so torn no one could recognize him any more.

Yusuf felt sickness rise up inside him. He turned away just before his stomach emptied itself. He was crying as he wiped his mouth on his sleeve. Tears spilled out of his eyes for a man he didn't know, a man who had tried to murder him. God made him shed these tears; God wanted him to mourn this man. He, Yusuf, had provoked the blasphemous struggle over the holy relics. He bore the guilt for the farmer's death. He had to bury this man. This would be his atonement to God.

He crouched beside the body. The man's shirt was torn out of his trousers, exposing a hairy belly. Yusuf was suddenly curious. He glanced around to make sure no one was watching, then gently undid the drawstring and pulled down the man's pants. The farmer was circumcised. So he had told Yusuf the truth. He had converted to Islam. He had indeed been a Muslim soldier marching from Istanbul to Jerusalem in the Ottoman army. Now he could be given a proper Muslim burial.

Yusuf undressed the farmer and packed his clothes into a bundle to throw into a crevice on the other side of the hill. He wrapped the body with his own cloak, then headed back to find someone to help him carry the massive body of a martyred soldier savagely waylaid, robbed, stripped, and shoved over a cliff.

* * *

A month passed. On Christmas Day, the Knights of St. John finally surrendered to the sultan in exchange for a safe passage from the island. On the first day of the new year, the Knights left Rhodes, vowing to establish themselves elsewhere and resume their struggle against the nation of Islam.

Yusuf settled on Rhodes and was granted a generous tract of fertile land along the coast, not far from the bluff where he and the farmer had their fatal encounter. He married a young woman selected by his Anatolian kinsmen. The couple got along well; they had sons; the farm prospered.

Yusuf looked often for the necklace, but in vain. God was still angry with him. The Muslim burial had not been atonement enough.

When his eldest son was fourteen, Yusuf went on a three-day hunting trip into the hills. It had rained heavily, the first rain of the season, and the dried topsoil was pried loose and washed away. As Yusuf was heading home on the third day, his dog chased a rabbit into the woods. Yusuf found her pawing at a burrow. There by her feet, Yusuf saw gold. The necklace! He picked it out of the mud and kissed it. He could hardly believe it. Had God forgiven him at last?

When he returned home, his wife rushed out and clutched his arm. Their eldest son had fallen ill. He was tossing and turning, she said, crying out in delirium. Throughout the following days poultices were applied, herbal brews administered, and charms muttered, but the fever refused to release its grip. In despair, Yusuf made the long trip to town to seek out the grave of the farmer. He knelt down, and with one hand on the headstone of the tomb, the other on the necklace of holy relics hidden inside his sash, he prayed harder than he had ever prayed. He implored God to spare his son, swearing he would do whatever God wished to pay for the death of the farmer.

That evening his wife greeted him with tears of joy. "He's asking for you," she said. "The fever has gone!"

Yusuf hurried inside. As he held his boy close, he thanked God for his great mercy.

Soon after, a field hand recovered from a poisonous bite. Yusuf had ministered to the man, and he was credited with the cure.

A miracle, said some.

The right hand of God, said others.

The sick began to search him out.

Yusuf kept the necklace hidden in his house. It was far too precious to sell. Eventually he would show it to his eldest son, but until then, no one except Yusuf knew of its existence. Yusuf never told his son how the necklace came into his possession. The struggle with the farmer was a secret he would keep his entire life.

He continued to visit the tomb of the "martyred soldier," where he would sit quietly for a good length of time. At first this habit was considered curious. With the passing years, as Yusuf's fame as a healer increased, the people of the area came to believe that the grave belonged to a holy man, that here lay the source of Yusuf's gifts. The tomb became a shrine, a place of pilgrimage for the sick. Yusuf did not thwart this custom. On the contrary, he took a particular pleasure in it.

When he died at eighty-two, Yusuf was satisfied that he had done all in his power to eradicate the stain he had brought upon the necklace of holy relics. Whatever remained, he would answer for it to his Creator on the Day of Judgment.

Chapter I

Summer, 1982. Andros (Greece)

By mid-morning the ferry to Andros was well across the channel. It had not yet reached the island's protection, so the winds that blew in earnest across the open sea held the boat in a permanent list to starboard. Every now and then the wind let up and the ferry lurched into upright position. The passengers had to pick themselves out of the laps of their neighbors.

On the upper deck, in the sun, four university students occupied the ends of two benches. Their neighbors, two families of three generations each, knew immediately that the four students were foreigners. Not only were they not speaking Greek, but one man and one woman were blond and blue-eyed, the second man had fine dark brown hair and a reddish glow in his cheeks, and each of their backpacks was decorated with patches showing, as the little boy with glasses proudly whispered all around, the flag of Switzerland.

The little boy watched them closely. These were the first Swiss he had ever seen. He wanted to go to Switzerland some day. His aunt and uncle and two cousins and his uncle's parents, on the bench across from him, lived in Newark, New Jersey. America was far away and certainly exciting but it was familiar. Did these Swiss have any chocolate? The boy wondered how he might ask them.

The brown-haired man took a roll of toilet paper from his pack and went off. He had already done this several times in the two hours since the boat left Rafina. The little boy wondered what the man had eaten. Maybe too much fruit or too many ice-cold drinks.

The other Swiss man kept twisting his golden beard, just under the chin. He was trying to talk with the yellow-haired lady who lay with her head back, looking up to the sky, her eyes protected by big sunglasses. The fourth student, a dark-haired woman with a ponytail, wrote in a little notebook from time to time. She was adding and subtracting. When the brown-haired man returned from the toilet, he argued with her and she waved the little book at him and wrote in it some more.

The boat was approaching the island. Soon the wind would die down and before long they would step off onto the dock at Gavrion. The dark-haired Swiss woman with the ponytail stood up to get her things in order. Noticing the little boy watching her, she smiled at him and said something in a very nice tone. He smiled back and, without warning, the word "sokolata" slipped out of his mouth.

"Schokolade?" replied the woman. "Nein." She shook her head. "No chocolate."

"She says she doesn't have any chocolate," said the little boy's uncle, translating into Greek.

"Chocolate out here in the summer?" laughed the boy's father. He patted his son on the leg. "It would melt into a gooey mess."

The boy sat quietly. They were close to shore and he was excited to return home, but he thought he should sit quietly to show these Swiss that he could be calm and polite. He hoped they would have a nice time on Andros. He wondered which hotel they would stay in.

* * *

The bus to Korthi was filled. It was Sunday, and many of the passengers carried sacks and packages from stores in Athens. Korthi was across the island from Gavrion. It didn't seem far on the map, but Nicole realized that all these twists and turns across the high spine of the island meant a long, tedious trip. She hoped Hans-Ruedi's medicine would hold him until they reached Korthi and another toilet. Too bad they had to stand the whole way.

Far more serious, her reserve wad of drachmas had disappeared. When they went out to dinner the night before she had taken her little purse with her and set it on the ground next to the table leg. She took it back to the pension, but this morning, when she looked inside the purse, the money was gone.

"We almost missed the bus on account of you and Hans-Ruedi," said Annelies, the blonde student, "and now we have to stand."

"He's sick," Nicole said. "Why didn't you save us seats?"

"Hey!" Peter tried to calm the two women. "Take it easy."

Annelies pulled at her halter top and looked out the window.

Hans-Ruedi had turned quite pale. Nicole couldn't begin to calculate how much wine he'd drunk last night. They should have stayed an extra day in Athens. Hans-Ruedi could have slept and she could have strolled around and people-watched. But Peter had insisted: Sunday they were leaving for an island.

Hans-Ruedi saw Nicole's concern and smiled. The bus was descending. The seacoast and Korthi couldn't be far off.

* * *

The hills outside Korthi were rocky and barren. There were almost no trees. Flagstone slabs set on edge marked property divisions, but no one was around, no animals were grazing.

Annelies stopped to take a sip from her water bottle. She was wearing a white cotton sun hat, but even so, the sun was crushing her. At least they had eaten a good lunch in Korthi and the toilet was clean. And a swim lay ahead. Peter had found a nice beach on the map.

She wiped her face with her bandana. If only Peter weren't so demonic about seeing every sight in the book! Annelies enjoyed visiting ruins and museums, and she wanted to linger, to sit on a block of ancient marble in the shade of a great tree and listen for the footsteps of Themistocles and Pericles. But Peter always looked at his watch and pulled her away.

The others were way ahead of her, but she could still make out Nicole's ponytail, swinging back and forth. She took another sip, then stashed her canteen and started up.

* * *

The stars shone brightly, silver dust suspended in the endless black. A wind had come up; it sent the sea slapping against the rocky ledge where the students were forced to camp. Annelies sat by herself, her knees drawn up to her chin, her arms clasped around her legs. She let the warm wind whip through her thick blond hair, pulling it, snarling it. Nicole and Hans-Ruedi had laid out their sleeping bag, and Peter had already fallen asleep in the bag that he and Annelies normally shared.

Annelies had her own sleeping bag, though, and tonight she intended to use it for the first time. She was thinking of returning to Korthi tomorrow morning alone, even of going on to Athens. The way the others had laughed at her tonight! She had knocked over the bottle of red wine at supper, and Peter called her a clumsy cow. She shouted back at him, then Nicole told her to go to hell and Hans-Ruedi yelled "Calm down!" Then all of them, Peter included, made mooing noises at her. When she went off to sit by herself, they laughed, but she was hungry, so she let them persuade her to come back. She pretended to make peace.

Peter tried to joke with her, but she didn't respond. She could feel his hostility. Maybe he would realize how angry and hurt she felt. But he said little to her for the rest of the evening and rolled out their sleeping bag as usual, got into it as usual, and now was snoring away...as usual.

In Zurich, before they set out, she had watched the excitement in Peter's face when he described Greece and spoke of the places they would see. She felt his joy; she wanted to live it. She dreamed of communing with the sea and the flowering hillsides and wise antiquity. Peter would be her perfect guide.

Annelies turned to look at her sleeping companions. Spilt wine and mocking laughter and their money stolen...that's all it had been.

* * *

The early morning sun could not soften the starkness of the landscape...thistles, clumps of prickly pear, yellowing grasses, jagged rock, and, in the distance, a small white church on the headland opposite, framed by the pale sky. The students left as quickly as possible, continuing north, in the direction of the church. Peter had convinced them that today they would find a stretch of seashore blessed with a tiny crescent of clean, light gold sand, with blue water so clear you could see your feet even when you were in up to your shoulders. Behind the beach they would see a fertile valley rising into the mountains, oak trees and fig trees and tall pointed cypresses and hillsides covered with twisted grape vines or olive trees with silvery leaves. Even Annelies succumbed to the vision.

They walked up to the white chapel. An enormous rusting padlock protected the entrance. When they peered in through the dirty windows, they could barely distinguish the outlines of the ritual furnishings. It all seemed drab and forlorn.

They kept going. It was already much hotter than when they left the cove. Annelies stopped to take a sip of water, but her water bottle was empty. She had forgotten to fill it from the large bottle Hans-Ruedi carried. Anger rushed through her. So stupid. Now she would have to wait until they reached the beach. She couldn't ask the others for water.

An hour later they reached the edge of a bluff.

"Oh, Christ!" said Nicole. "There's nothing."

As far as they could see, the coast was rocky, covered with scrubby vegetation, and plunged straight into the sea.

Annelies felt drained and desolate.

"Is this a joke?" Nicole's voice was getting louder.

Hans-Ruedi was already inspecting the map. Peter dumped his pack on the ground, picked up a rock and, with a curse, hurled it out to sea.

"Can't you guys read a map?" Nicole shouted.

"The map shows a beach," Hans-Ruedi said. "Maybe it's just hidden."

Annelies asked Peter for some water. "We should just go back to the mainland," he said as he handed her his canteen.

"And waste this trip to Andros?" Annelies looked at him with scorn.

"Hey! Don't drink all my water!"

Annelies threw the canteen at Peter. "Take your damned water," she said. "I've had it. I'm going back to Korthi."

"Wait!" said Hans-Ruedi. "If we walk on just a bit farther..."

But Nicole and Peter were already hoisting on their packs. Neither showed the slightest interest in Hans-Ruedi, the map, or the putative beach.

* * *

The sun baked the island. Since morning the rocks and the prickers that infested the fields seemed to have multiplied a hundredfold.

Hans-Ruedi had to stop. He took his toilet paper and rushed into the field. Nicole waited for him. A blister had developed on her right heel and she needed to put a bandage over it.

Peter went on ahead, staying even with Annelies. He tried to talk to her.

Annelies refused to answer. He was responsible for this miserable trip. She walked on, even though her throat was as dry as a desert and she wanted desperately to ask him for more water.

* * *

Nicole and Hans-Ruedi found Annelies and Peter sitting in the shadow cast by the chapel. Annelies was scratching patterns in the soil with a sharp-edged rock while Peter tossed pebbles out into the sun, trying to sink them in a small animal hole.

"What a mistake," said Nicole. She took out some bread, a little cheese, their water, and offered them to Annelies and Peter. They refused. They've already eaten, Nicole thought. She unscrewed her water bottle and took a drink. It was OK with her if they didn't want any. Her water had almost vanished.

Hans-Ruedi and Nicole finished, and Nicole packed everything away. No one made a move to go, no one said anything. A lizard crept out into the sun. Peter spotted it, picked up a medium-sized rock, but the lizard was too quick. In an instant it had fled.

Peter tossed the rock up into the air with one hand and caught it with the other, then he turned toward the church and heaved the rock at it. The window of the church burst into a shower of glass splinters.

"Peter!" Annelies cried.

He ran to the window. "Hey!" he called. "You've got to see this."

Nicole, Hans-Ruedi, and Annelies crowded around him. They saw a screen at one end, covered with pictures of saints. On the far wall of the chapel, just to the right of the screen, an icon was surrounded by a mass of tarnished mementos. Some represented parts of the human body, hearts, hands, legs, breasts. Some were plaques or trinkets.

Thank offerings for cures, Annelies supposed.

"Do you think they're silver?" asked Nicole.

Annelies and Peter looked at each other.

"No!" Annelies was alarmed by what she saw in his eyes. "No, don't do it!"

Peter stepped back from the window. "We're just going to have a closer look." He smiled a boasting little smile.

"I'll find another rock," Hans-Ruedi said.

"Wait!"

Nicole placed a hand on Annelies's arm. "Maybe we'll get something out of this trip after all," she whispered.

"What if someone sees us?"

"There's not a soul in sight," Nicole said.

Hans-Ruedi pounded at the padlock with a large brown rock. Each strike seemed like an explosion to Annelies.

"There!" said Hans-Ruedi when the lower part of the ancient padlock popped off in a spray of fine dark red powder. "Come on!"

Peter, Hans-Ruedi, and Nicole entered the church. Annelies wanted to run off, to run away. But where could she run to? She slipped inside behind them.

Sunlight filtered through the thick layer of dust that coated the windows. A small oil lamp burned on the altar. The church was not deserted after all.

Their eyes still adapting to the dim light, they scanned the worn decorations of the church. An icon on the right wall drew them closer, an elongated, elegantly robed man with a long, pointed gray beard and a halo of gold, raising his hand in benediction. Among the tarnished silver body parts arrayed as offerings around this image, one small object caught their attention.

It was gold.

Peter pulled it off its nail and held it out in the palm of his hand. It was not a body part, but a gold locket, a flattened oval about the size of a small hen's egg, with a green stone set in one side, surrounded by red stones. An emerald? Rubies? Peter turned it over. They recognized Arabic script, but none of them could read the inscription.

"I wonder what this was given for?" said Peter. He seemed

moved, all of a sudden, to be holding in his hand something so small, so old, so precious.

"It's glowing," said Annelies. "It's so beautiful."

"Let's take it!" Nicole said.

Annelies stared at her.

A seagull cried, just outside.

Peter's fist closed around the locket.

"Come on," Hans-Ruedi said. "Let's get out of here!"

Outside there was no one, only the seagull flying away and the sun that struck them savagely. The students cringed alongside the walls of the church until their eyes readjusted to the light.

Peter hid the locket in his backpack, in a dense layer of dirty underwear. They lifted on their packs and set off, walking resolutely under the hot sun.

Left, right, left, right, Annelies chanted to herself as she walked. One, two, three, four. What for? Why, why? Why did I take part in this?

She stumbled but recovered her balance. She had to leave Peter. He was bringing out the worst in her. As soon as they set foot on the mainland, she would say good-bye.

* * *

When they reached Korthi, they made a beeline for a restaurant with chairs, shade, and ice cold beer. They smelled sausages grilling. Would the Gates of Paradise open for them after all? When the sausages, fried potatoes, and salads were at last served, they ate ravenously.

"I think we should return the locket," said Annelies.

But they were going to sell it.

Where? In Greece? How could they sell it in Greece?

We'll take it with us to Zurich.

"We should give it back," said Annelies. "Stealing from a

church, it's not right."

Peter smiled. "I didn't know you were so religious."

"How can we return it?" said Nicole. "We can't go back to the church. We have to catch the boat."

"We'll mail it back," said Annelies, "so we won't be traced. We can send it from Athens in an anonymous package."

Hans-Ruedi looked at Nicole. "She's right. We need to start this trip over again. All we've been doing is arguing and complaining. Let's forget the locket. Let's forget the money."

Nicole glanced at Peter. He shrugged. She turned back to Hans-Ruedi and Annelies and smiled, embarrassed. "OK. Let's send it back."

Later, when she was standing on the upper deck of the car ferry for Rafina, watching the port of Gavrion recede into the east, Nicole noticed Annelies smiling at something Peter was saying. She leaned against Hans-Ruedi and put her arm around him.

"You and Peter just picked the wrong part of the island. Next time, let the women choose."

* * *

After spending the night in a pine grove near Rafina, the four travelers pressed on, hitchhiking northward toward Thessaloniki and their ultimate destination, Istanbul.

In the haste and excitement of the departure from Rafina, the locket wasn't sent and Annelies didn't say "good-bye" to Peter. Preparing a package and cutting short a love affair demanded special energy. Both would have to wait.

Chapter 2

Two weeks later. Istanbul

Oran Crossmoor stepped through the Beyazit Gate past the armed sentries into the crowded, noisy Covered Bazaar and headed for the jewelry stores at the heart of the old market complex. Up since dawn, he had been taking pictures for hours – fishermen in red and blue dinghies, sellers of charcoal-grilled meatballs, cars delivering mounds of long, spiky gladioli, pigeons massed at the entrance of the Spice bazaar, grime-encrusted mosques from the Golden Horn up to the university. He even got in a tall, tanned blonde carrying a backpack. Swedish, he thought. I wonder if she's free. From behind her a dirt-streaked man called out, "Annelies!" When she turned, Oran noticed the small Swiss flag sewn onto her pack. Not Swedish and – he realized with a twinge of disappointment – not free.

It was midday. After lunch Oran was expected on Buyukada for tea with Leyla Aslanoglu, a venerable acquaintance of his mother's. Until then he'd browse among the jewelry stores. With luck he'd find a good present for his mother. His friend Kemal had recommended one shop in particular, for old, unusual things. In Istanbul, Kemal had told him, if you look hard enough, you can find anything you desire.

Oran walked swiftly down the broad vaulted street. After four years away, he had forgotten what a keen feeling of pleasure it gave him to be able to blend into an Istanbul crowd. With his dark hair and dark complexion, he looked like everyone else. He spoke Turkish, too, because his Turkish mother had insisted on speaking her own language with her two sons even though her American husband knew only English. He was one of these people, and he felt at ease.

In front of him two women in dull-colored scarves and coats

were talking together while their children plucked pieces from a fresh loaf of bread and stuffed them in their mouths. Dodging the children, Oran passed a cluster of sunburned tourists in T-shirts inspecting leather jackets.

"Evet, efendim!" A hollow-cheeked man with a thick black mustache caught Oran's eye and gestured at his collection of wind-up ostriches. Oran lifted his chin slightly, indicating "No." In front of him and behind him boys carrying trays loaded with small tulip-shaped glasses of reddish-brown tea sped to answer the calls of shopkeepers. Two teenage girls, waiting for their mother to finish talking with an elderly gentleman in a white embroidered skullcap, eyed Oran slyly. Oran smiled back. The girls giggled and pretended to turn away.

Oran had come to Istanbul to take pictures for a book on cities of the Ottoman Empire. To do the book, he had taken a leave from his increasingly tedious job as a bonds analyst for Citicorp in New York. His grandfather was helping him out financially. Photography was a new profession for Oran, born out of Saturday-morning classes that followed his work week. For the final project each student had to record the emotional life of a family in the course of one day. Oran didn't think he could do much with such an assignment. Why would people he didn't know let him get close? If he were the subject, he would freeze up.

To his surprise, it went well. The photography teacher had assigned him her sister's family, Italians living in Brooklyn. Oran was amazed by their openness and pleased with the pictures he got. So was the teacher. She received many requests to do weddings, and some of these she passed on to Oran. Weddings intrigued him. He enjoyed trying to capture on film the mix of emotions that flowed with the champagne and music and the dancing. But weddings celebrated above all the commitment of the bride and groom to each other. What were they thinking? Through his camera lens Oran tried to penetrate their minds.

Just ahead, Oran saw the old fountain at the crossing of two streets, a bazaar landmark. At the section of the rug dealers, he stopped to get his bearings. He was anxious to avoid Ferid's store. After the painful visit with Elif's parents a few days before, he didn't want to risk seeing Ferid, not yet.

"Come in?" a dealer called out in English. The man beckoned toward the door of his shop. "Have a look? Just a look...no need to buy."

Oran shook his head and went on.

Oran and his girlfriend Elif had come to the Covered Bazaar four years ago, at the end of the summer, just before he returned to America. Elif had brought him to the rug section to meet Ferid, a favorite relative who had known her since she was born. She had dressed well for the occasion, and tied her dark blonde hair with a blue velvet ribbon. When the dealer welcomed Oran like a son-in-law, Oran was pleased but at the same time he felt uncomfortable, pushed in a direction he wasn't ready for. He liked Elif but he didn't want their relationship to be rushed.

Half a year later Elif was shot and killed at a demonstration at Istanbul University. A friend of theirs had called to break the news. The connection was bad. Oran would remember the loud crackling noises that filled the dreadful pauses. Like a storm. A storm of despair.

A few weeks later a letter arrived from Elif's father. "How can I understand it?" he wrote. "My son – you will always be my son – I feel God has betrayed me, taking away my wonderful daughter." A shroud of sadness had fallen over Istanbul. For four years Oran stayed away.

The street gradually sloped downward, narrowed, and became darker. Oran looked up at the smoke-blackened multi-domed Ottoman ceiling stretched high above him like a giant nomad's tent. Bits of sunlight filtered in through small openings in the roof, but neon signs and incandescent lamps inside the shops provided most of the light. Once, when he was a boy, Oran had been visiting the bazaar when the electricity went out. The store owners lit butane lamps, transforming the bazaar into a phantasmic nocturnal world. It scared him, it was so strange.

A gilded sofa sat in the middle of the street, blocking his path. His Turkish grandparents would have considered it ideal. Oran let his hand caress its bulging purple velvet upholstery as he walked around it.

The streets kept narrowing. Now the shops were devoted to jewelry. Each tiny shop had powerful, hot lights under which dozens and dozens of gold bracelets, lockets, and gold rings sparkled seductively.

The displays resembled each other from one store to the next. But Oran had a place to start, Kemal's friend who sold antique and nomadic jewelry, with a sideline in old furniture. He took out his notebook: Sedat Tufekcioglu. Sedat Son-of-a-Gun-Maker. Oran looked up and there was the shop, right in front of him.

Before he went in, Oran wanted to assess what Sedat's competitors had to offer. His mother had trained him well in the arts of the Middle Eastern shopper. He stuck his hands in his pockets, backed up a few steps, and glanced at the shelves of the preceding store. He crossed the street to inspect the display in the shop opposite. Only then did he feel ready to enter Sedat's.

A small man with thick glasses was sitting behind a red felt counter, smoking a cigarette. His shirt was white, his hair gray and perfectly in place, and his face heavily wrinkled. He seemed washed out, exhausted, bored.

"Sedat Bey?" Oran asked.

"Yes, efendim."

"I'm Oran. Kemal Erkan recommended your shop."

Sedat Bey looked at him with some interest, then stood up. "Kemal Bey. Yes." He smiled. "Are you an artist, too?"

"Sometimes."

"You are interested in the junk?" Sedat Bey pointed to a corner in the rear. "Scraps. Old metal belts, bits of sword, cooking pots.

That's where Kemal Bey prowls when he's about to start a new sculpture or dress his latest girlfriend for a gala event for the pleasure of the photographers."

"I'm a photographer," Oran said. "I'm not an artist like Kemal."

"No junk, then? Well, that's fine." He sat down behind the red felt counter. "What would you like to see?"

Oran glanced around the small room. Metal pitchers, cups, bowls, boxes, candlesticks lay jumbled on the shelves. They looked ugly, tarnished and covered with dust. He felt disappointed.

"The scimitar is not for sale, I must tell you." Sedat Bey pointed behind him to a corroded sword hanging by a braided cord with a large gold tassel. "Nor is that bronze candelabra standing in the corner. You see all the candles in it? That's my protection in case the electricity goes off and I can't get any butane for my lamps."

"I'm looking for a present. Something not too bulky, that I can carry back to America. Do you have any old jewelry?"

The question seemed to revive Sedat Bey. "What a thing to ask! I always have old jewelry." He went into a back room and returned with a simple metal box. He opened it and began to place objects on the red felt. A few pairs of gold earrings, and lots of jangly silver necklaces, many with amber beads, some with bright red stones.

Oran's mother already had a drawer full of things like this. He duly admired the beauty of each, but he was starting to think about catching the ferry to Buyukada.

"And then I have this," Sedat Bey said. "It's very unusual." He took a small pouch out of the box, removed a gold locket, and set it on the felt.

Oran picked up the locket: a flattened oval of gold, decorated on one side with an emerald surrounded by a circle of tiny rubies. An elaborate pattern of foliage was engraved into the gold, covering the entire surface except for a small rectangle on the reverse. In this plain space was an inscription in the old Arabic script.

Something tugged at his memory. A picture...

"Is something wrong?" Sedat Bey asked.

And a voice. GF's voice. His Grandfather Crossmoor.

Oran stared at the locket in his hand. He had seen it before. He was certain. He had seen this same flattened oval of gold, the emerald, the rubies. In the picture. And the letter.

"That's it!" he said aloud.

"What?"

Oran felt Sedat Bey peering at him. "It's..." Oran automatically put on the noncommittal smile his mother had taught him for masking keen excitement. "It's magnificent."

"Indeed it is," said Sedat Bey.

The picture in the album. Of course. In the old family album. And the curious letter.

Rainy days on Cape Cod. He can't play on the beach. GF brings in the old family photo albums. The bindings are crumbling, pictures have been jarred loose from their attachments.

How many times GF had described that necklace to him! The necklace...four oval lockets hanging from a chain...emeralds and rubies and four mystic words in strange writing... "From Jerooosalem," GF intoned in his British accent, as if he were singing a hymn.

Sedat Bey was watching Oran through his thick glasses. "Yes," he said. "A beautiful piece." He took a puff on his cigarette and smiled.

Oran looked up, hardly remembering where he was. He laughed and ran a hand through his hair as he tried to hide his confusion. The necklace had disappeared from his family at least half a century earlier. And the strange letter GF had received, the short, unsigned letter that mentioned the jewels, that beckoned

GF to come – what did it say, exactly? Did the writer plant this locket here?

Could this really be one of its four lockets lying here in front of him on a worn piece of red felt? GF who remembered it from his own childhood in Izmir now lay paralyzed from the waist down in his home outside Boston, but Oran could still see him in the damp Cape Cod house picking out picture after picture, reminiscing about his Irish grandmother, Oran's great-great-grandmother, the big-bosomed lady with the glowing necklace.

"Can you read this?" Oran held the locket out so that Sedat Bey could see the Arabic inscription.

Sedat Bey placed the locket on the felt and inspected it with a large scratched magnifying glass. His right hand was trembling, so he propped up the glass with his left hand.

"The first letter is a 'd'," he said. "It's Arabic, though, not Ottoman Turkish. I must check the dictionary again." He went into a back room and returned with a large, worn book.

"'Dum'u.' That means 'Tears'. This is a reliquary containing tears. Or whatever may remain of them."

"Tears from the Holy Land?" Oran asked.

"But from which holy person and for which tragedy?" Sedat Bey sat up grandly in his chair, clasped his hands in front of his chest, and looked skyward. "Profound sorrow," he declaimed. "A pure heart. That's all we can know."

"Bravo!" Oran said. Melancholy Sedat Bey had come to life. "You should have been an actor." Oran's mind was racing ahead. Tears. Had GF told him the four mystic words?

Sedat Bey laughed. "I wanted to be but my father said, 'Acting? Don't be silly'."

Oran couldn't remember the words. "Jerooosalem," that's all he could hear, and the longing of his grandfather for all that he had given up to go fight in the Great War, to marry an American heiress, to come settle in her country.

"In those days, if your father said 'No', you gave up on that tack and tried another."

Magic. It was magic. That's what the letter spoke about, the magic of the jewels.

"Sometimes I think I take after my uncle," Sedat Bey continued. "He could imitate anyone. He had a great talent."

This will make GF so happy, thought Oran. He's going to be thrilled.

"Uncle was useless in the shop. He couldn't add or subtract. Why did my grandparents force him to stay here? I never could understand it. He should have run off and done...oh, I don't know what."

Oran was calculating how much he could pay. Sedat Bey will ask the world if he suspects how much I want this locket.

Sedat Bey took a last puff and put out his cigarette. "So you like the locket, do you?"

"It's nice. I have to say so. It's nice."

Sedat Bey beamed at him. "Yes, it is nice!" He laughed. "Would you like some tea?"

He put the other jewelry back in the box, but slipped the locket into his pants pocket. He went out to order tea.

Oran stood up to stretch and take a few steps around the room.

Outside Sedat Bey started yelling.

He's upset about something, thought Oran. Good. That's an advantage for me.

Sedat Bey came in, sat down, and reached for his cigarettes. "The tea boy said someone tripped him. But I saw him. He was kicking a ball around while he was holding a fully loaded tray." He offered Oran the pack. "What does he think I am? A fool? And blind, too?" He massaged the cigarette in his fingers, loosening up the tightly packed tobacco, and tapped its end on the counter top. "We'll have to wait for the tea."

He pulled out his lighter and lit Oran's cigarette, then his own. He started to cough. He couldn't stop. Oran turned away, embarrassed.

A boy served the tea as Sedat Bey brought his cough under control.

Oran reached out for his tea as if nothing had happened.

Sedat Bey smiled a polite little smile, then offered him the sugar bowl. They stirred the sugar lumps around. Neither said a word. Sedat Bey took out the locket and set it on the red felt. "I've never seen quite this decoration before. It's rare. It's very beautiful. Very beautiful indeed." He contemplated it for a moment. "I know you think so, too."

Oran laughed.

"See, you can't hide it!" Sedat Bey said.

Sedat Bey had disarmed him after all. He had regained all his lost ground.

"How much would you want for this?" Oran asked.

A serious look came into Sedat Bey's face. "Such a locket might contain the tears of the Prophet Muhammad himself! It would then be priceless." Sedat Bey smiled, pleased at the thought. "But if it were, someone would have donated it to a mosque long ago. Let's invent a story, a compromise story: tears of joy shed by the Caliph al-Walid upon the completion of the Aqsa mosque in Jerusalem. A valuable pedigree, don't you think? Even if the museum authorities might prove skeptical. 100,000 liras."

"One hundred thousand Turkish liras?" Oran let his jaw drop in amazement. He calculated swiftly. It meant approximately US $7000 at the current rate of exchange. "Kemal would laugh at me if he learned I paid money like that for the fruits of your imagination. Let's forget the history and concentrate on the materials and the craftsmanship. I think 20,000 liras would be fair."

Oran sat back and fiddled with his cigarette. So far he was pleased. He was half-expecting a much higher initial price. Perhaps Sedat Bey had not paid much for it himself.

"If you only knew how many liras I spent for this," Sedat Bey said, "you would be laughing, too, at that ridiculously low figure you have just proposed. Do you realize how difficult it is to obtain old jewelry and antiques to sell? I've had to double my efforts to find new sources. The prices are soaring. And the other dealers are no longer the gentlemen of the past. I can't just give things away." Sedat Bey proceeded to reduce his asking price by several thousand liras, even so.

"How can I be sure of its age?" Oran asked. "Perhaps it was made for a lovesick maiden in a nineteenth century harem. I'm taking quite a risk! 25,000 liras."

Sedat Bey winced at the accusation. "Specialists, distinguished connoisseurs have bought medieval weapons and jewelry from me. They have been fully confident of their authenticity. I'll give you their names. Go ask them. I am honest, above all. This piece is much, much older, believe me."

"I'm not questioning your expertise, Sedat Bey. Dating jewelry can be a tricky matter. Certain types of decoration can have quite a long life. Like these floral motifs, for example. But you know that better than I do."

Sedat Bey took another sip of tea and stared off into space. "For the friend of a special client, I will sell the locket for 70,000 liras. I can't go any lower than that without sacrificing all possibility of profit."

"I'll give you 35,000 liras for it," Oran said. "I can't pay any more than that."

"You have been joking with me all along, then." Sedat Bey's laugh was laced with bitterness. "To end with such a price...you are insulting me. You are certainly not seriously interested in the locket."

"If that's so," said Oran, "then I think it's time for me to say good-bye."

As he was about to step outside, Sedat Bey said in a loud voice, "Yes, efendim, it is always possible that this locket was made somewhat later. Eighteenth century, perhaps?"

Oran turned around and smiled.

"55,000 liras," said Sedat Bey.

Oran kept smiling but headed again for the door. "37,500."

"You are showing a bit more respect for the medieval craftsman," Sedat Bey said. "But only a little. Would you care for another glass of tea?"

As they waited for the tea, they smoked cigarettes and watched the smoke curling up into the grayish atmosphere and discussed the costs of luxury goods in Europe and America. However high the tags might be in America on such items as a color TV, a Mercedes, or a blender, he would pay far higher prices in Turkey, Sedat Bey remarked, if the product could in fact be found. It was tremendously unfair.

"The essentials cost less here," Oran said. "I live in New York. Believe me, I know. A bus trip across Turkey, a hotel room, a meal in a restaurant...all are cheaper here."

"Perhaps. But if I make a lot of money, what can I buy with it here? A nice apartment with a spectacular view of the Bosporus? That's already worth several Mercedes. A dinner with imported wines or black market cigars? It's risky to be a conspicuous consumer here. I'd rather not excite the police. I don't want to tempt fate."

Tea was served. Sedat Bey asked Oran all about New York, one question after another. At last Oran finished his glass of tea. With a tone of regret he announced he had to leave.

Sedat Bey picked up the locket. "For 40,000 liras it is yours," he said. "You will take 'Tears', yes, but never forget that you leave me with my own tears for having made such a sacrifice."

Oran extended his hand and said as they shook, "That's fine, 40,000 liras. I'll pay it, even though I may be the biggest fool to enter this shop in the past ten years."

"No, no. You don't have to worry about that!" Sedat Bey went to wrap up the locket.

Now for the tricky part: the payment.

"I don't have the money on me," Oran said.

"I didn't expect you would."

"I'll have to get money wired from America."

"There's no hurry. Just leave me your address."

"Don't you want to make sure I am who I say I am?" Oran asked. Although Turkish shopkeepers habitually extended credit for favored clients, Sedat Bey had never seen him before.

Sedat Bey smiled indulgently, like a father to his little boy. "Oran, my friend, Kemal Bey told me you might be stopping by. Oran Crossmoor, from New York. American father, Turkish mother. Of course I know who you are."

Oran took the locket, thanked Sedat Bey, and stepped outside.

So Kemal had briefed Sedat Bey about him.

"Damn!" Oran swore softly. "And he just convinced me I wasn't a fool!" He laughed, shaking his head, as he made his way up the narrow street.

Chapter 3

Oran found a seat in the open air on the upper deck of the ferry to Buyukada. He wanted to see everything, the mosques and palaces of old Istanbul as they receded into the haze behind him, the Asian shore stretching out to his left, the Sea of Marmara and the little Princes' Isles ahead. The sun blazed strong and hot, but the wind, stronger still, kept him from baking.

When the ticket collector came by, Oran reached into his pocket for his ticket, and touched the little package from the Covered Bazaar. He felt certain this locket came from his family's lost necklace, but he wouldn't pay for it until his grandfather had confirmed it. GF needed to see a picture. As soon as he had left the bazaar, Oran found a quiet corner in the grounds of a nearby mosque and photographed the locket. On his way down to the dock he dropped the film off to be developed.

The boat wasn't crowded. It was a weekday afternoon, still too early for the commuters returning home from the city center.

He took out his wallet and unfolded the paper on which GF had copied the text of the mysterious letter he had received a few weeks before Oran was due to depart. "It is time to repent. Come find me. The jewels will show you the way. The beautiful, magical, tragic jewels." The letter, written in English, had been sent from Turkey, but the blurred postmark was illegible. His grandfather's transcription was small and tidy; the original's large, well-formed letters slanted to the right. "Look how fine the paper is." GF had held it up for Oran to see. "Who in the world could have sent me this?"

Oran put the letter back in his wallet. If the jewels were showing him the way, he had no idea where he was being led. To Buyukada? To Leyla Aslanoglu?

A vendor came around with a trayful of soft drinks. Oran took an orange soda to accompany the white cheese sandwich he'd brought and tried to recall Leyla Aslanoglu, the woman he was about to visit. His mother had assured him that once, long ago, when he was ten, he and his family had eaten lunch with Leyla Hanim and her late husband, Tevfik, at this very house on Buyukada.

"Don't you remember?" his mother said. "Tevfik Bey became so excited telling a story that he knocked a bottle of red wine off the table. Your tennis shoes were stained. You almost burst out crying!"

Oran did remember his sneakers getting ruined, but the rest of the day had disappeared from his mind.

Oran knew that Leyla Hanim and Tevfik Bey had been early and faithful supporters of Ataturk, which made them distinguished citizens of the Turkish Republic. And his mother had told him that Leyla Hanim knew Istanbul like the back of her hand, an accomplishment his mother found peculiar. "Wouldn't you find it strange," she asked him, "if a woman from Park Avenue knew New York like a taxi driver?"

"She'd be an exciting person."

"A bit eccentric," his mother replied.

Oran knew then he would enjoy meeting Leyla Aslanoglu.

It took the boat an hour to reach Buyukada, the furthest and largest of the Princes' Isles. The town behind the dock was bigger than Oran remembered. Leyla Hanim had told him on the phone that her house lay outside of town, much too far to walk, especially in the middle of summer.

He flagged down a horse-drawn caleche, the only type of taxi on the island. After passing through the town, the carriage continued on a tree-lined road that followed the coast. Soon it stopped in front of a large dark red wooden villa with gingerbread trim. Oran checked his directions. This had to be the right house, but it wasn't far from the dock after all. He could easily have walked. Leyla Hanim clearly had herself in mind, not a 26-year-old man.

Oran hopped out, paid the driver, and went through the gates. He could see a garden behind the house and the edge of a terrace covered with a grape arbor, just above the sea. No one seemed to be out there. Rose bushes lined the path to the front door. He knocked, striking with a large brass ring gripped in a lion's jaw. No one answered. The perfume of the roses drifted his way, and a large yellow swallowtail butterfly turned circles beside him, then floated off to a nearby stand of carnations. Oran knocked again. This time a thin, graying woman wearing baggy village pants opened the door. Yes, Leyla Hanim was in and was expecting him.

He waited in the entryway while the maid announced him. He listened for voices, but heard only a pair of magpies squabbling outside. His eyes were caught by an umbrella rack. It must have contained a dozen umbrellas. He pulled one out...canary yellow. He couldn't resist opening it...not all the way, just far enough to see the pattern.

"Please." The maid held open the frosted glass paneled door and motioned him to enter.

Oran tried to close the umbrella, but something stuck. Just as he was about to yank the thing shut, the maid took the umbrella out of his hands. "This was Tevfik Bey's favorite," she said. She closed it, put it back in the rack, and gave Oran a reproving look. She motioned again through the door. "Leyla Hanim is waiting for you in the salon."

Oran didn't enjoy being treated like a naughty child. He ignored the maid, stepping into a large cream-colored room with high ceilings and a majestic crystal chandelier, a room packed with dark furniture, tables, chairs, sofas, and two concert-sized grand pianos. Oran looked around. Where in all this confusion was he expected to go?

"I'm over here!"

Oran turned and saw a small figure with short white hair waving to him. He followed a trail through the furniture to the other end of the room, to an elderly woman sitting in a green velvet armchair beside a picture window overlooking the sea. She wore a simple navy blue dress and a necklace of pearls and gold beads.

"Oran Crossmoor?" she asked in a surprisingly strong voice. She offered him her hand. "This is indeed a pleasure."

"Madame Aslanoglu," said Oran, addressing her in the formal, European style of bygone days. He had meant to say the usual "Leyla Hanim," but somehow the huge room, the pianos, and her necklace of pearls and gold beads made him feel as if he had left the Turkish Republic.

"Leyla, if you please, not Madame Aslanoglu. I may be a relic from the Ottoman Empire, but I don't like to be reminded of it. Do sit down."

Oran saw that he had quite a choice of seats, even in this alcove by the window.

This amused her. "Here, take this chair next to me. I can hear you better. Normally we would sit outside, but today it's too windy. I've just recovered from a dreadful cold. I don't want to invite it back." She waved toward the window. "The sea view is almost as nice from here as it is from the terrace. These old ballrooms are perfect for the summer. Unfortunately I've had to turn this one into a warehouse."

Oran couldn't dispute that.

"I'm trying to simplify my life." She looked around. "It doesn't seem so, does it?" She smiled. "But I am. I'm preparing for my death."

Oran was startled. What a thing to admit to a stranger! Maybe his mother was right, after all.

"No." She reached out to reassure him. "You didn't say anything distressing. I did. But I'm telling the truth. I'm 82 years old, I know I'm going to die, and I intend to be ready."

"I hope you will live to be 100," Oran said. "God willing," he made sure to add.

"God willing," repeated Leyla Hanim. "If I don't go blind or deaf or senile, I probably wouldn't mind. All these chairs..." She indicated the whole room with a sweep of her arm. "My sister-in-law died five years ago and left me her house on Buyukada and everything in it. I haven't the slightest idea why, but she did. The house needed new plumbing, rewiring, and repainting. Such a bother at my age! I rented it out, for I didn't want to sell it, not wanting to be disloyal to the memory of my sister-in-law. But I made no improvements. Finally I got angry with myself for doing nothing. Then I became angry at the house. Simply ridiculous! I decided to sell."

"That sounds like the right thing to do," Oran said.

"They are gutting the inside and turning it into apartments. I'm storing the contents here until I can arrange the sale with an antiques dealer. All this was moved here only last week. I do apologize for the mess." She cleared her throat, then searched in a box on the table next to her. She popped a cough drop into her mouth. "Perhaps I am excessively anxious about my health."

"Not everyone can boast of reaching 82."

"I don't care a fig leaf how long I live. It's the quality of health. My family has always been concerned with health. But tell me, have you eaten?"

"On the ferry."

"A little sandwich, I suppose." She picked up a bell and rang it. "You speak excellent Turkish."

"My mother is Turkish."

"I know. We met years ago. But a Turkish mother in America, that doesn't guarantee you will learn good Turkish."

The maid came in. "Hanimefendi?"

"We'll have tea, Gul. And bring a big plate of cookies for our guest. He hasn't eaten a thing all day."

Oran knew it would be futile to protest.

When Gul had closed the door behind her, Leyla Hanim turned and looked carefully at Oran. "I knew your great-uncle

Edward Crossmoor in Izmir, years ago. He died in the fire of 1922, just after we captured Izmir from the Greeks. It was a terrible loss. He was a charming, distinguished man."

She peered at Oran, inspecting him.

Oran was surprised. The tone of her talk had abruptly turned somber. He wondered how she expected him to react. "My grandfather has never spoken much of him," he said.

In truth, Oran knew little about Uncle Edward except his grisly death. He must have been young when he died. Oran didn't think he had married, for GF surely would have mentioned a wife. But Edward was the last Crossmoor to own the necklace of four gold lockets, which GF mentioned every time he told Oran about the necklace. As the eldest son, Edward had inherited it. It had vanished, like him, in that fire of 1922. GF, then enrolled in university in England, had no idea what had happened.

"You don't look at all like him," Leyla Hanim said.

Oran slipped his hand into his right pocket. The locket was still there.

"He had a big mustache," Oran said, recalling an old photograph.

"And light brown hair, thinning on top, not like your thick, dark hair. He was pale. The sun burned his skin. But so distinguished. He carried himself well, he walked precisely, with a sense of his importance. How he impressed me!" Then she gave a tinkly little laugh. "That was so long ago, and I was young. The years do fly, don't they? And then we are finished, all of us. Edward, Tevfik, and then me." She waved the vision away with a flick of her hand. "We should talk of something else. Tell me about your projects. A book on Ottoman cities, is that what you told me?"

"I'm hoping you will tell me which spots have kept the flavor of Ottoman Istanbul. I mean the street corners and the little court-yards, not the great monuments."

"Oh, I do know Istanbul," she said. "The old parts, mind you, and Beyoglu, not all these squatter settlements sprouting up on the outskirts. When I was young, I wanted to write a guidebook. The Byzantine remains interested me in particular. We Turks have ignored them, by and large. I walked everywhere, read in libraries, and took many notes, but somehow I never wrote the book. I couldn't get started."

Oran smiled. "You have just described my entire college career."

"The things I learned. Did you know that Trotsky lived right here on Buyukada?"

In fact Oran did. Elif had mentioned it to him.

"For four years after he left Russia," Leyla Hanim continued. "You can still see the house. It had belonged to Izzet Pasha, the head of the secret police under Abdul Hamit II."

"That seems appropriate," said Oran.

"Doesn't it? The irony has always made me smile. I saw Trotsky once. He was gathering roses in his garden...he had just cut a large red rose...he held it delicately with two fingers, taking care to avoid the thorns...he brought it up to his nose and held it there. I stole away. I didn't want him to catch me spying.

"Yes, I know the real Istanbul. I know it too well, my niece Semra tells me." She laughed. "Semra can be so conventional! I think she is jealous of everything I know. But she hates to walk. She prefers to sit...whether at home or in the car, it's the same to her. Sitting, you can't learn very much.

"Now, of course, I'm too old to hike around even on smooth, level stretches, and I have all but given up on my favorite walk, from Taksim down Istiklal Street to the Markiz Pastry Shop. But..." Her eyes gleamed. "I have made sure that no one quite believes this. I tease my nieces and nephews and their children. I say, 'I think I will take a stroll down into Kasimpasha this evening,' or 'Tonight I would like to investigate social developments around the Galata Tower.' Everyone looks horrified. I am delighted."

Oran didn't know whether he should smile or not. The region below the Galata Tower included a thriving red light district.

"It's a joke, Oran! I would never set foot in such neighborhoods. I have become rather squeamish."

"What if your relatives call your bluff?"

"I doubt they will. They would miss the pleasure of being shocked."

They heard the door open.

"Beril? Is that you?" Leyla Hanim called. "Back already from the swimming meet?"

A well-built young woman with masses of long curly black hair made her way through the furniture. Oran stood up. She was almost as tall as he was. Good-looking, too. She glanced at him, then spoke to Leyla Hanim. "The race was cancelled. I was the only girl to show up." She bent down and kissed Leyla Hanim on both cheeks. Oran imagined her breasts swinging forward against the oversized T-shirt she was wearing.

"You're just in time to meet my guest," said Leyla Hanim. "Oran Crossmoor. This is Beril, my favorite niece."

"Hi," he said as they shook hands.

Beril gave Oran a friendly smile. "We haven't met before, have we?"

Oran smiled back. "I don't think so." He would have remembered her: statuesque...the word fit her to a T...and that hair.

She took a seat on the sofa opposite Leyla.

"Beril is actually my great-niece," said Leyla Hanim. "My brother's son's daughter. It's complicated, I know! Her mother is my niece by marriage, Semra, the adventurous soul I was telling you about."

"Oh, Aunt Leyla! No one admires you as much as Mother. Have you told Oran your latest proposal?"

"I didn't have the chance."

"She tried to persuade Mother to join her on an expedition to the Sulemaniye for the evening prayers on the Night of Power," Beril said to Oran.

"The mosque must have been packed," he said.

"It always is on the important nights in Ramazan," said Beril. "My mother hates crowds, especially religious crowds. She would have been hysterical, even in the women's section."

"I didn't insist, you must admit it," said Leyla Hanim. "Your mother was just returning from Ankara and she would have been excessively fatigued."

Oran smiled. "Does your mother always get teased like this?"

"We are hard on her, aren't we?" said Leyla Hanim. "She has many fine qualities. She cooks marvelously well. Even the stray cats benefit. They receive the tastiest leftovers imaginable. When she is in her own familiar setting, there is no one kinder than Semra."

"I understand your mother is Turkish?" said Beril.

"And my father is American."

"Of British descent," said Leyla Hanim. "You remember, Beril, I told you Oran's mother grew up in Bursa. Her family still lives there."

"Are you enjoying the Economics Department?" Beril asked.

"What?" said Oran.

Beril look surprised. "Aren't you studying economics at Istanbul University?"

"He's a photographer, dear," said Leyla Hanim.

"I'm taking pictures for a book about Ottoman cities."

Beril twisted her watch back and forth. "I must be confusing you with someone else."

"I have been working for a bank."

"That's economics, isn't it?"

"Close enough. If you saw an economist walking with a banker, you probably wouldn't be able to tell which was which."

"Could you?"

"I'm losing my touch. I've taken a leave from that job, to do this book. I work for Citicorp in New York. You've heard of Citicorp...Citibank?"

Beril and Leyla Hanim smiled politely...blankly...at him.

"I've been working there for two years."

"You'll go back?"

"Well..."

"And if the book is a success?" said Leyla Hanim.

"I took the job because I wanted stability," Oran said. "My father is a businessman, and he is incredibly stable."

"My father is a banker," said Beril.

"Then you might not believe me if I told you I was bored," said Oran.

"I probably would," said Leyla Hanim.

"My mind kept floating out the window. I wanted to travel, really get away. Three months in India, for example. You could really see India if you had three months."

"India!" said Beril. "That would be quite a change." She didn't sound taken by the idea.

This Turkish disdain for the rest of Asia annoyed Oran. "I've always thought India would be the most exotic, colorful, and profound country I could possibly visit."

Beril gave a little shrug, a questioning grimace.

"Beril would prefer Paris, I'm sure." Leyla Hanim's light but determined tone signaled Oran to return to courteous conversation.

He offered a conciliatory smile. "Sometimes I'd imagine myself in Paris, too." He glanced at Beril, awaiting her gesture of compromise. But she was watching him with suspicion.

"What are you studying?" he asked.

"Architecture."

"There's a lot of tedium in that, too," said Leyla. "All those precise drawings."

"But such a great subject to study in Istanbul," Oran said. "I saw a lot of buildings when I was here last. I spent two vacations here, in the summers of '77 and '78, and wanted to come back. But some of my friends got caught in political events. When I heard what happened..."

"I understand perfectly," Leyla said. "In those years of anarchy we all wanted stability, at any cost. We would have given our eye teeth for a humdrum life."

In her letters to Oran, Elif had related again and again her efforts to stay out of the clashes between the leftists and rightists. "I just want to read literature, attend lectures, and learn," she wrote him. "Is that so outrageous? I want to be neutral, but no one at this university will let me."

He learned later how friends talked Elif into joining them in a protest march. The bullet that struck her down might have come from either side. No one ever knew.

"Are you glad you have come back?" Beril asked.

Oran hesitated, then smiled. "I'd forgotten how much I enjoyed it here."

Gul came in carrying a tray. She set it down on the nearer piano while she positioned a small table in front of Beril and another in front of Oran.

"What do you like best about Istanbul?" Beril asked.

"Going swimming with friends at midnight, off these islands," Oran said. "I haven't tried it yet this visit. But I feel that freedom. I know if I wanted to go for a midnight swim, I could."

Gul poured glasses of tea for all three, then served Oran and Beril each a small plate of cookies and a large plate of meatballs, cigar-shaped flaky pastries filled with cheese, and vegetables mixed with mayonnaise. She stepped back to the piano and waited for them to take their first bites.

"Oh, Gul! I said I wasn't hungry!"

Gul smiled mischievously at Beril. "I made the Russian salad just this morning, to celebrate your first place in the swim race."

"I told you the race didn't take place."

"You can tell me whatever you want," said Gul, "but it's after three and I know you're starved."

"Gul is only doing her duty," Leyla Hanim said. "The choice is up to you, Beril." She turned to Oran. "Beril wants to look like a fashion model. She's perpetually fussing that she eats too much. Gul, on the other hand, is quite slender, as you can see..." She gestured toward Gul, who was as thin as a beanstalk. "...and has always been so, ever since she came to work for us twenty-five years ago. Gul, alas, has refused to accept that in modern Turkey a slender woman can be an object of envy rather than pity. And Beril..."

"Beril, alas," said Beril, "rejects the old-fashioned standards."

"To which she conforms most magnificently," said Leyla.

The three women looked at Oran expectantly.

"Thin or curvy, either is fine with me," Oran said. "Just as long as Turkish cooks don't abandon their traditions." He reached over and took a cheese pastry.

Leyla Hanim's eyes were alight with amusement.

Beril followed Oran's lead and picked out one of the meatballs. "Mmm...lots more thyme than usual and a good pinch of hot red pepper. If this is the consolation prize, I like it." She looked at Oran and they laughed together. Gul was smiling as she took the tray from the piano and left the room.

Leyla Hanim said to Oran, "I hope your mother hasn't lost her sense of Turkish hospitality after so many years in America."

"Nowadays she would have taken you at your word and served only that big plate of cookies."

Leyla frowned. "A pity. Your American father had no expectations, so your mother let standards slip. And with a kitchenful of time-saving machines, no doubt."

"Perhaps what my mother really needed was a Turkish maid." Beril laughed.

Leyla Hanim smiled wryly. "I'm sure Gul has a cousin who would love to work in America. Shall we ask her the next time she comes in?"

"It sounds as if his mother has adapted well to American life," Beril said. "Wouldn't you have wanted that if you had moved to America?"

"I'm not sure, Beril." Leyla Hanim looked thoughtful. "I can't picture myself as anything but Turkish, whether I'm in Rome or Paris or New York. I can't imagine myself other than a citizen of Istanbul. Yet I lived in Izmir when I was young. Look at my father, he grew up on the island of Rhodes, on a farm, only to move to the capital of the empire. Oran's grandfather, who was English, settled in America. These are radical changes, don't you agree? But we adapt so well, no matter what cherished things we leave behind." She smiled. "If I had gone to America I too would not have scorned frozen and bottled foods."

"You told me that great-grandfather's leaving Rhodes was a disaster for the family," Beril said.

"For the family, dear, not for him. There is a difference." Leyla Hanim turned to Oran. "My father, Beril's great-grandfather, made his career here in Istanbul. To move from a remote island to the grandest of cities, and to join the cavalry...surely an exciting and satisfying change. Yet his leaving Rhodes marked our family's end on that island, the end, after 400 years. He felt enormous guilt. He blamed himself for the collapse and shame of the family."

She sank back in the armchair. "You must understand, his own father was murdered by bandits. This tragedy turned his world upside down. He wanted to leave and try something new. Wouldn't you have done the same? When he set sail from Rhodes, the farm seemed safe in the hands of his uncle. How could he ever imagine that Rhodes would fall to the Italians in his own lifetime? That our lands would be seized? That the Ottoman Empire would crumble to dust?"

She sat still in her armchair, a blue flower fading inside its deep green foliage. She turned to look out the windows, not down at the sea, but off into the sky. Beril reached for her tea glass. She, too, was silent. Oran wondered whether it might be time to take his leave.

Beril sat forward on the sofa, set down her glass, and with a lightning-quick motion, popped a meatball into her mouth. She turned her eyes toward the others to see if they had noticed. Oran smiled. She had transformed a simple gesture into high comedy.

Beril inspected the plates in front of her. "When are you returning to Istanbul?"

A perfect exit cue, thought Oran. "Soon, I suppose."

Beril looked up, startled. "Oh, I'm sorry! I didn't mean you. I was asking Aunt Leyla!"

"Indeed!" said Leyla Hanim. "I haven't even talked to Oran about Istanbul." She stretched her arms out on the chair. "To answer your question, Beril, I'm leaving tomorrow in the late morning."

Beril turned to Oran. "Aunt Leyla never leaves Buyukada in the summer."

"Except in the most unusual of circumstances," said Leyla Hanim. "Suddenly, exceptional circumstances have been springing up all around me." She ticked them off on her fingers. "An old friend from Beirut is visiting Istanbul for the first time in years...Jacques Lebrun. Did I ever tell you about him, Beril? Then Alexandra Stephanides, one of my favorite pianists, is giving a recital in the Istanbul Festival. She's ancient, like me, and a Greek born in Izmir, but this is her first appearance ever in Turkey. A great event! We should all go. And, if I'm already going to one concert in the festival, why not see the Brazilian dancers as well? You can see I'm in danger of becoming addicted to the festival. My summer habits may well break into bits."

"What about all this furniture?" asked Beril, looking around the room. "Weren't you going to arrange for the sale?"

"I'm seeing Sedat Bey about it."

"Sedat Bey?" Oran interrupted.

"An antiques dealer in the Covered Bazaar."

"Sedat Tufekcioglu?"

"An old family friend," Leyla Hanim said.

"My father has been going to that shop as long as I can remember," Beril said. "He collects Seljuk and Ottoman metalwork."

"He must be well known," Oran said. "A friend gave me his name."

"It's a funny little place, though, just a cubbyhole," said Leyla Hanim.

Oran sat forward on the edge of his chair. "I happened to go to his shop this morning. I bought something really special." He took the package out of his pocket and started to unwrap it. "Let me show you." He held out the locket in the palm of his hand.

"Oh, my!" said Leyla Hanim. "It's magnificent. May I?"

Oran handed it to her. She inspected the locket and turned it over, showing it to Beril. "What fabulous stones! The emerald, the rubies." She cradled it gently in her hand. "Look, there's an Arabic inscription. It must be very old. Let me see if I can make it out. A word beginning with 'd'. Then 'm' and 'ain'...I can read the letters, but what does the word mean?" She asked Oran, "Do you know?"

"Sedat Bey read it for me," Oran replied. "It means 'Tears'."

"'Tears!' Are you certain? "

"Yes, he said 'Tears'."

"Ah."

"Ah?" said Beril, peering at her great-aunt.

"No, no, it's nothing." Leyla smiled. "Nothing, surely." She set the locket on the table, but she couldn't take her eyes off of it. "There is something mysterious about it, don't you think? Tell me, Oran, why did you buy it? What about it attracted you?"

"It's part of a necklace that once belonged to my family," Oran said.

"How extraordinary! Did your family own the necklace for a long time?"

"I don't know," Oran said. "I would have to ask my grand-father."

"If you have the opportunity, I would be grateful," Leyla said. "I would be most interested to learn more."

Beril leaned toward her great-aunt. "Why don't we go out into the garden?" she said. "The sun won't be so strong, and if the wind has died down..."

"What a good idea. It should be pleasant outside." She rose to her feet, then took Beril's arm. "Shall we, Oran? The flowers are lovely."

Now he needed to return to the city. He had made dinner plans.

"I'm afraid I must go," Oran said.

"So soon?" said Leyla Hanim.

"A boat is leaving shortly."

"Surely there are later ones."

"I'm meeting friends for dinner."

"Ah. Well."

Oran picked up the locket.

Leyla Hanim's eyes met his. "You are taking the locket?"

He was surprised by the question. "It's for my grandfather."

"Yes, of course. How silly of me." She stepped forward with him toward the door. "Do you have a picture of the locket that I might have?"

"Not yet. I'm waiting for my film to be developed."

"When the photos are ready, could you send me one? I would like to study it more closely. Who knows, perhaps Sedat Bey has other pieces, equally beautiful."

The door to the kitchen opened. Gul looked surprised to see the three of them standing together at the entrance. She glanced suspiciously at Oran.

"Everything is fine, Gul," said Beril. "No need to worry. Bring tea to the garden, just for Aunt Leyla. Could you get her a wrap, too? I'm going to take our guest down to the dock."

"I can find it," Oran said.

"There are some tricky turns. I think I should go with you," Beril said.

"We didn't even talk about old Istanbul, did we, Oran?" Leyla gave him a gracious smile. "We'll have to leave it for another time."

"You aren't returning to the city, are you, Beril?" Gul asked.

"No. I'll be back for dinner."

"We've run out of eggs. Could you bring back ten?"

Beril was already at the gate. "Come on!" she called to Oran. "You will miss the boat!"

"You must come back," Leyla Hanim said. "We have so much to discuss."

Oran smiled. "If you would like..."

"I would. Very much."

"All right, then," he said as they shook hands. "You can count on me."

He turned and ran. At the gate he waved to Leyla Hanim, then followed Beril out into the street.

Chapter 4

Leyla crossed the garden to the edge of the terrace. The wind was blowing steadily. It wasn't cold, but she pulled her shawl tighter. She leaned over the terrace railing and looked out over the choppy sea. Behind her, out of her view, the sun was descending. Its darkening light struck the houses on the Asian shore of the city not far off, enveloping them in a golden embrace that evoked the enchanted world of fairies and djinns.

"Tea, Hanimefendi."

Leyla had forgotten that tea was coming. Gul set the tray down on a table next to the white wicker chair, poured a glass, then returned to the house.

Leyla sat down, sinking back against the blue cushions that lined the chair. Was the locket really her family's? How strange that Oran Crossmoor should be the one to show it to her. Oran Crossmoor...Edward's great-nephew.

She reached over to pick up her tea glass. She would need to see the locket again, to inspect it. How could another meeting be arranged? Perhaps Beril has learned more about Oran, some helpful detail. An impetuous young man...and charming, too...polite...a good listener. He had certainly taken her by surprise. And yet for big surprises, how can anyone prepare? What would Father say? Or her brother Suleyman, or Tevfik?

She took a handkerchief from her pocket and wiped her eyes. It was cold in the garden...no...in July? She was imagining. She listened carefully and looked around timidly. No, she didn't see Death. He wasn't hiding in the garden, not today.

She laid her head back against the cushions and closed her eyes. The locket...gold, the emerald, the little rubies...if only Father could see it...

He paces back and forth in front of the window. His face passes in profile...his neat black mustache, that long straight nose, the slightly curved forehead, and black hair shiny with the oil that holds it down firmly on his head. He is smoking cigarettes. He smokes all the time, those gold-tipped cigarettes.

Her father had come upstairs to say good-bye. He was leaving Istanbul for Damascus, for the war. She was sixteen, her brother Suleyman four. Their mother was dead.

It was the last time she saw her father. Storm clouds were massing in the late autumn sky. The wind was pushing branches of the huge plane tree against their dark brown wooden house. A loose shutter kept banging in the wind. The electricity wasn't working. She had lit a kerosene lamp, but it still seemed dark.

He takes the necklace from around his neck and holds it up to the window. A golden star. Daylight, splintered through the panes of old glass, ripples across its surface.

"Muqaddas," he tells me, "Arabic for 'holy,' or 'blessed'. Blessed are the necklace and the family. Muqaddas, such is it written on this golden star. Our family was the guardian of this holy necklace. As long as we respected this duty, we lived in happiness. The necklace symbolized our prosperity. It stood for our particular gifts of healing. Some even believed it the very source of our good fortune. A superstition, perhaps. My father thought so. But superstition or not, when he destroyed the necklace, the family's fortune fell apart."

Yes, even if she had only glimpsed the locket before Oran took it away, she felt certain it was part of their special necklace. Her father had told her the story of the necklace, and now, as she remembered her last meeting with him, she recalled every detail of what he had said. Once there were four gold lockets as well as the star. Each one contained a relic from a holy shrine. Each was inscribed with a word beginning with one of the four Arabic letters used to write muqaddas: m, q, d, and s. He told her how his own father, his baba, had sold the four lockets.

Baba scoffed at Ottoman and Islamic traditions. He wanted to be modern like the Europeans. Men should put their faith in science and lead rational lives.

Baba mocked the necklace of relics. The relics weren't the source of his medical gifts; they couldn't make his family prosperous. He and his family were smart people, and they passed their knowledge and skills from one generation to the next. That's why they did well.

He would prove it by getting rid of the relics.

In the town of Rhodes he had met an Englishman, Sir George. As landholders, both were, in their way, gentlemen. But Baba felt Sir George looked down on him. How could a provincial Oriental hope to aspire to the rank of English gentleman? Eventually Sir George came to call. He suffered from many ailments. Most were imagined, said Baba. The Englishman was a fool.

He showed Sir George the necklace. Each locket contained a relic from the Holy Places, Baba told him. They cured illnesses. He swore it!

Sir George picked up the necklace with his long pink fingers. Baba could see at once that the beauty of the necklace enchanted him. But the healing powers surely attracted him even more. Baba could not help but smile. Sir George, the rational Westerner, would prove to be no better than a hysterical woman, whereas he, Baba, would be confirmed as a man of progress and dignity.

Leyla wished she had been in that room. She would have grabbed the necklace from those two foolish men and shouted, "No!"

Father brings his gold-tipped cigarette to his lips and inhales. "Sir George bought the lockets. My baba kept the star. I don't know why."

He sits down on the edge of the divan, takes my hand. I smell his tobacco. His own little cloud. I never see it and yet it is always there. My father's smell.

He was going to leave her. Leyla remembered how afraid she had felt. She threw her arms around him and cried.

Her father smiled sadly and hugged her. Then he started to pace back and forth in front of the windows, in the dim light of the stormy day, as he recounted to his daughter the disasters that struck, one after another.

A killer frost ruined the almond crop. A young farmhand went mad. And Uncle, Baba's brother, began to suffer from convulsions. Once a master healer, now Baba's command of the medical arts faded. Even elementary illnesses baffled him. Baba couldn't sleep. What was coming next?

One evening Baba called for his son Ismet, Leyla's father. Baba told him how he had sold the relics. Surely he had committed an impious act; nothing could explain their misfortunes except the anger of God. Baba was going to town the next day to find Sir George and buy back the relics.

He took the chain with the gold star out of a red leather box, grabbed his son by the wrist, and pulled him close. "Ismet! Swear to me that you will not be as foolish as I was. Swear you will never doubt the power of the holy places and of the saintly people who walked there. Should God in his mercy restore the lockets to you, you and your children and your children's children must keep them together as a sacred heritage. Forever, even until the end of the world."

The next morning Baba set out for town. The family awaited his return, but day followed day and he sent no word. The news came a week later. Baba's body had been found behind a cluster of boulders just off the road. Bandits had slit his throat.

Ismet went into town himself to find Sir George. But Sir George had set sail for England several weeks earlier and no one knew when he would return.

Ismet was devastated by the loss of his father. He thought of leaving the farm. He was still young, only seventeen, and he wanted to escape and start afresh. But he had no brothers and his uncle had no sons. Could he just abandon Uncle?

One day Ismet announced he was going to Istanbul.

Uncle didn't protest. He merely asked when Ismet would return.

In six months, Ismet said. He hadn't thought of his return. Six months seemed like a long enough time.

Uncle smiled sadly, then went to write a letter of introduction to a Jewish merchant who imported dried fruit and nuts from Rhodes.

That afternoon Ismet went into Baba's study. He lit a candle, took out the red leather box, opened it, and removed the chain with the gold star. He held it in front of the candle. "As you wear it and treasure it," he whispered to himself, "you will not forget your father, your family, or your land. Someday the star will lead you to the four holy relics, and peace will come to us again." He took the chain and the star with him.

A few days later he kissed his mother and aunt and uncle good-bye and promised them he would return in the spring.

"May God bless you and protect you," they said.

Leyla sighed. She wanted to weep with the relatives left behind. That departure had determined her life. She would be born in Istanbul, not on Rhodes as had three centuries of her forebears. She would never see the land to which they belonged.

Father looks out the window. The wind sends raindrops streaking across the panes.

"I never went back. Whatever we intend, a larger destiny controls us, just as the moon pulls the tides."

Her father worked hard for the merchant, loading and unloading crates of fruit, and the merchant kept a kindly eye on him.

Several years went by, and still her father kept putting off his return to Rhodes. He wrote home less and less. The farm was not doing well, Uncle wrote back. His own health was not good. As for Sir George and his family, no one had any word.

Eventually her father joined the cavalry. After he married, he and his young wife settled in Istanbul. The Italians took Rhodes in 1912. The farm was seized. Then Uncle died. His mind remained intact until the end, condemned to contemplate his family's ruin.

Her father told her he never heard a scrap of news about the relics. Were they still on this earth? Would they ever reappear? He wanted so much to believe they would.

Leyla brushed away a tear. She had longed for them, too. And today she had surely seen one of them. She could now hope to tell him, "Yes, Father, the lockets are coming back to us."

He sits beside me. He takes my hands and presses the golden star into them. He smiles at me. "As you wear this necklace, will you think of me so far away?"

"I will pray every day for your safe return, Father. I will guard the necklace for you."

He reaches out to hug me. "Good-bye, my precious daughter, my sweetest daughter, may God watch over you and bless you."

Then he is gone.

I feel cold.

I hear the rain. It is raining so hard. If I went to the window, could I even see the Bosporus?

Rain?

Leyla sat up with a start.

Rain? In July in Istanbul? Isn't it a sunny day?

She leaned over the arm of her white wicker chair and looked around. Where was she?

"I beg your pardon, Hanimefendi! It's the water pressure again."

She was on Buyukada. Her gardener was watering the plants with a hose. A few drops had splashed on her face.

It was almost dark. The sun had ceded its place to evening. It was late. How long had she been daydreaming?

She clucked her tongue and went inside to see if Beril had returned, if Gul had finished preparing the dinner.

Chapter 5

Leyla sat in her green armchair reading in a cocoon of light projected from a tall brass floor lamp. The rest of the ballroom was dim, although the nearly full moon outside was shining in through the windows.

She heard the click of the door opening, the scuffling of shoes. She looked up.

"Ah, Beril. At last. I have so much to tell you." Leyla set her book down and removed her reading glasses. "Do turn on the other lights. I can't see you."

An instant later, the room returned to life.

"Dinner has been ready for some time, my dear." Leyla's penetrating voice made clear her displeasure.

"I know, I know." Beril made her way through the furniture. "If only I hadn't run into Nadya." She sat down on the edge of the chair next to her aunt, pushed the hair out of her face, and smiled mischievously. "Guess what's happening to her."

"Well...I know she's getting married."

"The marriage is off! Nadya is going to be a movie star."

"What do you mean, the marriage is off?" Leyla was shocked. Nadya came from one of Istanbul's most distinguished families.

"Her fiancé signed on to explore for oil somewhere in the east."

"But that's his profession!"

"Nadya refused to go. They had a huge fight."

"She should respect her husband's career."

"But, Aunt Leyla! She had just won a part in a movie with Sinan Altay!"

"Oh, well!"

"She charmed Arif Bey."

"Arif! Why didn't you tell me it was Arif?" Leyla laughed with relief. "If only Arif had enough movie roles for all the women who charmed him."

"He never offered me a part," said Beril.

"I imagine you never asked him."

Beril smiled. "I've been hinting."

"That's like trying to fell a mountain goat with cotton-tipped arrows. If you want something from Arif, you will have to change your tactics."

"When he calls me up again, I'll ask him point blank," Beril said.

Gul came in and announced she was serving dinner.

Leyla rose from her chair. "At last." She looked at Beril. "Are you as hungry as I am?"

"You shouldn't have waited for me."

Leyla reached out for Beril's arm in a gesture of forgiveness. "But we have to talk!"

Together they crossed the ballroom and went out. Gul switched off the lights behind them.

The moonlight was now free to occupy the room, to linger in the silent alcove by the wide windows, on the green armchair and on Beril's seat, and on the chair in which Oran had sat earlier that afternoon.

∗ ∗ ∗

Leyla and Beril ate dinner at an old wooden table under the grape arbor. The wind had died down and the sea was smooth. In the moonlight that spilled across the water, a fishing boat headed southwards toward the open sea, its motor put-putting along. Beril found it pleasantly warm, but Leyla protected herself with a thick black wool shawl.

"So Oran has invited you to dinner," said Leyla. "The day after tomorrow! It's so soon." She took a sip of wine. "I must confess this surprises me."

"He wants to leave for Greece by the end of the week."

"He didn't tell me that."

"He didn't have much of a chance, did he?" Beril tore a piece of bread in two, dipped one half in the gravy, and took a bite.

"It was he who dashed off! But I'm hoping we'll have a chance to continue our discussion. Perhaps we could have tea with him tomorrow, in the city. Do you think you could telephone him?"

"Why are you so keen to see him again?"

"The locket, Beril. I am so thrilled! When Oran first showed it to us, of course I found it splendid, but there was something about it that kept pulling at me. And then, after you had gone, while I was sitting here on the terrace, the story my father told me the last time I saw him came back to me as clear as a bell. The locket is ours."

"What do you mean?" said Beril. "Oran told us it belonged to his family."

"I have no idea how Oran could claim it as his. The locket is part of our family's extraordinary necklace. I'm sure I remember telling you about it."

"No, you never have," Beril said.

Leyla poised the tips of her knife and fork on the edge of her plate and looked at Beril. "We need to get the locket from him, to buy it if need be. It is urgent that we meet with him as soon as possible."

"What is this necklace? I don't understand."

"Beril, sometimes you do exasperate me. You must not have been listening to me. I have certainly told you this story countless times."

Beril sighed. "If you say so."

"Our family owned a necklace for centuries, four gold lockets on one chain, with a gold star in the middle. I have the star. It is my greatest treasure."

"Did you ever see the lockets?" Beril said as she helped herself to a second piece of stewed lamb.

"No, but my father described them in minute detail. One of

the four lockets had 'Tears' written on it, in Arabic. And today, we saw it. You saw it. This was it. There can be no doubt."

Beril paused for a moment, resting her chin in her hand. "This is an amazing story," she said. "What happened to the lockets? Were they stolen?"

"No, they weren't stolen," Leyla Hanim said. "My grandfather broke the necklace apart. He sold the four lockets but kept the star. He sold the lockets for no good reason. It was a foolish thing to do."

"Why foolish?"

"He claimed it was superstition to think the lockets ensured the family's prosperity. By selling the lockets, he thought he would strike a blow against superstitious beliefs. It didn't work. In fact, quite the contrary. He tempted fate, and we were punished."

"Do you know who bought the lockets?"

"An Englishman. His name was Sir George. That's all I know. He lived on Rhodes for a short time, then vanished without a trace."

"Oran might know something about this Sir George."

"Indeed," said Leyla. "We might learn why he claims ownership."

"Perhaps you can meet with him yourself. I just want to have a nice, pleasant evening when we have dinner together. That's all."

Leyla inspected Beril's blank face. "He is handsome, isn't he?" she said.

Beril smiled.

"Will you be safe going out to dinner with him?"

Beril laughed. "We're going to the Secret Garden."

"Ah. Ibrahim Bey will watch out for you. That's good. Now..." She examined Beril's plate. "Do you want another helping, or can we move on to dessert?" She rang her little bell. "Don't rush, dear. I just don't want Gul to think we're spending the entire night out here." She took another sip of wine. "But first we have to do something else."

Beril looked amused. "Before dessert?"

Leyla laughed. "Another meeting in the city." She leaned toward Beril. "We must get Sedat Bey to tell us where he found this locket. Then we can work backwards from that source, and we'll learn what happened to the other three. Doesn't this sound exciting?"

Beril picked up her spoon and turned it over. "I think we should be realistic." She tapped the spoon lightly on the table. "You've had your miracle already."

Leyla reached toward Beril and looked earnestly into her face. "That's exactly the point, dear. It was indeed a miracle that this young man should bring us the locket, but this is not the end. Remember, I have the gold star. I'm sure this is a sign. The other lockets are bound to follow." She took hold of Beril's arm. "It's our kismet, our destiny. We have to pursue this. I'm counting on you. I am too old to track all the clues. I can only follow from my armchair."

"You mean command from your armchair."

Leyla smiled. "You are going to be my agent. I'm hiring you, I'm giving you a salary. Yes, indeed! Don't look so surprised."

"I do like treasure hunts," said Beril, looking up at the stars.

"Really, Beril! You make me seem like a schoolgirl in the playground. I'm deadly serious. The necklace had a special power for us. When the lockets were lost, we were cursed. My father told me the story the last time I saw him. My grandfather, who sold the lockets, was brutally murdered. Our lands were stolen from us. Then my father himself, shot dead in Syria. How can I forget all this, Beril, one tragedy after another? If we have the slightest chance to recover the lockets, how could I possibly not try? If we succeed, who knows what wonderful things will come our way."

Beril turned toward her great-aunt and smiled.

"Good! I knew you would help," Leyla said. "I will give you every assistance I can."

Gul came over with a tray and a dish of fruit.

"These are the peaches Gul's niece brought back from Bursa," Leyla said. "Gul is going to join me in town and her niece will watch over things here. Now, I'd like some linden tea. Beril?"

"A regular tea, please."

Gul cleared the table and returned to the house.

Beril inspected the peaches. She was smiling. "First I have to charm Oran," she said softly. She selected a pale yellow peach.

As they ate their dessert, a carriage came up the street. The clip-clop of the horse's hooves on the asphalt paving and the jingling of tiny bells grew louder and louder.

"Do you hear that, Beril? The music of horseshoes and bells?" Leyla's face lit up with excitement. "It certainly means good luck. Don't you think so?"

Beril cocked her head and listened to the night air. Bells and hooves fading away, a seagull cawing out over the sea, a sudden rustling in the bushes...she hadn't the faintest idea what message was being whispered to her, but she leaned toward Leyla and smiled and said, "Yes, Aunt Leyla, I'm sure it must."

Chapter 6

The next morning, as he was getting ready for breakfast, Oran received a phone call, from Beril.

"Oran? This is Beril. I haven't wakened you, have I? I wanted to catch you before you went out."

"We're still on for dinner tomorrow, aren't we?"

"Definitely. But I'm calling for another reason. Aunt Leyla would like to talk with you again."

"Not right now, I hope."

"It's about the locket."

"What about it?"

"I'll let her tell you herself. I'm just arranging your meeting. She's coming to the city this morning. Would this afternoon at 4:00 suit you, at the Divan Hotel?"

"Sure, that's fine."

It was nice to hear Beril's voice. She had made a great impression on him the previous evening. Just before getting on the ferry at Buyukada, on an impulse he had invited her to dinner. When she accepted his invitation, he was pleased. It could be hard to connect with young Turkish women, for parents, grandparents, friends, and neighbors monitored their every movement. Elif's conservative parents had been particularly vigilant. Whenever he visited her at her home, a third adult was always present.

It was odd, though, that Leyla Hanim wanted to meet with him. He'd sensed she was intrigued by the locket, but who wouldn't be? Gold, the precious stones, the inscription – small, but a luxury item of beautiful craftsmanship. He wondered if he should bring the locket with him. Maybe a photograph would do.

Later that morning Oran picked up the prints of the photos he had taken of the locket and mailed a selection "express" to his grandfather. In the accompanying note he asked GF to send him his opinion as soon as possible. And did he know when and from whom their family had obtained the necklace of relics? Had Uncle Edward ever mentioned a friend of his, a Turkish woman named Leyla? She said she had known him.

* * *

At 4 PM, when he reached the Divan, Leyla Hanim was already seated, looking off into space.

"I came a bit early," she said after he sat down. "Just in case any friends were here. I don't usually come into the city in summer, so if I had to explain my presence, I wanted to do it before you arrived. Two of my friends are here, so I have already prepared them for you. They do enjoy gossiping. Now, what would you like?" She beckoned to a waiter. "The pastries here are first-rate."

"I'll have some coffee with milk, and piece of chocolate cake," Oran said.

"For me, tea, please," said Leyla Hanim. "You must be wondering why I requested a meeting so soon. I hope you weren't too shocked to receive Beril's call this morning. I told her to call early in order to be sure of finding you."

"I am curious."

"Let me get right to the point. It's the locket. Do you have it with you?"

"Why do you ask?"

"I would like to see it again, to examine it. After you showed it to us, I couldn't get it out of my mind."

Oran looked around – no one sitting immediately adjacent – then put the locket on the table.

Leyla reached for it.

"To hold this, you can't know what this means to me. This is why I wanted to meet with you now." She peered up at him. "Are you sure this locket belonged to your family?"

"Quite sure. I've sent a photograph to my grandfather, for his opinion. Here, let me give you one of the pictures." Oran gave her a photograph.

"I would be most surprised if that were true," Leyla Hanim said, "because I am certain that this belonged to my family." She set the locket down on the table, between them.

"What do you mean?" Oran was astonished. "How could this be your family's necklace?"

"I had only an inkling when you showed the locket to us yesterday. But after you left, I kept thinking about it. Everything fell into place. My father had told me about a wondrous necklace our family had owned, a necklace of four lockets and a gold star. His own father had sold the lockets, in a silly gesture of anti-religious zeal, but he had kept the gold star. Our family fortunes plunged. Somehow, the necklace had been connected with our prosperity. I never saw the lockets, but my father described them to me in detail. He mentioned the inscriptions – 'Tears', in Arabic, was on one of them – that was the real key to this identification. I have the gold star. It is my greatest treasure. Of course I never dreamed I would see even one of the lockets ever again."

"There must be some mistake," Oran said. "I never heard of a gold star. Maybe they were two different necklaces."

"Two sets with the same inscriptions? I suppose that might be possible."

The waiter brought the tea, coffee, and cake.

"But there must be more of the story to learn," said Leyla. "How long did your family own the locket?"

"My grandfather showed me old photographs of his grandmother wearing it," Oran said. "That would have been some time in the later 19th century."

"When did it leave your family?"

"Uncle Edward was the last to own it. He died in the Izmir fire in 1922. His house burned; everything in it was lost."

"Clearly this locket escaped the fire. I wonder what happened."

"Let me ask you a question," Oran said. "If your grandfather sold the lockets, to whom did he sell them?"

"To an Englishman living on Rhodes. I remember only his first name, George. Sir George, my father called him."

Oran smiled broadly. "That must be my great-great-grandfather, Sir George Crossmoor."

"Crossmoor?" said Leyla Hanim. "Edward's family?"

"My grandfather's grandmother, the one wearing the necklace, was Sir George's wife. Your family sold it to mine."

"I'm astonished. Our families are so intertwined." She reached for her teacup, her hand trembling as she picked it up. "I had no idea."

Oran suddenly wondered, could she have written the anonymous letter to GF?

"If you are correct," said Leyla Hanim, "you are the owner, indeed twice over – from the 19th century, and now again from Sedat Bey. So now I must ask you. I wish to buy it from you."

For a moment Oran said nothing. He looked at her. Her small dark eyes held him in a firm grip.

"I don't want to sell it."

She laughed softly and waved lightly with her hand. "If it's a question of money, I'm sure we could agree on satisfactory terms."

"It's for my grandfather. This locket will mean a lot to him."

"Let me write him," said Leyla Hanim. "I'm sure we can reach an understanding."

"Haven't you written him already?" Oran asked.

She looked at him with such puzzlement that he realized at once that she was not the one who had sent the letter to his grandfather.

"Wait!" he said. "I'm not being clear."

"It's all right," Leyla Hanim said. "We'll ask Sedat Bey if he might find your grandfather another piece, equally beautiful, equally historic."

"I don't think my grandfather would agree." Oran picked up the locket and put it in his pocket. He wanted to explain why his grandfather would value the locket, that it stood for the world GF had been raised in, his family, Smyrna, British culture. GF cut those roots, but now, at the end of his life, perhaps he had regrets. Oran's own destiny had been colored by those distant actions. He sensed that he, too, had something to gain in the finding of this locket, even if he had no idea of what that might be.

"Clearly we will have to talk more about this," Leyla Hanim said. "In the meantime, I will write to your grandfather. For the first time."

Chapter 7

The next day

Leyla, well-protected against the sun with dark glasses and a wide-brimmed hat of pink straw, held onto Beril's arm as they entered the great maze, turning in the direction of the jewelers' shops. Inside the Covered Bazaar it was cooler. Leyla exchanged her dark glasses for her regular pair.

Leyla was impatient to talk with Sedat Bey. Getting the golden star from the bank had taken much longer than she anticipated. She felt hot, tired, and ill-tempered.

Beril was hungry. Breakfast was already a distant memory and lunch lay far in the future. When she spotted a simit seller, she steered Aunt Leyla in his direction and bought one of the ring-shaped sesame pretzels.

As they continued toward the Bedestan, the old heart of the bazaar, a bird darted down in front of them, then flew back up toward a small window high in the vaulted ceiling.

"Do you think he will escape?" said Beril.

Leyla stopped to watch the bird. "And what about us?"

Beril looked puzzled.

Leyla smiled. "The bazaar is like a giant birdcage. Sedat Bey has lured us in with the lockets. But don't worry. We'll take the bait and escape! I'm sure of it." She squeezed Beril's arm and they continued walking. "I remember when the sultan was deposed and his harem was opened. All the women inside were liberated. They could go home. But where was home? They were tame birds pushed out into the wild forest." She shook her head. "Can you imagine it?"

"Did savage beasts gobble them up?" Beril asked.

"Tasty quails that they were?" Leyla laughed. "But they had beaks and claws! They knew how to peck and scratch."

* * *

Leyla and Beril found Sedat Bey concluding a sale with two middle-aged German women. When he saw them in the doorway, he gave a cry of delight and guided them to some chairs.

Beril watched Sedat Bey as he attended to his German clients. "A fox in his lair," she whispered to Aunt Leyla.

"With two fat juicy birds," said Leyla. She and Beril exchanged smiles as they watched the tourists rummage around in their purses.

Tea was brought in and served. As soon as the tourists departed, Sedat Bey pulled over a straight-backed chair and sat down beside Leyla and Beril.

"Hanimefendi, this is a great honor," he said to Leyla.

Indeed, she had not visited the shop for quite some time. Months? Years? But Sedat Bey was genuinely delighted to see Leyla. He didn't stop smiling.

Beril couldn't recall seeing his teeth before. They were stained dark yellow and haphazardly positioned, but they all seemed to be there.

Sedat Bey asked Leyla about her family, and she inquired about his. After commenting on the weather, they ruminated over conditions in the bazaar. Leyla moved the talk on to her late sister-in-law's furniture and then, when the future of the furniture was arranged, she said:

"I was fascinated by an antique reliquary which a guest of mine showed us."

Beril watched Sedat Bey. He was still smiling innocently.

"A gold locket," continued Leyla in a businesslike tone, "decorated with an emerald surrounded by rubies."

"Yes, Hanimefendi, I remember." Sedat Bey's smile disappeared. He stood up to get his cigarettes from the counter. "A young man bought it."

"Oran Crossmoor."

"Half Turkish, I understand. A pleasant young man."

"And very determined, I might add. Now, I have brought something to show you." Leyla took the golden star out of her purse. She urged him to take it, to inspect it. "Do you see that leaf pattern? The locket is decorated with the identical motifs. Look! It's inscribed in Arabic. This star, Sedat Bey, is the companion piece to a necklace of four lockets."

Sedat Bey looked up at Leyla, not understanding.

"This necklace was my family's greatest possession. It had a mystical power that kept the family prosperous and happy for generations. You are smiling, Sedat Bey, but it's true! One hundred years ago my grandfather broke the necklace apart and sold the four lockets. Only the star was kept. It makes me sick to think of it. We were destroyed. We lost our land! We became like straw scattered by the wind. The great hope of my life has been to recover the necklace. You can understand, I'm sure, the emotion that overwhelmed me when I realized what Oran Crossmoor unwrapped in front of me the other day. The first of the four missing lockets!"

"Well!" Sedat Bey let out a quick, nervous laugh. "That's exciting, isn't it? If only you had told me..."

"So now I have told you." Leyla looked directly at Sedat Bey. Her voice took on an imperious quality. "You can help us find the other three lockets. If we can trace back the owners of the locket that Oran Crossmoor just bought, we should discover the fate of the rest of the necklace. First of all we need to know who the previous owner was. I wonder whether you might be so kind as to share with us the name of that man?"

Sedat Bey breathed out a sigh. "I'm afraid it's impossible, Hanimefendi."

"I see." Leyla smiled sweetly. "You would not break this confidence even for an old friend engaged in a project of supreme importance for her family?"

"For you or your family I would do anything, you know that." Sedat Bey lit a cigarette off the stub of the first. "But this case is ticklish."

"Ticklish? In what way?"

Sedat Bey returned to his chair. "The man who sold me the locket was neither a dealer nor a connoisseur. He had no idea of its date, other than that it looked old. At first he wouldn't tell me where he had obtained it. Then he changed his mind. He bought it in Tekirdag, he said. Now that, my friends, was an unfortunate choice on his part!" He beamed at Leyla and Beril. "My wife comes from Tekirdag and I know its bazaar. If such an object passed through Tekirdag, I would have heard of it."

"If you suspected he was dishonest, why didn't you tell him to go see someone else?"

Sedat Bey smiled. "You will understand, Hanimefendi, when I tell you I sense the rarity of the locket. Its form, its decoration, the inscription...everything was unusual. It was not, perhaps, sublimely beautiful, nor did it display the marvelous intricacy that marks the masterpieces of Byzantine and early Islamic jewelry."

Sedat Bey was speaking easily, expansively, now that he could rely on his expertise.

"In fact I wasn't certain it was so early. Your friend played on these doubts and pressed his advantage when we were discussing the price. Perhaps it is late, 17th or 18th century. Maybe you can tell me, Hanimefendi? In any case, I was fascinated by the locket and I had to have it in my shop. I had to buy it on the spot, for I knew the man wouldn't give me a second chance. Afterwards I made the usual checks. It was not listed as stolen merchandise, at least not in Istanbul. Friends in Ankara, Bursa, and Izmir had nothing to report."

"If you have no firm evidence that he was dishonest," asked Beril, "why can't you tell us his name?"

Sedat Bey inhaled deeply on the stub of his cigarette, then

exhaled slowly. "Because...if you must know...the man is a policeman."

"Ah!"

Well, so much for that, thought Beril.

"Yes, a policeman," said Sedat Bey. "Now you understand why I was hesitating. We must step with utmost caution. If he did steal the locket and he finds us prying, who knows what might happen to us."

"I can guess," said Beril.

"A policeman. Well." Leyla contemplated the problem. "Tevfik knew someone high up in the police department. If that officer is still there, I'm sure he would help us if your man turned nasty. I appreciate the difficulty, Sedat Bey, but I'm not going to let a policeman frighten us from pursuing the lockets."

"Hanimefendi, it's just too dangerous," said Sedat Bey.

"I understand your caution. The man sounds most unsavory. A policeman who says he buys medieval jewelry in Tekirdag. Imagine! Nevertheless, I want to approach him. I ask you in the name of our friendship of many, many years: who is this man?"

"I would lack gallantry if I sent such a venerable lady off into battle," said Sedat Bey, suddenly smiling.

Aha, thought Beril. He has decided to tell us.

"Venerable, because I keep myself battle fit," said Leyla.

"In spirit, yes. But the body?"

"I am proud to say that unlike you, I don't smoke, I drink only an occasional glass of wine or beer, and I take fresh air. Are you going to trail me in courage as well?"

"Perhaps in courage, but not in foolishness. But when is anything interesting accomplished without a pinch of foolishness? I will give you the man's name. I trust you to act with discretion. I put my life into your hands." Sedat Bey leaned forward and lowered his voice. "His name is Nusret Demir. You can find him in the Traffic Division at Security headquarters."

"Thank you, Sedat Bey," said Leyla. "We will not forget this."

She reached out to shake his hand. Then she laughed. "You think I am a tame old bird, unfit for this challenge, don't you? Well, you needn't worry. Hens like me can claw and peck!"

Sedat Bey couldn't help smiling. "I never doubted it for an instant. May I offer you more tea?"

Leyla shook her head. "You are most kind, but I have a busy afternoon ahead and I'm in need of lunch and a rest. Shall we, Beril?" She rose to leave.

"I wonder," said Sedat Bey. "Will your friend sell you his locket?"

"We are trying to activate his sense of decency," Leyla said.

"That's my job," said Beril.

Sedat Bey laughed. "Leyla Hanim, do you really expect these young men to act decently with Beril?"

Leyla snapped at Sedat: "What a thing to say!"

"I beg your pardon, Hanimefendi." He bowed his head in penitence, but winked at Beril as he raised it. "I may have acted recklessly, giving you Nusret's name."

"You have acted out of friendship for the sake of my family," said Leyla. "What greater motives are there than friendship and family?"

"Hanimefendi, you ennoble me with your eloquent language. May God bless you and preserve you." Sedat Bey showed Leyla and Beril to the door, shook hands with them, and wished them the best of luck.

Leyla hesitated before stepping into the street. She let out a sigh.

"My aunt is tired," Beril said. "Do you have a cart, something she could ride in?"

Sedat Bey smiled, held up a finger, and went across the street.

In a few minutes, a teenage boy drove up in an electric delivery cart. Sedat Bey showed Leyla to the seat next to the driver. Beril settled herself as best she could in the rear, on the flat part where freight was carried.

"Here, sit on this." Sedat Bey returned with a large brown cushion.

"All these decorations." Leyla inspected the dashboard. "It's just like a bus." Indeed, the boy had managed to cram in a photo of the entire Galatasaray soccer team, a cluster of red and yellow tassels, a picture of a bare-breasted blonde by a swimming pool, the name of Allah in intricate calligraphy, and a sticker that said in English, "No Smoking." A big radio-cassette player sat on the seat between the boy and Leyla. He turned the volume high, lit a cigarette, and started up the street. From their sonic cloud of zurnas and sazes and drums, Leyla and Beril waved back at the handful of onlookers who had stepped out to cheer these privileged visitors to the heart of the labyrinth.

Chapter 8

Oran paced back and forth in the vine-covered entrance court of the Secret Garden, waiting for Beril. He had reached the restaurant well ahead of time, because, he admitted to himself, he was eager to see her again.

Beril stepped into the entryway, a full five minutes early. She looked wonderful, elegantly dressed in white pants, a low cut red shirt, and gold necklace and earrings.

"Hi!" She smiled and reached out to shake his hand. "Am I late?"

"You're early," Oran said. This was a good sign. She was taking him seriously.

"Then you are, too."

"My watch must be fast." He gave his wrist a good shake.

Beril laughed. "Your watch and my taxi driver! Come on, let's find a table."

The Secret Garden had been a favorite of Beril's family for years. The restaurant used to have a fine view out over the Bosporus until the stately wooden mansion that occupied the lot just downhill burned one snowy winter night and was replaced by a tall, broad luxury apartment building. Outraged that half the view from his restaurant had been blocked, the owner, Ibrahim Selcuk, had two powerful loudspeakers installed just opposite the offending high rise. As long as his good friend Kemal ran the local police station, he could set the sound at full blast on selected evenings during the summer months and punish those who had bought apartments in the new building for their treachery, infamy, and barbarity.

Oran admired Beril's snug fitting white pants as he followed her into the restaurant and now, seated opposite her, he could enjoy her low cut red shirt. Two days before he had met Beril the athlete, back from her cancelled swim race. Tonight he was dining with a sophisticated city woman.

It was a warm, pleasant evening, still early. The restaurant was beginning to fill.

"Do you see the lights below?" Beril pointed to the scattered lamps that glowed in a denser garden. "That's another terrace of the restaurant. It's very calm and very private."

Oran looked down with interest.

"But you can only get tea, coffee, and snacks there," said Beril.

"I'm starved!"

"Then you're out of luck."

"After dinner, maybe?"

"I just want a light dinner," Beril said.

"I don't believe you!"

She laughed. "You already know me too well."

"Thanks to your maid and her meatballs, some things are easy to know."

"But other things are not," said Beril. "You, for example."

Was she joking with him? Oran thought his intentions were pretty transparent. Or could this be a serious statement? He put his arms on the table and toyed with a spoon. All of a sudden he was conscious of Beril's eyes on his muscular arms, his strong hands. He looked up at her, catching her off guard.

"Well," said Beril. "You invited me to dinner, for one thing."

"Can't you understand why I invited you?"

"We're enemies! You won't sell my great-aunt the locket."

"You said you understood my position."

"Did I?"

"I like your beautiful eyes."

Beril laughed and turned away.

A gray-haired man with a pale, fleshy face and a well-trimmed mustache hurried over to their table. "Beril! Welcome! How are you?"

Beril presented Oran to Ibrahim Selcuk. Ibrahim Bey took Oran's hand and shook it enthusiastically. Then he leaned forward, placing his pudgy hands on the table. "Celebrities are coming!" he whispered with excitement. "Gulizar Korkmaz has reserved a table for six!"

"Is she going to sing?" Beril asked.

"No. Just for dinner." Ibrahim Bey glanced back toward the entrance. "At least nothing has been arranged." He suddenly noticed their bare table. "Haven't you ordered yet?" He looked around for a waiter. "One second." He scurried off.

"He's jumpy," said Oran.

"Sometimes he gets carried away," Beril said.

A waiter came over, followed by an assistant carrying a large wooden tray loaded with assorted salads, cheese, pickles, marinated fish, and vegetables stuffed with herbed rice. Oran and Beril selected several, and ordered a baked fish with tomatoes, peppers, and onions as a main course.

"So you're studying architecture?" Oran helped himself to the appetizers.

"I want to restore old houses."

"Really?" With a mischievous smile, he added: "I thought maybe you were studying economics."

"Oh! That was so silly! I was sitting with a friend in the tea garden by the Beyazit Mosque. You happened to come near us. My friend indicated she knew you. 'You see that good-looking man?' she said. 'I met him at a party last week. He's studying economics at Istanbul University.' It never occurred to me she was lying."

"You have a trustworthy friend."

"To think I was jealous that she knew you!"

Oran laughed.

"I mean, a tiny bit jealous."

Beril seemed flustered, as if she had stepped too far.

"Tell me about the houses," Oran said.

"Aunt Leyla and my father have promised to let me take charge of restoring an old house they own in Bebek. Aunt Leyla grew up there."

"Who lives there now?"

"No one. And there's no furniture. Everything needs attention, the insulation and heating, the painting, the plumbing. But the house has beautiful woodwork and mirrors and old glass. When I've finished, Aunt Leyla and my father will give me the house."

"Wow! That's great. Are they paying for the restorations, too?"

"They are unbelievably generous. I'm really grateful."

Most of the tables in the garden were occupied. Boys in maroon shirts rushed around, setting and clearing tables, while waiters in white shirts and black bow ties took orders and served the food. Ibrahim Bey surveyed from the sidelines, making an occasional foray into the field of tables. From time to time he would look back toward the entrance, checking.

Beril passed Oran the plate of eggplant salad and the basket of fresh bread.

"I should move to Turkey," Oran said all of a sudden.

Beril looked at him with surprise.

Oran waved his arm to indicate the restaurant, the city, and the sea beyond, then turned to include Beril. "It's so beautiful."

"Would it be practical for you to live here?"

"What do you mean, practical?"

"Your career."

"I don't have a career."

"I thought you had become a photographer."

"Not really. I took classes. Then the book came along. But afterwards, I don't know. I can always return to the bank." He paused and took a sip of wine.

Beril watched him with curiosity.

"I want to find out why my father's family settled in the Near East," Oran said, "what it was that attracted them."

"Money?"

"They truly enjoyed living here. My grandfather said so."

"Didn't he leave?"

"By accident. He was wounded in the First World War and he was nursed by an American girl. She became his wife. But she didn't want to live in Turkey. She was very rich. She promised him a job with her father's company, so he agreed to go to America as soon as he finished his university studies. Only his brother Edward was left in Izmir."

Beril took a slice of white cheese. "I was surprised to hear that Aunt Leyla knew your Uncle Edward."

"So was I. I wonder if that might explain why she wants the locket so badly."

"I don't understand."

Oran reached for the dish of green beans. "Edward was the last in my family to own the necklace."

Beril looked at him with surprise. "Does Aunt Leyla know that?"

"I told her yesterday, when we were having tea at the Divan."

"She didn't mention it to me." Beril finished her glass of wine. "She has other reasons to want the necklace. She is terrified of dying a violent death. She hopes to die peacefully in her sleep, in her own bed, but she's convinced this is not possible."

"Lots of old people are afraid of dying."

"Several relatives have died violently, it happens."

"That's just bad luck."

Beril's voice rose. "Her grandfather was killed by bandits. Her father was tortured and executed by Arabs during the First World War."

"Wait!"

"Her brother and his wife, my grandparents, were killed when their car skidded off an icy mountain road. And then her husband collapsed right at her feet, not at home or in his office but in a muddy gutter during a rainstorm. You blame all this only on bad luck, but she has convinced me it's not so."

Oran turned up his palms, hoping for mercy.

"And she couldn't have children," said Beril. "For her maybe that was the worst. There were never any disasters like these before. Never, until the necklace was sold."

This was the opening he was waiting for. "And whom did your family sell it to?" Oran asked.

"Someone named Sir George, she told me."

"Exactly!" Oran smiled in triumph. "Sir George Crossmoor, my great-great-grandfather. We own the necklace. The title to the necklace is ours."

"What if your Uncle Edward sold it before he died?"

"He didn't."

"How do you know?"

"He would have told my grandfather."

"You can't know for certain."

"No, I can't," said Oran, irritated. "But I do know that you and your aunt don't have any valid claim to the necklace, no matter how far you stretch your imagination."

Beril looked off to the side, her chin held high.

A boy changed their plates and cleared a space on the table, just as a second boy brought the baked fish. The waiter arrived to serve the portions. Beril and Oran began to eat, in silence.

In an alcove at one end of the garden, the musicians were setting up their equipment, amplifiers and microphones, an electric guitar, and electric keyboard, and a set of drums. Because the alcove was being repainted, the musicians took care to avoid the walls and the painter's equipment.

Oran heard a meow by his feet. A black and white cat was staring up at him. Oran spooned out a chunk of the fish from right behind the gills and dropped it on the ground.

"You shouldn't feed cats in restaurants," said Beril.

"We have so much fish. Look! You're hardly touching yours."

"I told you I wanted a light dinner!"

"So you did."

Beril met his glance and smiled.

"Some more wine?"

She held out her glass. "Of course."

The people at the tables near Beril and Oran suddenly began whispering and looking down to the edge of the garden where three fancily dressed couples were making their way to a table. The women gestured broadly as they talked. Their jewelry sparkled. Ibrahim Bey hurried over to greet them.

"That's Gulizar Korkmaz!" Beril indicated the tall blonde in a purple satin sheath. "Do you see the man with the mustache and the while jacket?"

"He looks like Sinan Altay."

"That's right." Sinan Altay, Beril rushed to explain, was starring in a movie about Suleyman the Magnificent's siege of Rhodes in 1522. Sinan played one of the besieged Knights of St. John. Some of the shooting would take place in Istanbul and she intended to go watch. She knew the producer, Arif Bey, and the female lead, who happened to be her good friend Nadya. Somehow she would get on the set.

When the celebrities had settled at their table, the excitement caused by their arrival died down. The other guests in the restaurant turned back to their plates, to their own conversations. Oran and Beril started in on their fish again.

"I can appreciate your reasons for wanting to keep the necklace," Beril said. "But what will I do about Aunt Leyla?"

"She'll get over it."

"You don't know her. She won't talk of anything else. Now she wants to search for the other lockets...as if we'll find them!" She paused for a moment. "As if you would let us keep them."

"Why wouldn't I? Anyway, you're not going to find the lockets."

"How do you know?"

"Come on! What are the odds?"

Beril leaned forward. "We are already starting to look. I'm going to interview a policeman tomorrow, the man who sold the locket to Sedat Bey. I even have his name."

"You got his name? That's great!" Oran was impressed. "Did your aunt put Sedat Bey on the spot?"

Beril smiled. "He was helpless."

"You're not going to see the policeman yourself, are you?"

"Why not?"

"He won't tell anything to a woman. Why don't I come with you?"

Beril's face brightened. "But if we find the other lockets, they're ours."

"We'll work it out later."

"No, we should make an agreement right now. The other three are ours."

"If you don't want me to come..."

"I do! But I have to trust you."

Five musicians gathered on the platform and began their first number, a Westernized version of a classic Turkish love song.

Beril leaned forward and looked sternly at Oran. "We will take the other three," she repeated.

"When do we meet the policeman? What's his name, by the way?"

"Nusret Demir. How could I have made an appointment? I only learned his name this afternoon."

"Are you just going to go in and ask for him?"

"Do you have any better ideas? We're in a rush."

"Why?"

"Why are you so dense? Now that we've found one relic, we need to find the other three as quickly as possible."

"Mmm," said Oran. "This is one highly intelligent lady."

Beril suddenly realized he was teasing her. She reached across the table and gave his arm a swat.

When the musicians had finished a long introduction, a man in dark pants, brilliantly polished shoes, and a white shirt with fancy trim stepped onto the platform, took the portable microphone in his right hand, and smiled as he acknowledged the scattered applause. With a smooth baritone voice he began to sing of the passions aroused by the fleeting vision of a beautiful woman glimpsed high in the Taurus Mountains. "I saw you...then I saw you..." His voice quavered in a turbulent tremolo. "...and in my heart...and in my heart..."

A piercing whistle cut through the air. The music stopped abruptly, conversation ceased. Six policemen raced into the restaurant, found cover, and crouched with their guns held in ready position. Then four more officers ran in. The chief located Ibrahim Bey, who pointed to the table where the celebrities were sitting. The policemen surrounded the table. Two of them grabbed the statuesque redhead sitting across from Sinan Altay. She kicked and screamed. The chief officer took hold of her fabulous hair, but when he pulled, a wig came off in his hands. Her real hair was black and cropped short. Gulizar Korkmaz and the third woman at the table shrieked, and one of the men attacked the officer with his fists. With a flash of their guns the policemen put a quick end to this display of heroism.

Beril and Oran watched as the policemen led the three couples toward the exit.

"Sinan Altay arrested!" said Beril. "I can't believe it. We'll have to get all the papers tomorrow."

Suddenly the woman who had been wearing the wig broke free and darted through the dining tables toward the lower garden. Two policemen gave chase and quickly caught her. When the three reached the edge of the stage, just where the painter working on the alcove had left his equipment, the woman shoved with all her might. One of the policemen lost his balance and knocked over a bucket full of white paint. As he stumbled, he planted one foot right in the middle of the white flow. Without stopping he hurried forward to help bring the woman over to the chief. The chief officer exploded when he noticed the dripping white cuff and shoe. While the junior policemen listened with solemn faces, a torrent of insults poured from his mouth. At last, his anger spent, the chief ordered the agent with the white foot to join ranks. The entire group of policemen then marched the six prisoners out of the restaurant.

The garden burst into a buzz of chattering. The redhead must be a terrorist, said someone near Oran and Beril. An escaped convict, said another. A drug trafficker, a notorious madam, a transvestite... Waiters quickly cleared the table occupied by the group. The musicians picked up their instruments and started to play once more. Another waiter rushed over to remove the bucket of white paint and was rewarded with a round of applause by the diners near the stage.

"I wonder what Sinan did?" said Beril.

"Well, when we go to police headquarters..."

"Don't even think of asking," said Beril firmly. "We'll find our man, stick to the locket, and get out as fast as we can."

A different waiter cleared away the remains of the fish course, then brought a generous selection of fruit. "Part of an international theft ring," he declared. Oran and Beril looked up at him, a thin, middle-aged man with a pinched face and graying hair.

"Oh? Who said so?"

"The police. To Ibrahim Bey. What a disgrace, criminals in this restaurant. What a scandal." He walked off, shaking his head.

"That's Osman," said Beril. "He's always sour. He'll get over the scandal, though. They'll all get over it. The publicity value will be tremendous."

"The Secret Garden won't be so secret anymore," Oran said. "They'll have to find a new name."

When they finished their fruit, Oran paid the bill and they went out. The night was still warm. A slow breeze mingled the perfumes of jasmine, roses, and the sea as they walked down the hill. The amplified strains of love songs receded into the night, replaced by the honking of horns on the coast road, the growl of an affronted tomcat, the cries of seagulls roused from sleep.

Oran looked at Beril, at her strong, dignified profile. She had failed to win back the locket. That was one thing she could never achieve, but he admired her for trying.

Beril took Oran's arm. "What are you thinking?"

"Well," he said. "I'm wondering if it's going to rain tomorrow."

The sky was perfectly clear. They could see the moon and the stars.

Beril smiled. "OK, I won't ask any more questions."

When they reached the coast road, Oran hailed a taxi for Beril. As her taxi drove off, she turned and waved. He waved back, then crossed to the bus stop on the other side of the road. He still felt Beril's touch on his arm, and he smiled.

Chapter 9

A woman...a young woman...blonde hair, honey-colored skin...coming out of a movie theater near Lincoln Center...it's spring...early May, rainy and cool...we run to her apartment...she pulls her pink dress, her wet pink dress off over her head, takes off her underwear...my mouth is dry, I can't swallow...a sound, what is it? ... She faces me, her legs apart, and laughs...but she has black hair...olive skin, black hair...she throws back her head and towels her black curly hair...the sound, the telephone, she doesn't hear it... I'm undoing my belt, unzipping my pants...slipping off my shoes, ripping off my shirt...the telephone, the telephone...

Oran twisted around to reach the phone next to the bed.

It was Beril.

"Have you seen the papers?"

"What?"

"I woke you up?"

Oran sat up and looked at his watch. 7:30. "It doesn't matter."

"I'm sorry but I couldn't wait. Do you know who that policeman was who stepped in the paint?" Beril didn't wait for his guess. "Nusret Demir!"

"Who?"

"The man we're looking for. The man Sedat Bey named."

Oran tried to concentrate. "Nusret Demir?"

"The redhead was a high-class con artist," Beril went on. "No one else at the table knew anything about her. Her escort had met her only a few days earlier. The police released everyone else after questioning them."

"What about Sinan Altay?"

"He wasn't mixed up in this. Listen, Oran, I have some errands to do. Could we meet at 11 instead of 9:30?"

"Sure."

"At the same place."

"The New Mosque."

"Out in front, where the pigeons are."

"Fine."

"Oran?"

"What?"

"I'm sorry I woke you up."

I'm sorry too, thought Oran. "I'll see you at 11," he said.

* * *

While Oran was eating breakfast it came to him that they didn't know where Nusret would be. They might waste time tracking him down. Better to find him first by telephone and get an appointment.

In his room Oran made several calls to police headquarters. Nusret Demir was not in. Or he worked at another branch. Or the line went dead. And once, mysteriously, Oran reached a dentist's office.

But finally: "Nusret Bey?"

"Yes?"

Oran introduced himself and asked if they could meet.

Nusret wanted to know why.

Can't talk over the phone...

Why me? Nusret wanted to know.

"They told me I could trust you."

"OK," said Nusret. "OK."

But he had been given the day off and was about to leave the police station. Take a walk. Then head for home.

What if they met at 11, not too far from the police station? Say in front of the New Mosque?

"All right."

"By the women who sell pigeon feed."

* * *

Oran made his way down the steep streets of Galata, crossed a busy intersection through an underground passage, and emerged at the Karakoy docks at the edge of the Galata Bridge. Fishermen were selling fish from their red and blue painted caïques. Oran went to have a look before crossing the bridge to the New Mosque.

He never thought of it as a pontoon bridge, so its floating motion always surprised him. The traffic was heavy both in the road and on the sidewalks. A few beggars sat by the railing, displayed their deformities, and promised God's mercy. One vendor had spread a canvas over the dirty gray sidewalk and was selling white shirts. Another was showing watches, all the while keeping a lookout for the police. Oran passed women in smart western dress or in colorful, ragged gypsy skirts, women protected in cloth coats and scarves of the dullest desert colors; thin, slender, stocky, corpulent women. Women carrying packages, nets filled with groceries, holding little boys with heads almost shaved and little girls with thick braids and runny noses. Men in white shirts, dark pants and jackets, pink shirts, patterned shirts, walking quickly or sauntering, flipping little loops of beads, making them click, men with dark skin, some with pale skin, black eyes, black hair, brown hair, red or blond hair, blue eyes, piercing, wild blue eyes. Eyes from Hungary. Fierce Albanian brows. Syrian complexions, Tatar cheekbones. The legacy of the Ottoman Empire paraded with him across the Galata Bridge.

In the middle of the bridge, Oran took a few minutes to stare out across the Golden Horn toward the Topkapi Palace and St. Sophia and the Asian shore beyond. It was only 10:30. He put his arms on the cast iron railing and watched the seagulls hovering over the little boats of the fishermen. The smell of frying mackerel drifted up from the restaurants nestled among the underpinnings of the bridge. As he was looking out over the water, a man came up near him and leaned on the bridge's railing and gazed out to sea. He held a string of amber beads in his right hand and was quickly flicking the beads forward, one by one. His clothes were ordinary, brown pants, a dark jacket thrown over his shoulders. He was thin, not tall. He seemed neither old, for he had a head of dark hair still untouched by gray, nor particularly young, to judge from the lines on his face and from a certain weight in his stance. Something compelled Oran to keep glancing at the man. Did he know him? Surely not. Someone who worked at a shop near the bazaar, maybe? In his mind he walked through the shopping area on the slope between Beyazit and the Golden Horn, reviewing the faces of the store owners and their assistants. No. Someone encountered near his hotel? He tried to picture Beyoglu and Taksim and the people he might have noticed in those crowds. No one. He looked again at the man, his eyes traveling down to his feet. Flashy shoes. Party shoes.

All of a sudden he realized he was looking at Nusret Demir. Nusret, taking his walk, had stopped here in the middle of the Galata Bridge, just a few minutes from the New Mosque. Well, they would have their meeting earlier than planned.

Nusret was not in uniform. As for the shoes, he would have ruined his usual pair when he stepped in the paint. But he did look like his picture in the newspaper, small in scale and poorly printed though it was.

"Nusret?" Oran said.

The man whirled around, torn from his thoughts.

"I called you. I'm Oran."

"The New Mosque at 11?"

Oran nodded. "I was at the Secret Garden last night."

Nusret glanced away.

"An accident," Oran said. "It could happen to anyone."

"What do you want?"

"I need your help."

Nusret turned his head and looked directly at Oran,

inspecting him.

"I'm looking for a necklace," Oran said.

"You called me for this?"

"A necklace of four lockets with relics of the holy places, Mecca, Medina, Jerusalem."

"You're asking the wrong man," Nusret said. "I've never seen anything like it."

"My family owned it once. Then it was lost. We've been looking ever since." Oran paused. "This week we found one of the lockets in a jeweler's store in the Covered Bazaar. We asked who had sold it to him. He said you were the one."

"That's ridiculous! Who said that? Who is this man?"

"Sedat. Sedat Tufekcioglu."

"Sedat? That old granddad? His mind is falling apart!"

"I just want to find the other lockets. That's all."

"He has confused me with somebody else." Nusret turned away and leaned against the railing.

"I want the rest of the necklace. I need clues where to look," said Oran. "Can you tell me where you found the locket?"

Nusret looked around, angry. "Who are you anyway? How do I know you're not from security?" He scrutinized Oran's face, stared into his eyes. "Or a reporter?" He glanced at Oran's clothes, then he looked at them more closely. "Or a foreign spy?"

Oran took that as a joke. "Do I look foreign? I'm as Turkish as you are. I'm doing a book about Ottoman cities. I'm taking photographs of historical buildings."

"Where are you from?" Nusret wasn't satisfied. "I don't think you're from Istanbul."

"Actually I'm from America." Oran could have kept on with the lies, but he was afraid of getting tangled up in them. "I'm from New York. My parents met in New York when they were university students." That was true. "Listen. I want to be honest with you. Only my mother is Turkish. My real name is Oran Crossmoor."

"I thought so! You speak with an accent, did you know that? Very slight, but I could tell." He was inspecting Oran again. "So you're an American – a Turk from America. Do you like Turkey?"

"I love it," said Oran. "The people are friendly, the food is good..."

"Then why don't you move here?"

Oran looked Nusret straight in the eye. "Maybe I will."

"Good." Nusret turned back toward the Bosporus and placed his arms on the railing. A ferry from Haydarpasa was maneuvering to land at the dock. Oran and Nusret watched it as it turned a quarter circle, then swiftly glided alongside the pier.

"I don't know much," Nusret said. "I got it from some hippies. I was working earlier this summer at the border with Greece, at Ipsala. This group of hippies came through. Swiss."

Oran thought of the blonde girl, the one whose photo he had taken the day he bought the locket. What had her friends called her? Anna? No. Annelies, that was it.

"They looked suspicious, so we checked them for drugs. No drugs, but one of them was carrying that nice piece of jewelry. A fine gift for my wife. I offered to buy it, but at a low price. I'm not a rich man. I never believed they'd accept."

A likely story, thought Oran. He probably threatened to throw them in jail unless they gave him a present.

"Why did you sell it?" asked Oran. "Why didn't you give it to your wife?"

"I began thinking that maybe it was worth a lot of money. I could do a lot of things with that extra cash. I wanted to make a down payment on a car. I could get my mother a color TV. I could always throw in a nice ring for my wife. She would be just as happy with that as with the locket."

"You don't know anything about the other lockets?" Oran asked.

"Only one, that's all they had."

"Did they tell you where they found it?"

"No."

"Do you remember their names?"

Nusret lifted his chin.

"Or when they came through?"

"A couple of weeks ago. Mid June."

"I suppose it would be tough to find their names, to track them down."

"Yeah."

It looked pretty hopeless. "Could I offer you a tea?" Oran asked. "Or a beer?"

"No thanks," said Nusret. "I'm going to head back home." He took out a pack of cigarettes. "Like one?"

Oran refused.

Nusret pulled out a cigarette and lit it. "Sorry I couldn't help you."

Oran shrugged his shoulders. "It doesn't matter." He held out his hand. "Congratulations on last night's arrest."

Nusret spat out a piece of tobacco. "Thanks," he said as they shook hands. Then he leaned on the railing again and looked out toward the boats and the seagulls and the deep blue water.

Oran turned and headed across the bridge toward Eminonu, the New Mosque, and Beril. As he walked off, he felt certain that Nusret was watching him, waiting for him to disappear into the crowd.

Chapter 10

Oran and Beril took the elevator to the fifth floor, to Leyla's apartment in town. At first Oran had not wanted to come. "She will just get upset," he said. Beril had already made clear how annoyed she was that he had interviewed Nusret Demir by himself. He did not need a session with another angry woman.

But Beril swore that Aunt Leyla had specifically requested her to bring Oran along. Aunt Leyla had a special mission for him.

"Can't you tell me what this mission is?" Oran had asked.

No. Aunt Leyla insisted on telling him herself and Beril had agreed to keep the secret.

* * *

When she opened the door and welcomed them into the apartment, Gul smiled warmly at Beril, civilly at Oran. This cool greeting didn't bother Oran; he was thinking of the more important reception that awaited him in the living room beyond the hall. He and Beril were shown in at once. As they left the hallway, Oran caught sight of an umbrella rack. He smiled to himself. That was one thing he would steer clear of.

When they stepped into the living room, Beril went straight to greet her great-aunt. Oran looked around. What a contrast with the house on Buyukada! No furniture in transit here. Everything in place. The large room was pale green, with a beautiful carpet on the floor. A Shirvan? On the walls, a startling selection of art: two Japanese scrolls, a large oil painting of the Istanbul skyline, and, above the pewter-colored armchair at the end of the room where Leyla Hanim was seated, two portraits in the cubist style. Beyond this, windows and a double door gave out onto a terrace and a panoramic view of the Bosporus.

Beril was leaning over, giving Leyla Hanim a kiss.

Then Leyla spotted him. "Oran, my dear, how are you?" She rose from her chair and stepped forward to shake hands. She looked him squarely in the eye and gave him a cordial smile. "Do have a seat, both of you. Gul will bring us some fruit juice. It's so hot today."

She settled back into her armchair.

"Beril tells me you offered to interview the policeman with her. That is very kind. Do tell me the news. Did you find him?"

Oran described his conversation that morning.

"Surely he is lying," Leyla said. "Customs officials just don't *buy* objects carried by tourists, do they? At least not valuable antique jewelry."

"Should we ask your friend in the police department to check further?" Beril asked her.

"Zeki Bey? He could verify that Nusret was indeed posted at the Greek border. If Nusret did extort the locket from tourists, he probably knows nothing of its history. Exactly how he persuaded the tourists to sell need not concern us. Meanwhile, Oran, you are going to Athens!"

"Athens?" This wasn't at all what he had been expecting from this meeting.

"If you don't have other plans, of course."

"I hoped to be in Thessaloniki next week, taking pictures for my book."

"Beril told me. Actually, she said Greece, so I assumed Athens. Athens and Thessaloniki aren't too terribly far apart, are they? Have some juice. Apricot or sour cherry?"

Gul had brought in a silver tray with bottles of fruit juice, glasses, and cookies. Leyla supervised while Gul served.

Oran took a glass of dark red cherry juice. "What would I do in Athens?"

"I had tea yesterday with an old friend, a Frenchman from Beirut now living on Cyprus. I described the locket you bought – naturally, it's what's on my mind right now! Jacques – my friend

– told me he once had dealings with a Greek specialist in historical jewelry who had pieces of the sort I described. This was many years ago, he said, in Beirut. But the dealer later settled in Athens. Jacques noticed his ads, from time to time, in antiques magazines. The man's name is Konstantinos Tsellos. Jacques assured me his reputation is excellent – the perfect person for us to contact."

"Is he still alive?" asked Beril.

"He is," Leyla declared. "We have checked already. We found the number and telephoned the shop. Mr. Tsellos comes in regularly, although he has officially retired. So, Oran, I am sending you to Athens to interview Mr. Tsellos to see if our search can be advanced in any way. "

Oran looked at Beril. "Are you going, too?"

"I can't," she said. "I don't have a passport."

"Even if she did," Leyla said, "she would need a Greek visa, and that would take time to get. But you have an American passport. You can just go!"

"You are giving me free rein to follow these clues?"

"God has surely sent you to help us recover the necklace. I don't want to wait until Beril receives a passport. That could take weeks. I could go myself, but I simply don't have the stamina. So I choose to ask you. I sense you have a taste for adventure. There is a risk, I know." She paused. "You might, of course, find more lockets and disappear." She was watching him carefully. "Might you not?"

Oran thought for a moment. "Only if I decided to hand the lockets over to my grandfather."

"Beril is afraid of that," said Leyla.

"Then you would have to deal with my grandfather."

"I wish I could go with you," Beril said.

"To make sure I didn't run off?"

Beril tilted her head. "I've always wanted to see Greece."

Oran smiled, then turned to Leyla. "How can I be sure the

Greek jeweler will talk with me?"

"My friend Jacques Lebrun has written a letter of introduction. No matter that many years have passed since they last
saw each other. Such a letter has a certain authority, I assure
you."

"When shall I go?"

"I took the liberty of making a reservation for you on a
Turkish Airlines flight tomorrow morning. Can you go then?"

"I suppose so."

"And Thessaloniki?"

"My schedule is flexible," Oran said. "Besides, I'm sure the
Ottoman monuments will wait."

Leyla smiled. "Of course they will. Now, if you will excuse
me, I will get the money to pay for your ticket." She got up and
left the room.

Oran gave Beril a quizzical smile. "You don't trust me yet?"

"Someone has to play the devil's advocate," said Beril.

"I'd like you to come," said Oran. "But if you can't, you can't."

"Maybe you will forget us."

"What makes you think that?"

"You didn't agree to any compromise over the lockets," said
Beril. "I have to be realistic."

"I can't believe she's sending me to Greece like this."

"She has put her faith in you. She has such high hopes now."

Leyla Hanim returned with three envelopes and a piece of
paper. She gave Oran a fat envelope. "Here is the money. There
should be 7000 liras. Do count it to make sure. I have always
admired your American habit of using checks and credit cards.
We Turks are so mistrustful, so afraid of possible fraud – unless,
of course, we know someone personally."

Oran counted the money. All was there.

Leyla Hanim continued: "I have arranged at my bank for you
to get a certain amount of traveler's checks in dollars. Since you
are an American citizen, the transaction has been approved. In

addition, I have reserved for you a room at the Olympic Palace Hotel. It's not the most prestigious hotel in Athens, but my travel agent has a relative who works there and he tells me it's very nice. Here are the name and address of Mr. Tsellos, our dealer in antique jewelry." She gave him the piece of paper as well as two envelopes. "And the letter of introduction."

"What language am I going to speak with this man? I don't know Greek."

"Perhaps he speaks English. In any case, I'm sure that French will do. Jacques would certainly have conversed with him in French. You do speak French, don't you?"

"I'm out of practice," Oran said, putting his moth-eaten, high-school French in the best light possible.

"I'm confident your French will prove adequate. I learned French in elementary school and lycée and I still speak perfectly well." Leyla turned to Beril. "Are we all set, then?"

The audience had come to an end. Oran quickly finished his juice, then stood up. Leyla and Beril saw him to the door. And there they stopped.

"One thing more, Oran," Leyla said. "What will you do with 'Tears' while you are in Greece?"

"I'll take it with me."

"Aren't you concerned about thieves?"

"If I were you, I'd keep it in a safe place," said Beril. "Why don't you leave it here with Aunt Leyla?"

"Oh!" said Oran. So this was why they had trapped him in the doorway. "I could leave it with friends. Or with my mother's relatives in Bursa."

"It's a long way to Bursa," Beril said.

"I'm trusting you," Leyla said. "Won't you trust me?"

Oran felt hot with embarrassment.

"You needn't worry," Leyla said. "I have a great loyalty to the Crossmoor family."

Oran stepped toward the door. "May I think about it?"

"Of course. You have the rest of the day to decide," said Leyla. "This proposal must come as a complete surprise."

"That's for sure," Oran said.

"Surprises have a way of scattering one's wits. It can take time to collect them and put them back into place."

"Will you take lots of pictures in Greece?" Beril asked.

"If I get to Thessaloniki..."

"I'd love to see pictures of old houses, eighteenth or nineteenth century, from anywhere."

"When you return," said Leyla, "I want a full report."

Oran shook hands with both women. "A votre service, Madame," he said to Leyla. Then he smiled at Beril. "And yours, too."

"I am full of hope," Leyla said. "Oran, good luck!"

PART TWO

Prologue

September, 1922. The Island of Samos

On Samos, Yorgo Triandis, like everyone else, was waiting for news from Smyrna. Only two weeks after the collapse of the Greek army in central Anatolia, the Turks had recaptured Smyrna, after three years of Greek occupation. For the Greeks, it was a colossal disaster.

A few days after the fall of Smyrna, a boy brought Yorgo a message. The message was surely from Murat, Yorgo's Turkish supplier on the Anatolian mainland. Yorgo hadn't heard from Murat for days. "Who gave this to you?" Yorgo asked.

"A man."

"What man? What's his name?"

The boy knew nothing. Yorgo gave him a coin and he went off. Yorgo read the message. 'A Greek lady from Smyrna wants passage to Samos. She'll pay nicely. Mustafa's pier, 3 AM Saturday. Secret! Tell the boy yes or no.' The boy? Yorgo rushed outside. The boy was nearby, watching a thick line of ants entering a crack in the wall.

"Are you waiting for the message?"

The boy nodded.

"Yes," Yorgo said. "Tell them yes."

* * *

Yorgo had almost two days to wait. The excitement was unbearable. He was going to rescue a fellow Greek from the great catastrophe, but he couldn't tell a soul.

He set sail Friday afternoon and headed south around the east coast of the island. He would anchor his boat at an isolated cove and wait there until midnight. Then he would start for the

Turkish coast. Mustafa's pier was located in the shadow of Mt. Mycale, well to the south of the town of Kusadasi. Mustafa and his family lived there alone. Mustafa fished. His wife and children tended goats and a few cows and grew vegetables. He was involved in smuggling, too, Yorgo knew, but he hadn't yet been turned in. He had good friends, it was said.

A chilly north wind blew through the channel that separates Samos from the Turkish mainland. Yorgo waited in the shelter of the deck cabin and smoked cigarettes and thought of the payment he would be getting.

At midnight he set out. The sky was dark. Clouds hid the moon and the stars from view. When the boat left the shelter of land, it rocked back and forth in the waves, its wooden frame creaking and groaning. Yorgo raised the sail only halfway because of the strong wind.

As he approached the dock, he saw a soft red light swinging back and forth – someone with a lantern, signaling. Was there danger? He heard a whistle. In the distance a dog barked. Yorgo quickly lowered the sail. The boat touched the pier. The man with the lantern set it down and helped him tie up.

"Why is that dog barking?" Yorgo asked.

"Here!" whispered Mustafa. "They're coming now."

Two figures were moving quickly down the pier toward the boat...Murat and a woman enveloped in a black robe, her face veiled. She carried a small satchel. "Here she is," said Murat. "Get going!"

They heard three owl hoots. "Quick!" said Mustafa.

Murat helped the woman into the boat. "May God protect you, Madame."

Mustafa was already undoing the lines. Three more hoots filled the air. "Someone's at the house!" he said.

The woman turned to Murat. "I owe you a great debt, Murat Bey. I will never forget your kindness."

Mustafa had already tossed the lines onto the deck of the

fishing boat and was running back into the night. Yorgo steered the boat out to sea, out into the waves, into the moaning of the wind.

The woman went inside the cabin. Yorgo was thinking of his payment. He had not even seen her face. Could he trust her? Murat had said nothing about money. He must have been paid off handsomely, as the note indicated. Yorgo thought he should check right away. He called, ordering his passenger to come out.

The woman sat down near him at the stern of the boat. The wind was tearing at her robe. Her eyes, above the veil, watched him steadily and carefully.

"Are you comfortable?" Yorgo began.

"Yes, thank you. Thanks to you and your friends."

"The payment. Where is the money?"

"Ah, yes. The money." She reached into her robe and pulled out a little packet. "Here." She opened it. "A golden locket, with emeralds and rubies."

Yorgo cupped his hands and lit a match. The gold and the jewels glowed warmly in the tiny orange flame.

"It contains a relic from the Crusaders in the Holy Land. Keep it. If you sell it now, you will get a decent amount of money, but if you keep it, someday a collector will pay a fine price for it. It will make your fortune."

Yorgo was becoming conscious of her rich, polished voice. "But you? What will you do in Greece? How will you live?"

"My good fortune is to be alive, to be here on this boat, to be sailing for Greece. The rest will take care of itself." She placed a hand, a long hand with clear, smooth skin, on Yorgo's thick, rough fingers. "Don't worry about me. You are doing enough for me. Please, I am so tired, may I sleep a little now?"

"Tell me," said Yorgo, "what is your name?"

"Christina Markova."

"But you're Greek, aren't you?"

"With a Slavic name like Markova?" She laughed softly. "Yes,

I am. My mother is Greek. My father, though, was Russian. Please, if I could go inside and rest..."

He moved aside to let her pass. Alone in the wind, Yorgo contemplated the vision of the mysterious veiled woman, the honeyed voice, the hand with the long fingers, the lightness of her touch upon his hand. And her perfume. No, she couldn't be wearing perfume. Escaping, fleeing, who thinks of perfume? Anyway, how could he smell it out here in the wind? He was just imagining.

As he sat holding the tiller, guiding the boat across the channel, he thought he heard weeping. But the sounds mingled with the roaring and whistling of the wind. He couldn't be sure.

The boat reached the main harbor at Samos just as dawn was breaking. Yorgo woke his passenger and helped her off the boat.

"So I stand again on Greek soil." She tore off the veil and threw back the hood.

She was the most beautiful, most elegant woman Yorgo had ever seen. With those delicate, arched eyebrows and the wavy light brown hair, cut short, she came straight out of the fashion magazines his sisters liked to read.

"Would you like to eat something?" he said at last. "Do you need a place to stay?"

"If only I could lie down, if only I could sleep for a thousand years..."

They walked up to his family's house, a small house high on the hillside in the oldest part of town. Yorgo longed to ask her about the collapse of Smyrna. What horrible things had she gone through? But she was stopping frequently to catch her breath. All her energy was concentrated on the climb. It was no time for questions.

His mother, already up, welcomed the Greek refugee with a teary embrace. Then she went to prepare breakfast. Christina took off the black robe. Underneath she was wearing a simple dark woolen dress and stockings. "These are my only clothes. I had to leave so quickly. My mother, my sisters. I don't know what happened to them. I lost contact. I was so foolish."

Yorgo's mother brought in tea, bread, and white cheese. Christina ate hungrily. "I have the name of someone in Athens," she said, "a friend of my parents. I should go on to Athens right away. That would be best."

"First you must sleep," said Yorgo's mother. "Athens will wait."

Christina didn't protest. She let herself be taken to the room of Yorgo's sisters where, apart from a brief evening meal, she slept until the following morning. After waking up, she went to the harbor to buy a ticket. She returned to announce she would depart that same afternoon.

Yorgo accompanied her to the dock. A wind had come up. The harbor was filled with boats, and all – small, medium-sized, and the big steamer about to depart – were swaying back and forth. How could he let her go? Yet he was so young, so uneducated, so inexperienced. Such a beautiful, refined woman would never stay with him.

"I wish you were staying on Samos." The words burst out of him.

"If only I could," Christina answered. "But I'm a city person. I need to live in a city to breathe and work and feel alive."

Yorgo pulled out the locket. "Here. Take this back."

"No, no. It's for you. You saved my life."

"I can't take money for that."

"You are noble, Yorgo. Someday I hope you will realize how exceptional your generosity is. I want you to keep the locket, if not as a payment, then as a present from me. Yes, a present. A gift from me."

She smiled at him. Then she put her arms around his shoulders, looked him in the eye, and kissed him on both cheeks. Yorgo felt he was in the arms of the sun and the moon and the stars! She picked up her satchel and walked on board the steamer.

The gangplanks were pulled up, the whistle shrieked. She looked down at Yorgo and waved, and then the boat headed out to sea.

Chapter 11

Summer, 1982. Athens

The plane descended quickly. Oran reached across the middle-aged couple sitting next to him and handed his tray to the stewardess. He turned back to the view from the window. But at that moment the plane entered a billowing cloud and he couldn't see a thing.

He had left 'Tears' with Leyla Hanim. Was he crazy? He had extra prints of the picture he had sent to GF. He'd even brought them on this trip. But pictures were no substitute for the locket. What made him trust her?

The plane emerged into brilliant sunlight. Below lay a dry brown island, sparsely decorated with clusters of white houses.

After leaving Leyla Hanim's apartment the previous afternoon, Oran had stewed for hours about what he should do with the locket. Leyla Hanim and Beril were right. It would be risky to take the locket to Greece. But could he be sure that Leyla Hanim would give the locket back when he returned? What would GF say when he learned that Oran had left 'Tears' with Leyla Hanim? Would he think of the mysterious letter and wonder if the jewels were somehow making their way home?

Beril reminded him that Leyla Hanim had known GF's brother, Edward. "She knew him well," Beril had said. "That connection merits trust."

It was an instinct Turks would have. Oran's Turkish mother would think it a risk worth taking, and GF would no doubt agree. Beril had a lot of common sense.

The plane suddenly dropped. The woman next to Oran gripped the arms of her set. As soon as the plane recovered, the woman glanced at him, smiled, then turned toward her husband. Oran focused again on the view from his window. A large ship was turning into the deep bay, toward the port town at the far end of the barren island.

He was looking forward to seeing Beril again. When she made the comment about connections and trust, they had been out for a late afternoon stroll. He liked the way she walked. She was tall, and proud of it. She made jokes, she smiled and laughed. He could tell she wasn't putting this on to entice the locket from him. She did what she wanted. He liked independent women. He didn't want to dominate, but he didn't want to be dominated either. He wanted to be equal with the woman he loved.

Love? Why not...if wanting to be with someone all the time was love.

The plan was now following the coastline of what Oran assumed was the mainland. Settlements were increasing. Athens couldn't be far.

Oran smiled to himself. Beril had done it. She had made him believe that Leyla Hanim would honor their agreement and hand back the locket.

But maybe he should have kept 'Tears' after all. GF might give him a handsome reward. Of course Leyla Hanim would pay anything.

Did it come down to that – selling out to the highest bidder? Well, his ancestors were businessmen, all the way down to his dad. Love of money bubbled and hissed in their blood. Wasn't his Grandmother Charlotte's inheritance one reason GF agreed to live in America? But GF would never have sold the lockets.

Dad would have sold the lockets and reinvested the proceeds. In any case, he took no interest in his family's past and he disliked Turkey, which his wife had prodded him into visiting on a few occasions. The business world was capricious, erratic, vicious, exciting. He wanted his private life stable and relaxing. He liked to play tennis on crisp, cool days and work on his coin collection when the weather turned bad. In summer he would take charge of the barbecue, drinking a beer or two while the coals heated up. Like the business world, his wife could be capricious, but she ran his household smoothly, gave him excellent meals, and got him tucked away each night in their big bed. He would never consider leaping on a plane at a moment's notice, as Oran had just done, to go on some crazy assignment.

The airplane entered the approach pattern to the Athens airport. The air was hazy, but even so Oran could make out the Acropolis and the Parthenon. The height of the Acropolis astonished him. A flat-topped mountain rising above the vast city, holding high the famous relic of ancient Greece.

The structure of Dad's life seemed as enduring as the Parthenon. During his final semester in college, the stability of that life seemed particularly appealing. Elif was dead, shot in a demonstration she hadn't even wanted to be a part of. The universities in Turkey were barely functioning. Students could not finish their studies. The message was clear: a life without risk, that was the wise course.

But if he were to become a banker like Dad, would he end up being like Dad? He already resembled Dad in many ways. He owed much in his way of dealing with others to Dad's model: he treated people with reserve and distance, and he liked to imagine that he was scrupulously fair. In contrast, his mother either liked people strongly or disliked them strongly, and didn't care that she played favorites.

Shortly before his graduation, he had returned home for a weekend. Saturday afternoon, Dad asked him to join him for a drink. Together they built a fire in the fireplace, then settled into two comfortable armchairs. Dad's heavy red face and pale hair glowed in the firelight.

"You seem sad," Dad remarked, all of a sudden. "Is it Elif?"

Oran looked at him, surprised.

"You used to be such a happy guy." Dad paused, as if inviting Oran to speak.

Oran didn't feel comfortable discussing intimate subjects with his father. He smiled, then nodded.

"The healing takes a long time," Dad said.

"If only she had stayed at home," Oran burst out. "She would have been safe."

"Oran, nothing could have held her back." Dad reached for his drink. "I lost my first love, too."

Oran couldn't believe his ears. Dad never talked about such things.

"She refused to see me. All of a sudden. I couldn't understand it. She wouldn't talk to me or answer my letters. I learned later that my mother had bought her off." He took a sip of his drink. "Nancy's father was a janitor. My mother couldn't stand the idea of a janitor's daughter as her son's wife."

Oran remembered his Grandmother Charlotte's imperious bearing. He and his brother were always told to go play outside whenever they became restless in her presence.

"I couldn't forgive Mother."

But she did bring lots of big presents at Christmas, Oran thought.

"I couldn't forgive Nancy either," Dad went on. "For a long time I avoided women. Then your mother came along. She had a reckless quality I felt I could trust. What she said, she meant. She wasn't a schemer. She's still the only person I completely trust." He smiled. "Love will come again, Oran. Believe me, it will."

All of a sudden Oran was conscious of the stewardess talking to him. "Pull up your seat, sir," she was saying. "We're about to land."

The woman next to him was crossing herself. The plane was flying low over houses, approaching the Athens airport. In a matter of seconds the plane touched the runway.

When would love come? Was it coming now? Oran felt the sharp anguish of doubt. Did Beril even like him?

* * *

After settling into his room at the Olympic Palace Hotel, Oran went downstairs to find Dimitri Vranis, the relative of Leyla Hanim's travel agent. Mr. Vranis, a bookkeeper at the hotel, spoke good English; he had lived in Chicago for a few years. He was delighted to meet someone who knew his cousin in Constantinople, even if only second hand. He immediately ordered coffee. And yes, he would be happy to help telephone Mr. Konstantinos Tsellos.

Mr. Vranis eventually located Mr. Tsellos at home. He transmitted Oran's request, and translated the answers. Yes, Mr. Tsellos told Mr. Vranis, he had indeed lived in Beirut, and he vaguely remembered the name Jacques Lebrun – a French businessman? Ah yes, a distinguished man! He would be happy to meet a friend of Jacques Lebrun from Beirut. And a question about antique jewelry? Why not? After fifty years in the business, he knew a bit about the subject!

Since he lived a certain distance from the center of the city, he proposed to meet Oran not too far from the hotel, in the Plaka, the old section of town that hugged the north and east sides of the Acropolis. He was already downtown, in fact, so this would be convenient for him, too. They arranged to meet later that morning at Monakis's coffeehouse on Pritaniou Street. Mr. Vranis explained to Oran how to get there.

Oran left the hotel and strolled in the direction of the coffeehouse. The city seemed so white, so clean. What a contrast with dingy, chaotic Istanbul! The road began to climb toward the massive cliffs of the Acropolis. Soon he spotted the coffee house. Monakis, the sign read, in bright blue letters on a white background.

He entered a large room with high ceilings. Huge mirrors and old tinted photographs of stiffly posed gentlemen adorned the upper reaches of the walls. Everything looked in need of a good cleaning. Although the room was filled with tables, only a few were occupied. Two old men were talking softly. Others sat quietly, lost in their daydreams, a coffee or tea on the table in front of them, a cigarette between their lips.

None of them watched Oran with anything more than casual interest. Oran walked across the black and white marble checkerboard floor to the refrigerated display case at the back. "Hello," he called out. A man emerged from a back room, a middle-aged man with gray hair combed back over his head. "Oriste?" he said.

"Konstantinos Tsellos?" Oran asked.

"Ah, yes," the man answered in English. "This way, please." He indicated a door covered by a curtain of brightly colored plastic strips. They walked through a short passage and stepped down onto a little graveled terrace with a dozen or so tables shaded by large plane trees. A fig tree stood in one corner, its broad leaves splaying out over the whitewashed stone wall of the garden.

The man called out to an elderly gentleman seated off to one side. "Kyrie Kosta! He's here!"

Mr. Tsellos rose, smiling, and came over to greet Oran. "Bonjour, Monsieur. What a pleasure." He was a man of medium height, with little hair left on the top of his head. He wore a neatly pressed white shirt with lots of pockets, and brown pants belted above his prominent belly. "Please come sit down," he continued in French.

"My French is not very good, I'm afraid," Oran said.

"No problem at all! We'll manage, I'm sure. Would you like a coffee? Two coffees, Niko!"

Mr. Tsellos showed Oran to the table where he had been sitting and motioned him to a chair.

"Welcome to Athens," he said. "Clogged with people and pollution. Different from the old days, says my brother. You will see my brother soon, I hope. He is a priest. He is married to a cousin of Monakis, so he comes here often. I have only lived ten years in Athens, ever since my wife died. For a retired man like me, it's not so bad. When I want the peace of a country village, I come up here to the Plaka and sit in this garden and read the newspapers and drink coffee. I hope you will like Athens and take good impressions with you back to Turkey." He smiled expansively. "How nice to see a friend of Jacques Lebrun. It's kind of him to remember me. How is Mr. Lebrun these days?"

"To tell you the truth, I have never met him," said Oran. "He is a good friend of Madame Leyla Aslanoglu, the woman who sent me here. But I have a letter which he has written for you. I'm seeking information about a particular locket, gold, with rubies and emeralds, definitely an old piece. He seemed to remember you once owned lockets of this sort. Here, I have some pictures."

Mr. Tsellos put on a different pair of glasses to read the letter. "Ah, I see." Then he picked up one of the pictures and brought it close to his eyes. "Yes, that's it. I owned it, or one just like it. Of course I remember it. I'd be happy to tell you what I know. But why come all the way from Constantinople to find out a few facts which I could easily send in a letter?"

"Madame Aslanoglu gets impatient." Oran explained why Leyla Hanim considered his trip to Athens indispensable.

"I understand," said Mr. Tsellos. "She is a *grande dame*."

"And she is old," said Oran. "Maybe you get more impatient as you get older."

Mr. Tsellos folded his hands on top of his stomach. "Not all of us. We are not all of us so excitable. But she is right. If you have goals, you should pursue them with vigor."

Monakis brought them their coffees. Oran pulled out his cigarettes and offered one to Mr. Tsellos. After he respectfully declined, Mr. Tsellos added a testimonial to the benefits of giving up smoking. This was, he assured Oran, the main accomplishment of his retirement in Athens.

Oran lit his cigarette anyway, and led the conversation back to the locket. "Do you remember who bought the locket from you? I know it wasn't Mr. Lebrun."

"No, I don't remember," Mr. Tsellos said. "Not offhand. Who could it be? I will check my records. I certainly have the name there. Next you will ask me how I came across the locket, won't you? This I do remember, as clear as crystal." He hardly waited for Oran's assent to go on. "In Beirut. The war – World War II – was coming to an end, thank God. A Turkish woman came to see me. She had heard I was from Smyrna. Since she was also a native of that city, she felt certain I would take an interest in her case. She had the right thought, but unfortunately," Mr. Tsellos looked a little sad as he spoke, "I'm ashamed to say that the little Turkish I knew had almost entirely disappeared. I was only thirteen when the Turks invaded Smyrna and we fled to Athens. I had lived in the Greek quarter in Smyrna and I went to a Greek school, but I wasn't such a good student. I liked to play! I learned a bit of French though, and when I settled in Beirut I quickly built that up. I was learning Arabic, too, street Arabic, enough to get around, but not the beautiful language of the Koran. So when the woman from Smyrna came to sell me a piece of jewelry, we couldn't talk to each other. I had to find a translator.

"The woman had just buried her husband. He had dreamed all his life of making the pilgrimage to Mecca, and, at last, in his late sixties, he had the money. But the trip wore him out. On their return, they stopped in Beirut. He came down with a fever, and within a week he was dead.

"Murat – that was his name – had taken care of all the money arrangements for the trip. His wife knew nothing. When he died, she used up most of the cash she could find on him to pay for the funeral. Now, stranded in Beirut far from her home, what was she to do?" Mr. Tsellos spread out his arms and gave Oran a look of despair.

"The only valuable item they had brought with them was the gold locket. Since the name 'Medina' had been engraved on it, Murat felt it appropriate to take it with them to that holy city. The wife hated to give up this twice-blessed relic. 'May Murat forgive me,' she said. But she knew of no other way to return to their home in Kusadasi.

"I paid generously for the locket. A fellow native of Smyrna, a pilgrim, a widow in a far-off city...I found myself greatly touched by her story. As I held this piece of jewelry in my hands I felt a strange and powerful emotion." He cupped his hands as if the locket were actually in them. "The locket seemed to represent the aspirations and struggles of a man's entire life. I wanted to keep it with me always."

Mr. Tsellos suddenly remembered his coffee. He took a sip from the tiny cup. "Still warm," he said. "A hot day does have a few good features."

"Did Murat's wife tell you where her husband found the relic?" Oran asked.

"Indeed, yes, and that's quite a story, too." Mr. Tsellos set the coffee cup down on the table. "When the Turks attacked Smyrna, the harbor was choked with people desperate to escape. For a better chance at passage to Greece, some made their way to other ports along the Aegean coast. They were ready to pay good money for assistance. Murat, it seems, sheltered several refugees in Kusadasi before they fled by boat to the island of Samos. The locket was given him as payment by one of these refugees."

Oran leaned forward. "Did his wife know who this refugee was? His name? Anything about him?"

"Nothing. Murat never liked to discuss it. War is a nasty business, he used to tell her, and there the conversation would end. I'm sorry. I wish I knew more."

"Murat couldn't have been operating alone," said Oran. "Maybe I should go to Kusadasi."

"Grigori! Over here!" cried Mr. Tsellos. Oran turned around to look. A priest in a long black robe, a big heavyset man, had stepped out of the doorway. He approached their table, his shoes crunching the gravel. The priest and Mr. Tsellos hugged each other. Mr. Tsellos presented him to Oran. "My brother, Father

Grigori Tsellos. Mr. Oran Crossmoor, from New York. He speaks French. Friends of his in Constantinople are close friends of Jacques Lebrun." The priest looked puzzled. "You know, the French banker from Beirut."

"Oh, yes," Fr. Grigori pretended to remember. "Welcome to Athens," he said to Oran as they shook hands.

Oran smiled, enjoying once again the same words of greeting.

"Niko!" Mr. Tsellos yelled. "A coffee for the priest!"

The owner, sticking his head out the door, nodded in confirmation.

"How was the wedding, Grigori?" Mr. Tsellos explained to Oran that his brother had been away at the wedding of one of his wife's many cousins.

"I ate too much. I thought of my doctor. What would he say if he had seen me helping myself to seconds and then thirds of the desserts? But temptation overcame me."

"A fine way for a priest to act!"

"A tiny sin in the vast realm of evil. Anyway, I usually restrain myself. You know that."

"With Olga's cooking, no wonder."

"God didn't distribute talents equally. Not every Greek housewife can be a prize-winning cook."

"Olga's charred lamb chops and gluey rice certainly deserve a prize!"

"That happened only once, one disastrous night. How many times do I have to tell you? Her food is tasty and plentiful."

"I'm just teasing, Grigori! You know I love Olga. He is my younger brother," Mr. Tsellos explained to Oran. "He doesn't take jokes very well." He turned back to Grigori. "Oran here is tracking down antique jewelry and I have been helping him."

"I can see you have been hard at work here in Monakis's garden," replied the priest.

Mr. Tsellos ignored the jibe. "My friend Jacques Lebrun remembered I had shown him a locket which this man is now trying to recover. His sponsors in Istanbul once owned the locket, years ago."

"For this he has come to Athens? Not to see the Acropolis?" said Fr. Grigori. "This locket must be very special. What did it look like?"

"He has brought pictures. See for yourself."

The priest held the photographs by the lower right corner as he studied them. "Did you know that a piece of jewelry that looked very much like this was stolen earlier this summer from a chapel on the island of Andros?"

"Really?" Oran said.

"I don't believe it!" said Mr. Tsellos. "How in the world did you find this out?"

"I read about it in the papers. I only saw a newspaper photograph, and it was hard to see details, but it looks like the same piece to me. Don't you look at the newspapers, Kosta? I have a friend, a priest assigned to some town on Andros years ago. We used to trade stories about the offerings presented in the churches under our care. I remember his speaking of a small golden reliquary in one of his chapels. It stood out, he said, unusually flamboyant among the more modest thank offerings. When I read the newspaper article, I wondered if there was a connection."

"Is there any chance you could put me in touch with your friend?" Oran asked.

"Why not?" said Fr. Grigori. "We could go see him together. I'd like to. I haven't visited him for a while, and his health has been poor. I should telephone first, though."

"I'll be ready any time you are," said Oran

"Excellent! But he lives in Peiraeus, the port of Athens. I must warn you, it's a certain distance from here."

"Niko never brought your coffee," said Mr. Tsellos. "When you go inside to use the phone, ask him what's going on."

"Shall I order another round for the two of you?"

Mr. Tsellos and Oran declined. "I am thinking only of you, Grigori," Mr. Tsellos said. He folded his hands across his stomach and smiled benignly as his brother crossed the garden and went inside.

"Has your brother lived in Athens all these years?" Oran asked Mr. Tsellos.

"He was only five when we arrived from Smyrna. I was older, I hated the refugee camp, I planned to escape. But Grigori didn't know that life could be different. Apart from seminary in Thessaloniki, he has spent his entire life in Athens."

"You escaped from Athens to Beirut?"

Mr. Tsellos smiled. "I thought I was escaping to America! I was fourteen. I looked and looked for a job, anything that would take me out of the camp. I was trying all the ships in the Peiraeus and having no luck. Then I discovered that the cabin boy on the 'Queen Amalia' had come down with measles that very morning. The ship was about to sail. Was I ready to leave? the captain asked. Well, I said, I should go tell my parents. Where did they live? Behind Lykavitos, I said. Too far! he answered, and he turned away from me. Wait, I said. I'll come! Just let me leave word below, on shore. I ran down and found paper, then I realized I didn't even know where the boat was going. 'I have a job on a ship,' I wrote, 'headed for America, leaving today. No time for farewells, but I will think of you with all my heart. Pray for me.'"

Mr. Tsellos paused and looked down at his hands. Then he looked up at Oran and smiled. "I always feel sad, a little bit sad, when I remember this moment. The boat was not bound for America, but only for Cyprus and Lebanon. Beirut...that's where I got off and started my new life." He sighed. "Cyprus and Lebanon. All was determined then and there, in the twinkling of an eye. Yes, indeed. In the twinkling of an eye." He turned his head and looked out over the edge of the terrace, silent.

At that moment Fr. Grigori returned. "I reached him," he said as he sat down. "He lives with his sister Athena, a nasty old crow. She answered the phone. It took me five minutes to explain to her who I was and what I wanted, and then I had to chat five more minutes with her until her brother could come to the phone. Anyway, I can tell you right now that the stolen locket was the one in his chapel on Andros, and he has agreed to see us. Come, we should go now. He's busy later on."

Chapter 12

The taxi pulled up in front of a newly constructed apartment building in the Peiraeus.

"This looks magnificent," said Mr. Tsellos to his brother. "Didn't you tell me he lived in a rundown place by the waterfront?"

"They just moved," said Fr. Grigori. Oran paid the driver and the three got out. "The building at the shore was sold for a huge price," the priest went on. "Athena has been involved in real estate deals for years. This is her latest coup. They could live wherever they wanted. But here they are only minutes from all their old shopkeepers and neighbors."

At the door Fr. Grigori pushed the button marked Philippides and when an older woman's voice asked over the intercom who was there, he gave his name. The intercom crackled off. A loud buzz was heard; the door unlocked.

"They could have bought the apartment on the top," said Fr. Grigori as they rode up in the elevator, "but they wanted the insulation of an upper floor. I myself would have taken the penthouse. Think of the view!"

"Those thick robes protect you from cold drafts," said Mr. Tsellos. "Those of us who dress in twentieth-century styles are not so fortunate."

His brother rang the bell. The door was opened by a gaunt older woman with silvery hair drawn back into a bun. She was wearing a gray dress with navy blue geometric patterns on it, and slippers. "Come in, come in." She beckoned them into the apartment. "Welcome."

"Despina Athena, may I present my brother, Kosta." Fr. Grigori made the introduction in French. "I believe you have met, but some time ago. And a young American from New York who has recently been visiting friends in Constantinople..."

"Oran Crossmoor," Oran said as he shook hands with Athena Philippides.

"My brother is in the living room," she said. "He is not feeling well today. Or so he says. What else can you expect from someone who does nothing but daydream? He claims his left shoulder is acting up, that a restful day is what he needs. As if every day wasn't restful! He just wants attention. I made him an extra coffee this morning. He has been sitting in the sun, reading the newspapers, and is in quite a good mood for someone who is not feeling well, it seems to me."

She led them into the living room.

"Petros!" she cried. "The guests!"

In a comfortable chair in the sunlit edge of the room sat Father Petros Philippides. He stood up, a frail man with white hair and beard, dressed in dark pyjamas and a navy blue bathrobe. "I'm so glad you have come," he said. "My arthritis has been killing me this morning and I have been confined to this chair and the newspapers. How nice to have visitors!"

Mr. Tsellos presented Oran.

"The visitor from Constantinople," said Fr. Petros. "I am pleased to meet you." To Oran's surprise he was now speaking in perfect English. Fr. Petros was delighted to explain. "I learned French as a schoolboy," he said as he sat down. "But after the Second World War and our civil war, I was so grateful for British and American help in ridding Greece of Germans and commu- nists that I decided I would begin the study of English. I have continued ever since, to my great reward. Perhaps I should speak French, though, so we can all understand? Please sit down. Would you like some coffee? Some tea? It is almost lunchtime. Will you stay for lunch, too?"

"My brother mentioned you have an appointment?" said Mr. Tsellos.

"He doesn't have any appointment," said Athena. "He just wanted you to come as soon as possible. But don't worry, lunch is no problem. When I take the trouble to make a nice dish, I want people to eat heartily and enjoy it." She glanced at Mr. Tsellos's mid-section. "That shouldn't be difficult for you, should it?" She let out a laugh as she turned and headed for the kitchen.

"Athena is in an exceptionally fine mood today," Fr. Grigori said.

"Don't mind her," said Fr. Petros. "She's grumpy because I asked her to make me a second coffee this morning. 'So much to do,' she likes to say. But she looks after me well. I have no right to complain. Please, make yourselves comfortable." He examined Oran with a kindly expression. "So, young man, my friend Fr. Grigori tells me you are interested in the golden locket stolen from the chapel on Andros?"

"A week ago I knew nothing about it," Oran said as he took out his pictures. "Now it's the center of my life."

"So complicated," Fr. Petros said after Oran finished telling him the story of the four lockets and the golden star. "I had no idea." He handed back the photos. "Ever since you telephoned the memories have been rushing back to me. I can't clear up the mystery, no, not by any means, but I do know someone who can bring you closer." He settled back in his armchair. "Not long after the end of the war, I was assigned to a village on the island of Andros. The town was called Korthi. It lies on the southeast coast of Andros, at the bottom of a small fertile valley surrounded by high barren hills. As is typical, my parish included a number of remote chapels. Some were connected with distant farmhouses, but some stood alone, all by themselves.

"My parents had a good-sized farm on the mainland across the channel from Andros. I tried to visit whenever I could. They grew grapes and made wine. They also maintained a small herd of sheep. When we were young, my brothers and I used to take the sheep out to graze. By then, though, only one of my brothers still lived at home. With the unsettled conditions, it was difficult to find farmhands who would stay on for long. When I visited, I would always help out.

"On this particular day, I drove the sheep into the hills. Spring had come. The hills were green, and the wildflowers! How beautiful it was!

"I approached a cleft in the hills, a little valley watered by a spring. As long as I can remember, I have considered it a magical place. When I was a boy, I suspected that this valley still belonged to the pagan gods. Of course, Christ rules all, but perhaps the old gods lingered on in some remote spot just beyond God's all-seeing glance? Whenever I entered the grove and drank the sweet water of the spring, their presence seemed so strong. I used to look for their traces. Had these twigs snapped under the weighty footsteps of Zeus? That matted grass...had Aphrodite been sitting there after her bath, combing out her long, silken hair? If I were lucky, maybe one of the gods would smile and take my hand and fly away with me to Mount Olympus and show me wonderful things."

"Ah," sighed Fr. Grigori. "Spoken like a true poet."

Fr. Petros laughed. "You are kind to say so, but I'm no Homer, I'm afraid, just a simple Greek."

"That counts for a lot, doesn't it?" said Fr. Grigori.

"Some of us are mere mortals," said Mr. Tsellos. "I'm sad to say."

"Tut, tut, Kosta," Fr. Grigori said. "You'll be giving our young friend from Turkey strange ideas."

"Don't worry," said Oran, smiling. "Your secret is safe." He turned back toward Fr. Petros. "What happened in this magical place?"

"When I grew older, I no longer wanted to go into the valley," Fr. Petros said. "I had become a man. It was time to throw off superstition. But I must have been afraid, too, afraid of encountering one of the old gods, of being led by the hand and shown the most dangerous feelings and thoughts.

"On that day, as on all the others, I kept a distance between myself and the valley. As I walked by, the wind suddenly came up, a series of strong gusts that struck me from the front, blocking my progress. The whistling of the wind sounded like screams. I shuddered, even though it wasn't cold. Abruptly the wind stopped. In that instant a woman's shriek cut through the air, just as a jagged line of lightning rips through the blackness of a stormy night. I ran to the valley and entered the grove.

"A big, swarthy man was attacking a young woman. She fought back, but he threw her to the ground and tried to pin her on her back. The woman clawed at his arms, his face, his eyes, screaming incoherently. The man didn't hear me as I approached. I came up behind him and smashed the staff down on his back. He turned and looked up at me with an expression of shock. He raised a hand, but he was not quick enough to ward off a second blow. I hit him this time on the side of the forehead and knocked him out.

"The woman was huddling at the edge of the clearing. 'Let's go,' I said. 'Come with me.' I knew she could tell I was a priest from my beard and my hair. I explained that my family lived on a nearby farm.

"'He's my cousin,' she said. 'The bastard! He told me my brother was hiding here. My brother wanted to see me. I came all the way from Athens. Look at me now. How will I get home? What will I wear?'

"Her clothes were ripped and muddy, and her black hair was a mass of snarls. I told her to take my coat.

"She clutched my arm, weeping.

"'My family's farm is close,' I said. 'We'll take care of you.'

"When we reached the farm, my mother put her arms around the woman and led her off to wash and then to sleep.

"Later, at dinner, we asked her her name. 'Maria,' she replied. She ate a huge portion of the lamb stew. Her eyes shone in the uneven light of the kerosene lamp. Her hair was brushed back straight, not a strand out of place. Her high cheekbones and strong, straight nose gave her an austere beauty that touched the essence of heroic Greece. She was so beautiful. And I had found her in the magic valley."

The old priest shifted in his seat and examined his audience for their reactions. No one had a word to offer, not Oran, Mr. Tsellos, or even Fr. Grigori. He smiled. He cleared his throat and went on.

"Early the next morning, we set out for Athens. We walked to the main road and waited for the bus. We talked very little. She spoke briefly of her family: her mother; her late father, a merchant in Athens; and the brother whom she had not seen in years, off in the north fighting in the mountains, she thought, but for which side she couldn't be sure. She herself had spent much of the war on Samos, with her grandparents.

"When we arrived in Athens, she insisted on continuing alone. I never expected to see her again.

"The next spring at Easter time, I opened the door of my house in Korthi in answer to a persistent knocking. There she was. 'Despina Maria,' I cried. 'What are you doing here?'

"She had come to Andros to fulfill a vow she had made to St. George. I had rescued her last spring on the feast day of St. George. Surely it was a divine intervention. She decided to pray to St. George for his help in ending the turmoil the war had inflicted on her family. She prayed for the safe return of her brother, for a calming influence on her excitable mother, for enough money to assure good meals and clothes and shelter. And all this had come to pass.

"She herself had found work as a secretary for a shipping firm in the Peiraeus, where she caught the eye of a vice-president, a middle-aged widower with graying hair. He eventually proposed marriage. They would be married that summer.

"So Maria had much to be thankful for. She had vowed to St. George that if he answered her prayers she would offer him the most precious item she owned. When she learned that a chapel dedicated to St. George stood a short distance to the north of Korthi, she was pleased. She thought it fitting that her gift should go to a church under my authority."

All of a sudden Fr. Petros felt thirsty. He never talked this much. His throat was dry.

"Athena!" he shouted. "Athena!"

"Yes?" His sister quickly opened the door and poked in her head. "You don't need to shout. I haven't lost my hearing."

"Bring us some lemonade. Please." Fr. Petros loved fresh lemonade on hot summer days, and Athena made it so well.

"As you wish."

A pitcher and glasses were ceremoniously brought in on a tray. When Athena left the room, Fr. Petros continued his story.

"The object Maria intended to present...you have certainly guessed...was the gold locket you tell me you have recovered in Constantinople. I asked where she had obtained it.

"'From a friend.' That's all she said. I became suspicious. Had she stolen it? I asked her permission to copy the inscription, in order to find out what was written, I said.

"I discovered that the locket had a companion. Today you tell me it's one of four, but it seemed enough of a surprise to find a second. Theodoros Dimitriadis owned it."

"Oh!" exclaimed Mr. Tsellos. "The rich industrialist?"

"Indeed, one and the same," said Fr. Petros. "He kept his collection at his country house, his family's villa, but the house was vandalized by communists during the civil war and the locket was taken."

"How did you learn about this?" Oran asked.

"I had become suspicious, as I said, so I was keeping my eyes open for any clues. The break-in was reported in the newspapers. His important collection of antique jewelry had been stolen."

"I don't remember hearing about this," said Mr. Tsellos.

"You were living in Beirut," Fr. Grigori reminded him. "A foreign country."

"The locket wasn't named specifically in the news reports," Fr. Petros said, "but mention was made of a catalogue, a book. I made a special effort to find the book and check what sort of jewelry he had collected. I was lucky. He had owned a locket identical to Maria's. It was illustrated in the catalogue. It was definitely not hers, though. The inscription on her locket read 'Dum'u' which means 'Tears', but on his, 'Sitaar' or 'Veil.'"

The third locket, thought Oran, after 'Tears' and 'Medina'.

"Was it ever recovered?" Mr. Tsellos asked.

"Not that I know."

"Another casualty of our civil war," said Fr. Grigori. "Did your friend Maria in fact get to the chapel with her offering?"

"We went the next day," Fr. Petros said. "Maria presented the locket to St. George, hanging it on a nail not far from the icon of the saint. I spoke a prayer, and then we both prayed in silence.

"We went outside and ate our picnic in the shade cast by the church. Such an arid spot! No trees close by. I didn't mind. I had ideal company. At the end of the meal I was overcome with drowsiness – the wine, the heat, my heavy robes – and I stretched out to take a nap. When I awoke the sun was low in the sky. Maria had gone. I called her. But she had gone.

"This time I was sure I would never see her again. But I have. I ran into her by accident many years later in Athens. She had two sons and looked prosperous and content. Since then we have kept in touch. Her husband has died. Her sons are now grown, businessmen in Athens, married with children. She supports church activities, especially on Samos, where her mother came from. We meet every few months for a coffee. To tell you the truth, she and Athena don't get along. We might meet more often if they did."

"Where did she get the locket?" Oran asked.

"She never told me. But then I never pressed her. Perhaps she will tell you, especially now that the difficult moments of her life are far behind her."

"Could you introduce me to her?"

"It would be a pleasure. Let me write you a note of intro-duction. Her name is now Mrs. Petros Frontas. Her late husband and I share the same first name. Isn't that a coincidence? Do telephone her. Her English is good, thanks to her mother's encouragement."

The priest got up and looked for paper at a large desk set against the wall. Athena entered and said, "No, no, not there. Over here. You know I keep the writing paper in my sewing table."

"Ah, yes, Athena, how logical you are." He wrote his letter and gave it to Oran.

Now, where was lunch? He was hungry and he was certain his guests were, too.

"Are we almost at table, Athena?"

She glared at him. "You should know better than to ask questions like that."

"Has something gone wrong in the kitchen?" He thought he smelled burning.

"Of course nothing has gone wrong." She pulled out a cloth and started to dust off the top of the desk. "It's just taking longer than I expected."

The priest looked at her with alarm.

"I should never have hired that fool of a girl, she doesn't know a tomato from a turnip. She can't even keep an eye on the pot." Athena was rubbing every little crevice in the ornate dark wood desk.

The three guests were exchanging glances.

"Can I take everyone out to lunch?" Oran asked.

Athena stopped polishing. "How nice!" she said, beaming. "Petros, go change out of your pyjamas!"

And shortly Athena returned in proper street clothes herself. Fr. Petros took her arm, and together they guided Oran and the brothers Tsellos down the street to their favorite little garden restaurant. The meal and the conversation proved so pleasant that Fr. Petros's embarrassment at his sister's conduct quickly evaporated into the warm, dry summer air.

* * *

After lunch, Oran expressed a desire to climb the Acropolis. Mr. Tsellos and Fr. Grigori declined. After such a long morning and large lunch, a serious nap was in order. But they could all three take the electric railroad back into Athens. Oran could get out in the city center.

"And the person you sold the locket to?" Oran asked.

"Don't worry!" said Mr. Tsellos. "I won't forget to check."

For Fr. Petros and his sister Athena, a visit to the Acropolis was also out of the question.

"If I do any sightseeing these days, it must be from a car," said the priest. "How sad it is, in Greece of all places, not to be able to stroll among the ruins of antiquity, to hike in the beautiful rugged hills for hours and hours. Perhaps my character has benefited. A heart attack and now this arthritis have humbled me, have allowed me to see the limitations of man in this world. At least my ears and eyes still function well, and I think I am still sound in mind, whatever Athena might say. You go along and have a nice walk. I will think of you this afternoon as you make your way to the glorious place."

Oran thanked him heartily for his help.

"Do give Maria Frontas my best regards," said the priest. "And please, do not forget, our door is always open."

Athena, smiling at the memory of a satisfying lunch, praised Oran for his hospitality. "When you go back to Constantinople, you must teach the Turks some manners. If the Turks were like you, our two countries would be at peace."

"But I am Turkish," said Oran. "My mother is Turkish."

"Oh! I never would have guessed."

Fr. Petros smiled to see his sister so taken aback.

Oran shook hands with the elderly pair. "You must come and visit Turkey," he said, "and judge for yourself."

"Well!" said Athena. "Perhaps."

Oran then set off with Mr. Tsellos and Fr. Grigori to catch the train into Athens. Fr. Petros watched them until they turned the corner and disappeared. As his spirits sank, he sighed. "What a fine boy," he said. "We should have invited them all back for a sweet."

"Come now, don't think of it," said Athena, recovering her senses. "The morning was long. You need to rest." She took his arm and they made their way back to the apartment.

* * *

The priest drew the curtains, undressed and climbed into bed, pulled the cool sheet and the thin coverlet over him and laid his head on the pillow. It had been a long day and he was tired. He closed his eyes. Maria, he thought. His mind traveled back more than thirty years to Andros, to the dedication of the locket, to the picnic afterwards. Again, yet again. So many times...

They spread out the cloth for the picnic, set out the food, opened a bottle of wine. As they ate, they talked, they smiled and laughed. At the end of the meal, the talk turned to Maria's impending marriage. She looked across the hillside toward the sea. Then she turned to Petros and searched his eyes. His heart began to beat harder. His chest grew tight.

"It is you I love," she said softly. "You know that, don't you?"

Petros was paralyzed. The affection for this woman, the desire he had never acknowledged swelled up inside him. He wanted to take her in his arms.

"But a priest...you are ordained...marriage is impossible. Oh, Petros, it is so unfair." A tear ran down her cheek. She took out a handkerchief and wiped her eyes.

He took her hand and kissed it. How quickly it happened. "Please. Please stay with me."

He touched her cheek, its smooth pale skin, then he kissed her lips. To his amazement she responded, pressing her body against his. He put his arms around her and held her close.

Then gently but firmly he guided her to the ground. He put his hand on her thigh, under her dress. The perfume, the sweet softness of the skin...so sweet. So urgently sweet...

"No, Petros. No!" Maria abruptly rolled from under him. "We can't. We mustn't." She began to cry, burying her face in her hands.

He put an arm around her shoulder. "Don't be afraid. I love you. Yes, I love you." He put his other arm around her and kissed her on the cheek.

But she shook herself free. "If I give myself to you, then what? What is left for me?"

"I'll do anything. For you, anything. I'll leave the priesthood."

"You can't do that. To leave the priesthood for a woman? What shame you would bring upon yourself. It will not be me who will dishonor you before God." She pushed back her hair with one hand, then pulled at her dress, straightening it. "I want to go back now. Let's pack up the picnic things." She set herself to cleaning up.

"I'm sorry," he whispered when they were ready to go.

"Oh, Petros, can't we be friends?"

He tried to smile. "Yes, we'll be friends."

Lying in his bed, hovering on the edge of sleep, the old priest asked himself as he had so often whether she had offered any sign of encouragement after she broke off their lovemaking. Should he have pressed ahead? Should he have pursued her back to Athens? Would she have given in? It was possible. But the price, what would have been the price? He concluded, as he always did, that it turned out for the best. No need to invite chaos into your life when, unannounced, it intrudes so often anyway.

Sleep was carrying him off. How funny, he thought, that I should tell the Turkish boy I fell asleep after the picnic lunch and that Maria set off alone. Why did I say a thing like that?

He was so tired now, his brain seemed to be swimming.

Perhaps it is true after all. Perhaps I did fall asleep.

Dancing, leaping, quavering...stillness...the heat, the intoning of insects...the wind rustling the grass, a crow cawing...absence, emptiness, silence.

Which was the true story?

Chapter 13

Oran was sitting on the low wall on the south side of the Acropolis. In front of him loomed the cream-colored marble shell of the Parthenon. If he turned, he could look across the ruined Theater of Dionysos below on the south slope of the Acropolis out toward the Peiraeus and the sea. He had to sit awhile to take it all in.

But even as he inspected the ruins, guidebook in hand, even as he strolled through the Acropolis Museum, his mind wandered to the morning's interviews. The pieces of the puzzle of the lockets were falling into place – as if the anonymous letter writer were already hard at work: "The jewels will show you the way..."

But where, to whom? 'Tears', the locket he had bought in Istanbul, was traced back to a church on Andros and then to Maria Frontas.

A second locket, 'Medina', once belonged to Murat from Kusadasi, payment from a Greek escaping from Izmir to Samos. Mrs. Frontas had spent time on Samos. Mrs. Frontas couldn't be the refugee, could she? Oran calculated the years. Impossible. When the Turks took Izmir in 1922, she might not even have been born.

A group of Japanese couples scattered in front of him, taking pictures and admiring the view. They had small children with them, one of whom, a boy just learning to walk, was tottering toward him at full tilt. The boy's father ran over and scooped him up, laughing in apology. Oran smiled back.

That second locket, 'Medina', had passed from Murat and his wife to Mr. Tsellos. Soon he would find out what had happened to it.

And this morning a third locket had appeared: 'Veil', once part of the collection of Theodoros Dimitriadis, but stolen from his villa during the Greek civil war. After first looking up the

130

locket in the catalogue of the collection, Oran would contact Mr. Dimitriadis.

He had been lucky that Mr. Tsellos and Fr. Petros liked to talk. And Fr. Petros was so sweet. He clearly cast himself as a romantic hero. Living with that difficult sister must stimulate his fantasies.

It was getting on in the afternoon. By the time he walked back to the hotel, the Athenian siesta would be well over – a respectable hour to telephone Mrs. Frontas.

But when he rang the number the priest had given him, there was no answer.

* * *

Later that evening, after more unsuccessful tries to reach Mrs. Frontas, Oran went out for dinner and a walk. At some point he'd stop for coffee. Following tradition, the restaurant where he had just eaten didn't serve coffee. He would have to find a proper café.

The air was warm and dry. A faint breeze stirred, dissipating into the night the deadening exhaust of cars, trucks, and buses. Oran decided to climb Mt. Lykavitos, the other peak in the center of Athens. He wouldn't have to climb the entire mountain. A funicular railway enabled the less vigorous to reach the top. If the summit was further and higher than he anticipated, he might well count himself in that group.

As he walked along an arcaded sidewalk, he passed a chocolate store. He stopped to admire the carefully assembled pyramids of chocolates in the window. Elif had loved chocolate, especially chocolate syrup. She loved to eat profiteroles, clusters of little cream puffs awash in chocolate syrup. Funny, she never gained a pound. Beril would be another matter! He imagined Beril face-to-face with a plate of profiteroles. The anguish! The longing! He smiled as he turned away from the store window.

Well before reaching the funicular, he found himself in a small square on the hillside, Kolonaki Square. It had cafés. It looked like a good place to watch people. He sat down in a comfortable armchair, ordered a coffee, and lit a cigarette.

Lights shone around the square. People passed, a gray-haired woman with a thin black sweater draped over her shoulders and a young girl eating an ice-cream bar, a woman in bright yellow overalls walking a tiny white poodle, a pair of men wearing dark glasses who ran to their motorcycles, kick-started them, and roared off.

A silver Jaguar came to a stop in front of the café. A chauffeur in a black cap with gold braid opened the rear door. An old woman emerged, wearing a lustrous green dress. She had red hair and a gold necklace. Her face was heavily made up. An elderly man trotted up and kissed her hand and led her off to a table where a handful of people were sitting. Passers-by stopped to watch. People in the café whispered to each other. A man ran over from across the street, took out a camera, and flash! flash! flash! until he was chased away.

Oran hailed a waiter and, indicating the old woman, raised his eyebrows to ask, who?

"Mrs. Dimitriadis," he said. "Mrs. Theodoros Dimitriadis. Daidalos Industries." He rubbed his fingers together. "Very rich."

Oran tried to see her face again, but she was hidden behind the people seated next to her. Mrs. Dimitriadis! Should he approach her? She must know something about the stolen locket. He could have the waiter give her a note. But shouldn't he contact her husband first? If she's that old, he must be a fossil. If he's still alive...

While he was debating which action to take, Mrs. Dimitriadis stood up and, in the company of a well-dressed, middle-aged couple, returned to her silver Jaguar. She kissed her friends on both cheeks, then stepped into the car. The chauffeur shut the door after her, and the car glided off into the night.

Oran felt relieved.

He ordered another coffee, lit another cigarette.

* * *

The next morning, Oran cursed himself for not approaching Mrs. Dimitriadis. His timidity may have cost him valuable time. He must make a start on the Dimitriadis locket today. But before he did anything else, he would try Mrs. Frontas again.

While he was eating breakfast, a waiter came up to him and indicated he had a phone call.

"Yes?" he said, picking up the house phone in the lobby.

"Bonjour, Oran!" It was Mr. Tsellos. "How are you? I have checked my records. I sold the locket to Monsieur Henri Haddad on Tuesday, July 4, 1961. In Beirut. That is your American Independence holiday, is it not?"

"This Monsieur Haddad..." Oran began.

"A Lebanese gentleman. Well, Lebanese, at least. To tell you the truth..."

"Yes?"

"I do remember him, and..."

Mr. Tsellos was not normally at a loss for words. Oran wondered what the hesitations meant.

"I do believe he is dead."

"Are you sure?"

"Murdered, in fact. Henri Haddad took part in inter-clan feuds – those senseless medieval disputes that still tear poor Lebanon apart. Eventually he received his due."

"Was he just a hired gun," asked Oran, "or did he have a regular profession?"

"He was a trader in arms, and well off. His knowledge of weapons and his contacts made him invaluable."

"What can I do to learn what happened to his locket? Does his family still own it? How can I find them?"

"Much time has gone by since I sold him the locket," Mr.

Tsellos said. "Haddad is a common family name in Lebanon. And with the unending civil war in that poor country, who knows where the descendents might be."

"This sounds like a dead end," said Oran.

"Don't be discouraged," Mr. Tsellos said. "Families in Lebanon can be huge, with cousins closely connected. It would be difficult for Henri Haddad to disappear without a trace. I still have some contacts in Beirut. Perhaps they can help."

Oran thanked him, then returned to his breakfast. 'Medina', whose history he was learning with interest, had now vanished from sight. That was discouraging, no matter how Mr. Tsellos tried to soften the blow.

When he finished breakfast, he telephoned Mrs. Frontas. This time she answered. Oran introduced himself and mentioned the priest Petros Philippides.

"I'm sorry," said Mrs. Frontas in heavily accented English. "I can't see you today. It is not possible." She was leaving early the next morning for a vacation on Crete, she had many errands to do, and her baggage was far from ready.

Oran couldn't let her get away. "Can I come see you in Crete?" he asked in desperation.

Mrs. Frontas paused. Then she laughed. "Stop by late this afternoon. Around six. My suitcases will get packed one way or another." She gave him directions to her apartment and repeated that she expected to see him at six o'clock.

That gave Oran an entire day to research Dimitriadis's locket. First he should verify the description of the locket in the catalogue of the Dimitriadis collection. He consulted Mr. Vranis at the front desk. Any of the foreign institutes of archaeology would have the book in their libraries. Why not try the American School of Classical Studies? It wasn't far. As an American, he would surely get good service.

* * *

Oran sat at one of the ancient wooden tables reserved for visitors, banging his knees against the crossbar that connected the two wide supports below the table at either end. *La collection de Théodore Dimitriadis*, published in 1936, was a large format volume. When opened, it occupied half the table. The collection was housed in a villa at Mt. Pelion, Oran read. The public was permitted in on Tuesday and Thursday afternoons only, free of charge. He leafed through the section on Greek and Roman antiquities, slowing down when he came to the Byzantine objects. After a brief search he found a small black-and-white photograph of the locket. The accompanying description confirmed what Fr. Petros had told him: the locket was indeed inscribed with the word 'Sitaar', Arabic for 'Veil'.

Oran returned to the hotel, intending to telephone Mr. Dimitriadis. Mr. Vranis searched in the phone book. "Just as I expected," he said. "There are too many possibilities. Let me check with Madame Stella."

"He owns Daidalos Industries," Oran said.

"Oh, that Dimitriadis? He made his fortune during the First World War selling weapons throughout the Balkans. I can't imagine he's still alive. But let me check."

Mr. Vranis returned a few minutes later. "Theodoros Dimitriadis died seven years ago. However," Mr. Vranis held up his index finger before Oran had a chance to react, "he had a son. Iannis Dimitriadis is now president of the company."

"Could you call him for me?"

"Madame Stella is doing just that."

"Who is Madame Stella?" Oran asked.

Mr. Vranis smiled. "Our director of communications. She knows everyone. Everyone who can be contacted by telephone, that is."

A moment later the phone rang. Mr. Vranis picked it up. "Ahh...oh...wait." He put a hand over the receiver. "Mr. Dimitriadis is in Germany on business. But he is returning in a few days. Would you like to leave a message?"

"It's too long," said Oran. "I'll send a letter."

The son might well have control of the relevant documents, but the widow, Mrs. Dimitriadis, would have direct knowledge of the theft. Oran realized that he would have to contact each of them.

"I saw old Mrs. Dimitriadis, the widow of Theodoros, in Kolonaki Square last night," Oran said. "How can I reach her?"

Mr. Vranis went to consult with Madame Stella. When he returned, he smiled in apology. "Daidalos Industries refuses to divulge her address or telephone number. Don't worry. Madame Stella loves a challenge. In time we'll have it."

For now, contacting the son would have to suffice. Oran left the hotel in search of stationery. He sat down at a café in Syntagma Square, ordered a coffee, and, on the little round table in front of him, composed a letter to Mr. Dimitriadis junior, in which he related his mission and what he hoped to learn about the locket that once belonged to Mr. Dimitriadis senior's distinguished collection of ancient and medieval art. When he finished, he mailed it in the post office across the street.

*　*　*

Mrs. Frontas lived not far from Kolonaki Square. After a maid let Oran in, Mrs. Frontas came and greeted him. She was tall and well built, with beautiful silvery hair set in a wave. She was wearing a summer dress, red with scatters of tiny white flowers. She smiled and extended her hand. Her manicured nails were painted a matching red. A cluster of simple gold bracelets tinkled as she shook hands with Oran. Her grip was firm.

"I apologize for my initial hesitation," she said, "but preparing for a trip is always stressful. I don't know why. After all, my maid packs my suitcases. I only give directions. Even so, I like to have everything set well in advance. Otherwise I can't sleep. Come, let's go sit out on the balcony." She opened the sliding glass doors onto a large terrace. "It has been so hot today. Let's hope for a breeze." The apartment was high up on a hillside. Just below lay a little park filled with trees, surrounded by modern white apartment buildings.

"I even see a corner of the Acropolis from this edge over here," Mrs. Frontas said. "I have all Athens at my feet. Unfortunately truck drivers use this street as a short cut. Dawn is their favorite hour."

"An automatic alarm clock," said Oran.

"Set too early!" She gestured toward a chair, inviting him to sit down. "What would you like to drink? I have whiskey, gin, wine, beer, fruit juice..."

"Ouzo?"

Mrs. Frontas's face brightened. "Do you like ouzo? Of course I have some." She went inside.

The balcony was lined with shrubs and flowering plants of the sort Oran had seen in his grandfather Crossmoor's greenhouse: geraniums, gardenias, oleanders, a few tiny citrus trees. Across the park other people were sitting out on their balconies, reading newspapers, talking, or just watching the sun sink slowly after a fiery passage through the sky. Oran wondered what Beril was doing. Was she sitting on a terrace, watching the sunset over the Bosporus?

Mrs. Frontas returned, followed by the maid who wheeled out a little cart on which stood two glasses, napkins, bottles of ouzo, whiskey, and vermouth, white and red, and a bucket of ice with silver tongs. "Ouzo?" Mrs. Frontas asked. "You haven't changed your mind?"

"Ouzo."

"With ice?"

"Some water, too."

"Americans do like their ice." She poured in some water and the clear liquid turned cloudy. "The magic powers of ouzo!

Usually I resist. I prefer a little glass of vermouth." She served herself, then lifted her glass. "*Stin iyia sas*, as we say. Cheers."

The maid brought out plates of plump, shiny black olives, roasted peanuts, stuffed grape leaves, each packet stuck with a toothpick, and triangular pastries of flaky filo.

When the maid went back inside, Mrs. Frontas gave Oran a searching look. "So you have met Fr. Petros? If only you had seen him before his heart attack! He was always in motion."

"He seemed alert and cheerful," Oran said, "despite his sister."

"Oooh, that Athena!" Mrs. Frontas grimaced and gave a flick of her hand. "She's impossible. But you are absolutely right: his mind still works well and we must be grateful. Now I want to hear about these lockets."

Oran showed her the pictures. While he spoke, she listened attentively.

"I always thought there was only one locket," she said when he had finished. "Yorgo's. And now you tell me there are four. The man who gave me the relic, it is his story that will interest you. His name was Yorgo. Yorgo Triandis. But it's my story, too. Tell me, did Fr. Petros speak frankly to you? Did he speak of me?"

"He rescued you," Oran said. "He seemed proud of that. And he accompanied you to the chapel."

"Where I presented the locket. Did he go into much detail?"

"I'm afraid he did."

Mrs. Frontas caught Oran's eyes. Then she smiled. "He is such a sweet man. If he has told you all that, I will have to trust you, too." She took a sip of her vermouth.

Oran slowly let out his breath. He sensed she had been on the brink of turning angry, although he wasn't sure why. She could well have shown him the door.

"My mother sent my brother and me to Samos not long after war broke out in Europe," she said. "My father had died, leaving debts. My mother was terribly shaken. She had two children. War was coming. How would they live? She sent us to her parents, our grandparents. It was one less worry for her.

"We didn't want to go. Our grandparents were old-fashioned and very strict. We needed permission even to buy a once-a-week candy! But Mother held firm. We expected, of course, that we would soon be called back to Athens. But we were not to see Mother again until the Germans were chased from Greece. This tells you nothing about the locket, does it?" She smiled.

"I had not been long on Samos when I met Yorgo," she continued. "He was much older than I. About forty. He owned a small fleet of boats for fishing, transport, odd jobs. These ships he had acquired after years of hard work. Yorgo had started with nothing, you see. He was just a street urchin in Samos, the son of poor parents who only managed to live from day to day.

"He was not tall, but he was strong with big shoulders and a chest like a bull's. He had coarse black hair and a dark, dark face with deep wrinkles in his forehead and on either side of his mouth. I met him on the street one hot summer afternoon just after lunch, when most people were at home finishing their meal and getting ready for a long nap, and right then and there I fell in love.

"We were alone. He stopped and we talked about this and that. I never could quite remember what. I felt awkward and foolish. But he was so open and friendly, and he invited me...and my brother...down to see his boats.

"I went many times to see those boats. And one day he asked me to marry him. I accepted. I was in paradise. I was seventeen and engaged and I was in love.

"My grandparents, however, were not keen on the match. Yorgo was not of respectable family.

"I persuaded my grandfather to write my mother. It would take time to get a letter back from her! But Grandfather was practical. He knew his best hope lay in a long period of waiting. Our engagement might fall apart by itself.

"Contrary to Grandfather's expectations, our attachment grew. We saw each other every day when Yorgo was in port.

"One afternoon, as we were sitting in the shade of a tree behind my grandparents' house, Yorgo pulled out a small package, something wrapped in brown paper. He opened it up, and there was the gold locket. I was astonished.

"'Yorgo!' I said. 'Where did you get that? You didn't steal it, did you?'

"'No, I didn't steal it,' he said. 'I helped a Greek woman escape from Kusadasi to Samos. She gave me this in payment.'"

Oran sat up with surprise. "A woman?"

"Yes, that's right," said Mrs. Frontas. "A Greek woman from Smyrna, fleeing the Turks in that terrible September, 1922, escaping to Greece."

"A woman!" said Oran. "It never occurred to me. Did he tell you her name?"

"Yes, because I asked him. Christina Markova. A Russian name. A name I could not forget." She offered Oran the plate of filo pastries. "They are filled with a special feta cheese from Crete. Absolutely delicious. You must try them." He helped himself, and she went on. "While Yorgo was telling me this, he was looking at the locket with such a sad, tender expression that I realized, all of a sudden, that he had loved this woman. I almost burst into tears, I was so angry and hurt. But what good was it to be jealous of the past experiences of a forty-year-old man?

"He told me his Turkish business partner had smuggled this woman onto his boat. Yorgo couldn't refuse. He had just begun to work with this man, and the money promised to be good. This Murat – that was the Turkish partner's name..."

"Murat!" Oran said. "I heard about a Murat from Kusadasi just the other day."

Mrs. Frontas smiled. "It's a common Turkish name. Wasn't there a sultan Murat?"

"There's even a car named Murat," Oran said.

"This Murat, Yorgo's Murat," Mrs. Frontas said, "brought fruit and vegetables from the farmers and distributed them to the markets. If there was a surplus, he would often ship it to Samos, the island just offshore. When the Samian ship owner announced he was doubling his prices, Yorgo saw his chance and struck a deal.

"They worked together for years. Yorgo eventually bought his own boat, and several more besides. Murat was always very secretive about his money, Yorgo said. No one knew exactly what he did with it."

Mrs. Frontas paused. Her own glass was empty. She looked over at Oran's. "Some more ouzo?"

"No, thanks."

It was getting dark. Lights had come on in the apartments that lined the park. Mrs. Frontas turned on a porch light and called inside.

"It's warm, I know," she said when the maid placed a loosely crocheted white shawl around her shoulders. "But we all have our little habits." She sighed. "The story is quickly finished. Yorgo gave me the locket that day early in the war, when we were seated in my grandparents' garden. Two days later he slipped on his boat and knocked his head against a metal winch. He was in a coma when they brought him ashore. The next day he was dead.

"Never have I regretted the loss of anyone as much as I did Yorgo. He was my light, my essence. I cried bitterly for weeks. I ate nothing. I saw no one. But the war came and engulfed us all. Others were suffering just as much as I was. That sense of shared anguish brought me back into the world. Somehow we all had to go on.

"I treasured Yorgo's locket. I wore it around my neck. When I took it out to look at it, I remembered Yorgo and his hoarse laugh, his tanned, lined face, and his strong embrace. He would have wanted me to live, I knew, and in the locket I felt his encouragement through those black years. Afterwards, when all the fighting ended and my family was happily reunited, and with a proposal of marriage from a kind man who would allow me to begin at last a peaceful and ordinary life, I decided it was time to part with the locket. I would offer it in thanks to the God who had guided me safely through the dangers of death, of war, of poverty. I dedicated it in a chapel on the island of Andros. Fr. Petros had recently saved my life, so I chose a church under his care."

Oran felt sad for this handsome, gallant woman. "I have stirred up your memories."

"I am at a safe distance now. My marriage was happy. I have two fine sons, five healthy grandchildren, and no material wants. Do you know, for years the very thought of Yorgo frightened me? I felt it would be dangerous if I let those memories loose. How many years have gone by? Forty? I should be able to tell the story now, shouldn't I?" She fell silent, then picked up her drink, swirled it around a bit, and finished it off.

Oran wondered how deep a hole the death of Yorgo had made in Mrs. Frontas's life. Love destroyed, wiped out, just like that. Could anyone ever really recover?

"How odd," said Mrs. Frontas, "that events of forty years ago should still seem so real."

"Kyria Maria?" The maid was holding up a yellow dress.

Mrs. Frontas sat up, startled. "Yes, yes," she signaled.

"It's late," Oran said. "I've kept you from your packing."

"I was so silly on the phone, wasn't I? She will have done most of it by now."

"Did you ever learn anything more about Christina Markova?" Oran asked as they went inside. "She paid this Murat with a locket, too."

"Murat, of course, he would have had a locket. He, too, helped her escape. Perhaps Christina had all four. No, I don't know anything more about her. I have kept my eyes and ears open, but I have never spotted that name."

Chapter 14

Before preparing his letter for Mr. Dimitriadis, Oran stopped by the front desk to check with Mr. Vranis. Madame Stella was still trying to discover the telephone number of Mrs. Dimitriadis senior, Oran learned. Madame Stella's niece, a secretary for Olympic Airways, had a friend who worked as a bookkeeper at the Conservatory of Music. Madame Stella hoped this connection would bear fruit.

"What does Mrs. Dimitriadis have to do with the Conservatory of Music?" Oran asked.

"She still teaches piano there," Mr. Vranis said. "Someone must have her telephone number."

"I have something else to ask you," Oran said. "A real long shot. How can I contact the family of Henri Haddad, a Lebanese arms dealer who died some time in the past 20 years?"

"A Lebanese man? And dead?" Mr. Vranis gave Oran a curious look, as if he hadn't heard correctly.

"It's crazy to ask, I know."

"Why would I have any clue? Did this man have anything to do with Greece, perhaps?"

"He did buy antique jewelry from a Greek dealer, in Beirut. The dealer now lives here in Athens – Mr. Tsellos, whom I met the other day. You called him for me and translated. Do you remember?"

"Of course. And this Henri Haddad was a Christian, to judge from his name?"

"I'm not sure."

"Perhaps Greek Orthodox?"

"I could check with Mr. Tsellos."

"Is it because of the jewelry that you are interested in this man?"

Mr. Vranis was no fool. Oran told him about the locket, and

why he had come to Athens.

"One puzzle after another," said Mr. Vranis. "I trust you will let me share this question with Madame Stella?"

"I'm getting the impression she's a modern Delphic oracle," Oran said.

Mr. Vranis laughed. "Maybe she is! But let's wait and see, just to make sure."

* * *

While he waited for news, Oran took pictures, but they had little to do with his book on Ottoman cities. The Ottoman occupation had left few traces in Athens, which in any case had been a town of minor importance until selected as the capital of independent Greece. Northern Greece promised much more, but Oran didn't want to stray from his leads in Athens. So he settled for the little corners where a tree or a vine gave a timeless Mediterranean savor to the infinite repetition of grayish-white apartment buildings. If he were lucky, a distinctive person would step into the scene: the old man with a wide-brimmed straw hat who sat down on a park bench and soon dozed off, his head drooping forward, or the tall girl with the thick brown braid that reached to her waist and the curious sandals with straps tied criss-cross almost to her knees. This girl was carrying a plastic bag that read 'Zurich Airport'. She didn't look Swiss. She looked most definitely Greek. He remembered the blonde Swiss backpacker he had photographed in Istanbul. He had thought she was Swedish until he saw the Swiss flag on her pack. The beautiful blonde. Annelies, that was her name. The picture he had taken of her was probably back from the labs in Germany, waiting for him in Istanbul. He'd enjoy seeing her again, if only in the photograph.

Chapter 15

Istanbul

The night was clear but dark. The moon had not yet risen. On the balcony of Leyla Hanim's apartment, a yellow light glowed dimly. The French doors to the interior had been left ajar, the handle of one panel turned to keep the other panel an inch or two apart. Because the day had been hot and heavy, the evening breezes were invited inside.

One floor lamp lit the living room. But the room was empty. The dining room was dark. In the kitchen, the faucet slowly dripped into the sink. The smell of fried fish lingered, despite a vent that opened onto an air shaft. At the far end of the darkened hallway that led from the living room a crack of light cut across the floor, and loud voices, the voices of a movie or drama on a television rose and fell in a room beyond.

A man dressed in black stepped silently over the guard rail into the dark end of the balcony. He tied one end of a rope to the railing, leaving the rest coiled in the corner. He put on gloves, then slipped a mask of black cloth over his head. Holes were cut for the eyes, nostrils, and mouth. He moved toward the door to the living room. Did he hear voices? The old lady, Leyla Aslanoglu, had gone out; he and Dursun had watched her go. He reached inside the loosened doors and, with a twist, released the handle that held the two panels together. He hurried to the darkness at the edge of the dining room. Television voices. So loud he could almost distinguish the words. Someone was in. Who? He stepped forward and slowly opened the hall doorway just enough to peer to the end of the corridor. A crack of light. The maid? But she had gone out, too. How did she get back in?

Should he sneak out now? Or try anyway? The maid had shut herself in with her television. He had these soft-soled shoes. If he were quick about it, if he could find it right away...

But who knew when the old lady would return, when Dursun would whistle. He'd try the desk in the living room.

The top of the desk was neat. He pulled open a drawer. Letter paper, envelopes. Another drawer. Letters, stacked and tied with ribbon. The drawer on the right. A tin with a scene of windmills and ice skaters. He opened the box. Spools of thread. Needles. Bits of ribbon.

In irritation he shut the drawer. It must be in the bedroom. Down the corridor. Quietly, now. Quiet.

He opened the hall door and let himself in. He made his way slowly down the hall. With the faint light of the living room that passed through the frosted glass panel of the hall doorway, he understood he had passed the kitchen, a service room, and another small room, with a bed in it. He was now at the end of the corridor. The room with the television was on the left, another room on the right. He entered the room on the right. He could now make out the TV dialogue.

Man: "He came to you while I was in prison!"
Woman: "No!"
Man: "Are you denying it?"
Woman: "It's a lie, I swear!"

Had he seen that movie? It sounded very familiar. He turned on his penlight for a moment, to orient himself. He was in a large bedroom with a double bed in the middle. Small side tables flanked the bed. A massive dark wood wardrobe occupied one wall, a vanity table and mirror part of another. On the table sat a telephone.

Surely she'd keep it near the mirror. He turned off his light and advanced quietly toward the vanity table. He reached down and slowly pulled open the drawer.

Prrring! The telephone!

The man gasped, threw himself onto the floor, and slid under the bed.

Prrring!

The television sounds dropped. The man heard the swish of slippers.

Prrring!

"All right, all right!" A woman's voice.

An overhead light was switched on.

"That's odd."

Prrring!

The drawer shut with a bang.

"Hello? ... Who? ... What! ... How dare you!" The receiver crashed down into its cradle. "Crazy teenagers! Why can't the army take them when they're fifteen?"

The man in black was lying in a sea of dust balls. The dust was tickling the insides of his nose. He tried to hold his breath. A sneeze was building up. God no, not a sneeze!

The drawer was pulled open, the contents stirred around.

The man remembered a trick his mother had taught him. He brought his index finger under the bridge of his nose, and pressed hard. The sneeze calmed itself. Thank God! He took a slow breath. God bless you, Mother!

The drawer shut, the feet pattered over to the table by the right head of the bed. Bare feet in black slippers with embroidered pink roses. The feet were wide, but not long. Small, in fact. But ugly, from what he could see: thick, calloused, cracked, yellowed.

A smaller, flimsier drawer was pulled open.

"Ah."

Then shut again.

Could that be it? It must be. Once the maid left, the locket was his.

The footsteps padded out, the light was turned off. Soon the television voices were shouting at each other again.

The man crawled out from his hiding place, brushing the unseen dust balls off his hood, off his clothes. He turned on his penlight and went over to the right side table. He opened the drawer and saw a dark red leather box with gold initials engraved on it. He removed the lid. The locket! And something else, a gold star. It must have something to do with the locket.

He slipped the locket and the gold star into his pocket, replaced the lid on the box, and quietly closed the drawer. He turned off his penlight and stood, listening. Only the television. It was so loud, how could she hear the telephone ring?

He made his way to the door, then into the corridor that led back to the living room and the balcony. Now he heard clicks, little thumps, a door being unlocked, opened. Good Lord! Why hadn't Dursun whistled? A light came on just off the corridor, by the front door of the apartment, the man assumed.

"Gul!" a woman called. "I'm back."

* * *

Leyla had spent the evening out, invited to dinner by her nephew Metin and his wife Semra, Beril's parents. As she was riding in the taxi, returning to her apartment, she realized how happy this particular get-together had made her. She had a chance to tell them about the marvelous reappearance of the locket and enjoy their surprise. She told them about her campaign to recover the entire necklace. At first they irritated her with their lack of enthusiasm.

"It's such a long shot," said Semra.

"If the necklace is not recovered," said Metin, "you will be sad, but it won't be the end of the world."

Leyla bristled. "Don't you realize what an incredible opportunity this is?"

"We've lived all these years without the lockets. You would get over it, I'm sure."

"Listen to the two of you, so pessimistic," Leyla said. "I have two wonderful helpers, Beril and this young man from New York, Oran. They, at least, have the energy of youth."

"Is Oran suitable?" asked Semra.

"For this task?" said Leyla. "Absolutely."

Metin smiled. He knew exactly what his wife meant, knew that Leyla knew and would sympathize, but delighted in how his aunt had so deftly parried the question.

And Leyla knew from that smile that she could count on the two of them.

When she reached her apartment door, she took out her keys. She thought she had rung below, at the intercom at the building's entrance. But Gul had not answered. Maybe the intercom wasn't working. She opened the door, stepped inside, and called out, "Gul! I'm back."

* * *

"Gul?" the woman called again. "Where are you?"

The man froze in the darkness of the corridor.

The television was turned off. The maid stepped out of her room and switched on the corridor light. At once she saw the man in black. She swung her hands up to her head and screamed.

Quick! The balcony! He ran down the corridor, opened the door into the living room, and rushed forward. The old woman was standing right in his way. She gaped at him, her eyes wide with shock.

He had to get out. He shoved her down with all his might and ran outside. He heard whistling. Low whistles, like an owl. He hurried to the edge of the balcony and threw down his rope. Owl whistles? He scampered down the rope. He'd kill Dursun! Who could hear owl hoots when the TV was on?

As soon as he touched the ground, he ripped off his hood and ran off into the darkness.

Chapter 16

Athens

"Allô?"

"Samir? This is Antoine."

"Ah? I was just leaving the bank."

"Are you alone?"

"The secretaries have left. The office is quiet."

"Someone has been asking about Haddad."

"Our...?"

"Yes, our Henri."

"Who is this someone?" Samir asked.

"An American. With Turkish connections."

"What sort of connections?"

"Family. In Istanbul."

"Why the interest in Henri? He didn't have anything to do with Turks, did he? Or with Americans, either."

"Something about a relic from Medina," Antoine said. "A golden locket."

"This must be a cover. People weren't interested in Henri for things like that."

"My thought exactly."

"Let's lead him on a bit, and find out what he really wants. Is there anyone here in Athens who could follow him? Someone who knows what's at stake."

"Faysal is here," Antoine said, "with Prince Abdullah."

"Avoiding Lebanon these days, like the rest of us?"

"A holiday for the prince."

"In this heat? He must be losing his marbles. But Faysal, that's a good thought. He'll know what to do."

Chapter 17

Oran was finishing his coffee in the hotel's breakfast room when Madame Stella came in to tell him in person of her triumph: she had reached Mrs. Dimitriadis by phone and arranged for Oran to meet her.

"She'll see you tomorrow morning, at 8:30," said Madame Stella, a tiny woman with red lipstick and neatly set jet black hair. "For a few minutes only. Her schedule is very full."

That suited Oran. He was glad for any chance to talk with Mrs. Dimitriadis.

Madame Stella peered up at Oran through no-nonsense glasses with thick lenses. "Your name was the key. At first she said no. I said, 'Mr. Crossmoor will be disappointed.' She asked me to repeat your name, and then she said of course she would be interested in meeting Mr. Crossmoor." Madame Stella paused to light a cigarette, but kept her eyes on Oran. "You know what this means, I'm sure."

Oran shook his head.

"You are lucky to see her. She still plays concerts, you know."

Oran didn't understand.

"Alexandra Stephanides! The stage name of Mrs. Dimitriadis. You haven't heard of her, one of Greece's most famous pianists?"

"Stella!" Someone called from the back room.

Madame Stella shouted back in Greek. "You know the telephone," she said to Oran. "Never a moment's peace. Here is her address." She handed him a sheet of paper. "She lives in a villa behind the Hilton. I suggest you get there at 8:30 on the dot."

"Kyria Stella!"

"I can't believe it!" Madame Stella waved her hand with the cigarette back toward her office. "Alone for one minute and the poor thing's lost." She gave vanished through a rear door, leaving behind a fuzzy trail of smoke.

* * *

After breakfast, Oran prepared for another day of tourism and photography. His next stop was the National Museum of Archaeology. He had noted, though, that the city was full of modern sculptural monuments – mostly people, rarely abstract forms – planted everywhere, in squares, in little parks: the great and famous of modern Greece. He could get a good series of photos from them.

As he passed by the front desk, a man approached him. "Mr. Crossmoor? I would be grateful for a word." The man looked Greek. His clothes were elegant and impeccable, a dark suit, a red patterned tie – unusually formal for a tourist hotel on a summer day.

Oran glanced at the reception desk. Mr. Vranis caught his eye, and nodded ever so slightly.

"I am Faysal ibn Jinani, the personal secretary of his excellency, Prince Abdullah al-Wasf, from Saudi Arabia. Here is my card." His English was perfect, upper-class British. "I understand you are curious about my friend Henri Haddad. I would be happy to tell you what I know. Perhaps we might sit down, if you have a few moments to spare?"

"How did you find me?" Oran asked as they headed to armchairs in the far corner of the lobby.

"Henri was interested in antique jewelry." Faysal took a seat. "And so is Prince Abdullah, just as you are."

"I am looking for a group of medieval lockets with relics, Muslim relics, that once made up a necklace."

"Surely a necklace of great value. An unusual thing to search for, especially for a young man like you."

"For anyone to search for," Oran said. "Do you live here in Athens?"

"The prince has taken to spending a few months each summer on the outskirts of Athens, ever since the civil war in Lebanon made his holidays there too dangerous. He likes the trees, the flowers, and the quiet. But tell me, what is your profession? You can't be a full-time professional locket hunter, can you?"

"I am a photographer. And I work for Citibank."

"Oh? In what capacity?"

"Financial research, in the bonds department."

"What else do you know about Henri Haddad, besides his passion for old jewelry?"

"He passed away."

"That's true. A great loss."

"A violent death, I heard."

"A feud between prominent families. Henri had made himself some powerful enemies."

"He was an arms dealer, I understand," Oran said.

"Ah, you are well-informed."

"That's all I know."

"I could tell you about his clients," Faysal said. "If you're interested."

"I'm not interested. I don't know what kinds of weapons he traded. What I do know is that Henri Haddad once owned one of the lockets I am searching for. But he's dead. Where is the locket now?"

Faysal smiled. "It's time for you to speak about this with Prince Abdullah. His hands have held the locket you seek. He would like to meet you, for he, too, is curious about your search. Are you free for lunch today?"

Oran sat back in his armchair and looked at his camera bag, everything he had prepared for the day's outing. "Yes," he said. "Of course."

"Excellent. The prince's driver will fetch you here at one o'clock. The prince lives in Kifissia, some distance away. I will return separately, but I should be back for lunch." Faysal stood up and extended his hand. "It has been a pleasure."

Chapter 18

At 1:00 PM sharp, a dark blue Rolls-Royce pulled up in front of Oran's hotel. Prince Abdullah's chauffeur got out, requesting proof of Oran's identity. Only when Oran showed him his passport did he let him into the car. Oran asked him about the prince, how long he stayed in Athens, when he came. But the chauffeur's English had disappeared. Oran even tried the weather. No success. All he could do was watch the city roll past as they headed into the suburbs.

At last the driver spoke. "We are now in Kifissia."

They drove by cafes and restaurants under the trees in the center of town and passed a series of majestic old buildings that looked like hotels or retirement homes. The Rolls-Royce turned right and continued some distance to a massive wrought iron gate. The chauffeur spoke into an intercom. The gates swung open. The guard on duty waved them through.

The road wound its way through a forest of oak trees. The villa stood in a clearing in the forest, a large old-fashioned Mediterranean structure with ochered walls, tall shutters painted dark green, rust-red roof tiles, and classical Greek roof decorations. Broad beds of flowers lay in front of the house, white daisies, red geraniums, tall yellow dahlias, and countless others Oran couldn't identify, the whole immaculately tended.

Faysal ibn Jinani, wearing an Arabian robe and headgear, came down from the house to greet the car.

"Welcome." He gave Oran a solid handshake. "Did you have a pleasant ride from Athens?"

"Yes, thank you." Oran added: "Your chauffeur is quite a talker."

Faysal looked puzzled.

Oran smiled. "I'm being ironic."

"Ah, I see!" Faysal's face relaxed. "That's why we hired him.

Come, shall we go in? The prince will have finished his midday prayers. He is looking forward to meeting you."

Faysal ushered him up a few broad steps into the house. Inside it was wonderfully cool, thanks to the high ceilings and thick walls. Faysal knocked at a tall door at one side of the entrance hall. In the middle of the reception room an elderly gentleman rose from a high-backed Queen Anne armchair. The prince was short and thin, with sunken cheeks and a delicate nose. He was dressed in a white robe and a white head scarf held in place by twisted circles of shiny black cord. Over his robe he wore a tweed sports jacket.

"I am pleased to welcome you, Mr. Crossmoor," said the prince in carefully articulated English. Weariness showed in his deep wrinkles and the drooping pouches under his eyes, but his dark eyes examined Oran with vigor and intelligence.

"Please sit down." The prince motioned to an armchair near his. "We will be eating shortly. In the meantime, would you like a refreshment? A cola? Lemonade or fruit juice?"

"Lemonade would be great." The Athenian heat had given Oran quite a thirst.

Faysal nodded and left the room.

"You are in luck," continued the prince. "Ramadan begins later this week, did you know that? Of course you must, you are coming from Turkey. During the holy month of Ramadan, during the daytime when I am fasting...how can I say it...I am not in my best mood." He smiled. "I would have invited you for the evening meal, of course."

"Then I wouldn't have been able to admire the forest and the flowers," said Oran.

"You like my flowers, do you?" The prince beamed. "Flowers are one of my great passions. I receive a number of seed catalogues from various countries. Each year at least 50% of the new plantings must be of varieties I have not yet grown. The other half is composed of old favorites. I maintain a card file on all this, so my information is accurate. How I love flowers! In the bleakness of the Arabian desert the vision of my colorful Kifissia flowers sustains me for months. Do you like to garden?" He looked at Oran expectantly.

"I haven't had much experience."

"You must begin! Gardening gives such satisfaction."

A servant brought in two glasses of lemonade on a silver tray, set them on the coffee table in front of the armchairs, and withdrew.

The prince took a sip. "I am a religious man. That is why I found your story so intriguing. A family that owned and then lost a necklace of four medieval Muslim relics, all inscribed in Arabic, whose descendants are trying to find them again. But a Christian family! Crossmoor can't be a Muslim name, of course. Why would a Christian family want Muslim relics?" He held up his hand to keep Oran from answering. "I know. You Westerners, you collect anything and everything." He set his elbow on the arm of his chair, leaned his head on his hand, and frowned. "It never occurred to me that the locket was part of a set, not a single, unique piece."

"Did you own it?"

"Henri Haddad gave it to me. I understand you have been making inquiries about him." The prince peered at Oran.

"Only because he owned the locket."

"Henri Haddad was a difficult man. He started out as a prize fighter. God had given him muscles and agility, yes, but also a nasty temper on a short fuse. Since he is long gone, I feel free to tell you I didn't care for him. But liking him was beside the point. Our dealings were strictly business, and he knew firearms like no one else. Are you interested in guns, Mr. Crossmoor?"

"No, not really."

"I myself have a collection, a good one. My favorite is a flintlock blunderbuss that belonged to Count Alexey Orlov, Catherine the Great's commander-in-chief of the fleet that destroyed the Ottomans at the Battle of Cheshme. I would like to think he used the gun in that battle, but I can't be certain. And I have a Belgian Fabrique Nationale M 1910 semi-automatic pistol – the model used by Gavrilo Princip to assassinate the Austrian Archduke Ferdinand in Sarajevo, the shot that sparked the First World War. My real prize is...but perhaps I am boring you?"

"Not at all," said Oran, even though the prince had correctly anticipated what one or two more pistol stories would do. "Did Mr. Haddad find guns for your collection?"

"He did indeed. He was very good that way."

"Do you collect jewelry, too? Is that why Mr. Haddad gave you the locket?"

"Not exactly." The prince smiled. "I had helped him in a business matter. He was grateful, and he knew that I, a Muslim, would appreciate the gift. But I didn't keep it long."

"You no longer own the locket?"

"Ten years ago I gave the locket to my youngest son, Karim, on his twentieth birthday. He was a bright boy, innocent...like you. I thought a relic inscribed with the name of the holy city of Medina would be beneficial for him. I am not excessively super-stitious, not like some of my fellow countrymen, but still, it's foolhardy to neglect time-honored precautions."

"He's had a happy and fruitful life, I hope," said Oran.

"Happy I don't know, but fruitful, definitely not. My heart splits in two every time I think of it." He took another sip of lemonade.

Oran pulled out a cigarette. "May I?"

The prince consented with a wave of the hand. "My older sons are in Arabia. Each has a fine career, a fine family. The eldest is a doctor, a specialist in heart diseases, trained at the University of Pennsylvania. He is a professor of medicine in Riyadh. His wife comes from an excellent family and they already have two sons. My other son works for the Ministry of Oil. Having begun at the bottom so he could learn all about the industry, he now has a good position with much responsibility. He's a master of our traditional Bedouin horsemanship. He, too, is married, with a little daughter. So you see I have much to be proud of.

"Karim on the other hand...Karim has become a playboy. We all have our vices. The liquor and gambling, the women, the money spent on useless luxuries...I force myself not to let this upset me. What has roused my anger is the void at the center of his life. He devotes his serious efforts to mastering the game of bridge. Bridge!" The prince snorted. "How can a life centered on a card game be called serious? He no longer says prayers, doesn't fast during Ramadan, gives nothing to charity. As for the pilgrimage to Mecca, he told me he had no intention of getting trampled by hordes of ignorant Third World peasants. Such insolence to a father! And worse still: he has no wife, no children, and shows no interest whatsoever in remedying this situation. He honors neither God nor his family nor his country. He has shirked his duty as a man. It should not surprise you, then, if I tell you that Karim and I have rarely spoken in recent years. But I know what goes on. I have my sources."

There was a knock at the door. A servant entered and announced lunch. Refusing assistance, the prince took hold of a cane leaning against his chair and walked slowly across the reception room, through the hall and into the dining room. The room was lined on one side by tall French doors that gave out onto a sunny terrace bordered by trees and flowers as copious and colorful as those on the front side of the house. Prince Abdullah and Oran sat down at a massive wooden table. Faysal joined them. The first course was served, beef broth with tiny dumplings.

"I gave Karim the locket many years ago, and you can see the benefits it brought. But without the relic, perhaps his life would have turned out even worse, if that can be imagined. I never asked him about the relic. Do you know anything, Faysal?"

"No, Your Highness, the subject never arose in our discussions," Faysal replied in his formal manner.

"In that case," the prince said to Oran, "you will have to visit Karim and find out for yourself. Where would he be now, Faysal? On Hydra?"

"He has already spent several weeks on Hydra, Your Highness. I should imagine he has returned to Poros."

"Could you go see him on Poros, Mr. Crossmoor?" asked the prince. "An island, not far from Athens. You could easily make the round trip in a day."

"I'm free tomorrow, from midday on," said Oran.

"Good. Faysal, could you ring Karim after lunch and arrange for Mr. Crossmoor to visit? I do think you should see him in person," the prince said to Oran. "Critical business should never be carried out over the telephone. So much is conveyed in a person's body. And the eyes. Whatever message is given in words or tone of voice, the truth can never be masked in the eyes. That is one reason so many powerful Arabs wear dark glasses. They want to protect their secrets."

The servant cleared the soup bowls and brought in the second course, chicken grilled with thyme.

"Maybe he will tell you a simple, believable story," the prince went on. "It is equally possible that he will make up some ridiculous tale. Only if you are actually watching him will you be able to distinguish the truth from the lies."

He cut up his chicken with great care into tiny rectilinear pieces. Faysal, on the other hand, ate with surprising speed. Oran was already feeling quite well fed when the servant brought in a plate of sweet green peppers stuffed with rice, raisins, and pine nuts, served cold.

"Ah!" said the prince. "One of the priceless gems of the summer in the Mediterranean." But he waved the dish on to Oran and Faysal without taking any himself. "My doctor tells me I must restrain myself. When the doctor orders, we simple folk must obey."

After a dessert of lemon custard and fresh fruit, the prince invited Oran and Faysal outside for coffee. The servant held open the door for them as they walked out onto the terrace.

"It's so bright!" said the prince. "We must have some shade."

Faysal whispered to the servant, and a few moments later a large blue beach umbrella with 'Cinzano' emblazoned in red and white around the edges was inserted in a hole in the center of a round table. The prince put on dark glasses and positioned himself in the shade.

"This coffee is much, much stronger than Turkish coffee," said the prince while the coffee was being served. "It's flavored with cardamom in the Arab fashion. I do hope you will like it." The servant poured from an ornate brass pot with a long pointed spout. "The coffee pot has a core for embers. That's how the coffee is kept hot." The prince held the tiny cup to his nostrils. "What a divine aroma! I love coffee. I especially love to drink it outdoors. I don't know why. Perhaps its harsh taste reminds me of the pungent smell of earth or the crushing heat of the sun?"

Oran took a sip. So bitter! Fortunately his small cup had only been one third filled.

The servant brought a small silver dish piled with a neatly arranged assortment of Turkish delight, little squares covered with powdered sugar.

"Which ones have the pistachios?" The prince bent over, peering at the candies.

"Here, Your Highness."

"These are my favorite," said the prince. He took a bite. A shower of powdered sugar rained down over his coffee cup, and he laughed. "The first bite is always dangerous."

Oran and Faysal helped themselves in turn.

"Oh, yes, that kind is good, too," said the prince, noting that Oran had chosen a piece with walnuts. He took another sip of coffee. "How idyllic! The heat of the summer penetrating my bones, the coffee making my blood race as if I were a young man, and in the sweetness of the candy I taste perfection. You remember, Faysal, how Latifa – my late wife, Mr. Crossmoor – how she loved her coffee and sweetmeats? Such an irony. Her tongue could be so sharp. We all felt its sting. But then, after her meal, there she would sit nibbling on candies or pastries, in ecstasy, at peace with herself and with the world."

The prince fell silent. A pair of swallows frolicked nearby. The buzz of the cicadas seemed to grow louder. Oran felt his eyelids getting heavy.

"Faysal," said the prince, rousing himself from his reverie. "Would you try Karim? We must get an appointment for this young man."

"Do you think Karim will agree to see him about the relic?"

"Why shouldn't he?"

"I am thinking of Miss Morse, Your Highness."

"Ah, I see. Karim will think we are sending someone under false pretenses once again." He turned toward Oran. "You don't write for scandal sheets, do you?"

"I want to ask about the relic and nothing else," Oran said, meeting the prince's gaze.

The prince turned back toward Faysal. "You are quite right. The relic might scare Karim off. He would believe it a cover that only we could provide. So how can we get Mr. Crossmoor in the door?"

"A bridge fanatic from New York?"

"No! Nothing to do with cards, please!"

"Why not a book about bridge?" Faysal went on. "An American preparing a book on the different styles of bridge games in Europe and the Near East? Interviews with the Italian Blue Team, the Egyptians, and so on. Karim would find it perfectly natural that he should be included."

"Perhaps that's not such a bad idea after all," said the prince.

"I don't know a thing about bridge," Oran said.

"It doesn't matter," said Faysal. "Let me take responsibility for the deception. I know how to deal with Karim."

Oran didn't like the smell of this little plot. Despite all the assurances, the maneuver was bound to backfire. His best asset was his openness. Even the policeman in Istanbul seemed to trust him.

A short while later Faysal returned. "As I expected, Karim is on Poros, resting, he said, after an exhausting month on Hydra. He wants to see no one, he said, absolutely no one. But when I mentioned Mr. Crossmoor, the bridge expert, he expressed interest. I arranged an appointment for tomorrow, around lunch time."

"Wonderful," said the prince. "Get me some paper, Faysal. I'll write a note to Karim while you give directions to Mr. Crossmoor."

While the prince prepared his letter, Oran learned where to catch the boat from Peiraeus to Poros and which roads to take once he reached the island. Faysal recommended that he walk to Karim's house. It would take thirty minutes, but the route was particularly attractive.

The prince had torn up one sheet and was now beginning the letter once again. After quickly filling most of a page in his large, rhythmic Arabic script, he stopped, lifted up his pen, and, with a flourish, added his signature in the lower right hand corner. When the ink had dried, the prince carefully folded the letter and put it into an envelope. "I do hope your meeting with Karim will be successful." He smiled benignly.

"Thank you very much." Oran rose.

"I am so pleased that you could come," said the prince. "My chauffeur will drive you back." The prince accompanied Oran to the front door. "May God grant you all that you are seeking."

* * *

When Oran returned to the hotel, the clerk handed him a

telegram.

"Aunt Leyla hospitalized, critical, return at once. Beril."

What had happened? Oran went up to his room and sat down in an armchair and re-read the telegram.

I must call, thought Oran. If she died...how sad.

Yes, sad.

He was surprised. He hardly knew her. But that's what he felt.

He walked over to the window and pulled back the curtain. Traffic was picking up in the late afternoon.

I'd have to cancel my meeting with Prince Karim. My last lead.

The telephone rang. Istanbul calling, said the operator.

"Oran?" Beril said. "Did you get my telegram?"

"What happened?"

Beril could barely hold back her tears. Aunt Leyla had surprised a thief in her apartment, she explained. When she returned from a dinner the night before, he attacked her and threw her to the ground, knocking her out.

"How is she now?" Oran asked.

"Nothing broken, thank God, but she suffered a concussion. She's still slipping in and out of consciousness."

"Where was Gul?" Oran asked.

"She was there all the time but hadn't heard a thing!"

Gul had turned the volume of her TV up high, Beril went on, as she did whenever Aunt Leyla was out. When she heard Aunt Leyla return, she stepped out of her room only to surprise the thief in the hallway. She screamed and screamed, and the thief ran away. When she found Aunt Leyla unconscious on the floor, she called the police and an ambulance.

"And I haven't dared tell her the worst," said Beril.

"The 'worst'? What do you mean?"

"He took the locket."

"What?"

"And the gold star."

"You're joking!"

"I know, it's awful," said Beril.

Oran felt sick. "Who did it?"

"I don't know. He was wearing a black hood."

How could he have trusted them with the locket? What would he tell his grandfather?

"Come as soon as you can, Oran. I need your help."

"The locket is gone. What can I do?"

"Talk to her, tell her what you discovered in Athens. You have learned something, haven't you?"

The passion in Beril's voice alarmed him. It was demanding a commitment. "What good would it do?"

"She's dying the violent death she always feared. And now the locket is gone. Please."

"But there's only one flight a day and it's the tourist season." Oran felt foolish saying it. But he was angry, too. It was their mess. They had lost the locket. "I'm not sure I can get a seat."

"Well, try!" She hung up.

Why should I? He replaced the receiver on its cradle. Ordering him around, telling him what to do. What right did she have?

He leaned back against the pillows. He imagined Leyla Hanim lying on the floor, a small pool of blood under her head, dark liquid seeping into the ornate Oriental rug. Oran tried to banish the picture from his mind, but he couldn't.

He forced himself to get up, and soon he was outside. He walked by a travel agency. He went in to see about a ticket for the next day. The flight was full. He could get a seat for the following day, if he wished.

"What about stand-by?" Oran asked.

"It's possible," said the agent. "But I wouldn't count on it."

"I'll go the day after tomorrow, on Sunday."

He would see Prince Karim after all. He would have more results to take back to Istanbul, and he wouldn't have to arrange a second, special trip to Athens for another appointment with this touchy man.

He didn't want to telephone Beril. He didn't want to hear her voice. Tomorrow, maybe, or the following day, before he left.

He felt depressed and lonely. Coffee, cigarettes, a newspaper, he thought, that's what I need. Or just a long walk.

He reached Syntagma Square, but he didn't feel like stopping. He needed to move. Mt. Lykavitos lay just beyond. Maybe this time he'd find that funicular railway to the top. He bought an International Herald Tribune and a pack of Aroma filter cigarettes and headed up the hill.

Chapter 19

Oran made sure to arrive on time at Mrs. Dimitriadis's house, just as Mme Stella had urged. In fact he had arrived early, not knowing how long it would take him to get there. He strolled up the street then back down until his watch showed 8:30 AM.

As soon as the maid closed the door behind Oran, traffic noises seemed far away. The entrance hall of the large, cool house and the spacious living room were filled with the muted sounds of piano playing. The maid gestured to him to wait and went into another room.

The music broke off, and the door opened. An elderly woman with an aureole of copper-colored hair stepped in to greet him, the maid just behind.

"Mrs. Dimitriadis," Oran said. "It's very kind of you to see me."

"This is an unexpected pleasure, Mr. Crossmoor," she replied in excellent English. "Most unexpected."

Oran was surprised. Why unexpected? They had an appointment.

She looked at him keenly with her coal black eyes. She was shorter than he, but she stood absolutely straight. Her wrinkled face was expertly made up. She wore an austere black tunic, white pants, and a necklace of intertwining gold strands.

"Do come in," she said. She followed Oran into her music room, then closed the door behind them. She continued to examine Oran. She was smiling slightly, but said nothing.

Oran felt uncomfortable. "It's not too early, I hope," he said, just to say something.

"Not at all. I wake up very early these days, even after I give a concert. It's something that comes with age, I'm afraid." She gestured toward the sofa behind the shiny black concert piano. She sat down facing him, her right leg drawn across the seat, her right arm placed across the back of the coffee-colored sofa. "You even have a Mediterranean complexion. Yet with a name like Crossmoor, the family must come from England. Isn't that so? Now, tell me. How can a Crossmoor look more Greek than I do?"

Oran observed her long fingers and painted fingernails trimmed short, the liver spots on her hands. Then he met her glance. She watched him with a strange expression, those dark eyes embedded in the heavily wrinkled face with lashes powdered in black, thin arched lines for eyebrows, tall forehead, and the halo of dark red hair. She was waiting for an answer.

"My mother is Turkish."

Mrs. Dimitriadis gave a little smile. "Aha. Yes."

"And my father..."

She leaned forward slightly, her head erect, her eyes alert.

"My father is an American."

"And your father's family?"

"Part American." Oran paused. He looked at her, inspecting her, trying to read her thoughts. But all he could see were her lips slightly parted in the little smile, her even white teeth. "My grandfather is British. His family were merchants in Izmir."

"Izmir. Smyrna?" She kept her smile. "How fascinating." She looked off, away from Oran, out through the sliding glass doors toward the sunlit garden beyond. "Merchants in Smyrna..." Her voice had fallen to a whisper. "How fascinating." She turned back, looking at him with a warm, almost tender expression. "What is your Christian name?"

He told her.

"You weren't named for your grandfather, then?"

"No, his name is Frederick."

"Frederick..." She said the name softly. Then she broadened her smile. "Frederick Barbarossa. Frederick the Great. A fine name. Tell me, did he have brothers?"

"Only one brother, Edward. And no sisters."

"Edward? Edward Crossmoor? Well." She fell silent. Then she

roused herself and got up from the sofa. "Please excuse me. I have been very rude. Would you like some coffee?"

He had to catch a boat, he explained.

"Don't worry, my driver can take you to the harbor." She stepped out to give the instructions, then returned to the sofa. "I am giving one more concert this season before I go to my summer house near Mt. Pelion. Next week I'm playing in the Istanbul Festival. To think this is my first concert ever in Istanbul. Isn't that silly? I live so close by."

Oran remembered how much Leyla Hanim wanted to hear Alexandra Stephanides in concert. Now she wouldn't be able to go.

The maid brought in coffee for Oran. Mrs. Dimitriadis kept talking. "I practice a few hours in the morning, a few hours in the afternoon. I try not to go out. I don't want to waste my energy in small talk and gossip. I must concentrate on the music. I am a maniac when I'm preparing for a concert. But someday it must stop. Someday I will play only for myself, someday, here in this room and in my big, airy living room at Mt. Pelion, just in these two places. But tell me. Where does your grandfather Crossmoor live now? Surely not in Izmir."

"In America," Oran replied. "Outside Boston."

"Are you close to him?"

"He understands me better than my own father does. I never have to explain myself."

"That's lovely. I wish I could say my grandchildren felt the same about me. Is he well?"

"His mind is sharp, but he is partly paralyzed from a stroke. He can no longer walk."

"I'm so sorry. I trust he is well cared for?"

"He is in good hands." Oran, although smiling politely, began to feel impatient. Time was running out. He had to get to the boat. Yet he still hadn't asked her a single thing. Even if there was no gracious way to do it, he had to step in.

"Your summer house near Mt. Pelion," he said. "Your husband's art collection was kept there, wasn't it?"

The question wrenched Mrs. Dimitriadis from her thoughts. She sat up and glared at him.

"The golden locket," said Oran, "that was stolen from the collection."

"Ah, yes. The beautiful medieval locket."

"I wanted to ask you..."

"You may ask me anything you want."

"Did you ever recover the locket?"

"I...why no, we never did. It was stolen during our civil war, by communists. They took everything north, to Bulgaria, as far as we could learn. And then silence. Nothing has reappeared."

"I suppose it would be impossible to search for it in Bulgaria," Oran said.

"For anyone without sterling communist credentials, indeed, it would be. Perhaps, though, with a miracle..."

Oran smiled at the thought. "I have another question. Where did your husband find the locket?"

"Don't you believe in miracles, Mr. Crossmoor?"

"Well, no, not really. Do you?"

"Looking at the events of my long life, I can only say yes, miracles happen. Moments when all seems lost, then suddenly you are saved."

"Perhaps I need to be older to have the right perspective."

"No!" she exclaimed. "Not at all. Miracles can happen to the young, too. Keep your mind open. You will see."

Outside the music room a clock chimed. "Oh, my! Nine o'clock already!" Mrs. Dimitriadis stood up. "I'm afraid it's time for you to go. My chauffeur will be waiting for you."

"I still have much to ask you," Oran said. "Can we meet again? Perhaps in Istanbul, when you are there for your concert? Let me give you my address." He tore a sheet out of the notebook he had with him and took out a pen. It wasn't elegant, but it would have to do.

"I look forward to hearing from you," he said as he handed her the paper.

She smiled. "Will you attend my concert in Istanbul? If you do, you will certainly hear from me."

Oran looked puzzled.

"My piano," she explained with mischievous delight. "You will hear me through my playing."

Chapter 20

It was early afternoon when the ship reached the harbor at Poros. Oran checked the schedule of boats returning to Peiraeus, as Faysal ibn Jinani had advised, then set out through the town for the coast road beyond, to the west.

As always, Oran had his Leica with him. He stopped to take a few pictures of the narrow streets and the whitewashed houses with brightly painted doors and dark red tile roofs. So what if these were standard tourist shots seen on postcards everywhere. He was seeing these Greek village streets and houses for the first time and wanted to capture these images for himself. The colors were so pure. Beril would love this architecture. And over there, two old ladies in black, one fat, one thin, knitting and talking furiously!

But first he should see Prince Karim. Then he could wander around and take pictures at his leisure. Even so, he couldn't pass up the old ladies. He found the face of the fat woman in his telephoto lens and snapped the picture.

It was a hot day and the road seemed long. From time to time a car roared past. Perhaps he should have hired a taxi.

At the fork in the road that Faysal had indicated, he turned uphill. Ten minutes later he reached an ivy-covered gate with the number 8 on it. Why 8? There were no other houses nearby. He pushed open the gate and started to climb steps.

A dog barked. Oran stopped. This dog meant business.

"Sit! Jimmie, sit!" A man appeared at the top of the stairs between the big bushes on either side. "Oran Crossmoor?" he called down. "Hi. I'm Karim. Come on up, I'm holding the dog." A Doberman pinscher was poised to attack. Oran circled the dog and shook hands with Karim.

Karim was as tall as Oran, but thinner. He wore a yellow and red striped rugby shirt, loose white pants, and Ho Chi Minh sandals. A pair of dark glasses had been tipped up to rest in his thick black hair.

"Don't worry about Jimmie," said Karim. "He's here to keep out the unwanted. Let's sit on the terrace." Karim released Jimmie and led Oran around to the side of the house. Before turning the corner, Oran glanced back. Jimmie had sprawled out on the warm pavement, his head resting on one of his forelegs, ears alert.

"What a great view!" Oran said when they reached the terrace. The sea was magnificent, spreading across the horizon beyond the forest below.

"This is where I come when I'm ready to crack. Even friends can wreck your nerves if you see them too much. You must be thirsty. What can I get you? A beer?"

"That's fine."

Karim returned with two beers and a bowl of nuts. Oran took that first long, cold swallow and immediately felt a thousand times better. Karim watched him and laughed. He started in on his own beer.

"Let's follow Goren," he said abruptly. "I open with two spades. You have a six point hand not counting distribution, a singleton diamond ace, a singleton spade, four hearts, jack high, and seven clubs, jack high. What do you respond?"

Oran avoided Karim's gaze while he rummaged around in his hazy memories of casual college bridge games. "Three clubs."

"If I continue with 'Four no trump'?"

Oran rarely played a round where the bidding had ascended this high. Slam was in the air. The very word made him panic. What should he say? Did you indicate your second best suit, your weakest suit, or your best suit once again? Or should he stop at Karim's game bid? With what he hoped was convincing confidence, he said, "Five hearts."

"I will then say 'Six clubs,' since the hand I'm thinking of has three nice clubs, the ace through the queen, and seventeen additional points in high cards alone. Of course we would have to see the distribution in all four hands to make sure.' Karim gave Oran a hard look. "You're a fake. I heard those hesitations. And 'Five hearts' instead of 'Five diamonds'. Don't you know the convention for showing how many aces you have? What's going on with you and my father?"

Oran felt two inches tall. "You're right. I'm not a bridge player."

"They are incredible, my father and Faysal," Karim said in a low voice. "They really are."

"The real reason I came was to ask you about an antique gold locket."

Karim looked surprised.

"I traced it to your father. I went to see him in Kifissia. He gave it to you some time ago, he said, ten years ago."

"Why didn't Faysal tell me? Did they think I'd refuse to see you?"

Oran handed over the prince's letter. "Your father explains it all."

"They think I'm a spoiled boy who likes nothing better than to slam doors in people's faces." He opened the envelope and read the note. "Let them rot in hell!" he shouted. He tore the letter to bits and threw it to the ground. "Faysal turned my father against me. Do you know why? A woman! A little fortune hunter had him on a leash, then traded him in for me. He tried to win her back, sent flowers, telephoned again and again. All this from a so-called respectable married man with grown children.

"If my father had found out, he would have fired Faysal on the spot. Faysal still blames me for stealing her away. She's long gone, but I'm still here right in the heart of the family he serves. He's afraid some day I'll reveal his secret. Maybe I will!" He stood up and walked to the edge of the terrace. "He began to criticize me in front of my father. The criticisms were well received. I study bridge. I lead a casual life. My father can't stand it. He says at least I should have children. But why? Should children enter this world just to satisfy my father's vanity?"

He put his hands in his pockets and sat down on the low wall that lined the terrace. "I try to live honestly. My father isn't against honesty, but he firmly believes that life should conform to pious Muslim traditions. Thanks to the poisoned tongue of his secretary, he's convinced I'm neither pious nor honest. I'm a stain on the family honor." He indicated the shreds of his father's letter lying on the ground. "I can't even be trusted to receive a guest with traditional courtesy."

Oran hoped the outburst had come to an end.

"I'm hungry," said Karim, snapping out of his dark mood. "Let's go inside and see what there is." He was on his way before Oran could remind him about the locket.

"It's a mess," said Karim, once they were inside the kitchen, a spacious room with a large raised fireplace at one end. "I've just let everything pile up since I came back from Hydra. The maid comes in two days, but I can't wait that long. I'm going to clean it all tonight."

The sink, the counters, the table in the center of the room were covered with dirty dishes, vegetable peels, partly eaten pieces of bread, and crumpled paper napkins. "I should have put the butter away this morning," said Karim as he grabbed a dish with a yellow puddle in it and popped it into the refrigerator. "At least I keep the wine corked." A half-empty bottle of red wine stood on the table, its cork in place.

Together they cleared off the table, stacking the dishes on the counter near the sink. From the icebox and from various stashes in the room, Karim assembled hard-boiled eggs, cheese, salami, yogurt, cucumbers, tomatoes, fruit, and cookies. He told Oran to start slicing.

"Wait!" he said. "You'll need a knife." He pulled open a drawer and took out a long, heavy carving knife. He smiled apologetically. "The small knives are all dirty." Then he looked around. "We need bread. If only you had picked up a loaf in town. It doesn't matter. I'll toast some of this old stuff. You take the food outside. We'll eat under the big tree."

It was well into the afternoon, and Oran was hungry. He loaded up a tray and carried it out to the end of the terrace where a wooden table stood in the shade of a tall, spreading tree. Karim brought bread, paper plates, plastic utensils, and more beer. The two men sat opposite each other and helped themselves.

"Do you work out?" asked Karim. "You've got great shoulders."

"I don't do anything special. I played a lot of sports in school."

"I did, too. Did you know I have an American high school diploma?" Karim said as he started in on his food. "I went to a prep school in Massachusetts. Andover."

"That's where you started playing bridge."

Karim smiled. "You guessed it."

After a few more glasses of beer it was time to ferret out the truth. "Do you still own the relic your father gave you?" Oran asked. "The one with 'Medina' written on it?"

"Why are you so keen on this relic?"

Oran explained the reasons for his search. He ended with the news of Leyla's accident.

"So you think she will be protected if you collect all four lockets?" Karim said. "Her family has just gone through a long period of bad luck. It will change. Luck always changes, in one direction or the other.

"Look at me," he continued. "I gave 'Medina' away, a present to a friend. Nothing happened to me, one way or the other."

"Your father told me he hoped the locket would act as a good influence over you."

"It didn't work. But I only kept it for a few months. I never told my father. I didn't want to hurt him."

"Not then, in any case," added Oran.

Karim smiled.

"I have spent a lot of time tracking these lockets." Oran spoke seriously.

"You have even come all the way to Poros, just to see me."

"You gave the locket to a friend? I'd like to contact him...or her."

"Him. I don't think he would appreciate being asked about it."

"Why not?"

"It would stir up memories."

"I don't care what happened ten years ago," Oran said. "All I want to find out is whether he still has the locket. If he does, I want to buy it. If he doesn't, I want to learn where it is."

"Yes, yes, it's all so simple, so black and white."

"Who is he?"

"What's the hurry? How about another beer?" Karim rose from the table. "Or a coffee? I'm going to have a coffee. You'll join me?" He was already on his way to the kitchen.

Oran got up and started clearing the table. He wasn't supplying gossip to newspapers. So they had a fight ten years ago. Who cared?

He carried the tray inside and set it down with a bang.

"Easy!" said Karim.

"They're only paper plates," said Oran.

Karim grunted. He was making Turkish coffee in a little metal pitcher with a long handle.

They took their tiny cups of coffee outside and sat down on the terrace wall. "I don't want to disappoint you," said Karim, "but I don't think you should intrude on the privacy of my friend." He took a sip of coffee. "Why don't I contact him for you? If he has the relic, I'm sure he could sell it anonymously through a dealer. That way he would avoid embarrassment."

"Embarrassment?"

"Let me get in touch with him. You give me your address, and when I get an answer I'll write to you at once."

Oran watched Karim go off to the house for his address book. He wondered if Karim would follow through.

When Karim returned, Oran wrote down his address in Istanbul. "I'm counting on you," Oran said firmly. Then he remembered what Prince Abdullah had said about truth, falsehood, and the eyes. But Karim's eyes looked openly at him, perfectly candid.

"I'll write," said Karim, smiling. "Don't worry."

Oran finished his coffee and stood up.

"Where are you going?" asked Karim.

"Back to Athens."

"You can't leave now! We haven't seen Laura."

"Who's Laura?"

"A good friend of mine. We arranged to meet this afternoon. You can always catch the boat this evening."

"I wasn't invited, was I?"

"I told her you were coming. She loves to meet my friends."

Oran didn't much like being counted as one of Karim's friends. "I have to go."

Karim grabbed him by the arm. "She's great fun, you'll see. We'll have a drink, and then I'll take you down to the boat. We can go swimming. She has a great set-up for swimming."

Oran had brought a swim suit in the hope he might get in a dip somewhere. It was hot and Karim was insisting with such enthusiasm. Maybe Karim would write his friend after all. Oran didn't want to jeopardize that possibility. "All right, I'll come."

"Great!" said Karim. He gave Oran a pat on the shoulder and went to lock the house.

As they were walking along the road, Karim said, "I've got to clean that kitchen tonight. Why don't you stay over and help me? We could grill some prawns, have some wine..."

"Another time," Oran said. "I want to get back to Athens."

"Why don't you just say outright you hate to wash dishes? If everyone made a point of telling the truth, think how much better the world would be, cleansed of poisonous double-dealing."

Oran kicked a small rock down the road. "Sometimes it's better just to keep silent."

"I disagree. I value honesty above all else."

Oran saw a glint of white up on the hillside among the trees and wondered if that was Laura's house.

"We must be brutal with ourselves," Karim went on. "We cannot fear the truth."

"Tell me about Laura," Oran said.

"She's a goddess. There's no other way to describe her."

"Does she play cards?"

"She hates cards. Laura plays other games." Karim gave Oran a knowing look. "She's older than I am. She must be in her mid thirties. She spends most of her time sailing. She takes part in long-distance ocean races, designs boats, and writes books about her experiences."

"What's she doing here?"

"Taking a vacation. Escaping from the world, like me. It's her mother's house. Her mother comes from Crete. Her father was an American, from South Carolina." Karim gestured to the right. "Here's where we turn. Now the road starts to climb. It's a white house. We could see it earlier. I should have pointed it out."

"You were concentrating on more important things."

"Was I?" Karim peered at Oran to see if this was a joke or not. "The old man died, and Laura's mother married again. A Swede this time. This villa is their vacation home in Greece."

"Is Laura married?"

"She was once. He was a champion sailor, with a red face and lots of money. He called her arrogant, and she claimed he drank. But she told me his real problem was he couldn't get it up." Karim looked at Oran and raised his eyebrows. "She has ruled out marriage. But don't misunderstand. Laura loves men. She feels at ease in our world. She likes our directness, our sense of action, our independence."

This men's world sounded military. Oran tried to imagine Karim fitting this description...Colonel Karim...marching crisply in front of the reviewing stand.

They had reached the gate of the villa. They were sweaty from the climb. Karim pushed at the gate, but it was locked. He rang a bell. "In a nutshell, Laura is charming and determined. Isn't that exactly what you would expect from a woman half Charleston, half Crete?"

Oran couldn't help smiling.

They heard footsteps coming down the stairs. Oran watched eagerly as the fruit of this exotic alliance came into view and opened the gate. Indeed she was magnificent, tall and tanned with short-cut, honey-colored hair and large gray eyes.

"Hello, Karim" she said. "I see you have brought a friend." She looked directly at Oran, smiled, and shook his hand firmly after Karim introduced them. "Come on up."

Oran followed her up the steps, watching her shoulders and hips swing smoothly from side to side.

"Mother and Sven have gone to Athens for the weekend," Laura said.

"That's convenient," Karim said.

"Isn't it?" She glanced at Oran. "I thought of joining them. The number two at the American Embassy is giving a party. He's leaving to become ambassador to Venezuela, and I wanted to tell him how much I will miss his bad jokes. But my vacations are sacred, as you know. No parties when I'm resting." Oran came up beside her and she explained, "I'm about to sail around Africa, Tunis to Tunis."

Soon the three reached the house, a rambling structure in traditional style, thick walls plastered white, large windows with brown shutters, a red tile roof. Laura and Karim led Oran along a tree-lined terrace around to the side.

"Do you like bathing?" Laura asked him. "Karim does, I

suppose you know."

Bathing? That must be British for swimming. "I brought a suit," Oran said.

"Oh." Laura glanced at Karim, who smiled back ever so slightly. "You certainly are well-organized, Oran. You come prepared for anything"

Oran caught the look between them. Prepared for anything? That was an odd thing to say.

They walked through an overgrown garden and reached a rusting wrought iron gate decorated with grape vines. Laura pulled open the gate and let the men go in. She stopped Oran with a light touch on the shoulder. "Our swimming area," she whispered in his ear.

A large pool lay sheltered inside a tall fence covered by masses of purple bougainvillea. Copies of antique statues stood around the deck, Aphrodites, Apollos, Amazons, nymphs, and satyrs. The water was limpid blue. After the hot climb it looked most inviting.

"Our bathing area is behind this."

Oran was puzzled.

"Come on, I'll show you."

Through a gate at the far side of the pool, they entered a small, dim brick-lined room lit only by a skylight. A mosaic of black and white diamonds covered the floor.

"A miniature Roman bath," Laura said. "My parents loved immersing themselves in water: the ocean, waterfalls, saunas, Japanese pools, everything except the old-fashioned bathtub in a frigid British hotel where only the towel rack is heated. When they bought this house, they decided to build an ancient bath complex." She smiled at Oran. "Adapted to the modern world, of course." She began to loosen her red halter top. A moment later, when she bent over to remove her skirt, her breasts swung free.

Oran stood there, astonished. He didn't have to imagine anymore. Here she was, naked. The pale skin around her breasts looked so soft.

Oran glanced over at Karim. He was already stripping, putting his clothes in one of the compartments along the wall.

So the two had set him up! British bathing indeed. 'I even brought my swim suit,' he had said. What an idiot! And now what? For an instant he hesitated. He looked at Laura and Karim, then back at Laura. She was smiling at him. Well, OK, he thought. He took off his shoes. Then he brought his fingers up to the front of his shirt and began to undo the buttons.

"Don't be shy," Laura said. She came over to help him.

"I can do it."

She stood next to him, her hands on her hips, watching until he stepped out of his pants. "Nice!" she exclaimed, admiring his body. "Put your clothes over here, by ours."

He followed her into a small square room. What was he doing? He felt drops of sweat run down from his armpits.

"We wash here before settling ourselves in the hot bath," Laura explained. At one side of this second room was a large marble basin. Warm water poured into it from a spigot. A wide shallow bowl filled with big sponges stood next to the basin. "Take one. Wash with soap and water, then rinse off. I'll wash your back when you're ready."

Karim was bending over, squeezing out a sponge. Oran watched him. His buttocks were so pale in contrast with his dark brown back and legs. Suddenly Karim turned his head. His eyes met Oran's and held them fast.

Laura came over with a sponge dripping soapy water. "Ready?" she asked Karim. He looked down at the rest of Oran's body, then turned away so Laura could wash his back.

Oran let out his breath. For an instant he had felt afraid.

Laura stepped over to Oran. She filled his vision, and he was grateful. His eyes swept over her breasts, the long smooth curve of her hips and thighs, the dense hair below her flat stomach. She caught his glance, and they smiled at each other. Oran felt a surge in his groin. He reached for her.

Laura laughed as she caught his arm and deftly turned him around. "First things first," she said. She washed his back, massaging hard with the sponge. "Now you can rinse off."

Oran loaded the sponge with water, held it above his head, and squeezed it. The warm water cascaded down his body. He repeated the process again and again until all the soap had been washed to the floor, to disappear in a drain in the center of the room. He went over to Laura and with quick, thick strokes of the sponge, washed her back.

"Karim is already in the caldarium," she said. "I'll join you in a second."

Oran went through the door into the third room – round, marble-lined, with a domed ceiling. Like the changing room it was lit by a skylight, but the opening was larger, the space brighter. In the center was a small, round pool. Oran stepped in and sat down on an underwater bench beside Karim. His feet touched the bottom of the pool. The water was barely warm, not hot at all, as he had expected.

Oran tried to brush off the disturbing shock he had felt when Karim stared at him. He smiled as if nothing had passed between them. "She's really something."

"There's no one quite like Laura," Karim said, echoing Oran's jaunty tone.

Dripping water, Laura joined them in the caldarium. She flipped a switch and suddenly the water began to bubble and swirl. "Sven insisted on having a Jacuzzi," she said, "even though it's hardly authentic." She brought over a bottle and shook in a generous quantity of powder. Lemon scented foam quickly rose up to the level of Oran's neck. Laura stepped into the pool and sat down on the other side of him.

She let out a sigh. "How completely, totally, utterly relaxing!"

"Sitting in a hot bath on a hot summer day?" said Oran. "It's crazy."

"Who's crazier," said Laura, "the ancient Romans or we moderns? They sat in hot water. We go lie on hot sand and grill ourselves."

Oran inched toward Laura.

"But you like to look weather-beaten," said Karim.

Laura gave him a nasty look. "I like to have a nice tan like everyone else, but I'm not going to work at it. I do what I like. I sail, I swim in the ocean. I take whatever the sun gives me. If my tan turns out a bit on the red side, I won't break down and cry."

Oran's shoulder touched hers.

"What about these baths?" asked Karim. "You don't get a tan here."

Oran felt Laura's fingers on his thigh.

"The baths are reserved for special occasions."

"For guests," said Karim.

"Honored guests," she added, smiling.

Laura was caressing Oran's leg very lightly with her fingertips. He was aware of Karim's presence to his right. Did Karim suspect anything? At least the foam hid everything from view.

"I want to learn something entirely new," Laura said, tilting her head. "A new language, I think, one completely different from our European tongues. Which one do you think I should study?"

Oran moved his left thigh toward Laura's leg and made contact. It felt long and smooth.

"I vote for Arabic," said Karim.

"Why not Turkish?" Oran said. His fingers crept over, tickling the inside of her thigh. "It's completely different."

"I already know something about the Middle East." She poked a foot up out of the foam, wiggled it for an instant, and then brought it down with a splash. In the waves that followed, Oran's hand lost its place on Laura's thigh, and Karim drifted up against Oran.

"I'm attracted by Chinese and Japanese," Laura said. "Once I took part in a regatta in Japan's Inland Sea. The area was gorgeous. But the culture seemed so remote. I've never felt anything so foreign in my life."

The waves had subsided, but Karim's shoulder had not retreated from Oran's side. It was warm and soft, like Laura's. Oran wondered if he should protest.

"What do you think?" asked Laura. "Would you recommend Chinese instead?"

Laura's fingers were moving slowly up Oran's thigh. Then Oran felt another hand, on his right knee. It, too, began to travel upwards.

"Ohhh," he groaned. He stood up, his body concealed by foam. "My leg! It has gone to sleep." He hopped around in a circle, then sat down on the other side of Laura, a safe distance from Karim. Karim, smiling, moved in close to Laura.

"I often choose languages to study on the basis of a country's food," Laura said. Her fingers quickly located Oran's thigh. "I've done French, of course, and I took Latin in high school."

Oran, meanwhile, was trying to cup her left breast without agitating the layer of bubbles that floated under her chin.

"You haven't tried ancient Roman cooking, have you?" asked Karim. "I thought they liked sauces made of sardines that rotted under the sun."

"Rotting under the sun, like sunbathers?" said Oran.

"No, no, not that," Laura said to Karim. "That's disgusting! I'm thinking of modern Italian cooking: spaghetti, grilled scampi with garlic butter, prosciutto con melone, gorgonzola."

Oran abandoned Laura's breast and moved his hand down her belly. "So which do you like better?" he asked. "Chinese food or Japanese food?"

Laura's hand was moving in small circles upward on Oran's leg. "I like them both. That's my problem."

"In that case, you should study both languages," said Karim.

Laura's exploring hand at last reached its target. Oran plunged his own hand into her bush. But he touched another hand, descending from the opposite side. At once all hands retreated. After a moment of silence, Oran, Laura, and Karim peeked at each other, then burst out laughing.

"Isn't it a marvelous day, gentlemen?" Laura rose from the bubbles and, turning around, stretched in front of her guests. "The bath, the whirlpool, the perfume, the company of two handsome men...I'm beginning to feel like a whole woman once again." She scraped some of the foam off her body and threw open her arms. Oran and Karim jumped up and the three bodies joined in a soapy, slippery embrace.

Then Laura lost her balance. With a shriek she brought all of them crashing down in the water. Rising from the foam, they reached for the bench, they reached for each other. Oran found himself again in the middle, between Laura and Karim. He was caressing Laura, now with urgency, while trying only halfheartedly to shake off Karim's determined hands.

"Tell me, Oran," Laura said as he was kissing her on her shoulder, "why did you come to Poros? I never even asked." She inched backwards on the bench. "Karim has never mentioned you. Are you an old friend of his?"

"He came today, with a message from my father," said Karim.

"I thought you had nothing to do with your father."

Oran brought his face up close to Laura and smiled. "I'm on a private mission. Prince Abdullah suggested I contact Karim."

"What sort of mission? A business matter?"

Karim sat up, releasing Oran. "A sale of antiques," he said. "Medieval antiques. They want to make a trade. Nothing important."

"Antiques? I love antiques." Laura tried to sit up. "What kind? Furniture?"

"Jewelry," said Oran. He passed a hand around her back. He didn't want her to sit up, not yet. He had her in such a promising position.

"My mother collects old jewelry. You knew that, Karim. Why didn't you tell me your father did, too? I thought he only bought guns, and maybe religious artifacts, manuscripts of the Koran, things like that."

"And reliquaries," added Oran.

"Quiet!" Karim snapped. "Or you can forget our agreement."

"What agreement? What are you talking about?" Laura pushed Oran away and sat up. "Karim, what are you keeping from me? I thought we told each other everything."

"Let's change the subject!"

Laura pressed ahead. "You had a reliquary once. You told me about it. A small gold locket decorated with precious stones."

Karim sat stunned as Laura's words poured out.

"The one you gave to that man who's now the Turkish film star."

"What?" It took Oran a moment to digest this news. "Which one? What's his name?"

"Don't you have any sense?" Karim shouted at Laura. "Can't you keep quiet?"

"What does it matter?" Laura yelled back as Karim stepped out of the pool. "You said that affair was over long ago. You always told me to speak honestly with you. So I did. Why should I watch what I say in front of your friends?"

"He is not my friend," said Karim coldly.

Oran climbed out of the pool and confronted Karim. "Tell me his name."

Karim was trying to get out of the room, but Oran blocked his way. "I promised you I would write him," Karim said. "Isn't that enough?"

"You don't even know where he lives," said Laura.

Oran grabbed Karim by the arm. "Who is he?"

Karim broke away from Oran's grip. Oran made a grab for his leg and caught him, just barely. They crashed down together onto the mosaic floor. They scrambled up, eyeing each other.

The rays of the sun, penetrating through the skylight, fell on the two opponents, illuminating their dark bodies and the bits of white foam that still clung to them, throwing their shadows onto the scenes of dolphins and cupids who frolicked in the tiles on the floor. Laura had been enjoying this skirmish between her lithe, smooth-skinned friend and the muscular, hairy-chested visitor, but now the conflict was turning serious, threatening to ruin her afternoon.

"Enough, you two! Tell him the name, Karim. What does it matter now? Oran will be discreet, of course he will, won't you, Oran?"

Neither man paid her any attention. Suddenly Karim broke from their deliberate dance and darted toward the doorway. Oran leaped after him. He grabbed Karim's shoulder, spun him around, and, seizing him by the arms, tripped him and sent him down. He threw an arm lock on him. Karim grunted in rage. Oran crouched beside him and, with one knee pressed against his back, pulled the twisted arm.

Karim groaned in pain. "I'll tell you." He was breathing heavily. "Let me go."

"The name," said Oran.

"Sinan Altay," Karim said in a choked voice.

"Sinan Altay!" Oran released Karim's arm and stood up. "You must be joking."

Karim was silent as he got up, massaging his sore arms.

"That's the name, now I remember," said Laura.

"You had an affair with Sinan Altay? The great ladies' man of the Turkish cinema?"

Karim was already heading for the door.

"Karim, don't leave us." Laura got out of the pool and followed him through the doorway. "Don't be angry." She pressed herself against him and began to caress him. "Don't go."

"You bitch." Karim shoved her aside and stalked off toward

the changing room.

Laura returned to the center of the caldarium. "He's gone," she said to Oran. "A fit of anger at my frankness." She stepped back into the pool and sat down on the underwater bench. "So much for his principles."

The room seemed darker, as if the sun had suddenly fallen.

Oran hesitated. What had come over him? Why had he been so brutal?

Laura turned to see why Oran hadn't joined her. "Come sit down," she said. "Then we'll go swimming outside."

Oran felt silly standing there naked. He came over and sat just above her on the edge of the pool, his legs dipped in the water, his feet touching the bench.

"He still smarts from the memories," she said. "He was young, on vacation in Istanbul. Sinan was an unknown, a singer in a night club. Karim fell for him and invited him for a drink. Karim may have been innocent, but Sinan was not. Before he came for that drink, he discovered who Karim was. A prince! An Arabian prince! And once there, it didn't take him long to figure out what he had to do to tap into that wealth.

"But the affair lasted only a while. Sinan milked Karim for more and more money. One day he asked for the locket, which Karim had showed him. Karim handed it over. Then something snapped in him. That was the end. He didn't want to see Sinan any more. Sinan threatened blackmail. He'd tell Prince Abdullah! Karim didn't care. He walked out of Sinan's apartment and the next day returned to Arabia. Sinan didn't bother to carry out his threat. Arabia was too far away. Karim has never seen him since."

She climbed out of the pool and sat next to him.

"He wouldn't have written him, then," said Oran.

"Of course not."

"Why did he lie to me?"

"Because you are handsome and he wanted to have a hold over you."

"A narrow escape."

Laura smiled. "I, too, find you handsome." She ran her hand over his chest. He turned toward her, but before he could embrace her she stood up and went over to the cupboard and took out several dark cushions, blue like the sea. When she had arranged them on the floor, she beckoned to him. "Come here," she said. She stretched out on the cushions, on her back. When he lay down beside her, she closed her arms around him. She laughed softly.

"Mmmm," he said, burying his face in the crook of her neck. "I smell lemon blossoms."

She traced his spine with her fingernail. "Escapes can be dangerous, don't you think?" she whispered.

Oran passed his hand slowly, softly along the outline of her wet body, from her shoulder over her breast to the inset at her waist, then out around the curve of her hips and down her thigh as far as he could reach.

PART THREE

Prologue

September, 1922. Izmir (Smyrna)

Enver closed the Silver Dolphin on the eve of the Turkish entry into Izmir and took his family to the farm of his brother-in-law, beyond the southern outskirts of the city. He posted a trusted waiter at the restaurant, to keep an eye on the place.

When the waiter heard knocking at the door, he was afraid. He would ignore it. The knocking continued insistently; he opened the door a crack. A veiled woman insisted she had to talk with Enver Bey. It was urgent, she said, desperate! He could tell from her accent that she was not a Turk, but a Greek. Enver would hardly thank him for entangling them in the affairs of a Greek.

The woman fell to her knees and grabbed his arm. "I'm a friend of Enver's; he won't refuse me."

* * *

The woman did not go straight to the farmhouse as the waiter had directed, for she didn't want the rest of Enver's family to know she was there. She hid in a clump of trees not far away and sent a small boy who was playing in the field to Enver with this message: "Loyal patron of the Silver Dolphin needs help."

Enver couldn't contain his curiosity. He sneaked out to see who it was.

Christina Markova. He remembered her at once; she had even figured in his dreams. Reddish brown hair, the most wonderful dimples when she smiled...

She had come for help, she told him. Her family had already disappeared in the confusion. She knew he had many contacts. Surely he could indicate an escape route to Greece. She would pay, she said. She pulled out a gold locket studded with an emerald and rubies. "Here," she said, forcing it into his hands. "It's yours."

Enver was stunned. He had never held such a sumptuous jewel. Of course he would help her. He had never been able to resist the plea of a beautiful woman, with or without money. Moreover, he was flattered at this recognition of his importance. If she had the good sense to appeal to him for help, he would do all in his power to demonstrate the correctness of her judgment. He assured her he would fetch her in a few hours and drive her in a horse-drawn cart to Kusadasi. From there a friend of his would arrange for passage to Samos, the nearest Greek island.

She wanted to know how dangerous the trip would be. The Turkish army would be fanning out southwards toward Kusadasi, Enver thought. She would travel as his wife. In appearance, she could pass for a Turk, even without her robe and veil. But if she spoke, her accent would give her away. She had to keep silent.

He returned in the middle of the morning with the cart. The back of the wagon was loaded with empty packing boxes. He told his family that he intended to load up with fruits and vegetables in Kusadasi and sell them in Izmir. People would be desperate for food. He would make a big profit. His family thought he was mad. His wife begged him to stay home. But he had made up his mind.

Enver thought it best if Miss Markova rode in the back. There was shade, and the packing crates would conceal her. He himself was armed with two pistols, but he didn't think to give her one. She wouldn't know how to handle it.

For some distance they rode along slowly on a dusty, rutted, poplar-lined track, a back road Enver picked because only locals used it.

Suddenly two Turkish soldiers stepped out of the trees and stopped the cart. Enver was panic-stricken. They would search the wagon!

The soldiers questioned Enver and inspected his papers. They had odd accents. Enver judged they came from the East, far away. They would be unfriendly. One of the soldiers, a dark, thin man with an oversized mustache, walked around the wagon, inspecting it. Then he climbed in the back.

"Hey!" he shouted to his comrade, a heavy-set man with rust-colored curls peeping out from under his cap. "There's a woman back here."

"My wife!" Enver cried.

"What's your wife doing wedged in behind a pile of boxes?"

"She's sick. She has a fever."

The soldiers looked at each other. "Why are you taking her on a trip? Why isn't she home in bed?"

Enver was thinking furiously. What could he reply? "I'm taking her to her family. They'll watch over her."

The heavy-set soldier hoisted himself into the wagon and whispered to his comrade below. The second man climbed up, and together they peered in at those boxes. "We want to see her," the thin soldier said. "Unveiled. Take off her robe and veil."

"This is my wife, gentlemen," Enver protested.

"We don't mean any harm."

"Just checking," said the heavy-set soldier. He smiled, very slightly. He stepped closer to the woman. "Get up," he ordered. "Take off the robe."

Enver watched frozen with terror as Miss Markova slowly rose from her corner and stepped out in front of the soldier. Her back was to him. He could see the faces of the two soldiers, the heavy-set man right in front of her and the taller dark-complexioned soldier standing below.

She reached up to her face and undid the veil. The soldiers watched intently. She pulled the robe over her head. Enver could hardly bear to look. But she was wearing a plain dress with simple stockings. How fortunate! Her clothes would arouse no suspicions.

The soldiers exchanged glances. They look embarrassed. Disturbing a virtuous Turkish wife...where were their manners? "Put your robe back on," they said. Enver let out his breath in relief. The soldiers climbed off the rear of the wagon, then came around to the driver's seat. "We've fallen behind. Could we ride with you for a while?"

Oh, God, no! thought Enver. "Of course." He forced a smile. "Please."

The soldiers got up and sat on the bench beside him. The heavy-set man stank as if he had spent the night on a dung heap. Enver flicked the reins and off they went. The soldiers talked of the war, of victory. Enver joined in. But all the time he could feel sweat drenching his shirt.

Not much further on, the wagon was flagged down by a peasant woman.

"Enver!" she called out in astonishment.

Enver recognized the wife of a friend of his, a tobacco farmer. He greeted her as cheerfully as he could. "Yeter Hanım, how are you? Are you and Ali Bey getting on all right?" He was ready to babble anything that came to his lips.

"We're looking forward to victory, at last," the woman replied. "The Greeks around here have all fled...on the heels of their soldiers." She laughed. "But what in God's name are you doing here?"

"Ask his wife," said the thin soldier. "She's in the back."

"Hatijeh? Here?"

"Be careful," said the other soldier. "She's come down with a fever."

"A fever?" The woman hurried to the side of the wagon and looked in. "Hatijeh? How are you feeling?"

There was no reply. She asked again. Silence. "Why won't you answer me? Enver, why isn't she talking?"

"She's weak," said Enver.

"Why are you taking her out into the country with you? With

the fighting going on, you might be caught."

"He's taking her to her family," said the first soldier. "He didn't say where. Kusadasi, maybe."

"Hatijeh is from Izmir! Her brother's farm is just outside the city. You've long since passed it."

The soldiers glanced at each other. "Come here," the dark, tall soldier looked at the peasant woman. "You will identify his wife."

The village woman was looking at Enver. He signaled to her. Ever so slightly. With his lips. He was telling her to be quiet. She would not see Hatijeh behind the veil. She smiled briefly at Enver, indicating she understood. She would not betray him. Accounts could always be settled later.

She went around to the side of the wagon. The soldier told the woman in the corner to get up and remove her veil. "Is this the man's wife?"

The peasant woman examined the face.

"Why don't you answer? Is this his wife or not?"

The village woman glanced at Enver, then looked back at the woman standing in front of her. Their eyes met.

"Yes," she said. "This is Hatijeh, his wife. She has lost weight. I hardly recognized her. It must be the illness."

Miss Markova attached her veil and sat down in the corner. The peasant woman went over to Enver. "Have a good trip. May God protect you."

"When the fighting has ended, come see us in Izmir. You and Ali Bey."

"Yes, Enver, we'll come, God willing. We have much to discuss."

The soldiers climbed back onto the driver's bench. Enver waved to the village woman. The road became narrower, hedged in by low stone walls and poplar trees that lined the farm fields on either side. The fields looked dry, the wheat stalks yellow and brown at the end of the hot, rainless summer. To the east, hills rose up, with craggy peaks in the far distance. They rode along in silence, the cart jostling through the potholes. Enver wondered what the two soldiers were thinking. He prayed that this was the end of their danger.

It was by now early afternoon and Enver was getting hungry. But he didn't dare say a thing.

"Stop!" ordered the dark, thin soldier when the wagon reached a small clearing by a stream, just before the road took a sharp turn into a pine forest. Enver pulled on the reins. The soldier jumped to the ground and gave Enver a hard look. "Where are you really going? If your brother-in-law's farm is back near Izmir?"

Enver was stunned.

"She didn't even greet her friend. I want to hear the lady talk."

The worst was about to happen. If only he were a better liar! She should have put her trust in someone more clever.

The second soldier hopped off the wagon.

With his trembling hand Enver groped for his pistol.

The soldiers climbed onto the rear of the cart and made their way through the boxes. They pulled Miss Markova to her feet. The first soldier ripped off her veil. "Talk!" he shouted. "Say something!" He slapped her. "Talk, damn you!" The soldier struck her again, harder.

"Animals!" she cried, the tears running down her cheeks. "Leave me alone!"

"A Greek!" They turned toward Enver. "So you're smuggling a Greek out of Izmir. And such a beauty!"

Enver jumped up on the driver's bench and pointed his pistol at the soldiers. "If you don't get off this wagon, I'll kill you."

The two soldiers laughed nervously. "We meant no harm," the heavy-set soldier said. They looked at Enver with contempt as they backed up among the crates.

"Funny, isn't it?" said the tall, dark-complexioned soldier

with thick black eyebrows. "We're trying to push the Greeks into the sea and here you are, a good Turk, saving one for yourself." He and his comrade laughed again. "What's the matter? Turkish women aren't good enough for you?" He spat at Enver.

Bam! The tall, thin soldier fell over onto the wooden boxes. The heavy-set soldier spun away from Enver and pointed his rifle at Miss Markova.

Before he could pull the trigger, Enver shot him dead.

He stared at Miss Markova. He could see the hole in her robe. The bullet had made it when she fired the first shot. "You had a gun," he said.

"Hurry." Miss Markova took her pistol out from under her robe and set it down. It was small, and its handle was inlaid with mother-of-pearl. "We must carry them to the woods. Quick, before anyone sees us." She looked up at Enver, frozen on the bench, staring at her. "For God's sake! Take hold of yourself."

He climbed down. Together they lifted the bodies off the wagon and dragged them one after the other into the pine forest, to a hollow filled with pine needles well out of sight of anyone traveling on the road. After covering the bodies with pine needles and leaves, they washed their hands in the stream.

"They would have killed us," said Miss Markova. "Sooner or later."

"I suppose so." Enver's voice was leaden.

"We'd better get going."

"Yes," said Enver. "It's getting late."

When they got back to the wagon, Miss Markova touched Enver's arm. "You saved my life," she said. "How can I ever thank you enough?"

"Let's go." Enver wanted to put it all out of his mind. Killing Turkish soldiers! And yet, if she hadn't fired so boldly...

Miss Markova collected her pistol and climbed back among the crates. Enver installed himself once more on the driver's bench. The fading light of the long September afternoon cast a warm glow on the scenery he knew so well, the dirt road lined with low stone walls and poplars and the occasional fig tree or pomegranate bush or silvery cluster of olive trees, the tobacco fields beyond, here and there a modest stone farmhouse. He saw no one, though. Most of the farmers in this district were Greek. Had they all fled, the Turkish farmers, too? As he drove into the evening, he kept asking himself why he was doing this. She had touched him softly and smiled. But the picture of her standing over the dead soldiers came back to him, her face cold and hard. She had pulled that pearl-handled revolver from under her robe. He hated to admit it, but he was afraid of her.

* * *

It was night when they reached a concentration of houses and gardens inside low whitewashed walls – the outskirts of Kusadasi. Enver sent word to his friend Murat, the produce wholesaler, to meet them there, at the edge of town. Murat came promptly, surprised that Enver should appear in this dangerous time. He was even more surprised by Enver's explanation. Enver presented Miss Markova as a faithful client of his restaurant, a person to whom he was much obliged. He knew he could count on Murat for help.

The woman was beautiful. Murat had known Enver for a long time, and he immediately understood the situation. Murat agreed to hide Miss Markova in a nearby warehouse. She would have to wait a few days, he made clear, until he could make contact with an associate on the island of Samos just across the channel, a man with a boat who might well agree to come fetch her and sail her back.

"Why did you get mixed up in this, you fool?" Murat asked Enver as they drove into town.

"I must have lost my head."

"We have a good chance of literally losing our heads. The

Turkish army is about to take Kusadasi. The Turks here are wild with excitement. If we're discovered..."

"I'm appealing to you as a friend."

"You put a heavy strain on friendship, Enver."

"She'll pay you well."

"Mmmm..." Murat was never one to sneer at gain. "What's she going to pay with? I won't take paper money."

"She'll pay with another piece of jewelry." Enver took out the little packet wrapped in a black velvet rag, and slowly pulled open the cloth. "Just like this one."

Murat whistled.

"The Greek woman posed as my wife," Enver told Murat. "A villager I know stopped us and saw her, but I didn't have a chance to explain. If there are any questions, say that I arrived here alone."

"All right."

"Also, I need a truckful of produce to take back to Izmir."

"With soldiers running around the countryside you think the farmers have been calmly harvesting their crops?"

"But I told everyone this was the purpose of my trip!"

"You may run your restaurant well, Enver, but there are times when good sense deserts you."

"My wife will kill me if I return empty-handed."

"You deserve it." Murat laughed and slapped him on the back. "Cheer up. We'll find something to load in your wagon even if we have to go pick it ourselves."

Chapter 21

Summer, 1982. Istanbul

Osman, a waiter at the Secret Garden restaurant, was smoking a cigarette at the close of the afternoon. Osman was sitting outdoors in a shady corner, just below the office of Ibrahim Selcuk, the restaurant's owner, relaxing before the first of the evening diners arrived. As always, he had pushed back the exuberant ferns to clear a seat for himself on the low stone wall that held in the flower beds here by the office. As always, he had hissed away the dirt-streaked orange cat who napped here each day after polishing off the plate of stale bread moistened with broth that the cook set out for it. While he smoked, Osman heard the yells of the boys up the street who played soccer when they came home from school, kicking a little ball around, adeptly dodging the cars whose drivers would honk, then stop, lean out, and scold them before roaring off. Directly above, a jet flew over, its waves of rumbling sounds crashing around him. And then, in the ensuing calm, someone sneezed not far away, something smashed on the ground and, after an instant of dead silence, the air rang with the curses of the outraged cook. Osman grimaced, then took another puff on his cigarette.

He thought back to the police raid of the previous week, the arrests of Sinan Altay and Gulizar Korkmaz, and the policeman who idiotically knocked over the bucket of white paint...that glorious evening had fueled conversation for days among staff and clientele alike. But the excitement was abating as the busy summer routine of the restaurant reasserted itself.

Osman watched the yellowish smoke of his cheap unfiltered cigarette swirl upwards to be carried off by the breeze. For years and years, the same routine. It was getting to him. Stingy tippers and drunks, abusive orders, disgusting table manners. If only he could break away.

Ibrahim Bey should treat us better, he thought. We deserve better. For all those hours we put in, what's our reward? A pittance. He even makes us responsible for our tuxedos. Unbelievable! It's true he drove me to the hospital when I had the appendicitis attack. And he let Ismet off on paid leave to go to his mother's funeral in Eskişehir. But these were exceptions! Definitely exceptions. We need benefits, regular benefits: insurance and sick leave and paid vacations, all spelled out in a written contract. And our wages should be indexed to inflation. Why not? If the waiters at the Captain's Table get that, why shouldn't we?

Hearing the squeaking and bumping of the restaurant's veteran wheelbarrow, Osman looked up to see one of his colleagues pushing a load of garden trimmings out to the garbage bins by the street. Why doesn't Ibrahim Bey oil that wheel? he wondered. If I owned a restaurant, I'd certainly do things differently.

He lit another cigarette off the stump of the first one. Where could I ever get the money to open a restaurant? If I have to depend on what I earn here, I'll never make it. It's true, I've dipped into the till. But what could I do? I tried the drawer. It was unlocked. So I pulled it open. A pile of bills lay there. Ah, I thought. How lovely! My heart was pounding. I looked at the bills. And they looked back at me. 'Take me, take me,' they said. How could I refuse? But I only took a few. I didn't want to alarm Ibrahim Bey. I swore that was the end. But the following week I tugged on the drawer again. Had the drawer been open by accident, or did Ibrahim Bey make a habit of such carelessness? I was curious to see. Ah! Again temptation! Why, Ibrahim Bey, why? I helped myself to more cash. Not too much, of course. Just enough to treat my family to an extra meal of meat, and myself to an extra bottle of raki. A few days later I had to go into his office to get the "Paid" stamp. 'Why not?' thought I. I pulled...but it was locked. Just when I was improving my standard of living! Ibrahim Bey should give us raises, all of us, right now, on the spot. Then we wouldn't have to stoop to dishonest acts. I always test the drawer now, but it's always locked. The poor never have any luck. That's what my father always said: "What a rotten life it is for us poor."

Osman put out his cigarette, splitting the paper that encased the stub, leaving a pile of tobacco, some charred, some unsmoked, in the center of his red plastic ashtray. Two more minutes, he thought, then I'll go set the tables on the terrace. He heard voices inside the office. One voice, anyway. Ibrahim Bey's. Ibrahim was there, talking as usual...but rather softly. Unusually softly. He was on the telephone.

"35,000 liras...yes...I hope so..."

What would Ibrahim Bey be doing with 35,000 liras? Osman sat up.

"If it's convenient for you...this Friday? I prefer the morning...no, earlier than that. I'll be there by nine."

Perhaps I have time for one more cigarette, Osman thought.

"It is a fine piece of jewelry...yes, I keep it safe, don't worry...naturally...I agree...and to you, too, Sedat Bey. Thank you very much...yes, of course...good-bye."

Osman heard the click of the receiver placed back on the hook. His mind was racing. What extraordinary news! He had understood correctly, hadn't he? Ibrahim Bey was going to sell a piece of jewelry for 35,000 Turkish liras. To someone named Sedat. 35,000 liras! A nice sum of money. A jewel he has been keeping safe...somewhere...here in the restaurant? No! It's not safe here. Where, then? Not in his apartment, not if the apartment is as small as they say it is. But think of all the terraces and gardens here at the restaurant. Lots of good hiding places. 35,000 liras! I could start a little restaurant, open up a shop for that. What could Ibrahim Bey need with all that extra money?

"Osman!" Somebody was yelling for him. He crushed out his

cigarette in the ashtray.

"Coming!" he shouted. Stop dreaming, he said to himself. Put that jewelry out of your mind. They'll throw you in jail! He stood up and straightened his black bow tie. I could never find it anyway. I don't even know what it is! A ring? A brooch?

"Osman! Where are you?"

"Over here!" He bent down to collect his cigarettes and the red ashtray. This Friday? Today is Monday. I have most of a week. Maybe I can find something out. I will keep my eyes and ears open.

"I'm coming!"

With an unusually light step he headed toward the terrace and the section of tables under his charge.

Chapter 22

Oran called Beril from his hotel before he left for the Athens airport. She sounded eager, but he kept the call short, announcing only the time his flight arrived in Istanbul. Not that he wasn't pleased to hear her voice.

He regretted not having called the previous morning. Then he could have spoken with sincerity. Now it was difficult. He felt ashamed, and angry too. He had pulled a fast one and he had to hide it from her. He had considered not phoning at all. But he couldn't disappear from sight. He had promised to come see Leyla Hanim in the hospital, and even if the discussion about the stolen locket would be painful, he felt obliged to keep his word.

To tell the truth, Beril had barely passed through his mind the previous afternoon. He had been stranded on an island, tricked by the locals, and swept off his feet by a goddess. He would have stayed the night, but Laura wanted him to take the last boat to Peiraeus. She drove him to the dock herself.

"Let's keep in touch," she said.

He remembered their last kiss before he got on the boat. She said again, "Let's keep in touch."

* * *

"If that's how you feel, I won't take you to see Aunt Leyla." Beril folded her arms across her chest and looked straight ahead toward the front of the Turkish Airlines bus. The bus had just passed beneath an imposing late Roman aqueduct and was heading down toward the Golden Horn. Beril, who always admired this view, was too angry to pay attention.

Oran shrugged his shoulder. "If she's recovering anyway..."

Beril didn't answer. They had talked about this already, before they climbed into the bus. And to think she had been so excited to see him there at the airport, only an hour ago! He had great news that almost made her forget about the stolen locket. Sinan Altay with one of the relics! Her eyes had almost popped out when Oran told her that. She still couldn't believe it. And all those other people Oran had managed to interview. He had learned a lot. He'd made a giant step forward. Aunt Leyla would be thrilled to hear it all. It would give her hope after the crushing news of the theft from her apartment. As soon as the airport bus reached the terminal in town, Beril had intended to take Oran directly to the hospital, by taxi.

But something was wrong. At first he seemed happy to see her. His smile, his eyes, so warm, alive. The stories poured out of him, the dealer, the priest, the well-to-do widow, the Arabian prince with the gun collection, the old pianist Alexandra what's her name that Aunt Leyla had so wanted to hear...

Then came the prince's son, Karim, his last interview, only the day before. He started telling her the details, but his body stiffened, shifted awkwardly, just a touch. What was it? Did he glance at her, then look away too quickly?

This meeting with Karim was the best part of his entire trip. That incredible story about Sinan Altay! She sat forward, eager to soak up every last detail. It wasn't quite clear to her, though, exactly how Oran learned that Sinan owned one of the lockets. Karim hadn't wanted to tell him.

"So Karim's friend steered the talk in that direction?" she had asked. "Wasn't Karim angry with her?"

"Of course he was," Oran said. "What do you expect?"

"I was only asking!"

"So we left." Oran looked down at his hands.

"Oh?" said Beril.

He turned and looked at her with a curious cold expression. "You're lucky I'm doing all this for you."

Beril stared at him, astonished.

"I didn't have to come give you a report," he went on. "I don't need your help. I could take off and find all the lockets myself. And I wouldn't leave them out for thieves to stumble over."

Beril gripped the strap on the back of the seat in front of her. She was furious. "Well!" she said in an exaggerated voice. "I wouldn't want to stop you!"

"I'm the one who's turned up all the clues," he said.

"Like discovering the name of the policeman who sold Sedat Bey his locket."

He couldn't answer that. He just sat there sullenly. That's when Beril decided not to take him to see Aunt Leyla. He would only insult her and make her angry. Aunt Leyla certainly didn't need that sort of treatment when she was lying in a hospital bed trying to recover.

The bus reached the Sishane terminal. When Oran had picked up his suitcase and was waiting for her lead, Beril said to him, "I'm going alone to visit Aunt Leyla." She paused so he could have a chance to protest. But he said nothing. He stood there dumbly. So she went on: "You just keep collecting your clues. In a week you'll have the entire necklace."

She turned and walked down to the main street and hailed a taxi. As the car drove off toward the hospital, Beril could barely check her rage. She wanted to scream and let loose her tears. How could he? She had trusted him. Aunt Leyla had trusted him. Now he was holding back valuable leads. He'll find the other three lockets himself. He'll disappear. They would never see him again. He had tricked them. Betrayer! She kept repeating that word to herself, to fan her indignation, to keep her anger alive.

* * *

"You have done all you could, Beril dear, so stop crying." Aunt Leyla spoke softly. She was reclining on a mound of white pillows. The crown of her head was wrapped in bandages. "You have been nice to him and you have spoken frankly with him. If he doesn't like us, what can we do? It's unrealistic to expect that everyone will like us."

"I was so sure he would come tell you what he had learned. I wanted it so much for you." Beril reached into her pocket for a tissue. "Especially after the attack."

"When I saw that masked hooligan raise his arm against me, I knew Death had come to cut me down. But look, I'm alive! Doesn't that cheer you up? Come here, dear, let me hold your hand. There. Let's forget Oran for a while. Let him continue his search alone, if that's how he wants to do it. In the meantime, we will carry on by ourselves."

"It's all finished," Beril said.

"We can outfox him," said Leyla. "You talk with Sinan Altay yourself. You don't need Oran. Go see Arif Bey. They must be filming now. He will arrange a meeting. Or your friend Nadya? We are lucky, aren't we, that Oran told you about Sinan before the two of you had your argument."

"And then?" Beril stood up and drifted toward the window.

"And then...we'll just have to see."

A nurse stepped into the room and came over to arrange the covers. "You should sleep now," she said to Leyla.

Leyla didn't protest. In fact, she smiled at the nurse. "Yes, I think I should. I am tired, it's true." She left the nurse help her into a comfortable sleeping position. "Will you excuse me, Beril?"

"She is making good progress," the nurse whispered to Beril after Leyla had closed her eyes. "She was even singing to herself earlier this morning."

Beril smiled.

"Beril?" Leyla asked in a low, dreamy voice. "Beril?" She looked up toward her niece. "Tell me again, the woman who escaped from Izmir, what did Oran say her name was?"

Beril took Leyla's hand. "Christina Markova."

"Christina Markova...ah..." She was almost asleep.

Beril kissed her hand and went outside. The nurse followed

soon after.

* * *

That evening after her dinner, as she was listening to a concert on the radio, Leyla whispered to herself, "Christina Markova...Christina Markova. A Russian? Should I know her?" She looked thoughtful for a few moments. "No, I didn't know any Russians. Wait. Yes, I did, Vera and Celeste...they always ordered napoleons with chocolate icing...Celeste ate so quickly...so quickly..."

The luxuriant music of Tchaikovsky swelled up and embraced her, and soon she drifted off to sleep.

Chapter 23

A handful of people were sitting outdoors at the Secret Garden, sipping tea in the late morning. They didn't need much attention, so Osman spent most of this time sitting too, smoking and resting in anticipation of the busy lunch hour ahead.

An entire day had passed and Osman had discovered nothing more about the piece of jewelry Ibrahim Bey intended to sell. He knew he should put the subject out of his mind. There was absolutely no chance that he would stumble across the jewel, so why should he spend all his time daydreaming of quick wealth? He was just torturing himself.

"It's going to be windy today, isn't it?" Ibrahim Bey came over and sat down next to Osman.

"No. It's going to be hot and still. Oppressively hot and still." Osman inhaled deeply on his cigarette, held his breath, then exhaled quickly. "I can feel it in my bones."

Ibrahim Bey smiled and slapped Osman on the thigh with his pudgy hand. Osman's bones could always be counted on to offer a contrary opinion. After ten years he was used to it. It had become a bracing tonic.

"We had a good crowd this weekend," said Ibrahim Bey.

"That dog did pick the right moment to chase the squirrel through the place," said Osman, recalling Saturday evening.

"Our expenses are ballooning, though. The inflation is killing me."

"What about us waiters? I'm sure you're not losing profits at our expense."

"You're not responsible for this place. You don't know the meaning of the word 'worry'. I worry all the time. Will I or won't I be able to make ends meet?"

Osman was all too familiar with Ibrahim's handwringing. It usually preceded an announcement that salaries would not, could not, be raised in the near future. "Why don't you take up another business on the side?" Osman suggested for maybe the thousandth time.

Ibrahim sat up, startled. "How did you know?"

"Know what?" Osman had difficulty recalling what he had just said.

"I'm expanding my business."

"What?"

"Not here. There's not much I can do to improve business here." He lowered his voice. "I'm buying a new restaurant."

"You are?" Osman looked at Ibrahim with surprise. "Where?"

"Out at the beach. At Buyuk Cekmece. A small place. It needs fixing up. But the location is fabulous. Right on the shore."

"By the time you get it ready, summer will be over. Why are you buying it now?"

"The owner wants to sell out. His heart's bad. He's just had an operation. In order to sell right away, he's cut the price."

"With all the money problems you keep telling me about, how are you going to buy it?"

"Well, Osman..." Ibrahim cast a glance around. "Between you and me, I'm selling an old piece of jewelry in order to come up with the down payment."

Osman tried to appear as calm as possible. "Oh?"

"A medieval locket made out of gold. On the back it says 'Qur'an', in Arabic. There is probably a sample of the Holy Koran inside, a verse written on a scrap of parchment. But I'm not going to crack the thing apart just to find out!"

"Have you owned this locket a long time?" Osman asked.

"I won it years ago. I used to gamble when I was young." Ibrahim winked at Osman and slapped him on the leg again. "Nowadays I keep it under control."

Osman saw in his mind the string of doubtful characters who visited the office at the Secret Garden from time to time. If they received no encouragement, why did they keep returning?

"A man once owed me a lot of money. Another restaurant owner, in fact. All he could pay me with was the locket. I hated to take it, a sacred object, as payment for a gambling debt. But an obligation is an obligation."

Osman lit another cigarette. Ibrahim joined him.

"Do you have a buyer?" Osman asked. "Such things must be hard to sell."

"I asked around and learned of a dealer in the Covered Bazaar who specializes in old jewelry. Everyone spoke highly of him. I called him up. He became very interested when I described the locket to him."

"Perhaps you asked for too little money."

"The price seems fair to me."

Osman paused for a moment before saying, "Could you show me the piece before you sell it? If it's convenient, of course. You might keep it in a bank vault, for all I know."

"You'd like to see it?"

"It must be beautiful," said Osman.

"Well...sure, why not?" replied Ibrahim. "Come into my office and we'll have a look."

Inside the office, Ibrahim opened the wall safe and took out a little box. He brought it over to his desk and removed the top. There, nestled in cotton, was the locket. Ibrahim lifted it out and handed it to Osman.

"Ahh!" said Osman, smiling with delight. It was indeed exciting to hold such a magnificent object.

"I hate to give it up. But I need the money. I have to think of my wife and children." Ibrahim put the relic back on its bed of white cotton, then locked the box back in the safe. "In a few days it will be sold, and then I'll forget all about it. There's no use being sentimental."

"I hope everything turns out well."

"The new restaurant should be a surefire success, right there on the beach. Oh!" He looked at the clock on the wall. "It's almost lunch time!"

Ibrahim closed the door behind them and hurried off to greet a businessman who had just come in, while Osman went over to his section of tables.

He could not get the locket out of his mind. Even as he took orders, served food, and directed busboys, Osman kept thinking about that gold locket, dreaming about all the money it would bring.

* * *

A young woman was sitting in a sheltered corner in the lower garden, sipping an orange soda and enjoying the sun. A dark blue scarf concealed most of her hair and dark glasses hid her eyes.

For once she was left alone, and for that Annelies was grateful. You'd think she was a freak the way Turkish men kept accosting her. It had never occurred to her before this summer that being tall and blonde and attractive might have some serious disadvantages. Fortunately the trip was almost over and soon she would be back in Zurich.

A breeze blew lightly through the garden, making the branches and leaves sway and dance. Annelies set her soda on the little round table and leaned back in her chair. The temperature was ideal. What a wonderful place, this restaurant and tea garden. If only they had discovered it sooner.

The trip hadn't been so bad, really, once they got into the country. That policeman at the border...the way he kept staring at her! Thank God she had her friends with her.

She sighed. It's a good thing I didn't leave Peter. I couldn't possibly have traveled around this country by myself. He's not so bad, really. Just a bore. A big bore. We'll get back to Zurich and that will be the end.

She reached forward and took a sip of her orange drink and

looked around. A scattering of people occupied tables here and there among the bushes and the trees. And no one was watching her. How much better this was than going on a shopping expedition. Let them shop all day, all three of them, she would be happy right here. Maybe she could even get a job here. She wondered what sort of person owned the restaurant, what the waiters were like. But no...she hadn't seen a single waitress during her entire trip in Turkey. How odd, no women waiting on tables.

She reached down into her bag and pulled out her novel and in an instant was back where she really wanted to be, on board the Orient Express heading westward across Bulgaria...

* * *

35,000 liras! Osman thought about the money all afternoon as he moved around between the tables outdoors and the kitchen inside. Ibrahim Bey certainly was lucky. If only he, Osman, could have such luck! Was there any way he could take the locket without anyone finding out? He would have to hire someone to help him. He couldn't do it all by himself, could he? Either the safe would have to be cracked or Ibrahim Bey would have to be waylaid Friday morning on his way to the bazaar. If the safe were robbed, Ibrahim Bey would know exactly who did it. But anyone could ambush him on Friday morning. No one would suspect Osman. Of course, he'd have to work up a good alibi. What if Ibrahim Bey got hurt, though? Osman didn't want Ibrahim Bey to come to any harm. He'd have to make sure the hired thief didn't rough up Ibrahim Bey too much.

Was this realistic? It came down to this: could he really capture the locket and sell it without attracting suspicion? All day he kept turning the question over in his mind.

* * *

"I want to know the truth, Beril," said Semra as soon as she had dropped her shopping bags on the ground and settled her large self on the little chair. "Arif didn't give you any trouble, did he?"

Beril laughed, shaking her curly black hair. Her mother looked so concerned! "He sat behind his desk the whole time. Of course his telephones kept ringing. I was lucky to exchange even a few sentences with him."

"Thank God for modern technology. If it weren't for those telephones... Ah!" A waiter passed near them and Semra Hanim flagged him down. "Two teas. And I want a grilled cheese sandwich. All this walking. I have never been so hungry." She looked inquisitively at Beril, who smiled back, nodding. "Make that two sandwiches," Semra Hanim told the waiter.

It was late afternoon and the lower terrace was well filled. Beril had agreed to meet her mother here at the Secret Garden. After refreshments and a rest, they would return home together.

"Arif has become a dangerous man," said Semra. "Almost 70, and with his wife dead only a few months! However did your grandfather make such a friend?"

"I don't think he started chasing women only when his wife died," Beril said.

"These movie people! Really, I don't see how Nadya's parents ever let her sign up to be a movie star." Semra Hanim shifted herself on the chair. "And with a good marriage right in front of her."

"I'm going tomorrow morning to watch the filming of 'The Conquest of Rhodes'. Arif Bey has agreed to present me to Sinan Altay."

"Oh, my! First Nadya, then you. Who's next?"

The waiter brought their sandwiches and tea. Semra Hanim lit into her grilled cheese sandwich. Then a thought struck her.

"Isn't Oran Crossmoor going, too?"

"We have had a parting of the ways," Beril said dryly.

Semra looked astonished. "But he was the one who told you

215

about Sinan, wasn't he?"

"Fifteen minutes later he declared he could find all the lockets himself. He didn't need our help."

"How ridiculous!" said Semra. "Doing all the work himself when the necklace is ours in the first place." Then she paused. "So Oran will be talking to Sinan Altay. Not this evening, I hope? Beril, dear, you will have to get there first. We can't risk losing any more of the lockets. Aunt Leyla would be devastated."

"He won't see Sinan today," said Beril. "He doesn't even know how to find him."

"Look what he uncovered in Athens in just a few days!"

"You don't think he could locate Sinan that quickly, do you? He returned to Istanbul only this morning."

Semra Hanim smiled contentedly. "If he gets to Sinan first, you will just have to go back into partnership with him. Aunt Leyla told me he was a most presentable young man, and his mother comes from a good family."

"Mother!"

"I keep your best interests at heart, dear, as I always have."

"I can do it all myself."

"Yes, yes, I'm sure you can. Now, you haven't forgotten that Aliye Hanim is coming for tea tomorrow afternoon? She is extremely busy right now organizing the Festival so it's really very kind of her to stop by. She was quite shaken to hear about Aunt Leyla." Semra finished her tea and called the waiter over to get the bill. "So please, Beril, don't dawdle on the film set tomorrow."

"Yes, Mother." Beril sighed and then stood up to help her mother with her numerous bags and packages.

* * *

The vision of the relic would not leave Osman. The small gold oval decorated with jewels, nestled sweetly in the white cotton.

Could it truly be his?

Plans. He needed to make plans. What would he have to arrange? He would have to make sure he could sell the locket. He did know a man who smuggled things...tape recorders, radios, calculators, kitchen appliances. He would have good contacts.

And he had to find an accomplice. Perhaps he could find someone at the bar he went to late at night, after work. Some of the men who came in there looked pretty rough.

Well, he thought, it all seemed possible, didn't it?

In the late afternoon, he went into a grocery store several blocks away and asked to use the phone. The grocer didn't know him. But he was standing near him, behind the counter. Osman would have to watch what he said. He would have to disguise his request, make it sound absolutely ordinary. He dialed the number.

"Hello, Sadik? This is Osman, Bülent's friend...I'm fine, how about yourself? ... I'm calling about some jewelry. I want to sell a small gold piece, a family heirloom. I want to sell it later in the week, on Friday. Can you recommend a buyer? That's Friday, mid-morning. Oh, good. I'll be there." He hung up.

The grocer barely looked at him.

But Sadik would know what kind of sale it was. Why else would anyone get in touch with Sadik? Sadik lived on the Asian side, in Uskudar, not far from the ferry landing. So Osman would cross the Bosporus by ferry. He'd be back at the restaurant by lunchtime.

* * *

The sun had gone down, and the darkening sky was filled with the amplified voices of muezzins calling Muslims to prayer.

Oran was finishing dinner in the upper terrace under a string of colored lights. He ordered another beer. What the hell? He'd had a few already, just a few, but he was still thirsty. In fact he seemed to be getting thirstier and thirstier. He should be drinking water. But beer tasted so good. Much, much better than water.

Why wasn't Beril there? He had to talk to her. He thought for sure he'd find her at the Secret Garden. Why didn't she come?

He helped himself to more peanuts.

Why had he acted so stupidly that morning? He really had been glad to see her. But he didn't realize it. It didn't hit him until afterward, until it was too late.

She looked fabulous. She had such a great big smile. He forgot all about Laura.

Who is Laura, anyway?

I told Beril everything I had discovered. She was so excited, smiling, taking it all in.

But I couldn't tell her about Laura. I wanted to tell her the truth about everything and then right at the end of the story there was something I couldn't tell. I should have lied, I should have made up a story, why didn't I just slide over it? But I couldn't lie, not to Beril. So I got angry instead.

He pitched down some more beer.

Fair and square, that's how I like to treat people. Like Dad. He taught me about principles. But sometimes you can't stick to your principles.

Dad didn't teach me about that.

He should have!

Suddenly Oran felt morose.

I'm never going to see Laura again.

The thought shocked him. But he recognized it as the truth.

I can't complete with the America's Cup races or rounding the Cape. Or a man in every port.

The beer was going fast. Another one? To have or not to have...

It's late and it's dark. I want to go to bed!

He lit a cigarette. I'll have a cigarette and nurse the end of this beer and then get the bill and go back to the hotel. By taxi. No, I'll walk.

But of course, Monsieur! Tabii, Beyefendi!

I need a walk. Tomorrow I can walk, too.

Tomorrow...what about tomorrow?

I've got to see Sinan Altay. How can I find him? I don't even know where he lives. No one gave me his address.

One locket gone. Stolen. Lost. They lost it. I trusted them. But they trusted me, too. We trusted each other. Poor Leyla Hanim, I should have gone to the hospital. I have a lead on a second locket, I would have told her that, and if Mrs. Dimitriadis comes through, information on a third. I've got to write GF again...why hasn't he answered my letter?

He finished off his beer.

What if I find those other lockets and then they're stolen, too? That's it. Dead end. I might as well go back to my pictures. Photographs of Ottoman cities. Cités ottomans. Or is it cités ottomanes? I think you say 'villes'. Oh, hell, I can't remember.

He let out a belch. Oh, God...

A woman at the next table glanced at him. Not a friendly glance.

OK, I've had enough beer.

What if I call Beril tomorrow morning and apologize and join forces with her to find the other lockets? Wouldn't that be the easiest, the noblest, the sensiblest thing to do?

Just as the waiter brought over the bill, Oran reached out toward the ashtray and knocked over his glass. Shit, he thought.

This was one shitty evening.

* * *

After the Secret Garden closed that night, Osman went in search of someone to help him. He went to that little restaurant he had been thinking of, not too far away, and ordered a glass of raki and a plate of fried potatoes. He looked around the room. Tuesday was a slow night and there weren't many customers.

Even so, the air was thick with cigarette smoke, dimming even further the weak fluorescent lighting.

It didn't look promising.

The raki and potatoes were brought over. Osman salted the potatoes, then began to eat. The anise-flavored raki burned agreeably in his mouth and he felt calmer.

A man came in and sat down at the table next to Osman. He was medium-sized, with a round, fleshy face. He hadn't shaved. He wore a badly frayed leather jacket.

As soon as he sat down he shot Osman a glance. "Could you spare some money? I'll pay you back tomorrow."

Fat chance, thought Osman.

But this might be his man!

"Sure," Osman said. "Have whatever you want."

The man called over the waiter and ordered grilled liver, rice, and a small bottle of raki.

Osman sipped his raki and inspected the man.

The waiter brought the raki, pouring out a serving, and added water. The man took a big swallow. He pulled out a pack of cigarettes. "Like one?"

"Thanks," said Osman. The man took out his butane lighter and lit both cigarettes. Osman noticed the cracked fingernails, the black stained hands.

"What kind of work do you do?" asked Osman.

"Auto mechanic."

"Where?"

"Out in Levent. But I was laid off last week."

"What happened?"

"I took too long to get things done. That's what the manager kept saying. For weeks he kept laying into me. One day I couldn't hold it back any longer. I told him to shove it." He paused. "I grabbed a crow bar and went after him. Some guys rushed over and held me until I calmed down. But the owner fired me on the spot."

"Was he right? Did you take too long with the repairs?"

"I try to do good work."

"You'll get another job."

"I'd better. My money's almost gone."

His food was brought. He put out his cigarette and attacked his meal.

"Don't eat so fast," said Osman. "You'll get sick."

The man smiled. Two gold teeth, Osman saw. "Yeah, I guess I should eat more slowly."

"You're a pretty good fighter?" Osman asked.

"I can take care of myself."

"I thought so. You've got big fists."

"I don't like to pick a fight. But once I get going, I'm hard to stop."

"I've got a fight on my hands," said Osman, "and I need someone to stick by me."

"I don't want to mess with your troubles."

"I'd pay you."

The man looked up. "What kind of fighting?"

"A man took a piece of jewelry. I want to get it back."

"If he stole it, why don't you call the police?"

"Well...this is just a little quarrel between us. The police don't need to know about it."

"I see." The man kept eating.

Osman sipped on his raki.

"What's in it for me?" the man said at last.

"2,000 liras."

"Oh."

"It wouldn't be serious fighting. I don't want any harm done to the man."

"Is he strong?"

Osman laughed. "Strong enough to get his big belly up the hill. That's all."

"When?"

"Friday morning, early. Not far from here."

"Will you pay me part now?"

"You'll get paid when you show up."

The man kept eating. "I want an advance. 500 liras now."

"No! I'll give you the advance when you appear Friday morning, and the rest at the end of the job."

The man thought about this. He drank some more raki and then ate the large sprig of parsley that garnished his plate. "Maybe I'll get a job and I won't be able to come. If you give me the advance, I could always arrange to make it."

Osman knew he shouldn't pay anything until Friday. But he wanted everything fixed now. Friday was too close.

"How do I know you'll show up?" Osman asked.

"I'm a man of honor. Don't you trust me?"

Osman peered at him. "Give me your name and address."

The man told him.

"Show me your identity card," said Osman. "I want to make sure." When he had verified the man's name, Osman took out 500 liras and handed them over. "OK, Temel. Six AM, Friday. At the Besiktas dock."

"I'll be there," said Temel.

They shook hands. Osman called over the waiter and asked for his bill.

"Hey!" said Temel. "What about my dinner?"

Osman gave him a sharp look. "You've got cash. Pay for it yourself."

He glared at Osman. "The dinner is part of the deal."

Osman pursed his lips with irritation. "All right." After he settled at the owner's desk, Osman walked out into the street and headed uphill and then across toward his home. It's all set, he kept saying to himself. It's all set. He should feel excited, or vastly relieved. Instead, he just felt bone-tired at the end of this long, long day. And the raki had gone to his head. He stumbled over a dip in the sidewalk and almost fell. Son of a bitch, he muttered. He recovered his balance and continued on.

Chapter 24

The next morning Beril took the bus from Bebek a short way up the Bosporus to Rumeli Hisar, the fifteenth-century fortress where "The Conquest of Rhodes" was being filmed. First she would look for Nadya. She assumed Nadya would be here, but come to think of it, Arif Bey hadn't mentioned her. That was odd, for she had a starring role along with Sinan. Beril was annoyed with herself. If she hadn't been so entertained by the eyes Arif Bey was making at her, she would have asked.

Mehmet the Conqueror had built the fortress on a steeply sloping hillside. Its massive crenellated walls rose and fell, following the irregular terrain like a strange slinky beast. It was a perfect place to film Suleyman the Magnificent's siege of Rhodes, Beril thought, if you couldn't make it to Rhodes.

The interior of the castle lay open to the sky, a pleasant park planted with trees and grass. By following a string of cables, Beril found the movie crew ensconced in the far end of the area. People were milling about in a copse of cameras and lights on tall stands, not far from a small caravan that seemed to be the company's headquarters. A medium-sized, round, faded red tent stood nearby, among the trees.

Two actors in medieval costumes posed by a flight of steps while klieg lights were adjusted. The points of the halberds they were holding caught the sunlight and sent beams flashing toward Beril.

"Hey!" a man with a tool-laden belt shouted. "You're not allowed here."

"I'm looking for Nadya," said Beril.

"Who?"

"Nadya Gursel. The star of this film."

"What?"

"Isn't this the film about the siege of Rhodes, with Sinan

Altay?"

"You got that right."

"She's the nun," said one of the actors holding a halberd. "You know, she brings Sinan water during the battle."

"Oh, that one! We did her a few days ago, didn't we?"

Beril smiled. Nadya a nun! Aunt Leyla would enjoy that. "Is she here now?" she asked.

"She's finished."

"What?" said Beril, not understanding.

"That was her bit. She gave Sinan the water. We filmed it three times."

"And that's her part? Only that?"

"You got it."

I can't believe it, Beril thought. Just a walk-on, after preening like a peacock. Mother is going to be terribly disappointed. Beril glanced around. "Is Arif Bey here?"

"He'll be back any time."

"And Sinan Altay?"

"You can't see him, if that's what you're thinking. He stays in his dressing room until his scenes are set up." The technician nodded toward the red tent.

Beril wondered what Sinan was doing inside his tent. Playing backgammon with himself?

"No visitors without appointments," the technician added. "He's strict about that."

"He must be afraid of his fans."

"If they thought they could get in to see him, they would trample down this entire castle."

Beril smiled. "I suppose they would." She turned away, deciding to take a stroll until Arif Bey arrived. She walked over to the ramparts and climbed a steep set of stairs up to the battlements that overlooked the Bosporus. As she caught her breath, she leaned against the wall and watched the boats pass by. And Oran, where was he? She remembered how he had hugged her at the airport. She had felt wonderfully strange inside. She wanted to kiss him, a real kiss. Why hadn't she dared?

For God's sake, what was she doing? After their argument in the taxi she had sworn she would wipe Oran from her mind. But it was impossible. She had been thinking about him all day long.

A big truck rumbled by on the coast road below. A group of teenage boys filled the back, some dancing in line formation with their hands joined, their leader holding high a white cloth, others clapping and chanting. One of the boys spotted Beril and waved to her. She was so caught up in the celebration that she didn't hear the footsteps on the staircase.

"Beril!" said a man's voice.

She spun around. "Oran! What are you doing here?"

"I've come to see Sinan. What about you?" He came over and leaned against the wall, crossed one foot over the other, and, tilting his head slightly, smiled at her.

"How did you know Sinan was here?" Beril made no attempt to hide her irritation.

"I just guessed it."

"No, you didn't."

"I went out drinking last night and when I woke up this morning, my head pounding, I thought 'castle'."

"I don't believe you."

"My head felt like a cannon. A medieval cannon of Mehmet the Conqueror. That's the truth, I swear."

His eyes did appear bloodshot.

"That was stupid of you to get drunk," she said.

Her remark hit him like a slap, but she didn't care. "How did you really find out?" she asked.

"A production of 'Midsummer Night's Dream' is about to open in the outdoor theater here. Did you know that?"

It rang a bell, Beril thought.

"Part of the Istanbul Festival," continued Oran. "This film crew with all these cables and generators and garbage was supposed to be out of here long ago. Of course they're behind schedule. But the producer..."

"Arif Bey."

"...the producer knows the head of the Festival so the movie crew can stay until the very last moment."

"How did you find this out?" Beril asked crossly.

"When I went to the café for breakfast, what did I hear? 'Just because it's a Sinan Altay movie...' I raced over and grabbed the man and ordered him to tell all."

Beril couldn't help smiling.

"His son designed the lighting for the play. He's been leading the complaints about the film crew not leaving. I shook the father's hand up and down. I bet he thought I was nuts."

He looked so pleased with himself. It was catching, Beril thought. And in his white shirt, blue jeans, and black loafers...

A commotion lower down in the castle caught their attention. A man was walking briskly toward the area occupied by the film crew, with a flock of retainers scurrying alongside him.

"That's Arif Bey," said Beril. "He's going to introduce me to Sinan. I arranged it myself."

"May I come with you?" Oran asked.

"I thought you didn't need my help."

"Well, sometimes," he said, smiling.

"I want you to keep that in mind," she said, her anger melting away. "Let's go find Arif Bey."

The producer was standing behind the cameras, talking with a tall, well-dressed man. Arif Bey himself was fairly tall, but unlike his colleague he had an ample mid-section. He was dressed in white: white shirt, white pants, belted high, and white sneakers – except for his dark glasses with black frames. His sparse silver hair had been artfully deployed across the top of his head.

When he spotted Beril, he beamed and stretched out his hand.

"Beril, darling! I'm so glad you came. A touch of sanity, at last!

You're looking gorgeous today."

"To match the weather," replied Beril. She turned to the tall, thin man. "Hello," she said, giving him a smile.

"Ah." Arif Bey was obliged to present him. "My director, Orhan Friedlander. Turkish mother, German father. An excellent director."

"This is my friend Oran Crossmoor," said Beril. "Turkish mother, American father."

"Oh!" said Arif Bey, taking notice of Oran. "Another creative combination. Can you direct?"

"I'm a photographer."

"Wonderful. Sometime we'll have to discuss your future. At the moment I'm about to go gaga. I've just learned that Ali Akhan, our Suleyman the Magnificent, stepped on his son's roller skate and sprained his ankle. To tell you the truth I didn't think things like that really happened. Now we have to rearrange the entire shooting schedule and I'm tearing out every last hair on my head."

Beril gave him her most charming smile. "Could you introduce us to Sinan?"

"What?" Then Arif pretended to pout. "You came to see Sinan, not me?" He burst out laughing. "Come to think of it, I don't even know if he's here. Attila!" He called to a man sitting nearby.

"Sir?"

"Sinan is here, isn't he?"

"He's in his tent, sir."

Arif Bey turned back to Beril. "His scene doesn't come up for another half hour or so. Shall we go see what he's doing? Later we can watch the filming and I'll tell you all about making movies."

As Arif marched ahead of them over to the red tent, Beril whispered to Oran, "Arif Bey thinks I only want Sinan's autograph."

"So he'll be there with us, all the time?"

"I'm afraid so."

"Sinan?" Arif Bey called out when he reached the tent. "May I come in?"

A deep, rich voice boomed out, "Lasciate ogni speranza..."

Arif Bey rolled his eyes. "Another useful phrase from those Italian script girls." He pulled back the flap and went inside.

"Our Sinan is a real multinational," Oran said. "Italian script girls, Arabian princes. I wonder what he thinks of Turkish architecture students?"

Beril laughed. "We'll see."

Arif Bey looked annoyed when he came out of the tent. "He's not in the best of moods. We shouldn't stay long."

Beril and Oran followed Arif Bey inside. The interior glowed dark pink. The air was thick with cigarette smoke.

Sinan Altay, wearing a white shirt and black pants from centuries past, was sitting on a long, wide couch, his legs propped up on it. He was barefoot. His leather boots and black stockings lay on the ground near the sofa.

He kept on reading his newspaper, smoking his cigarette, barely glancing at the three intruders. To judge from the pile of newspapers scattered at the foot of the sofa and the butts that filled the nearest ashtray, he had been reading and smoking for quite some time.

"Sinan," said Arif Bey. "I would like to present Beril and her friend, Oran."

Sinan put down his newspaper and inspected his visitors. After giving them the opportunity to admire his dark, handsome face and thick black mustache, he graced them with a smile, revealing perfect teeth. "Have a seat," he said, waving to the simple chairs scattered around. "The tent is Ottoman...replica Ottoman...a war tent. But my producers and directors refuse to sit on cushions, so we have chairs." He spoke with contempt. "They have surrendered to the West."

"Indeed," said Arif Bey with a twinkle in his eye. "If this very day studios in Hollywood and Cairo offered you a contract, naturally you would pick Cairo."

"Of course!" Sinan broke out in a smile. He looked at Beril and Oran. "You are friends of Arif's?"

"Beril is the granddaughter of a boyhood friend of mine," said Arif Bey.

"You are old enough to have grandchildren? You seem so young to me, so energetic. A lion!" Sinan threw his head back and roared with laughter.

Arif Bey drew himself up and gave Sinan a gracious smile. "I do my best... Your Excellency."

"I hate filming," said Sinan. His face had taken on a stormy expression. "The cameramen fiddle with their cameras. I sit around. I do a fifteen-second sequence five times, ten times, fifty times until the director is satisfied. After that, back to the tent for another wait. I'm bored out of my mind."

"Why don't you work in the theater?" asked Oran.

Sinan looked at him with surprise. "The money, of course! I can't resist the money. Ask Arif. He knows as well as anyone how I like to have rivers of cash flowing into my bank account."

Arif Bey smiled benignly.

"I understand you're not playing the hero in the film," said Beril.

"Arif Bey didn't offer me the best part, Suleyman the Magnificent. He didn't even consider me for the leader of the enemy, the last Grand Master of the Knights of St. John. At first I turned him down flat."

"We're trying to broaden your image," said Arif Bey.

"And pound and flatten and squash it."

Arif Bey ignored him and turned toward Oran and Beril. "Sinan is playing the most interesting character in the drama, Andreas d'Amaral. For the Knights of St. John, who ruled Rhodes from their fortified citadel, Andreas was a traitor. He made a deal with the Ottomans, they thought. He was denounced and executed. But we are rehabilitating him. We see him as a warrior of supremely realistic vision: would not a deal with the Ottomans be preferable to a valiant but wasteful stand to the end? As it turned out, Andreas's judgment was vindicated by the later actions of the Knights. When it became clear that the Ottoman siege of Rhodes would end in victory, the Knights accepted the offer of Sultan Suleyman. They would surrender in return for safe passage off the island. And on New Year's Day, 1523, that's exactly what they did."

Oran leaned forward. "So the conflict of the besieged Knights of St. John will be reflected in the personal drama of Andreas d'Amaral."

"Exactly. This is a great part for Sinan..."

"A challenge, Arif called it," said the actor.

"... which he will play with brilliance." Arif Bey added a flourish with his hand.

"My family came from Rhodes," Beril said. "They arrived with Suleyman the Magnificent."

"Really?" said Sinan. "This film will have a special meaning for you." He reached over for another cigarette, but the pack was empty. He crushed it in his hand and tossed it into a waste basket. He looked plaintively at the producer. "I'm out of cigarettes, Arif."

Arif Bey sighed as he rose to his feet. "That's a tragedy. And we don't want any tragedies around here, do we?" He winked at Beril as he went out to find the boy who supplied the staff with tea and cold drinks.

"Here," said Oran. "Have one of mine."

"Thanks." Sinan helped himself.

Beril pressed ahead: "My family had a farm on Rhodes, not far from town."

"I hear Rhodes is a beautiful island," Sinan said. "I'd like to see it. Before doing this film, I had barely heard of the place."

"They worked the farm for centuries. The land was fertile and they lived well, until…"

"Did the Greeks kick them out?"

"The Italians confiscated the land during the First World War."

"The Italians? Were they down there, too?"

"But the farm was already in difficulty."

"You just said everything ran smoothly."

Sinan seemed caught up in the story. So far, so good.

"Something odd happened." Beril paused. "Our explanation isn't modern, it's not scientific."

Sinan smiled with understanding. "All our mothers attached blue beads to our cradles to keep away the evil eye. You and I would do the same for our children, wouldn't we?"

"Well, if you're interested."

Sinan sat up in a crosslegged position. "I've already read today's newspapers inside and out ten times and they all say the same things. Tell me your story."

Beril glanced at Oran. He signaled encouragement with his eyes.

"My family was noted for the gift of healing. One member of each generation was blessed with special powers, and people would come from all over the island to consult with him. The family attributed the healing skills and our good fortune to an unusual necklace, a necklace of four gold lockets, each containing a holy relic, and a gold plaque in the shape of a star."

"But then…"

"My great-great-grandfather didn't believe in the connection between the necklace and the family's fortune. He sold the lockets to an Englishman."

"Aha!" said Sinan. "He was a fool. I can see that right now."

"So it seems," Beril said. "The family's well-being came to an end. Bad luck began to plague us. The farm is no longer ours. No one is left on Rhodes, and violent death has followed us ever since. Death in war, horrible accidents, long and painful illnesses, more frequently than any family could reasonably expect."

"You should find these lockets and put the necklace back together again," Sinan said.

"That's exactly what we're trying to do."

"In fact, we've found one," said Oran. "But only one."

"Good for you."

"In the Covered Bazaar, here in Istanbul. It matched perfectly the descriptions we had." Oran was watching Sinan while he spoke. "A small, oval locket made of gold, covered with an engraved floral pattern, on one side a large emerald surrounded by rubies, and on the reverse, a word inscribed in Arabic." He reached for his wallet, opened it, and pulled out a photograph. "Like this!" Oran held up the picture in front of Sinan.

Sinan's eyes widened suddenly. He recovered quickly, keeping his smile in place.

Oran went on. "We are prepared to pay well for any others we can find."

"Recovering the necklace will mean much to you," Sinan said smoothly. He stretched with princely languor. "I have to put on the rest of my costume. My scene's coming up soon." He put his bare feet down on the ground and gave Oran and Beril a hard, cool look, waiting for them to go.

Oran sat back in his chair. "I've just returned from Greece, where I ran into an old friend of yours. Prince Karim al-Wasf."

"Karim?" Alarm flashed across Sinan's face. Just as quickly a smile came back. "I haven't seen Karim for years."

"So he said."

"How is he?" Sinan had risen from the couch.

"He plays bridge and goes to parties. I think he enjoys himself, in his own way."

"He learned what he wanted out of life," Sinan said. "That's the secret, isn't it? Now, if you will let me get ready."

"We're going," said Oran. He and Beril stood up. "I would like to ask about one thing Karim said."

"I can guess. Bridge-playing Karim...fantasy was always his strongest suit."

Oran might have enjoyed the joke had Sinan's eyes not found a gold-hilted dagger on the dressing table beyond the sofa and lingered there an instant before returning to his two guests. Suddenly Oran felt apprehensive. He glanced at Beril. She, too, had followed Sinan's eyes to the dagger.

Sinan's face had turned dark and cruel. But Oran plunged on. "He said he had given you one of the lockets about ten years ago. He described the circumstances."

"Lies!" Sinan shouted. "He lied to you! I helped him find a house on the Bosporus. He gave me the locket as a reward, a commission."

"That's exactly what he told me," Oran answered calmly.

Sinan was stunned.

"Isn't that true, Beril?"

Beril nodded gravely.

"So you did have the locket," said Oran.

"Well, yes, or one similar."

"Do you still own it?"

Sinan seemed confused. "Yes," he mumbled. "Yes, I do."

"Could we buy it from you?"

"But I like it. Yes, I rather do. And as a token of my friendship for Karim..."

Oran smiled sardonically. "Karim told me you were close."

Beril stepped in. "Don't you find our family's story reason enough to sell?"

Sinan sat down. The silence in the tent hung like a thick, heavy curtain.

"I'm not sure," he said at last. "If I did sell it, how would I know the price? I would need the advice of an expert."

Beril held her tongue.

"I'd want secrecy, complete secrecy. Do you understand?" Sinan spoke with icy formality.

"Absolutely."

"Arif Bey shouldn't know a thing."

"You'll contact us directly, then?" Oran asked.

"Yes," Sinan said. "If I decide to sell."

Beril took out a piece of paper and wrote down her name, address, and phone, and Oran added his phone as well. "I hope the film is a success," said Beril.

Sinan gave them a frosty smile. He held up the flap of the tent so they could leave.

* * *

Arif Bey approached Oran and Beril, Sinan's cigarettes in hand. "I hope Sinan didn't snarl at you."

"We had a nice chat," Beril said.

"He has so much experience," said Arif Bey. "He's been in the business a long time. And he's a great actor. You can tell that just by talking to him, can't you? We're counting on him to make this film a success."

"We really are enormously grateful," said Beril. She gave Arif Bey her most charming smile.

His face lit up. He loved it. "You must stay for the next scene," he said eagerly. "Andreas...that's Sinan...is going to pace the battlements."

They waited to see Sinan emerge from his tent, accompanied by members of the costume and make-up staff. After putting on his breastplate, he climbed the steps to the top of the walls and practiced his brief scene. The director called, "Action!" and the cameramen sprang into motion, their cameras pointed upwards to record the controversial knight from the fortress of Rhodes, lost in contemplation, his dark hair and proud profile etched against the brilliant blue of the sky.

* * *

Oran and Beril crossed the shore road in front of the castle and looked out over the Bosporus. Near them, a group of boys were jumping off the rocks into the water, shouting and splashing and throwing a ball around. A bit farther on, a heavy-set man with graying hair adjusted the hooks on his fishing line.

Oran turned to Beril. "I was a fool," he said, "yesterday in the bus."

Beril glanced at him, then turned away.

"I shouldn't have blown up like that. Will you forgive me?"

She looked at him. The sleeve of his shirt moved slightly in the breeze, the white shirt over his brown arms...the sunlight hit one side of his face and left the other in shadow. She made a slight motion forward, almost a step.

"I'll try," she said, smiling

Oran threw his arms around her and kissed her, a full, deep kiss. Right there in public, in broad daylight, before she could utter a word of protest.

She felt crushed against his strong chest, but in an instant she was reaching out to hold him closer still.

Someone blew a whistle.

Beril broke loose. They were kissing in public view!

They looked around. A watchman was warning the boys they were swimming too close to the fisherman.

How silly of her! No one was staring at them. She couldn't help laughing.

He was smiling, too. He took her hand.

I'll forgive you, she thought. Of course I will.

* * *

After the filming of his walk on the battlements, Sinan returned to his red tent and lay down on the sofa. He could still see those two cold faces staring at him. How did they outmaneuver him so neatly?

How low of Karim to send blackmailers! After all these years. He had to sell that locket. He had no choice. Nowadays only the savory scandals from his past could be released for publicity.

Even so, he didn't have to be walked over like a doormat. He took out the piece of paper the blackmailers had given him, inspected the names and addresses, and decided what he would do.

When he was free late that afternoon, Sinan changed out of his costume, put on dark glasses, combed his hair in an unusual way, and went out for a pack of cigarettes.

And to use a telephone.

Everyone needs a contact in the underworld, don't they? If you want to stay afloat, you certainly do.

This Oran, this Beril, maybe they won't say anything. But who knows? A warning wouldn't be out of place.

And no one knows how to deliver warnings better than Ahmet.

* * *

The telephone rang. Nusret answered. "Hello?"

"This is the Flea, calling in an alert." Before Nusret could answer, the man at the other end of the line went on, speaking rapidly in a deep round voice. "Two students, lots of questions. Oran Crossmoor and Beril Rodoslu. Oran Crossmoor, speaks Turkish, and Beril Rodoslu." Nusret was too startled to say anything when he remembered that Oran Crossmoor was the man who tried to trip him up on the bridge.

"Check on them." The man read out their addresses and phone numbers. "This is a warning!"

The line went dead. Nusret looked at the receiver, then slowly put it back on the telephone.

Who was this Flea? What would Ahmet say when he came back from the market and found out that he, Nusret, had been talking with the Flea?

Nusret sat down at the table and poured himself another glass of raki. Of all the days to come to Ahmet's for a pre-dinner snack.

Oran Crossmoor, what was he up to now? Nusret felt uneasy. Had Sedat Bey told him anything?

Nusret took a handful of roasted chick-peas. He'd have to be very careful, very careful indeed.

He reached into his pocket, pulled out a small package, and unwrapped it on the table. The beautiful locket and the gold star, too. Gold, emerald, rubies. He deserved them. Sedat Bey had betrayed him. When Nusret first brought him the locket, Sedat Bey promised never to reveal his identity. Nusret smiled, remembering Sedat Bey's look of panic when confronted with his betrayal. And Sedat Bey squeaking back that he hadn't told Oran, he had only told his friend Leyla Aslanoglu...who was at that very moment safeguarding the locket while this Oran was away. His dear friend, Leyla Aslanoglu. An old lady with an apartment a child could break into.

And now Ahmet would sell the locket for him. Not to Sedat Bey, but through his own reliable channels. What these connections were, Nusret had his suspicions, but he knew probing questions would not be welcomed.

In exchange for selling the locket, Ahmet wanted Nusret to make one last delivery.

Chapter 25

Beril and her mother, Semra, listened while Aliye Hanim recounted the blunders committed during the planning of that year's Istanbul Festival. The three women were sitting in the garden of Semra's house. Tea would be served shortly.

Aliye Hanim frightened Beril a bit, this old friend of Aunt Leyla's, admired violinist and famously strict, successful teacher at the Istanbul Conservatory of Music. She had always struck Beril as rather dry. She still wore her hair in bangs in front and pulled into a bun in back, and this summer's khaki dress differed little from its predecessors. When she gestured, her bony elbows and wrists poked and jabbed the air.

And yet her fingers moved fluidly and delicately. At heart she was a conductor. The people she met were all players in her orchestra. The only person still alive before whom she felt humble was Leyla Aslanoglu, who had sponsored her music studies first in Istanbul and later in France. Indeed, her respect and affection for Leyla explained this exceptional visit to the house of Beril's parents. Aliye Hanim had come to express her outrage at the attack on Leyla and to inquire after her condition.

As soon as she heard the favorable prognosis, she breathed a sigh of thanks for God's great mercy and moved on to the topic that truly absorbed her: the organization of the Istanbul Festival. Already in the entry hall of the house, then through to the back door and into the garden, she fumed about her incompetent, foolish colleagues.

"I told him a thousand times he had to find a new piano," Aliye Hanim said. "That decrepit Pleyel needs a complete overhaul."

Beril quickly lost interest. The crimes of the organizers weren't enormous at all, merely minor mishaps.

Then she heard Aliye Hanim say, "At least they listened to me when I proposed we invite Alexandra Stephanides."

Beril sat up. Alexandra Stephanides...the pianist? Oran's pianist? All at once she was back in the conversation.

"Why shouldn't they have?" asked Semra, one eye locked on the back door of the house to monitor the arrival of tea.

"Because no one had ever invited her before!" Aliye Hanim rose halfway from her seat in her outrage. "I wrote and asked her if she would like to give a concert in Istanbul. She accepted with pleasure. What a surprise, she said, to be invited at last."

"Why wouldn't they invite her?" Beril asked.

"Why would a famous Greek pianist want to perform in Turkey?" Aliye Hanim said sarcastically. "Far better to accept the higher prestige and fees of Europe and America!" With a flick of her hand she dismissed those foolish Istanbul impresarios.

"Ah! Here we are." Semra had spotted the maid coming out with a large tray. She roused herself from her chair to assist in the presentation of the tea.

While Semra was fussing over the refreshments, Aliye Hanim folded her hands in her lap and inspected her surroundings. Beril followed her glance. The garden wasn't large, but it was well-tended. Marigolds and petunias lined the brick path from the house. Behind them were rosebushes and oleanders and, in a distant corner, two gnarled, woody geraniums with coral red flowers. Beneath them reclined a black cat, slowly waving its tail.

"I met Madame Stephanides years ago, in London," said Aliye Hanim. "My dear father had suddenly fallen ill. I was worried sick. But I was to give a recital; somehow I had to concentrate! Madame Stephanides came to the concert and afterwards introduced herself and told me how much she had enjoyed it. It was so kind of her to say that."

Semra served her a cup of tea. "Is she playing with an orchestra here?"

"She's giving a solo recital. Don't you have tickets? It's in just a few days."

Semra looked flustered. "Metin usually gets the tickets for such things. He has been in Germany."

"I'll take care of it, Mother," Beril jumped in. "I'll go tomorrow."

Aliye Hanim smiled. "For you, there will always be tickets. Call me if the box office tells you the concert is sold out." She relaxed back into her seat and sighed. "It's so peaceful in this garden. What a perfect tonic, just what I need. As soon as Madame Stephanides leaves, I'm going to Buyukada for a long weekend." Suddenly her face brightened and she sat up. "Do you remember, Semra, how I first came to Buyukada, a young violin student from nowhere, from a village on the Black Sea? Leyla Hanim and Tevfik Bey took me to their summer house. I was so enchanted, I must have played like an angel all summer. There is something special about islands."

"My husband's family came from Rhodes."

"Yes, I'm sure Leyla Hanim told me," Aliye Hanim said. "Have you been? I've always wanted to visit the Greek islands."

"Metin has collected pictures. Why don't you stay for dinner? I could show you the albums."

"I'd love to," said Aliye Hanim. "But the festival..."

"We haven't seen you for so long."

"This summer, I promise." Aliye Hanim smiled as she stood up. "Here, or else on Buyukada. But in either case, after the festival." She crossed the garden, heading for the house.

Beril followed her. "Do you think I could meet Madame Stephanides?"

"I don't see why not," said Aliye Hanim. "She's arriving in a few days. Perhaps we should ask her son and daughter-in-law. They will know her schedule."

"How can I reach them?"

"They're staying at the Sheraton. Mr. and Mrs. Ianni Dimitriadis. Shall I give them a message?"

"That would be wonderful!" Beril couldn't wait to tell Oran.

After Aliye Hanim left, Semra went into the kitchen to inquire about dinner, and Beril went for a walk, down the hill to look at the boats tied up in Bebek Bay...and to get some ice cream. Whatever her mother might think of desserts before dinner, the day's progress deserved a proper celebration.

* * *

"Sedat Bey just telephoned," Semra said when Beril returned. "He insisted on speaking with you."

"Is he at his shop?"

"How should I know? He wouldn't tell me a thing."

"He must have been in a rush," Beril said. "Here, why don't you read the newspaper while I call him." She settled Semra into an armchair and then went into the little telephone room under the stairs.

Chapter 26

Nusret felt lousy. He had a headache and his stomach felt queasy. Normally he stopped drinking raki before he hit the danger point but last night he got carried away. Why didn't he stop for a bowl of tripe soup like everyone else? It was the only surefire way to stave off a hangover.

Now it was too late. He'd have to feel like shit the rest of the day.

He washed his face in cold water and put on his dark green uniform. He had to go to work. He had to pretend things were normal.

How had he got himself into this corner? Money. His wife reminded him every day.

"If only we could get a new stove," she'd say, "with an oven that works." Always "if only."

He had begun by taking bribes from applicants for driver's licenses. Then he was transferred to Customs. Very fertile. That's where he met Ahmet. Ahmet appreciated the smooth transit of his shipments when Nusret was handling the paperwork. But, said Ahmet, if Nusret wanted bigger rewards... So Nusret had ended up running drugs for Ahmet.

And now stealing that locket, knocking out an old lady, just to get revenge on that jeweler for giving out his name. Nusret thought he'd sell it again, get more money.

Last night Sedat had called him. "I know who robbed Leyla Aslanoglu and sent her to the hospital," he said. "But if you get that locket and star back to me, I won't press charges. If you don't..."

Sedat Bey didn't sound scared anymore.

Nusret tried to reach Ahmet. He had given the locket and the star to Ahmet to sell for him. Now he had to get them back. All night he kept phoning, but Ahmet was out.

Nusret went into the living room. His wife had tea ready. He stirred in two lumps of sugar and lit a cigarette.

His younger boy, the five-year-old, ran in and grabbed him around the waist. "Daddy, Daddy," he cried. He was still in his pyjamas.

My boys! thought Nusret as he hugged his son. Oh, God, what will happen to my boys?

I've got to find Ahmet!

* * *

The red and beige city bus headed up the Bosporus road toward the Black Sea. Since it was mid-day, the bus wasn't crowded. Even though they could have had seats, Peter and Annelies stood at the back of the bus, guarding everyone's packs. Nicole and Hans-Ruedi were sitting nearby.

Annelies worried they were cutting things too close. They had tickets on the Orient Express for the next day, but now, instead of staying near the train station as she had urged, they were going to spend their last night in Turkey up the Bosporus at the furthest point you could go before the military zone stopped you. Peter had proposed they camp out at a spot overlooking the water. It would be a romantic way to end the trip. Nicole and Hans-Ruedi thought it was a great idea. They could ride the ferry back to the center of town! It landed just a few steps from the train station.

But the ferry trip took hours. They'd have to catch an early boat. What if they overslept? Annelies knew she would be checking her watch all night. She wouldn't get a wink of sleep.

* * *

When he had finished photographing Ottoman tombstones in the cemetery attached to the great mosque of Suleyman the

Magnificent, Oran sat down on a low wall, pulled out the letter he had received that morning, and read it once again. GF had typed it on his electric typewriter, all except for his quavering signature.

Dear Oran,

Indeed you have found one of our lockets! Bravo! I was so thrilled I almost kissed Mrs. Tinker (my morning nurse). I knew you would find important things in Turkey – and I'm not even thinking of the mysterious letter dangling beautiful, magical, tragic jewels in front of us! I sensed this trip would be crucial for you, but now I understand how crucial it is for me as well. I am old, my body has given out, but inside I still feel very much alive.

To return to your question, How did the locket escape the Smyrna fire? Whatever did my poor brother Edward do with it? I suppose these are questions we will never be able to answer.

And no, I never heard of Edward's friend, Leyla. But I moved to America soon after the war (World War I, for you), and knew nothing of Edward's private life.

Should you need some wherewithal to pay for this or any other lockets that might appear (I don't rule that out!), ask me. And while you are in Istanbul, a request: I would love a picture of the Bosporus at dawn. Rosy-fingered, of course. Could you take one for me?

Your loving
GF

Oran folded the letter and replaced it in the handsome gray envelope. Of course he would chase Dawn as she tiptoed over the Bosporus. He'd get on the earliest ferry the next morning and find that perfect picture. But how could he tell GF about the theft?

He sighed and looked around. An old man with a grizzled beard and a white skull cap walked slowly toward the octagonal mausoleum of Suleyman the Magnificent. A plump woman in a brown coat waddled close behind. His wife, no doubt.

Perhaps GF would accept the news stoically, with the Oriental fatalism he claimed he had adopted only once he left Asia Minor. He would be disappointed, even so.

The finding of the locket had clearly lifted GF's spirits. Perhaps GF regretted the choices he'd made in his life. Maybe his marriage to the rich American nurse hadn't brought him happiness. Oran remembered his Grandmother Charlotte in her perfectly tailored gray suit, with the little hat to match, removing her gloves finger by finger. Marriage to her could not have been easy. Now GF was too frail to visit Turkey; death might not be far off. Could this be why he was so keen for Oran to come?

The elderly couple removed their shoes and stepped inside the sultan's tomb. Oran imagined them inside, their hands raised in prayer. A curious thing to do, it seemed to him. the sultan was no holy man. Elif would have understood. She had always enjoyed visiting this cemetery. It wasn't far from the university. She liked to contemplate the resting place of the great sultan, in the shadow of his imposing mosque, and think of the vanished glories of the sixteenth century.

"It makes be proud to be a Turk," she had told him. "And you?" She took his hand and gazed expectantly at him. "What makes you proud to be a Turk?"

"Well...I'm not sure."

He had never thought about this particular question. Oran always felt the intellectual challenges of Elif's remarks. He had learned a lot from her, but sometimes she was too teacher-like. She wanted him to commit to his Turkish half. How could he? He was an American. Couldn't she see that?

After the old couple emerged from the tomb of Suleyman, they had crossed to examine the companion mausoleum of Roxelana, the sultan's favorite wife. Since the tomb was locked, they stayed only a moment before turning back.

"I never visit the tomb of Roxelana," Elif had said. "She wrecked the empire." Roxelana was a Russian, Elif explained.

She had twisted the mighty sultan around her little finger. She persuaded him his favorite son was plotting against him. After this prince was strangled, her own son became the uncontested heir to the throne.

"Do you know what her detestable son would be called? The sultan who would tip the Ottoman Empire into its long decline?" Elif grimaced, as if she were holding out a piece of soiled laundry. "Selim the Sot."

All were dead now, Oran thought, Suleyman, Roxelana, Selim the Sot, the Ottoman Empire...and Elif. Elif, buried in a small cemetery up the Bosporus. He had made a trip there soon after he returned to Istanbul. It was a peaceful place with beautiful trees.

Small blue irises had taken hold by the headstone of the tomb nearest him. Oran reached out and touched the delicate flowers. Then he touched the headstone. Tears sprang to his eyes. Elif is gone, he thought. Gone, truly gone. He bent his head under the sudden weight of his knowledge and let out the sob that had been building inside.

A strong breeze rose up, rustling the leaves of the tall trees. It was chilly. Oran didn't know how long he had sat there on the old stone wall of the cemetery. He shivered, then stood up. He wanted to go, he wanted to be somewhere else. As he turned to collect his equipment, he knocked his knapsack onto the ground. Out fell the envelope of photographs that had arrived in the mail together with his grandfather's letter. Oran remembered one of the pictures. He picked it out and held it up. The Swiss girl, the tall, tanned, blonde backpacker. Blonde...like Roxelana? She didn't look like an evil schemer, just forthright and healthy. A sort of blonde Beril. A blonde Beril! He laughed at the thought. But Beril wouldn't stroll through a Middle Eastern city in shorts!

All of a sudden he longed to see Beril. Straightforward, happy Beril. But where would he find her?

He gathered up his equipment, stashed it away, and walked quickly out of the cemetery.

Chapter 27

Osman arrived at the Besiktas dolmus stop a few minutes before six in the morning. The sun had risen, but it was still cool. Osman hadn't worn a jacket. He paced around the taxi area waiting for his accomplice to appear.

Temel was late. Sleeping off a hangover, Osman decided, or gorging himself on breakfast at someone else's expense.

At 6:30 it was clear that Temel was not going to show up. Osman couldn't wait any longer. Soon Ibrahim Bey would be coming to the Secret Garden to get the gold locket and take it to the dealer in the Covered Bazaar.

Osman set off for the restaurant, walking rapidly up the hill. He was furious. Didn't he suspect this would happen? He shouldn't have given Temel any advance. Not to mention the free dinner!

"Hey!" someone shouted behind him. Osman turned around to see Temel with his round, red face racing up toward him. "Here I am, I made it!"

"Don't shout like that," Osman hissed. "What happened?" He kept on climbing the hill.

"The bus, it didn't come and it didn't come."

"You should've taken a taxi," said Osman. "I know you have the money."

"You didn't tell me to take a taxi."

"It's an emergency! Didn't I make that clear?"

"We'll make it, sure we will."

"If we don't, I want those 500 liras back."

When they got close to the restaurant, Osman stopped at the edge of a building just where the street made a bend.

"We'll plant ourselves here. He'll come out of the restaurant and head straight towards us."

"How do you know he won't turn uphill?"

"The closest taxis are down on the coast road."

"Do you think he's in there now?"

"Shhh! Get back!" Osman pulled Temel back into the shadows as Ibrahim Bey came down the street from the upper end, unlocked the gate to the Secret Garden, and went inside.

"He almost saw us," said Temel. His breath smelled of onions and beer.

"You have to be more careful," Osman said.

"What if someone else walks by?"

"At this hour? In this back street?"

"Did you bring masks?" asked Temel.

"I've got two stockings, with eye holes," said Osman. "Now, here's the plan. The man comes out and walks by us. We grab him and pull him over here. You do the talking. I don't want him to recognize my voice. He'll be carrying a gold locket. That's what I want, the gold locket. You ask for it. If he doesn't give it up, we'll keep roughing him up until he does."

"What if he still refuses?"

"He'll hand it over. I'm sure of it."

"I brought these along." Temel took out a set of brass knuckles.

Osman's eyes widened. He had never seen brass knuckles close up. "I don't want any bad injuries! Is that absolutely clear?"

A faint smile came to Temel's lips. "I know how to control myself."

The two men stood back in the shadows and waited. Osman strained his ears for telltale sounds.

The loud banging of the gate hit them like an electric shock. He was coming out! As soon as they saw Ibrahim shut the gate of the restaurant, Osman and his partner ducked behind the building and pulled the stockings over their heads. Osman could feel his heart beating. The seconds ticked by, five, ten, fifteen. Ibrahim Bey, where was he?

"He must have gone up the hill," Osman whispered.

They dashed out of their dark corner to chase Ibrahim Bey up the street. But he was still standing there, just around the wall from them, fiddling with something. His key chain? Osman stopped just before he crashed into him. Ibrahim Bey looked up. In an instant his air of distraction changed to terror. He turned and ran.

Temel and Osman grabbed Ibrahim and dragged him into the corner from which they had stalked him.

"Your money!" said Osman's accomplice in a low, growling voice.

Ibrahim Bey hurried to take out his wallet.

Temel removed the wad of bills. Osman stuck out his hand and took charge of the money.

"What else do you have?"

"Nothing."

"I bet you have something else on you."

"I don't. I swear." Ibrahim Bey's pitiful tones repulsed Osman. He liked Ibrahim Bey. He didn't want to humiliate him. All he wanted was the locket.

"Let's take a look." Temel frisked Ibrahim Bey. He stopped at his pockets. "What do you have in there?"

"Nothing. Change. Some medicine."

"Let's see it."

Ibrahim hesitated.

"All of it." Temel reached into his own pocket, pulled out the brass knuckles, and slipped them on.

"Here!" said Ibrahim as he took out a little packet of brown paper.

Osman snatched the package and unwrapped it. The gold locket!

"Very nice!" said Temel when he caught sight of the gold. "What else are you hiding from us?"

"That's everything, I swear!"

Temel smashed Ibrahim with his fist. Osman watched with

horror as Ibrahim gasped and clutched at his belly, then fell to the ground.

"Let's go!" Temel said to Osman.

Osman thought he was going to be sick. "You've hurt him."

Temel tugged at his arm. "We've got to get out of here!"

Get out. Escape. Hide. Osman followed Temel downhill, racing over the irregular cobblestones.

"In there," Osman called out. The two ducked into the dark entry hall of a decaying apartment building. The hall stank of urine and rotting garbage. A pair of kittens stopped swatting at each other and scampered up the stairs into the darkness. The men yanked the stocking off their heads. Osman counted out 1,500 liras and gave the bills to Temel, who immediately counted them again. Satisfied, he put the money in his pocket and smiled.

"Why did you hit him?" asked Osman. "He'd already given us everything."

"He'll recover."

"Do you really think so?"

Temel looked carefully at Osman. "You weren't a friend of this guy, were you?"

Osman said nothing.

"Well, so long." Temel saluted and disappeared out the door.

"So long." Osman gathered up the two stockings and threw them onto a pile of garbage.

He touched his pocket to make sure the locket was still there. In the other pocket was Ibrahim's cash. He'd return that when he got back to the Secret Garden.

He stuck his head out of the hall, glancing up and down the street. An old lady was trudging uphill, her eyes fixed on the ground. Osman slipped out and started toward the dock. The old woman looked at him. He met her eyes and felt a stab of fear.

He wondered how Ibrahim Bey was. Had someone already found him and taken him in? Osman hoped he wouldn't be too discouraged, now that the restaurant at the beach was down the drain. If Ibrahim Bey could only know that the money would be going for a better cause.

Osman reached the dock just as a ferry was pulling in. The express to Eminonu, he learned at the ticket window. He'd better get on it. From Eminonu he could always get a second boat across to Uskudar. It would be safer to wait in Eminonu. No one would think to look for him there.

He crossed the dock and stepped on the long white ferry with the dark varnish trim. He found a seat upstairs. How comfortable it was to sit down. He was ready for a good sleep. But the whole day still lay in front of him. It wasn't even eight o'clock in the morning.

The dockhands undid the thick ropes and the sailors hauled in the gangplank. The ferry glided off, heading for Eminonu in the heart of the city. Osman looked around at the passengers: businessmen, office workers commuting from their homes up the Bosporus. No one seemed to take an interest in him. He signaled to a waiter who circulated with a large tray loaded with glasses of tea. After stirring in two lumps of sugar he took a sip. He pulled out a cigarette, lit it, and inhaled deeply. Tea and a cigarette – breakfast at last.

A controller came by and punched his ticket. Osman inspected him, but the controller didn't show the slightest sign of suspicion. The man across from him couldn't be an undercover agent, could he? Even with those torn pants and black plastic shoes? What about that smartly dressed woman with her cascading hennaed hair? Or that young man by the railing, with his red shirt and khaki pants and the camera with the big lens...was he merely pretending to watch the shore line as it passed by? No, no one betrayed any interest in him whatsoever. No need to get worked up, he hold himself. He finished his cigarette and immediately lit another, then turned to examine the passengers on the other side of the aisle.

* * *

Oran stood by the railing, his eyes fixed on the European shore. It was like watching a wonderful movie, this steady unrolling of houses and villas and docks and boats. And the pictures never grew stale. With each ferry trip, the spectacle changed slightly.

The ferry was now passing in front of the Dolmabahce Palace, the long, low, cream-colored rococo home of the sultans in the middle of the nineteenth century. From the sea and in the sunlight, it was one of Oran's favorite buildings in Istanbul. He liked its long line, its symmetry, the undulating crest of the cast iron fence at the water's edge, and the harmony of the colors of the palace, the garden that surrounded it, and the sea at its feet. He had already photographed it, before his trip to Greece. He'd hired a small boat to take him out into the Bosporus in the late afternoon, when the descending sun made it glow in golden light. Those pictures had to be good.

Today he had gotten up early, really early, before sunrise, and taken a taxi up the Bosporus to Tarabya and photographed the little harbor at dawn. The colors were lovely. He'd pick one of these pictures to send to GF. When he finished in Tarabya, he found another motorboat to take him as far as Bebek, so he could shoot rolls and rolls of the old waterfront houses in the early morning light. He was favoring his 85mm lens, he noted, and because the ride was bumpy, he had to use fast shutter speed and high speed film. On his way to Bebek, though, a slight haze developed. The light was no longer good for the sharp pictures he preferred.

Now he was heading back to Eminonu, to the center of town, to go to the apartment where he was staying, sleep for a few hours, and get out of this red shirt he'd been wearing for days. Then he'd try again to find Beril.

* * *

Annelies was sitting on a bench inside the ferry, keeping one hand on her back pack, trying to stay awake. You never knew when something untoward might happen; you had to be alert. Her three friends were asleep next to her. They had delegated her to play watchdog during the boat ride so they could get some sleep. As if she hadn't been dancing and talking and drinking all night long, too! As soon as they got to the train station and confirmed their seats on the Orient Express, she'd settle in a corner, lean up against her back pack, and take the nap she had earned.

It had been a beautiful evening. But how oddly it had started! She had felt apprehensive. Frightened, really. They had gone all the way up the Bosporus to spend their last night in Turkey. But they didn't know where they would camp. There weren't any secluded spots, so privacy was out of the question. No matter where you set up, someone was bound to come along and stare and say things.

They had found a nice spot overlooking the Bosporus and started to eat a picnic dinner. Some men came along and wanted to talk German with them. There was no way to get rid of them. One of the men kept his eyes locked on her. She had her hair hidden beneath a black scarf, and she looked in all directions except toward him, but it didn't make the slightest difference.

One of the other Turks kept urging the four of them to come along to a restaurant where he knew the owner. They would all have dinner together. The last thing she wanted to do was have dinner with complete strangers, especially men who couldn't get enough of her blondeness. Her friends thought otherwise. Speaking in Swiss German, which the Turkish men couldn't understand, they argued that out here on this bluff they weren't going to have any peace. When these men left, others would take their place. Annelies stood up and brushed off the seats of her shorts. Her friends were right. They might as well accept the invitation.

At the restaurant, they drank more and more beer, got sillier and sillier, and little by little became friends. Annelies stayed glued to Peter. She even made him accompany her to the bathroom. That way an unwanted admirer wouldn't try anything funny.

What a change from the start of the trip! When that policeman at the border gave them a hard time and forced them to pay him off with the little gold locket, she was ready to go straight back to Greece. Fortunately she didn't. Everything had gone well in Turkey. Even Peter had changed for the better. He didn't know the country, so he couldn't play powerful leader. She liked him much better this way.

Now, if only they would get to the train station so she could get some real sleep.

* * *

Nusret was standing by the snack bar drinking a glass of hot tea. He had boarded the ferry in Besiktas for that final stretch down to Eminonu. He wasn't wearing a uniform. His friend Ahmet was expecting an envelope from someone on the boat. Ahmet didn't want to collect it himself. He thought he would be recognized. So he asked Nusret to pick up the envelope. Nusret would drink tea at the bar and a man would come up and say, "It's cooler outside, and it's not even crowded!" and Nusret would make his way into the crowd waiting to get off the boat, take the envelope offered him, and reply, "See you at the wedding!"

It sounded simple enough, even if the passwords didn't make much sense. And in return for the envelope, Ahmet had promised to give back the locket and the star.

* * *

Approaching the dock at Eminonu, the ferry turned in toward the

Golden Horn and slowed down. Passengers began to get up, check their belongings, straighten their clothes. Some headed right for the exit.

Annelies shook Peter awake and called out to Hans-Ruedi and Nicole. She put on her back pack and stepped out into the aisle, into the flow of people moving down toward the exit.

"Hey!" Someone tapped her on the shoulder. "Your pack is about to come undone."

She turned around and saw a good-looking young man in a red shirt. He was speaking in English, though, not German, not Turkish. And he was smiling at her, almost as if he knew her. That was all right. He didn't look dangerous, somehow. She took off her pack and tightened the main strap. Sure enough, it was about to pop open. As she put her pack on, she smiled at him, too. "Istanbul?" she asked.

"And New York," came the answer.

"Ach, so," said Annelies. She glanced around to see if Peter were nearby. He wasn't, so she tried another smile and wished she spoke better English and that she had had a bath recently.

* * *

As the ferry glided into the dock, Nusret was waiting by the exit. His contact had found him by the bar, as planned. And now he was pushing through the crowd, heading Nusret's way. Nusret recognized him by the scar on his forehead. In the moment before the boat touched the landing, the contact stepped close to Nusret and slipped him the plain white envelope.

Just as Nusret was about to say "See you at the wedding," he spotted blonde hair, fair skin, and blue eyes. Then he recognized her, and the man in the red shirt she was talking to. He turned to hide his face. The Swiss hippie from the border, and the American who kept nosing around! They knew each other. Was Sedat in on this? Nusret panicked. They'd get him! Where could he hide? He looked for his contact, the man with the scar. But he had vanished.

Just at that moment the ferry hit the dock and the crowd surged forward toward the gangplank. As Nusret turned to escape, someone knocked into him and the envelope fell from his hand.

*   *   *

Osman set his tea glass on the bench, touched his pockets to make sure that the locket and his wallet were still there, and stood up. He advanced slowly in the mass of passengers funneling toward the narrow staircase that led to the exit downstairs. The hennaed woman, the man in the torn pants, and the young man in the red shirt were at his elbows. They made him uncomfortable.

He descended the stairs and approached the exit.

The boat struck the dock. A group of passengers next to Osman struggled to remain upright. But he was shoved sideways so abruptly that he lost his balance and fell against a mass of ropes, crates, and other equipment. His left pocket caught on an iron bar and ripped open. He watched aghast as the gold locket dropped to the floor and was kicked away. The brown paper wrapping had been torn, and the gold could be seen. He had to recover the locket. But people kept pressing forward onto the dock. He couldn't get through them.

Then someone was shouting, "Thief! Thief! Police!" The young man with the red shirt was brandishing the gold locket and yelling at the top of his lungs! Suddenly Osman's arms were pinned. He couldn't move. Oh, good God! A wave of fear and embarrassment engulfed him. I'm caught. My God, I'm caught!

"Hey! I know you! You're Nusret!" Osman heard the man in the red shirt cry out. "You're a policeman, arrest this man."

The spectators looked up, behind Osman. A blonde foreign woman screamed, pointing at Nusret, now on his knees straining for a white envelope just out of reach.

People followed her lead and started to shout. "Catch that man! He's trying to sneak away! He's the one who shoved the old guy. Get him!"

The old guy? What old guy? thought Osman. Who's being chased now? Why were they still holding him? What in the world was going on?

It was with a certain sense of relief that Osman allowed himself to be led away some time later by two policemen in honest-to-goodness dark green police uniforms, along with the man in the red shirt, another man in a pale green shirt, and a group of filthy foreigners with shorts and back packs. At least the confusion would come to an end. And maybe amidst these mysterious complications he might even be able to talk his way to freedom.

* * *

As they walked along, Osman heard the young man in the red shirt denounce him. Gold locket. Couldn't possibly be his. Stolen! The police turned to him. "Is it yours?" one asked.

Osman thought quickly. What could he tell them? They couldn't know already of the assault on Ibrahim, could they? "It belongs to my employer. He's selling it. I'm delivering it to the dealer." Osman tried to be as indignant as possible. "This is an outrage!"

"Which dealer?" asked a policeman.

"Ah...Sedat Bey, in the Covered Bazaar."

"Impossible!" said the young man in the red shirt. "Sedat Bey would have told us. This is one of the lockets my friends and I were intending to buy. Look." He pointed to the writing on the back of the locket. "It's in Arabic."

"Naturally," said Osman. "Why shouldn't it be?"

"And the arrangement for the sale..."

"Who are you, anyway?"

"...what do you know about that?"

"At the bazaar, of course," Osman said. "This morning."

"Who's your employer?"

This young man wouldn't let go, like a mad dog! "He couldn't make it so early," Osman said. "He'll be joining us later."

"I don't believe it," said the young man.

"It's true," said Osman. "You'd better release me," he said to the policemen. "Arrest on trumped-up charges...you could get into a lot of trouble! He's the one you should be arresting, whatever his name is, for all his lies." He pulled out a cigarette and lit it as calmly as he could.

The policemen looked confused. The four Swiss students anxiously huddled together. Nusret stared at the ground. The crowd of on-lookers that surrounded the entire group of policemen and captives watched, fascinated.

"My name is Oran. Why don't we go see Sedat Bey together?"

"I have an errand to do first," Osman said. "Urgent business at the bank."

"I want this story checked," said Oran.

The policemen whispered to each other.

"I must go," said Osman. "The dealer is waiting for me at the bank."

"Isn't he at his shop?" said one of the policemen. "Isn't that what you just told us?"

"Yes, yes. He's waiting for me at his shop to leave for the bank," replied Osman. "Can I go now?"

"My friends know a police commissioner," said Oran. "I want to see him."

"Which commissioner?"

"I can't remember. If I saw a list of names, it would come back to me."

The policemen smiled. Osman laughed scornfully. "Isn't this ridiculous? This young man thinks he's so clever."

"Clever! That's it!" Oran shouted. "Zeki!" The Turkish word for clever. "Zeki Bey! I want to see Zeki Bey!"

The attitude of the policemen changed at once. "Zeki Bey? Of course. Let's get going." They grabbed Osman on either side.

"Where are you taking me?" cried Osman. "My appointments! The bank! The bazaar! You're arresting an honest man!"

"Don't make a fuss," said one of the policemen. "You don't want to be charged with resisting an officer, do you?"

As they led him to a waiting car, Osman realized his cigarette had been knocked out of his hand. He turned to look for it. But all he saw was grimy, littered pavement and a crush of shoes and boots and slippers.

Chapter 28

As Oran and the other members of the motley procession entered the decaying Ottoman building occupied by the police, the guard in the little room just inside the entrance and the two men standing with him turned their heads and stared. They must have recognized Nusret Demir, although Oran had no idea if this was Nusret's office. Nusret, his face drained of color, was keeping his eyes fixed straight ahead. Next came the middle-aged Turkish thief, gripped on both sides by policemen. He looked dazed and afraid, like a trussed goat that knows its end is near. Beside Oran walked Annelies, her three scraggly friends following behind. Oran had been delighted when he recognized her on the ferry as the Swiss backpacker he had photographed. Now he realized they wouldn't have much of a chance to get to know each other. Annelies didn't speak good English, but her companions did. They were apprehensive. They hadn't done anything wrong, they insisted. The Turkish man had thrown away the envelope with the powder inside, not them. They had intended to leave that very afternoon on the Orient Express. They had tickets!

The policemen marched the group up two flights of stairs and down a corridor. A man playing with a string of amber beads sat on a chair outside the door where they stopped.

"Is Zeki Bey in?" asked one of the policemen.

"He's busy." The attendant stared at the Swiss backpackers in their shorts.

"For long?"

"He's signing documents. Should be through soon."

A policeman emerged with an armful of folders. The attendant indicated they could all go in. A thin man with bristly white hair, a mustache, and a deeply wrinkled face was seated behind a large desk stacked with papers, reading. Above him on the dingy green wall hung a tinted photograph of Ataturk in evening dress. The window was open and a small portable fan by the window blew air into the room. Nevertheless, the smell of tobacco was strong.

Zeki Bey looked up. He had thick white eyebrows and gray eyes. He took in his visitors, then set down his pen and crossed his arms on the desk. "Nusret," he said at last. "What is this? You look as if you've been arrested."

Nusret smiled. "It's nothing, sir. I was off duty, taking the ferry, when this old man fell." He gestured toward Osman

"Nusret Bey tried to run away, sir," said the policeman on duty. "Some men caught him. They said Nusret Bey shoved the old man against the cabin."

"But I didn't!"

"Of course we didn't know he was a member of the police force, sir, since he wasn't in uniform. This envelope was found nearby. That foreign woman with the blonde hair claimed Nusret Bey took it out of his own pocket and tried to throw it away."

Zeki Bey reached for the envelope, opened it, and took a sniff. He reached under the desk and pushed a button.

"Heroin, Nusret?"

Nusret stared down at the ground.

"You know what this means, don't you? Look at me! You know what this means?" Zeki Bey's face was turning dark with fury.

The door opened and the attendant came in.

"Sir?"

"I want Mustafa here immediately."

"Yes, sir."

"Who are these people?" Zeki Bey asked Nusret. "Are these your accomplices?"

"We don't have anything to do with him," said Oran.

Zeki Bey stared at Oran.

"I'm a friend of Leyla Aslanoglu," Oran said.

Zeki Bey turned to the uniformed officers. "What the hell is going on?"

The policeman on duty who spoke earlier stepped forward, indicating Oran. "This man claims the older man stole a gold locket."

"A locket? What locket? What are you talking about?"

Oran took out the locket and gave it to Zeki Bey.

"Did the old man steal it from you?" asked Zeki Bey.

"Not from me. He claims he was taking it to sell in the Covered Bazaar. But I don't believe him."

"How do you know Leyla Hanim?"

"She's an acquaintance of my mother's," said Oran.

"Her late husband was a friend of mine. Tevfik. Did you know him?"

"No, sir."

A little smile came to Zeki Bey's face. "Too bad. Quite a man. How is Leyla Hanim? I understand she was attacked by a thief."

"She's doing much better."

"That's good. Still in the hospital?"

"She should be out soon."

"I'm glad to hear it. Now, tell me again what happened."

"When this man tripped on board the ferry," Oran explained, "he hit something that ripped open his pocket. The gold locket went flying out onto the deck. It's a locket from a long-lost heirloom necklace that Leyla Hanim, her niece Beril, and I have been searching for. Incredibly, there it was, right at my feet."

Zeki Bey examined the older man in the custody of one of the policemen. "What's your name?"

"Osman."

"Your identity card?"

Osman showed it to him.

"Where do you work?"

"At the Secret Garden. A restaurant."

"In Besiktas? I know it. Ibrahim Selcuk's place. We raided it a while back."

"It's one of Istanbul's finest restaurants," said Osman.

"Where did you get this locket?"

"He says his employer couldn't get to the bazaar this morning and gave him the locket to bring to the dealer," said Oran.

"We should be able to resolve this quickly," said Zeki Bey. He reached into his desk and pulled out a tattered telephone directory. "We'll call up Ibrahim Bey and then the dealer...what's his name?"

"Sedat Bey."

"Sedat Tufekcioglu?" He smiled. "I should have known." He turned to Osman. "What do you have to say for yourself?"

Osman smiled weakly.

Zeki Bey began to hunt for the numbers.

"I needed the money." Osman spoke softly, to no one in particular. "My salary was so low."

"Shut up," said Zeki Bey. He dialed. "Hello? Secret Garden? Get me Ibrahim Bey...what? ... Have the police been contacted? Hello? This is Commissioner Zeki at headquarters. How is Ibrahim doing? I see...I see. Thanks." He hung up. "Ibrahim Bey was attacked by two hoodlums. He made it inside and called the police. We have his testimony. Ramazan!"

The attendant entered. "Sir?"

"A robbery took place this morning just outside the Secret Garden restaurant in Besiktas. I want a copy of the report as soon as possible."

"Yes, sir."

"The doctor has given Ibrahim a sedative and ordered him to rest for the entire day," Zeki Bey said.

"Is he badly hurt?" Oran asked.

"No. It's mostly the shock of being attacked. Tomorrow he'll be better."

"I didn't want to hurt him," said Osman.

"Who punched him?" asked Zeki Bey. "You or your friend?"

"The other man did. I only wanted the money. I deserved it!"

"Why didn't you ask him for a raise?"

"Ibrahim Bey wouldn't have given me a cent."

"You should have threatened to quit, to go on strike. Shake him up a little. Not this."

Osman was silent.

"Let's call Sedat Bey." Zeki Bey reached for his telephone.

Nusret was staring blankly out the window. The Swiss students looked ill at ease. Peter, the taller of the two men, caught Oran's eye. "What's going on?" Peter whispered.

"First the locket and this thief," said Oran. "Then he'll get to you."

Peter didn't look reassured.

"Hello, Sedat Bey? Zeki from police headquarters. A gold locket was stolen from Ibrahim Selcuk this morning. No, we've recovered it. An inside job, a waiter at the Secret Garden. Ibrahim is resting, no injuries. A friend of Leyla Aslanoglu is here with me." Zeki cupped his hand over the receiver. "What's your name?" he asked Oran.

Oran told him.

"What?" Zeki Bey looked at him with surprise.

"Oran Ka-ros-mor."

"Yes, indeed, Sedat Bey, he speaks Turkish just like a Turk. All right...if that's what you wish. Yes, fine, I'll tell him." Zeki Bey hung up the phone. "Sedat Bey wants you to meet him tomorrow at the clinic where Leyla Hanim is recuperating," he said to Oran. "He will have Sinan's locket, the one marked 'Medina', and he wants you to bring this one. Ibrahim Bey was indeed going to sell it to him. Here, take it."

Oran couldn't hide his surprise.

Zeki smiled. "You think I should check with Leyla Hanim, too, don't you? Why should I trust you with the locket?"

Before Oran could reply, Zeki Bey indicated Osman to one of the policemen with a flick of his head. "Take this man away."

Osman suddenly came to life. "What?"

"We'll press charges as soon as we can review the report on

the attack," said Zeki Bey.

The policeman took hold of Osman and marched him out of the room.

"You would surely like some tea," Zeki Bey said to Oran. "Ramazan!"

The attendant hurried in. "Yes, sir?"

"Two teas."

"Yes, sir." He backed out of the room.

"Now." Zeki Bey turned to the students. "What are they doing here?" he asked Oran.

"They've had a run-in with Nusret."

"What kind of run-in? Shall we hear what the foreigners have to say, Nusret?" Before Nusret could answer, Zeki Bey asked Oran to put the question to them.

"They say Nusret forced them to pay him in order to enter Turkey," Oran reported.

"A bribe?" said Zeki Bey, eyeing Nusret.

"They had marijuana," Nusret said. "They were trying to sneak it in. I had them searched."

Oran translated for the students, then asked if this was true.

"That's a lie," said Peter. "We didn't have any pot. We had a gold locket. Old. An antique. It was valuable."

"Are you serious?" Oran asked. "You were hiking around Greece carrying an ancient treasure?"

"That's what this guy wanted," Peter said, "as soon as he laid his eyes on it."

Then Oran remembered what Nusret had told him that morning on the bridge. Nusret claimed he'd bought 'Tears' from some Swiss hippies. And here they were.

"Well," Zeki Bey asked Oran, "what did he tell you?"

"Nusret searched them himself," Oran said. "They didn't have any drugs. That's a lie."

"What are you telling him?" asked Peter.

"Don't worry," Oran said. "I'm just translating what you told me."

"Are they changing their story?" Zeki Bey asked Oran.

"No, no, it's OK," Oran said. "He's nervous, that's all."

Zeki Bey stared at Peter. "He's hiding something from us," he said to Oran.

"They had a gold locket, just like this one, and Nusret made it clear they had to hand it over."

"These hitchhikers were traveling with an antique golden locket? Do you think that's normal?" Zeki Bey asked Oran.

"It was damn curious," said Nusret, "and that's why I knew I should confiscate it."

"And hand it over to the Department of Antiquities and Museums, as of course you did," said Zeki Bey. "What did you do with the locket, Nusret?"

"He sold it," Oran said.

"Oh?"

"To Sedat Bey."

Zeki Bey smiled as he reached for his cigarettes. "I see."

There was a knock at the door. The attendant came in, followed by a large man with bushy black hair and glasses.

"Mustafa, we need this powder analyzed." Zeki Bey handed him the white envelope. "Quick."

"Yes, sir." The man left the room without asking any questions.

"We'll talk later, Nusret," said Zeki. "We have lots to discuss. Take him away."

The remaining policeman took hold of Nusret and escorted him out. Nusret gave Oran and the students a look of hatred as he walked by them.

Zeki Bey picked up a metal letter opener and turned it around in his hands. "In many ways I'm a very naïve man," he said. "I'm still surprised to see how effectively money corrupts. Not just the desperate, but the wealthy, too. I only see the criminals, of course, those who have given in. I tend to forget the honesty that lies beyond our sight." He looked up at Oran and smiled. "Honesty does exist, doesn't it?"

"I never see the criminals," said Oran. "Not knowingly, anyway."

Zeki Bey laughed. "What disturbs me is that I've become accustomed to crime. Little attacks like this waiter's, a blow to the gut and a theft...that's nothing. We see that every day. Cheating, fraud, lying...arrest them, book them, try them, throw them in jail...it's all routine." He waved his hand at the Swiss students. "Look at these four," he went on. "Dirty, messy, indecently dressed. They want to see our country; we let them in, why not? There's no reason not to. Typical student tourists. And yet they have a golden locket with them. A grandmother's bon voyage present? A tourist trinket? But where's the bill of sale? Ask them, would you, where they got the locket?"

Peter answered Oran's question.

"He says..." Oran paused.

"Well?" said Zeki Bey.

"He says a Greek priest gave it to them as payment for cleaning up an old, musty chapel."

"And that's why they're looking at each other so nervously, like a bunch of chickens?"

"I'm just repeating what they've told me."

"They're lying. I know it and you know it. Shall we keep them here a while and find out what really happened?"

Oran glanced at Annelies. So she, too, had taken part in the theft of 'Tears' from the old, musty chapel. She seemed so frightened. And pitiable. "They were leaving Turkey today," Oran said.

The attendant entered with two teas. Zeki Bey dropped two lumps of sugar into his small glass and began stirring. "Or is it worth the bother? Why should we care if a priest got himself robbed in Greece? After all, what do the Greeks care if someone throws a rock at a mosque?"

"They have tickets on the Orient Express," said Oran.

"Maybe we should just let them go," said Zeki Bey. "I wonder if they would like some tea. Yes, let's give them some tea." He stood up and shouted, "Ramazan!"

The attendant stepped inside. "Yes, sir?"

Zeki looked at the students and smiled broadly. "Chay?" he said as he lifted up his glass toward them. And then he reached into a drawer and pulled out a box of candy. "Bonbon?" he asked, holding out the box in their direction.

The students looked at each other, puzzled.

"It's all right," said Oran. "You'll soon be free."

Chapter 29

Sinan groped for the phone. "Yes?"

"Flea?"

Ahmet. Sinan sat up, glanced at his companion in the bed. The woman shifted slightly. Daylight filtered in through the curtains. She'll wake up! But no, her breathing continued thick and steady.

Sinan cupped his hand over the receiver. "What is it?"

"I'm going on a vacation, a long one..."

Something has happened, someone's been caught! Sinan panicked. Was he implicated?

"...but you can stay here, enjoying your work."

I won't be named. Thank God!

"A friend left me a present. I'm sending it to you."

No! No more presents!

"Tiny. Nice for your mother."

OK, that's OK. It's not drugs, not porno. I can handle it. It must be something valuable. Like a diamond.

"Keep it for me. Or sell it and send me the proceeds. You know where I like to take my vacations."

Germany. The Turkish ghetto in West Berlin. What a great vacation spot.

"Ciao, baby."

"Ciao."

But why was Ahmet sending him this diamond? Selling jewels wasn't his line. He recruited others for drugs.

He lay back on the bed. Tiny...sparkling...his mind wandered through the wonderful world of jewels...diamonds... emeralds...gold...

Suddenly he tensed.

Gold?

Wait!

Emerald and rubies? On a tiny locket? It couldn't be possible. He sat up.

It can't be that locket, can it?

The woman started to snore, then shifted her position and resumed her smooth breathing.

Sinan glanced at her, got up, went to the window and peeked through the curtains. Still early...the garbage truck was at the far end of the street.

I'm just imagining. What would Ahmet have to do with that locket?

Smiling, he gave his chest a caress and turned back toward the dark-haired woman only partly covered by the sheet.

Nothing. Nothing at all.

Chapter 30

Leyla sat in her hospital bed, propped against a pile of pillows. Beril and Sedat Bey and even Oran were coming to call. They had a surprise, they said. Leyla knew quite well what that surprise would be, and she couldn't wait. They had announced they would come at 2 PM, and it was already 2·15. What had happened? They were going to visit yesterday, but Ibrahim Bey, who was participating in the surprise, although exactly how Leyla couldn't figure out, had been attacked by thugs. She had read about it in the papers this morning. How dreadful! Why should anyone want to attack him, poor man?

He wasn't seriously injured, Sedat Bey had said, and he insisted on coming along to the clinic. But how could Ibrahim not be badly hurt? Look at her: she had been attacked by a thief, and here she was almost one week in the hospital! She'd had quite enough of the place, too. She didn't care what the doctor said, tomorrow she was going home.

Someone was knocking on the door. At last! Leyla pulled the bedcovers smooth around her. In came Beril and her mother, followed by Sedat Bey and, yes, Ibrahim Bey, pale but on his feet.

Semra and Beril came over and kissed her on the cheek, then Sedat Bey kissed her hand and pressed it to his forehead, a sign of respect, and Ibrahim Bey did the same. With the help of the nurse, bouquets of flowers were pushed aside and chairs brought in.

"You look much, much better, Aunt Leyla," said Semra.

"I'm quite well, thank you," said Leyla. "The doctor doesn't agree, of course. He thinks I need a few more weeks of absolute rest. I'll do my resting at home, I told him. I gave him no chance to protest. Tomorrow I'm going home."

"You will come stay with us in Bebek?" said Semra. "We insist."

"That's very kind of you, but I'm going to my own apartment. Gul can take care of me perfectly well. I asked her this morning to describe the view...the boats, the dawn, the sunset. I will find the best relaxation right in my own apartment. My own bed, my books, television and radio, and my chaise longue out on the terrace."

Sedat Bey was watching her with his droopy eyes. "What if a thief enters again and your maid is watching TV with the sound turned up high?"

"Gul never watches television with the sound turned up high when I am at home! As for the robber, it was just bad luck. The first break-in, after all these years."

"May it be the last," said Sedat Bey.

"God willing," added Ibrahim Bey.

"God willing," said Leyla, looking at him. "Sedat Bey told me you were viciously attacked yesterday."

"Just outside my restaurant. But I was more fortunate than you, Leyla Hanim. I didn't have to stay in the hospital."

"Praise God," Leyla said. "You were in fact on your way here to see me when you were robbed?"

"I was coming to bring you something."

"The thieves took it?"

Ibrahim Bey nodded.

"Is that so?" Leyla said. "I'm so sorry."

She suddenly felt apprehensive. Was this the surprise, this bad news? She looked at Sedat Bey and Beril. "I thought you were bringing me the locket and star stolen from me. Weren't they recovered? Wasn't that to be the surprise? A happy surprise?"

"Ibrahim Bey's locket is coming, Aunt Leyla," said Beril. "I'm sure it's coming."

"Oran is bringing it," Semra said.

"Oran!"

"He caught the thief on the ferry yesterday, the thief who robbed Ibrahim Bey," said Beril. "If it hadn't been for Oran..."

"Where is he?" asked Leyla. "Wasn't he coming with you?"

"I thought so," said Sedat Bey.

Leyla sank back into her pillows. She felt terribly disappointed and, all of a sudden, dreadfully tired. What poor taste to come with such fanfare, only for this!

Sedat Bey stood up. "But I really do have a surprise."

"What do you mean?"

He spoke in a grand voice. "'Medina', Leyla Hanim." He pulled out the locket from his briefcase. "'Medina', from Sinan Altay."

"Oh!" Leyla sat up, her face suddenly alight with excitement. "I can't believe it!" She took the locket in her cupped hands.

"And," Sedat Bey continued, "'Tears' and the golden star."

"Oh, my goodness!" Leyla Hanım felt her eyes grew moist. "I don't know what to say." She set the two lockets and the star on the bedcovers, in her lap, and gazed at them. "Where did you find them?"

"How did you settle with Sinan Altay?" Semra Hanim asked. "It can't have been easy."

"In the end," Sedat Bey said, "not so difficult. Our policeman friend Nusret gave a most interesting statement yesterday. He mentioned a flea. A Mr. Flea. What a curious name! When I told Sinan about this testimony, he realized that it was in his best interest to sell 'Medina' as quickly as possible. I might add, Leyla Hanim, that we bought it at a very attractive price.

"Then, this morning, moments before I was to leave, a courier ran into my shop. He gave me a package and ran out. No names. I opened the package: 'Tears' and the star. I can only conclude that 'Tears' and the star were bonuses from the same sources: Mr. Flea and Nusret...and the crime lord who controlled them both."

"My, how amazing!" Leyla smiled blandly. She had no wish to explore how Sedat Bey knew about crime lords and men named Flea, no desire to probe into his special relationship with the police. Sometimes it was best to remain ignorant. She turned to

Ibrahim Bey. "You, too, owned one of the lockets, I gather?"

Ibrahim Bey held his fleshy palms up, empty. "I wanted to present 'Qur'an' to you, Leyla Hanim, but it's not here."

"Oran is bringing it," said Beril. "I hope." She looked at Sedat Bey for confirmation.

Sedat Bey was fingering his string of prayer beads. "I hope so, too."

Leyla asked Ibrahim Bey how long he had owned the locket.

"Ever since I was a young man. I won it gambling. All that's behind me now, I'm happy to say."

"Did you win it here in Istanbul?" Leyla Hanim asked.

"In Izmir. I grew up in Izmir."

"Do you remember anything about the man from whom you won it?" asked Beril.

"I don't know much. The man who paid me with the locket owned a large restaurant in Izmir. His name was Enver."

"The name Enver means nothing to me," said Leyla Hanim. "Perhaps I might recognize the name of his restaurant." She looked at Ibrahim Bey. "When I was a young woman, I lived in Izmir."

"Is that so?" Semra asked, startled.

"You are surprised, Semra! I understand. I've never spoken of those years. Four years...such difficult years. But tell me. What was the name of the restaurant? Do you remember, Ibrahim Bey?"

"The Silver Dolphin," he said. "How could I forget it? That's where I went one stifling summer afternoon to claim my winnings, in the dark, cool owner's office. My best take ever!"

"The Silver Dolphin!" Leyla said. "I ate there several times. An admirer...a friend...took me there. How extraordinary! So one of the lockets was there close by while I enjoyed my meals."

"When did you live in Izmir?" asked Semra. "It must have been before you married Uncle Tevfik."

"I left Izmir shortly before Atatürk's forces entered the city."

"Did I know you lived in Izmir during the Greek occupation?" Semra asked. "I was sure you never left Istanbul."

Leyla smiled. Semra was getting so excited! Such delicious gossip, and so unexpected from her husband's aunt! Leyla could see that Beril, too, was hanging on every word.

"I worked as a secretary and interpreter for a British import-export firm," said Leyla. "I knew little English when they hired me. But I spoke and wrote Turkish, French, and some German. That made me useful. I worked hard at English, and within a year I was competent."

"But when did you come to Izmir?" Semra was determined to get to the bottom of this.

"Toward the end of the First World War, not long before the Greeks marched in. My parents were dead. I'd finished lycée in Istanbul. I had no prospects for marriage. My aunts decided to send me off to Izmir for an extended visit with some cousins. I found the job fairly quickly. I enjoyed my work."

"Your relatives must have objected," said Semra. "In those days a woman from a good family working."

"My aunts were shocked. Our Izmir cousins, on the other hand, supported me. When I said I didn't want to stay around the house all day, Auntie understood. She herself taught in a girls' lycée, and she was sure she could find me a teaching position. But I was sick of school, so she persuaded Uncle to find me work in business."

"But eventually you left Izmir," Semra said. "You gave up the job. Really, I can't imagine you in business!"

Leyla took a sip from a glass of water on the little table beside her bed. "The story is more interesting than that, Semra. Just before the collapse of the Greek army, I made my way secretly to Ankara. In the event of a Turkish victory, my firm wanted its support for the new regime made clear. I fully intended to return to Izmir. But that was not to be. After the victory I was kept busy in Ankara. I met Tevfik, who was also devoting himself to the new government. Two years later we married and moved to Istanbul."

"The company sent you, a woman, to Ankara, at the height of the war?" said Semra. "It must have been terribly dangerous! Couldn't they have sent a man?"

"Foolhardy, my dear Semra, but not dangerous. I circled the battle zones. I went first to Istanbul, where a British tobacco merchant arranged passage for me on a Black Sea freighter to Samsun. I traveled as the companion of the mother of a Turkish associate of his. From Samsun, I went south to Ankara, just as Ataturk had. It was a risky trip. When Uncle found out about it, he thought I had lost my mind. But you see, Semra," and she fixed her with her eyes, "I was in love. And for love one often does things which in normal circumstances would qualify as mad."

Everyone was silent. She could not possibly be referring to Tevfik Bey.

Leyla glanced at Beril and smiled. "Yes, I was in love," she continued, "but I had to disguise my feelings, even in front of Auntie. The man I loved was not Turkish, you see. He was British...Edward Crossmoor, the son of the founder of Crossmoor and Tipton, the company for which I worked. The ancestor of Oran Crossmoor."

"Aunt Leyla!" Beril looked stunned.

Semra shifted in her chair. "Oh, my!"

"Yes! His great-uncle." Leyla's fingers played with the gold lockets on her lap as she spoke. "Marriage seemed in the air. He hadn't yet proposed, but I was ready to do anything for him. He was so polished and witty. When I heard that the company was anxious to promote itself with the nationalist government in Ankara, I offered to go. I wanted to prove myself to Edward."

"How could he allow you to do this?" said Semra.

"He refused to send me. But who else would go? So one day I just left. When I reached Ankara, I wrote him a letter explaining why I had set off on this adventure." She looked down at the necklace. "I don't know if he ever received my letter. I learned later that he died during the destruction of Izmir. He was identified by means of his dental records. There was no question that it was he." She raised her head. "You understand now why I had no particular desire to return to Izmir. Izmir was dead for me. I was in mourning."

No one spoke in the room, not Beril, Ibrahim Bey, or Sedat Bey, not even Semra.

Leyla lightened her voice. "This is all past. I must apologize. But the mention of the Silver Dolphin...Edward used to take me there for lunch, to the special room reserved for Europeans, where women could eat with men and no one would look askance. I felt so chic!"

She smiled, then she picked up the lockets. "Sedat Bey, can you attach these to the gold chain?"

"I came prepared." He took a pair of pliers out of his briefcase. "But don't wear it until I can attach them solidly." He attached the lockets and the star with a few deft twists.

Leyla held up the necklace for all to see, the two gold lockets with rubies and emeralds and the gold star. "Isn't it magnificent?"

"Oran isn't coming," Beril said suddenly.

"Do you think he's been attacked?" said Ibrahim Bey.

Beril sniffed. "I doubt it."

"Maybe something did happen to him," said Leyla. "We should check."

Beril lifted her head and tossed her curly black hair. "I'm having tea with Mr. Ianni Dimitriadis this afternoon. I'm not sure when I will have time to check."

"Beril!"

"Of course she will look into it," said Semra.

"I trusted him, but he didn't show up. What's he doing with that locket?"

"I, for one, am not worried in the slightest," said Leyla. "And you'll be getting new information from Mr. Dimitriadis. He might even know where the last of the lockets is."

Sedat Bey glanced at the others and stood up. "We shouldn't let Leyla Hanim tire herself out."

Beril suddenly smiled. "She might be too tired to go home tomorrow."

Leyla laughed. "Even if I lie awake all night, I'll still have the energy to go home."

* * *

Leyla sank back into the pillows. She was tired. How strenuous, unexpectedly so, waiting for this visit, then the presentation itself, and now, telling them about Edward. Had she tarnished the memory of Tevfik? She had never mentioned Edward to Tevfik. She had nothing to be ashamed of. Her relations with Edward had been completely innocent. God willed her to marry another. Oh, but his gruesome death...if only he had been spared that.

Maybe their love would have died and they would have drifted apart. Their love? She assumed he loved her. Had he ever said so? Surely he had! He was older than she, ten years or more. Why had he not married? He certainly had the money to marry. Had he loved before, but been rejected?

She rang for a nurse and ordered a tea.

Why think about it now? I am only agitating myself.

She looked at the necklace, still in her lap, then brought it to her lips. Oh, Father, if only you were here to see this necklace in my hands. You wanted this so much. What was it you told me when you took the gold star from your Baba's study? 'Never forget your father or your family.' Was it that? 'Someday the star will lead you to the four holy relics, and peace will come to us again.' Yes, Father, the star is leading me to them. And I will never forget you. Never.

Chapter 31

Ianni Dimitriadis looked out the window of his room at the Sheraton Hotel. Although he made regular trips to Istanbul, this was the first time he had seen the magnificent panorama of the Bosporus from the twenty-first floor. So high up. He felt like a bird.

His wife, a native of Istanbul, had gone off to see relative and family friends. He himself found it tedious to make conversation with her relatives. She understood, or at least pretended she did, and consequently was forcing him to attend only one large gathering This afternoon, in exchange for freedom from the family visits, he was expected to meet a woman who wanted to discuss a gold locket his father had collected years ago. But why? His wife had merely passed along this odd request from Aliye Balkaner, the violin professor who headed the Conservatory's concert committee. He had to accept. It would help promote good relations between Greeks and Turks.

He went into the bathroom and checked his tie and carefully combed his hair, the graying fringe that remained. His surviving hair habitually received the greatest respect.

Just as he was reaching for the doorknob, the phone rang. How annoying! He went back and picked up the receiver. A man named Oran Crossmoor. Something urgent needed to be discussed.

He should have arranged for incoming calls to be screened.

"What is it?" He pushed his glasses up with irritation. "I'm in a rush. I have an appointment."

The caller explained his concerns.

"Not the locket!" cried Mr. Dimitriadis. "Not again! Why is everyone interested in this locket?" He reached out with his right hand, his palm upraised, imploring God for an answer. "I'm about to meet someone right now who intends to ask me about it." A thought occurred to him. "Why don't you come along? We can all three talk and settle everything together. Her name is Beril Rodoslu."

* * *

Oran wondered how Beril found out where Mr. Dimitriadis was. Maybe she telephoned Daidalos Industries in Athens as he had, to ask where Mr. Dimitriadis and his mother were staying in Istanbul. That must be it. She was pretty sharp.

Beril would be surprised to see him. And angry at him for missing the meeting at the hospital. Well, he was angry, too! He had started out late from a distant section of the city on the Asian shore. Then the dolmus, the shared taxi he was riding in, was hit by a red Renault. The dolmus driver implored him to stay to give his testimony. That took what seemed like hours. As soon as the accident had been duly reported, he called the hospital. Leyla Hanim was sleeping. Her visitors had left. When he tried Beril's home, no one answered.

He got into another dolmus and crossed over to the European side. Surely the traffic on the Bosporus bridge had never been heavier. As the dolmus crawled along, Oran calmed down. He'd find another time to return 'Qur'an', Ibrahim's locket. In the meantime, he thought, why not contact Mr. Dimitriadis?

* * *

Mr. Dimitriadis was delighted to be sitting down with Beril. Through the years he had developed a soft spot for tall, ample women with untamable dark hair. His wife was small, slender, and fair, and although she dressed with elegance and acted with refinement, qualities which he appreciated in principle, she didn't excite him anymore. She was in her fifties. Her career took up all her time. She no longer dropped everything to answer his every call. Yet everyone else was paying him more attention. They, at least, knew that with each passing year his importance was increasing.

With reluctance he left off gazing at statuesque Beril in order to direct his fork into his chocolate éclair. As soon as the first bite was safely in his mouth, he looked up again.

Beril gave him a radiant smile. "Will you be staying long?" she asked.

"Only into next week," he said. "Unfortunately." He peered into her eyes, searching for sympathy. "It's a difficult city to leave, isn't it? I'm lucky to be able to come here regularly. My wife was born and raised here. She has relatives..."

"Your wife is an Istanbul Greek?"

"She grew up not far from here, on the other side of Taksim, in a large apartment that looked out toward the sea."

"My great-aunt lives in that area," said Beril. "She has been there a long time. Perhaps they were neighbors."

"It's possible."

"She wanted to join us, but she's still resting in the hospital."

"I'm sorry to hear she's ill."

Beril recounted Leyla's encounter with the thief. "It was a miracle that she didn't break any bones. But since she's old, she must get a good rest."

"Indeed." Mr. Dimitriadis took another bite of his éclair, but his eyes were on Beril.

"She has to take her convalescence seriously."

"I hope she will take it more seriously than my father did." Mr. Dimitriadis set down his fork. "My father became childlike toward the end of his life. He loved to drive. Even though he had lost an arm in a car accident, he had an automobile specially outfitted for him. When he was older, no one would ride with him, except his exceedingly well-paid chauffeur. Everyone was scared to death. Yet no one had the courage to take away his driver's license. Finally my wife was delegated to persuade him to stop driving in Athens, to drive only near Mt. Pelion, where we go for vacations. Oh, yes, he said. But a few days later, Father backed into a parked car while trying to retreat from a one-way street he had entered from the wrong direction. We were furious. 'I intended to visit a friend on the outskirts of town,' he replied. 'A taxi would have cost too much.' This from a man who could have bought the entire fleet of taxis in Athens!" He pushed up his glasses and laughed.

"I hope Aunt Leyla will act sensibly," said Beril. "But she'll probably start to play tricks like your father."

The waiter served them more tea. "The éclair was delicious," said Mr. Dimitriadis. "The pastry is the real reason I return to Istanbul so often." He smiled at Beril.

She tilted her head and laughed, her black curls shaking seductively. "You aren't staying til next week just for the pastry, are you?"

"Well, I..." He smiled. "I'm in partnership with a Turk to import heavy farm equipment."

"Between business, your wife's relatives, and the pastry, you have many reasons to stay," said Beril.

"I can think of others, too," said Mr. Dimitriadis, looking pointedly at Beril.

Beril smiled innocently, then quickly lowered her glance.

"What is it?" asked Mr. Dimitriadis.

"Nothing, nothing at all."

Mr. Dimitriadis looked behind him, only to see a broad-shouldered young man weaving his way through the tables directly toward them.

"Mr. Dimitriadis?"

Mr. Dimitriadis remembered with distaste that he had agreed to share stunning Beril with someone else.

"I'm Oran Crossmoor."

"Delighted, I'm sure," said Mr. Dimitriadis in his best textbook English. "Do you know Miss Rodoslu?"

"We have met," said Beril. She extended her hand. "How are you, Mr. Crossmoor?"

"Fine, Miss Rodoslu," said Oran. "And you?"

"Do sit down, Mr. Crossmoor," said Mr. Dimitriadis. "Miss Rodoslu and I... "

"Call me Beril. That's the Turkish way."

"Beril and I were having tea and pastry while we chatted." He flagged down a waiter. "You will have some tea, won't you?"

Beril said to Oran, "I was just about to ask Mr. Dimitriadis..."

"Ianni, if you please."

Beril smiled at him most graciously. "...if he had ever met my great-aunt Leyla Aslanoglu or her husband, Tevfik. You know my Aunt Leyla, do you not, Mr. Crossmoor?"

"Do call me Oran."

"I don't believe I've met her," said Mr. Dimitriadis. He wondered why Beril and this young man were acting in such a theatrical manner.

"It's a large city," said Oran. "Why should they meet?"

"But you know my aunt," Beril said to Oran.

"Sheer chance. I had an introduction."

"You were even going to visit her this afternoon, I believe." Beril looked crossly at Oran. "But you didn't come."

"I was held up. An accident."

"You didn't even phone."

"I did! But I was too late. Don't worry, you'll get the locket."

"Lockets?" said Mr. Dimtriadis. "Aren't we here to talk about lockets?" These two were practically at each other's throats. If he didn't get rid of this person in short order, this tea, which had started with such promise, would be irretrievably wrecked.

Beril seemed to have the same thought, he was gratified to see. "A small gold locket in your family's collection," she said. "Aliye Hanim explained our interest in it, didn't she?"

"Not that my wife reported. Why are you so interested in these lockets?"

"They're family heirlooms," said Oran. He quickly recounted the history of the necklace.

"The fourth locket is definitely ours!" said Mr. Dimitriadis. "The locket was presented to my father by this same Christina Markova who plays such an important part in your story."

"Why? Did your father help her after she left Samos?" asked Oran.

"He did indeed. Her parents had met my father. He urged them to come visit him in Athens. When she fled from Smyrna, she remembered his name. She arrived on his doorstep and begged for his assistance. Her beauty and grace charmed him. He gave her shelter, food, and money."

"And she gave him the relic in return?" asked Beril.

"She gave it willingly," replied Mr. Dimitriadis. "You see, within the year they were married. Christina Markova is my mother." He smiled, pleased by their complete astonishment. "If you wish, I would be happy to introduce you to her this week. She arrives tomorrow in Istanbul. She is a pianist, and she's giving a concert here on Tuesday."

"Now I understand," Beril said. "She is Alexandra Stephanides."

"Yes, that is the performance name she chose for herself."

"Aliye Hanim told us about the concert. I've bought tickets."

"She still plays well, even at age eighty-two."

Alexandra Stephanides, Christina Markova. Beril wondered why she never guessed they were the same person.

"I should add that she has kept this locket for herself," said Mr. Dimitriadis.

"But wasn't your locket stolen during the Greek Civil War?" Oran asked.

"Yes, when the villa at Mt. Pelion was vandalized by communists. But we recovered it, thanks to my father's Bulgarian connections."

"Where does she keep her locket?" asked Beril.

"She wears it when she plays a concert. As long as I can remember, she has always checked for it when she gets dressed, and then again when she arrives at the concert hall."

"Would she sell it to us?" asked Oran.

"I doubt it. It has become her good luck charm, a reminder of her youth, her escape to Greece, and her good fortune."

"That's just a superstition," said Oran.

"I'm sure she would agree. But it's absolutely vital." He took another sip of tea. "Achh, it's cold. Let's get some hot tea." He waved for a waiter. "Shall we have more pastry?"

"No, thank you," said Oran.

"Beril?"

"Well, all right I give in."

"Wonderful. Another slice of chocolate cake and another éclair, please." Mr. Dimitriadis smiled at Beril. She smiled back, most marvellously.

"How did your mother get the lockets?" asked Oran, interrupting yet again. "What's her claim to ownership?"

"She bought them from a dealer in Smyrna." Mr. Dimitriadis pushed up his glasses. This relentless prying was annoying him. And he could no longer deny that Beril was as eager an interrogator as Oran Crossmoor.

"When she was so young? Was she wealthy enough to afford such a necklace?"

"Her family gave her the money as a twenty-first birthday present. She wished to spend it on jewelry."

"She made a strange choice," said Beril. "I would have picked something contemporary, not ancient reliquaries."

"It is odd, I agree," said Mr. Dimitriadis. "But I can only tell you what she said to us."

Oran pressed ahead. "Did your mother ever name the dealer in Izmir?"

"There was no reason for us to know."

"Perhaps we should ask your mother ourselves," said Beril.

"I'm sure she would tell you all she remembers," said Mr. Dimitriadis. "Insofar as her memory permits, after sixty years."

"Memories do fade, it's true," said Beril.

Mr. Dimitriadis glared at Beril. What a rude thing to say about someone's mother! "My mother is very alert. She won't sell you her own locket. You can be certain of that." He finished his éclair and tea and looked at his watch. "Oh! You will have to excuse me. We are invited out. My wife will be back at the hotel, wondering where I am." He rose from his chair. He smiled coldly at Oran and Beril. Yes, even at Beril. She had been so friendly at first, but then she betrayed him. Look at the two of them! At first they were snapping at each other. Now they're exchanging smiles!

Beril looked him squarely in the eyes and said in a warm, full voice, "Thank you so much, Ianni."

He was about to correct her. "Mr. Dimitriadis!" he was about to say. But her lips and breasts were close and warm.

Beautiful Beril.

Without any difficulty he summoned up his most charming smile. "It has been a pleasure," he said as he took her outstretched hand.

The honorable Christian must always be ready to forgive.

PART FOUR

Chapter 32

Istanbul

Mrs. Dimitriadis was returning to Turkey after nearly sixty years, and she was afraid.

She paused on the upper landing of the steps that had been pulled up to the Turkish Airlines jet. She wore a gray suit and a beige silk blouse with a big bow. Her copper-colored hair was protected with a scarf, her eyes hidden behind large dark glasses. She looked around at the airport buildings, the sea in the distance, up at the cloudless sky. A gust of wind tugged at her. She gripped the railing. Holding her handbag closely, she descended from the airplane, the slow progress of the sinewy hand with its manicured, short-clipped, red nails and gold ring matching the advance of her steps.

At the terminal, she joined the line of passengers waiting to have their passports stamped. The policeman at the control desk flipped through her Greek passport in search of the Turkish visa. He checked her statistics, ticking them off on the entry form she had filled out.

He must have noticed I was born in Smyrna, she thought. But he doesn't say anything. Doesn't this mean anything to him? For heaven's sake, Kiki, be realistic! He must stamp the passports of countless Anatolian Greeks. And he is young. The burning of Smyrna in 1922...for him it's just a victory recorded in history books. Nothing more.

On her way to the baggage claim area she opened the passport and looked at the Turkish stamp. Am I really here? Alexandra Stephanides has come to Turkey. Mrs. Theodoros Dimitriadis? No. She glanced around nervously. It's Christina Markova...Kiki...who has returned home.

* * *

Her son, her daughter-in-law, and Aliye Balkaner, the professor of violin, were waiting to greet her.

Later, at the hotel, Aliye Hanim took her leave. The schedule for the next few days had been arranged en route from the airport.

"I was right to come, Ianni," Mrs. Dimitriadis said as she watched Aliye Hanim drive off in a taxi. "Isn't she friendly?"

Her son, in conversation with a porter, barely nodded.

"I was apprehensive. What would I find? Of course I knew it would be different." She turned to Anthi, her daughter-in-law. "You grew up here. You come back often. Tell me, are you really more comfortable in Istanbul than in Athens?"

"I've become an Athenian. That's where I blend in," Anthi said. "But this city is my true home. When I'm here, I wake up. I come alive."

"It's a visit to Mt. Pelion that restores me. The quiet and the isolation. How can a noisy, crowded city like Istanbul bring you to life?"

Anthi laughed. "You may be surprised."

"Everything is settled," Ianni said. "Shall we go up?"

"My brother has invited us to dinner," said Anthi.

"It won't be a late evening, will it?"

"I'm sure not," said Ianni as he guided his mother into the hotel.

"I don't like distraction before a concert."

"The food will be wonderful," Anthi said.

Mrs. Dimitriadis smiled. "Of course it will be, dear."

When they reached the twenty-first floor, Anthi wished her mother-in-law a good nap and then disappeared. Ianni showed his mother into the adjacent room.

"What a marvelous view!" exclaimed Mrs. Dimitriadis as she looked out the window. "And there's a little balcony. Let's go out." But the wind was still blowing hard, so they quickly came back in. Mrs. Dimitriadis sat by the window. She took off her scarf and dark glasses and patted her hair back into place.

Ianni stood over her. "There is one more thing," he said.

"More? Besides music, relatives, and, I trust, sightseeing? I'm only staying a few days."

"I have been pursued by a local family – Turkish – and their American friends about medieval lockets, especially the one you wear, the one from Father's collection."

She sat up. "The lockets? Why are they interested in the lockets?"

"Family heirlooms, they claim. They are determined to get them back."

"Mine they won't get. Not at any price."

"I told them that."

"And?"

"They seemed to accept it calmly."

"What else can they want from me, then?"

"Information on how you obtained the lockets."

"Through a dealer in Smyrna, of course. You knew that. Didn't you tell them?"

"I did." Ianni sat down on the bed. "But they want to know more."

"Is one of them Oran Crossmoor, by any chance?"

"Do you know him?"

"He came to see me in Athens about these lockets." She reached out to reassure her son. "Something of a pest. I told him very little."

"This Oran Crossmoor and his Turkish friends have now obtained three of the four lockets."

"Three of them! Really? Do they know I owned them all?"

"They know you escaped from Smyrna using the lockets as payments."

"I kept the fourth one. I didn't buy anything with it. Why did you tell them I had it?"

Her vehement tone startled Ianni. "I saw no point in hiding the truth."

"I want to keep it! Do you understand?"

"Then we'll just say that you're not interested in meeting Madame Aslanoglu and her family."

Mrs. Dimitriadis took a cigarette out of a silver case and lit it. "I didn't say I wasn't interested in meeting these people. What I refuse to do is give them the locket."

Ianni stood and walked over to the window.

"I am curious to meet them," Mrs. Dimitriadis continued. "I rather liked young Oran Crossmoor, and he and his friends have discovered so much about me. But I want to learn their story, why these relics mean so much to them. I'll tell them what I can, of course, what little more there is to be told...the name of the dealer, the price I paid..."

"Will you show them the locket?"

Mrs. Dimitriadis took a puff on her cigarette. "I don't know. It depends. Who knows, perhaps I won't like them at all."

"I met Beril Rodoslu. She's very striking."

"And this Madame Aslanoglu?"

"Beril's great-aunt? She's the head of the family. She's the one intent on recovering the relics."

"What's she like?"

"I haven't met her. She has been in the hospital recuperating from an attack."

"An attack?"

"In her own apartment. She surprised a burglar. He knocked her out."

"How dreadful! The crime these days is unbelievable."

"She wasn't badly hurt. Fortunately."

"And now, the standard prescription for old people, rest and more rest?" She flicked a long tube of ashes off her cigarette. "I must visit her," she said with determination. "I will pay a call on this courageous lady. I'll wish her the best, and tell her every-thing I know about the lockets."

"I don't know if she's well enough to receive visitors."

Mrs. Dimitriadis put out her cigarette. "I'm talking only with her. The others...I just don't care to be interrogated by the others. Only by an aging lady. She is old, isn't she?"

"I'm quite sure."

"An old woman like me...confined to a bed, thanks to some criminal. I could just as easily be in her place." She rose from her chair. "It's settled. You will arrange it?"

"When should we say? Tomorrow? The next day?"

"After the concert. Wednesday morning. I already have the city and Anthi's relatives to visit, distraction enough before the concert. Insist on Wednesday."

* * *

When her son had left, Mrs. Dimitriadis looked out the window, at the water and the boats, the steep, undulating hills, the rooftops decorated with laundry lines and TV antennas, here and there a mosque with domed roof and towering minaret, and the late afternoon sun reflecting off distant window panes, turning them into panels of gold.

Had sixty years really gone by since she'd last seen this city? She felt as if she had spent her entire life here. It was so beautiful, so much like Smyrna with its long bay surrounded by hills.

Smyrna. She smiled. Izmir, they call it now. I will have to watch myself. "Izmir." She spoke the name out loud. I wonder what you look like today? I wonder. Shall I go see?

No. I can't! No. Impossible. I couldn't bear it.

She turned back into the room, away from the window, and sat down on the edge of the bed and began to undo her earrings.

Still, I came here, didn't I? After years and years of saying No and No and No. But no one ever invited me to perform. When

Aliye Balkaner asked me to come, I wrote back at once, 'Yes, I would be delighted.' I left Smyrna; I went to Greece. I played concerts all over the world, in Berlin and Buenos Aires, in New York and Tokyo, but never in Turkey. 'I would be delighted to play in the Istanbul Festival,' I wrote her, just like that, without reflecting.

Then I saw the book. It was just a nice present, a beautiful birthday present. But when I looked at those old pictures of Smyrna, I burst into tears, I couldn't stop crying.

She started to undress.

When she had changed into her nightgown, she folded the clothes she had just taken off. She sat down at the dressing table and stared at herself in the mirror. Mrs. Theodoros Dimitriadis...Alexandra Stephanides...distinguished concert pianist...at the end of her career...a wrinkled face...vision fuzzy in one eye...red hair, not her own color...like a funny, shriveled clown. And Kiki? Where is she now? Poor Kiki, poor foolish Kiki is dead. She died in Smyrna, in 1922, at the age of twenty-three.

After carefully removing her make-up, she opened a little jar of moisturizing cream from her red leather case, massaging the white cream into her cheeks, her forehead, her chin and neck with her powerful fingers. Then she applied the cream onto her hands, rubbing them together deliberately and thoroughly as she did every day. She got up to close the curtains, then pulled back the covers of her bed, and got in. She leaned over and turned out the light. Now I must sleep, she thought. I must sleep. Sleep. I must sleep.

She turned onto her side. She shifted the pillows, returned to her original position on her back. Her breathing was shallow and uneven. "Why can't I sleep? I must go to sleep." A sonata by Mozart began to play in her head, the sonata she had scheduled for Tuesday's concert. No, not now! The music stopped. Then it began again, but at the start, not at the place where it had left off, and much, much louder. It played on and on and on.

In despair, she gripped the covers and swept them back. She put on her robe and slippers, pulled the curtains open, and sat in an armchair by the window. She propped her arm on the edge of the chair, resting her head in her hand. She sat without moving, without thinking. After a while she lifted her head and looked out the window. A magical view, truly. She closed her eyes, trying to relax. Her heart was beating fast. But why? It was only the hour of the afternoon nap, the gentlest time of the day. Think of hot summer days in Greece when you retreat into a darkened room to sleep after the midday meal. The shutters are latched, the house is still, you slip between the sheets and sink down and down. In Greece...at Mt. Pelion, even in Athens...and in Smyrna, too...in Smyrna, so long ago...at noon, when the streets were quiet, when the shops had closed and even the one-eyed man who sold fresh almonds went off for lunch and a rest.

Once again she was in the cool, darkened drawing room of the large house painted white which stood in the center of a garden where jasmine grew unchecked. In Edward's house, in Smyrna.

No, she said to herself. No! But the remembrance swelled and took command of her mind. She felt the anxiety of that day, the scene unfolding in her mind.

I slipped into the house unseen. Not even Chapman spotted me. Is Edward here? I pause at the edge of the salon, listening. A dog barks outside, but he stops and I hear nothing more. The room is heavy and somber. At the far end a window is ajar. A wedge of sunlight cuts into the gloom, exposing a slice of the parquet floor. The rest lies in shadow, but I know it well: high ceilings lined with elaborate moldings, crystal chandeliers, immense dark carpets, drapes the color of Burgundy wine, weighted down with gold rope and gold tassels.

All is silent. Silence? In wartime? I have taken off my gloves and knead them with my fingers. He is my fiancé, isn't he? He will protect me and get me on a British warship...won't he? The minor melody of a Chopin nocturne fills the room like a delicate perfume. Who is playing the ebony piano? Not me. Who else would be playing? No...no. I'm imagining. No one is playing.

I walk quickly across the room, tap at the door, and let myself in. The curtains are drawn, the windows open, a breeze stirs the curtains and rustles the papers on the desk. The room is full of light and air.

He is sitting in his armchair in the corner, in front of the bookshelves that rise all the way to the ceiling. He is reading and smoking a cigarette. He doesn't look up. Surely he has heard me come in.

"Edward. My love."

He turns around. "Kiki, darling!" he says loudly. "What a surprise!"

"Don't call me Kiki!" I say. "How many times!"

He laughs. "Christina, darling."

"That's better."

"Come here."

I go over and sit on his lap and give him a kiss.

"Everyone says the Turks are advancing," I begin.

"Nothing's confirmed."

"If the Turks invade and the British are evacuated, you will take me, won't you?"

"Of course! You know that." He smiles. "How many times...?"

I smile and stroke his mustache. "I love your mustache."

"And more, too, I hope."

I bend over and kiss him. "It tickles. Will I ever get used to it?"

"Maybe I should shave it off."

"Oh, no! It makes you look so dashing."

"I'm not the only mustachioed man in town. Perhaps others have caught your eye?"

"Edward, what are you saying?"

"I don't have to watch out for a rival, do I?"

"Of course not!"

He laughs but looks away. What can he be thinking?

"My love." He is shifting himself in the chair.

I get up. "Am I too heavy?"

"What in the world did you have for breakfast?"

How crude! He has never said anything like that before.

He stands up and takes out his pocket watch. "I have an appointment, a luncheon engagement."

"It's Monday. You always save Monday for me."

"This came up all of a sudden, just this morning. It's quite urgent."

He lights another cigarette and collects some papers from his desk.

"Edward!"

"Yes, darling?" He is annoyed, I can tell.

"Is it the war?"

"The appointment? Yes, of course. British contributions to hospital care for wounded soldiers." He keeps searching through the papers. "Women's Auxiliary."

A woman! There is a woman! "Who is she?"

He has promised marriage. But there has been no engagement, no publicly announced engagement. He says we must wait until the war ends. He's concerned about the war. Everyone is. But other couples are getting engaged.

Edward glances up at me with exasperation. "Do you remember Mrs. Phelps? Red Cross?"

An ugly fat old thing! Thank God! I almost spin around with joy. I reach for his arm. "Dearest Edward ..."

But my mind swirls with doubts. He is still kind and warm, but not entirely, not as he used to be. Sometimes he's far away, sometimes he seems cold...

He has lied! I'm sure of it. He's not having lunch with Mrs. Phelps. Lady Elizabeth! It is she! He spoke to her at the Red Cross reception last week. How they looked at each other when he held the door open for her!

She's English, like him. They'll escape together. He'll abandon me here. He'll leave me to the Turks!

Edward is smiling at me. I look down at my hands, my big piano player's hands. I laugh loudly, masking a sob.

"I have something to show you." He takes me by the hand and leads me over to a large window. "Here." I see only a palm in a large ceramic pot.

I don't understand. "A potted palm?"

He grabs the palm at its base and tugs, lifting it out of the pot. He pulls a packet out of the pot, replaces the palm, opens the package and takes out a magnificent necklace which he spreads out on some white paper on his desk.

Gold, emeralds, rubies!

"It's for you."

"Oh, Edward!" I throw my arms around him. How could I have doubted him? "Is it really for me?"

He kisses me on the forehead. "The most precious object I own. For my most precious love." He fastens the necklace around my neck. He steps back and smiles. "It's stunning!"

"I love it." I do a pirouette by the window, in the sunlight. "But why do you keep it in a flower pot? People always hide valuables in flower pots."

"Only keys, darling...outside the house. Besides, there are so many plants indoors. The choice is endless. Aren't you going to ask where I got the necklace? Or whose relics they are? Saints' relics from the Near East. They have healing powers." He seems so serious, so earnest. "Whoever owns the relics has a mysterious capacity to cure the illnesses of others. Or so my grandfather thought."

"Your grandfather?"

"Sir George Crossmoor. He claimed that after he bought the relics from a Turkish family on Rhodes he no longer suffered from colds and headaches."

"Did the healing powers pass to you?"

Edward looks ill at ease. "I don't know."

Suddenly I am terribly afraid. "Edward, why are you showing this necklace to me now? Is this to protect me from some danger?"

"To protect you...and free you."

I quickly take off the necklace. I don't want to wear it any longer. Edward wraps it up, puts it back in the flower pot.

A knock at the door. Chapman enters. "A gentleman to see you, sir. Mr. Davies, from the consulate."

"What the devil could Davies be doing here?" says Edward. "One moment."

A moment...a minute, an hour? I can't think of time. Protect me, free me? What did he mean? It's hot, my dress is sticking to me. I can't sit still. I move around the room, first to one window, then to another.

The drapes, grandly suspended from the top of the window high above, are velvet. Thick, smooth velvet. I bend over and smell the cloth. Dusty, but cool, a trifle damp...perfect for the great hall in an English country manor, like the ones I have read about in novels. When we are married, will we live in such a house? Will I play the piano in an oak-paneled drawing room, with a fire blazing at one end, ancestral portraits on the walls, heraldic banners hanging from the rafters?

Edward steps into the room and closes the door. "Davies came to tell me that the Turks have defeated the Greek army near Afyon. They're chasing the Greeks westwards in this direction."

"God help us!" I grab his arm.

"The news is spotty. I don't know what to believe."

"The Greeks will regroup. Surely they will defend Smyrna."

"Davies says we should prepare for the worst."

"Are you leaving the city?"

"I don't know. The British will be evacuated, if necessary."

"You will take me with you, won't you, your fiancée?"

"Of course," he says in a low voice. He puts his arm around

me. "Don't worry."

I break away from his hug. I dare not look into his eyes again. Has he not spoken the words I want to hear?

"I must go," I say.

He takes my chin in his hand, and guides my face up to his. His eyes find mine. He seems terribly shaken. "Don't worry, dearest." He kisses me lightly on the lips. "We'll be safe."

* * *

Mrs. Dimitriadis opened her eyes and gazed out the window. By now the sun was low and threw its golden shadows onto the sea. Was it still windy outside? She couldn't tell. She was too high up to see if the trees were bending or not. Whenever the wind blew she trembled. The day of the great fire the wind had swept her to disaster. Now she was trembling again: did catastrophe lie ahead? No, not with her son next door, not with her music. How foolish! She looked at her hands and wiggled her fingers. She was alive, she had survived. She had repented a thousand times, and then a thousand times more.

Since that terrible day she had kept her emotions under tight control. It had been unfair to old Theo, a wife who never let herself go. But she had never done anything untoward. A wife beyond reproach. She repeated it to herself, a wife beyond reproach.

No one knew. In the next life she would pay, of that she was certain. Unless...unless her letter might condemn her first...

How could she have done it? After she had closed the book of photographs, that innocent birthday present, after she dried her tears, after she discovered that Frederick, Edward's brother, was still alive, she had written to him. She didn't dare to sign her name, for the short message sounded so strange, even demented. Frederick would have no idea what she was talking about. Yet now they were here in Istanbul, Frederick's grandson and his friends, with three of the lockets in their hands, and she had agreed to meet with them.

Dear God, what have I done? She sighed deeply, then began to play the Mozart sonata, her fingers moving in the air, the music resounding in her head. Music, my beloved music. It is to you I have given my heart. She stopped her fingers, but the music kept on, accompanying her, serenading her even as she removed her robe and slipped into bed.

Chapter 33

"There's no time for dessert," said Oran, folding his napkin. "The concert begins in half an hour."

"The theater's only five minutes away," said Beril.

"Oran is right, dear," said Semra Hanim. "We have to find the waiter and pay the bill."

"How about dessert afterwards?" Oran said.

Beril looked annoyed.

"We'll be able to eat slowly," said Oran. "You don't want to get indigestion, do you?" He signaled to the waiter for the check.

Beril gave him a little smile, then got up to go with her mother to the rest room. Oran lit a cigarette. It was 7:30 on a Tuesday evening and people were just now beginning to arrive in large numbers.

Oran was starting to feel outmaneuvered. What should he do? What would he end up with for GF?

After the tea with Mr. Dimitriadis, Beril had tried to persuade him to go see Aunt Leyla as soon as possible and present her with Ibrahim Bey's locket. No one was angry with him for not showing up at the hospital. A car accident! Of course she understood why he hadn't come. So when could he call on Aunt Leyla?

He had to see Mrs. Dimitriadis first, he said.

Mrs. Dimitriadis has agreed to visit Aunt Leyla the next morning, she replied. Everything was falling right in Leyla Hanim's lap. After trying to reach Mrs. Dimitriadis for hours, all he had to show for it was the curt message: Madame Dimitriadis was not receiving visitors.

Some champion he was for GF's interests!

What if he lay in wait for Mrs. Dimitriadis at the Sheraton?

Or he could call on Leyla Hanim when Mrs. Dimitriadis was there. Then he could plead his case, his family's case, to both women and persuade them that his grandfather, Frederick

Crossmoor, brother of Edward Crossmoor, the last known legal owner of the four lockets, had the right to reclaim his heritage.

Would Beril agree to his coming? Or would she consider this a ruse? If he knew Beril, he'd best broach the subject after the concert, over a nice, big, sweet dessert.

* * *

Oran, Beril, and Semra Hanim were shown to their seats in the center of the main hall at the Ataturk Cultural Center. Soon after, Beril spotted Aliye Hanim making her way to a seat in the front row, greeting people as she advanced. Mr. Dimitriadis and his wife followed her.

"I should go check about tomorrow's meeting," Beril said. She pulled her dress straight and headed down to the front row.

As she talked with Mr. Dimitriadis, Oran could see Mr. Dimitriadis's eyes turn toward him ever so briefly. But Mr. Dimitriadis didn't reveal a thing.

Beril was excited when she returned. "We're invited backstage after the concert!" she said.

"Even me?" asked Oran.

"I had to ask." Beril looked embarrassed. "At first he said no."

"Maybe I shouldn't go."

"I told him you only wanted her autograph."

"What I really want is to see her locket close up."

"That's what Mr. Dimitriadis said."

"I don't want to frighten her. Do you think I scare her?"

Beril smiled. "Maybe you scare Mr. Dimitriadis."

"But he likes you." Oran folded his arms across his chest. "Let me think about it."

Beril glanced at her mother for help.

Semra Hanim was settled peacefully in her chair. "Why get upset now?" she said in a soothing voice. "Why spoil the music? Let's discuss it later, after the performance."

* * *

The houselights dimmed, leaving the stage brightly illuminated. The shiny black concert piano gleamed under the strong lights. After a moment of silence, Mrs. Dimitriadis...Alexandra Stephanides...stepped out from the wings and walked slowly to the piano. She wore a turquoise-colored dress, long-sleeved, floor length. Her coppery hair seemed to glow like a halo. When she reached the piano, she caught hold of it with one hand and, steadying herself, turned toward the audience to acknowledge the applause. As she straightened up from her bow, the spotlight caught the jewel hanging from a black ribbon around her neck: a gold pendant studded with precious gems. The last of the lockets. Oran felt thrilled to see it. A miracle, no doubt whatsoever. The emerald was flashing back at the audience, at Oran and Beril and Semra Hanim. This green glint of reflected light...a good omen?

Mrs. Dimitriadis sat down on the bench, settled herself until she was comfortable, and began to play. She filled the hall with clean, strong, beautiful tones, breathing her passionate life into the rich sound worlds of masters of western music, Bach, Mozart, modern Greek composer Marios Varvoglis, and finally Chopin. Each time she rose to acknowledge the applause of the enthusiastic audience or to retire to the wings, the golden locket around her neck came into view.

At the end of the concert, huge wreaths of flowers were brought to the stage, tributes from the conservatory, the Greek consulate, and the directorate of the festival. The applause never let up, so Mrs. Dimitriadis sat down and played first one encore, and then a second. The public was enchanted. The public wanted more. But after a few more bows, Mrs. Dimitriadis waved to the audience and walked slowly to the wings. The houselights came on, the long black piano returned to lusterless shadow, and the concertgoers got up to leave.

* * *

Oran, Beril, and Semra Hanim waited in the lobby for Mr. Dimitriadis, his wife, and Aliye Hanim. But Aliye Hanim was completing the greetings begun earlier that evening. Such courtesies took time.

"Shall we go meet the pianist?" asked Ianni Dimitriadis when at last Aliye Hanim arrived. He cast a jovial smile even on Oran. As he and Aliye Hanim led the group backstage, he continued to chat as if he were with his best friends.

"What a maniac," whispered Oran.

"He's just relieved his mother got through a concert," said Beril. "Performing in your eighties must be almost as risky as going down a one-way street the wrong way."

"What?" Oran stared at Beril.

She laughed, and gave him a poke.

* * *

A small crowd of well-wishers had already gathered outside Mrs. Dimitriadis's dressing room. Mr. Dimitriadis broke through and reached his mother.

"A wonderful concert," he said, kissing her on both cheeks.

"Thank you, Ianni."

"I have Aliye Balkaner with me, and the Rodoslus, just outside."

"The Rodoslus? Yes. How nice of them to come."

"And Oran Crossmoor."

"Oh?" Then she turned to a couple standing at her side. "Ianni, you do remember the Greek consul, Mr. Zirotas, and his wife? We met the other night at Rosa's, very briefly."

"This is a great moment for Greece," said the consul as he shook hands. "Your mother is a great artist. She played magnificently."

"Yes, didn't she?"

"Did you like the Varvoglis?" asked Mrs. Dimitriadis.

"Very nice," replied the consul with polished sincerity.

"I make a point of scheduling Greek composers on my programs. How else will they reach foreign audiences if we performers don't promote them?"

"You are quite right, Madame," said the consul.

Mr. Dimitriadis excused himself and went outside to fetch Semra Hanim, Beril, and Oran.

"This is a great honor," said Semra Hanim when she was introduced to Mrs. Dimitriadis.

"How kind of you to come backstage." Mrs. Dimitriadis examined Semra and Beril with frank curiosity.

Oran kept his eyes on the locket.

Mrs. Dimitriadis couldn't help but notice his interest. "'Sitaar,' that is the Arabic word written on it...the 'Veil'." She held it up for him to see. "My faithful companion whenever I perform. Isn't it beautiful?"

"Magnificent."

"We will be talking about it tomorrow, I'm sure."

Oran glanced at Beril.

"You are coming to Madame Aslanoglu's, aren't you?" said Mrs. Dimitriadis.

Beril looked surprised, but kept silent.

"It depends," said Oran.

"But you're a Crossmoor, and I may never see you again. You must come. Of course, if it won't tire Madame Aslanoglu to receive us."

"No," said Beril. "She is counting on it." She paused. "She'll be pleased to see you both."

"I want to offer my encouragement for her recovery. But I will try not to stay long." Mrs. Dimitriadis looked around the simply furnished room. "Can I offer you something to drink? I have fruit juice. Perhaps there's some wine, too."

"Thank you so much, but we must be returning home," said Semra Hanim.

Mr. Zirotas stepped forward. "There is a reception at the consulate. I'm sure Mr. Dimitriadis would be delighted if you joined us."

Mr. Dimitriadis pushed up his glasses. "Yes. Please. You will be most welcome."

"You are most kind," said Semra Hanim. "But it's already quite late."

* * *

Mr. Dimitriadis followed them out. "You must forgive me for not mentioning the reception at the consulate. It was very much a last minute affair."

"Think nothing of it," said Semra Hanim.

"Mostly for musicians and members of the Greek community here."

"Naturally," said Semra Hanim. "We understand."

"We'll see you tomorrow?" asked Beril.

"Of course." Mr. Dimitriadis took her hand.

"At my great-aunt's apartment. It should be easy enough to find."

"Where do you think we are, in the African jungle?" Mr. Dimitriadis said. "Of course we'll find it."

He gave Beril's hand a kiss.

Chapter 34

Leyla sat on the terrace of her apartment in a wooden armchair well-bolstered with red cushions. Despite the warmth in the air, she wore a sweater and a shawl. She could tell a good breeze was blowing by looking at the white sheets hung out to dry on top of a building across the street. They were flapping like banners at a regatta. Even though her terrace was now sheltered, one never knew when the wind might switch directions. Precautions were always essential.

She was glad to be home again, but she did feel terribly weak. She couldn't concentrate. Her mind would go white and she'd doze off. It was all she could manage to flip through the European fashion magazines Semra had collected for her. Of course she kept thinking of the approaching meeting with Alexandra Stephanides...Mrs. Dimitriadis...Christina Markova from Izmir, owner of the fourth and last of the relics and once, almost sixty years ago, possessor of all four. Leyla was eager to meet her. At the same time she felt anxious. After all those drowsy days in the hospital, how could she possibly summon the cleverness to persuade Mme Stephanides to part with her locket?

But if Mme Stephanides has no intention of selling, as Beril reported, why, then, has she agreed to come see me?

Leyla turned the page of her magazine. Bathing suits. Look at them, with all those low-cut backs and peek-a-boo windows! Fortunately her old navy blue one-piece suit still served her well. To be honest, though, she had to wonder whether her swimming days were over. She used to love swimming, but now she was frightened of slipping on the rocks or steps, of her muscles going rigid from the shock of the cold water, of being swept away or pulled down into some dark green grotto filled with sea urchins and sea weed. Perhaps it was time to leave the sea to Beril.

Inside the telephone rang. Gul stepped out to say that Beril was on the line.

"Oh!" said Leyla, looking up. "Well, bring me the phone." She wondered why Beril was calling.

When Gul finally reappeared, Leyla almost snatched the receiver out of her hands. "Beril, dear? What is it?"

"I'm going to be late," said Beril in evident distress. "Mother has had an accident and we're waiting for the doctor."

"Good Lord, what happened?"

"She was just sitting down to breakfast when her chair collapsed under her."

"Oh, my!"

"I've helped her to the couch. She thinks she has thrown something out of joint."

"Poor Semra! You must stay with her. Don't worry about me, dear. I can manage quite well. Is Oran coming, do you know?"

"He was coming separately. Oh, Aunt Leyla, I'm so sorry! I promise I'll get there as soon as I can."

"You needn't worry at all, dear. Truly." Leyla hung up. She had been counting on Beril's support during the meeting with Mme Stephanides and Oran. Even if she didn't say much, her presence would have been reassuring. But she couldn't abandon her mother. Poor Semra! Leyla imagined Semra piled on the floor amidst the wreckage of the chair. A smile came to her lips. How naughty!

"Leyla Hanim!" Gul stuck her head out of the living room.

Leyla started from her chair, catching her magazine just in time. "Don't tell me they're here!"

"Oran Bey is here."

"Oran? Is he with an old lady?"

"He's alone."

"I was so sure everyone would arrive together! Show him out here to the terrace. But keep watching from the bedroom. I don't want Madame Stephanides to catch me by surprise."

* * *

If it weren't for Beril, he wouldn't be here tempting fate, Oran thought. Somehow Beril and Leyla had put him on a leash. He went to Greece for them. He shared all his great clues with them. And now he had agreed to still one more meeting. Where was his freedom?

He rang the doorbell to Leyla Hanim's apartment.

Leyla Hanim now had two lockets, including 'Tears', Beril had told him. He had one, Ibrahim's 'Qur'an'. Leyla Hanim would put pressure on him to return it. And if Mrs. Dimitriadis sold hers to Leyla Hanim, what would he have for GF?

The truth was he'd become attached to these women, to Beril. In New York he had played the field. But Beril...so many things about her he liked. He wanted to know her better. Was he risking disappointment? When he first arrived in Turkey, he would have said 'Yes' and backed off. He didn't think of risks anymore. It was a need.

The maid opened the door and let him in.

"Hi, Gul," he said.

She nodded back.

And there was the umbrella rack!

"I wonder if rain is predicted?" Oran said. "In this place, squalls can come up just like that."

He felt Gul watching him as he reached over and pulled out a waxed paper parasol.

"From Japan," she said.

Oran opened it and then quickly closed it with two smooth gestures. "Works pretty well, doesn't it?" He winked at Gul.

She smiled back as she opened the door into the living room.

Whatever might happen, Oran thought, I'm prepared. He headed out to the terrace.

"I'm delighted you have come," said Leyla when she saw him. "I wonder...could it have been the view?"

Oran smiled. "How could I turn down a chance to see all this?"

"So that's it!" Leyla laughed. "I am pleased you're here. Do sit down. Madame Stephanides should arrive at any moment."

"And Beril, too?"

"Later on, I'm afraid." She explained what had happened to Semra Hanım. "I'm sure she'll be fine. She's been startled, that's all. Could I offer you some tea?"

"I'll wait, thanks. I've just had breakfast."

"A rather late breakfast, wasn't it?"

"I get up late when I can."

She leaned over to arrange the magazines on the table next to her. "Have you brought Ibrahim Bey's locket with you?" she asked.

Oran was surprised. He didn't expect her to bring up the subject so quickly.

"I would love to see it," Leyla said.

"Let's wait for Beril."

"If that's your wish, why not?"

Oran had other things to find out. "Beril told me you were once engaged to my great-uncle Edward."

"It's true," said Leyla. "I was."

"Did you know he owned the necklace of lockets?"

"I had no idea."

"What kind of man was he?"

"Edward? What can I say? He was charming, he carried himself well."

"Was he a dreamy person? My grandfather, his brother, gets lost in his memories."

"Not at all. Edward lived in the present. He was a businessman. I wish I could tell you he was someone of vision and ambition, but he wasn't. What he really valued was his early evening stroll along the waterfront and a whiskey at his club. He could be crafty. He wasn't always scrupulously honest. I know it...I worked in his firm. But I wasn't bothered. That's how people are. With me I felt he was honest. That is what matters, isn't it, how you deal with your family."

"If you almost married Edward," said Oran, "then we are almost family."

"Almost," said Leyla, smiling. "Almost, but not quite. Years ago, when your mother came back to Istanbul with her married name of Crossmoor, I wondered. In casual conversation I learned she had married into Edward's family. But I couldn't ask too many questions. My husband Tevfik knew nothing. What would he think?"

"And thanks to my Turkish mother," said Oran, "Crossmoor and Turkey have been united." He was strangely moved by the thought.

Leyla laughed softly, shaking her head. "It was fated."

Gul came out onto the terrace. "They're just getting out of a taxi!"

"Don't shout, Gul! I'm not deaf."

"An old woman and a middle-aged man."

"That must be them," Leyla said as she got up from her chair and looked around for that cane she had just started using. "My hair, Gul, is it all right? And the cake! Is the cake ready?"

* * *

Mrs. Dimitriadis leaned on her son's arm as they went up the few steps leading into the building. Normally she didn't mind steps, as long as there weren't too many, but this morning she felt tired. It was the concert, and perhaps the thought of the airplane trip this afternoon.

She wondered why she had consented to come to this meeting. Her son thought it was crazy. Maybe he was right. She didn't want to give up her locket. She didn't want questions asked. And with social calls to make, he couldn't even stay with her to back her up.

She smiled, shaking her head almost imperceptibly. Of course she knew why she had come.

When a maid opened the door to the apartment, Mrs. Dimitriadis and her son stepped into a small foyer in which stood an umbrella rack filled with umbrellas.

"Look, Ianni!" said Mrs. Dimitriadis. "Look at all those umbrellas. She is a collector, just like your father. We must be wary, don't you think?"

The maid showed them into the living room, where Leyla Hanim was seated in a large armchair, with Oran Crossmoor standing to one side.

"Madame Stephanides! How nice of you to come. I am Leyla Aslanoglu." She was speaking in English. "I believe you know Oran Crossmoor?"

"Yes, indeed." Mrs. Dimitriadis came over and shook hands. The size of her hand and the strength of her grip surprised Leyla. "May I present my son, Ianni?"

"It's so kind of you to come," Leyla said once again as she looked into her adversary's eyes. "Please sit down. I hope you won't mind if we sit indoors? It's rather breezy on the terrace."

"Not at all. This is perfect." Mrs. Dimitriadis took a seat in an armchair near Leyla, then looked up at her son. "Are you sure you won't stay, Ianni?"

"An old school friend lives nearby," Ianni explained to Leyla, "and this is our only chance to meet. So if you will excuse me..."

"I understand," said Leyla. "Friendships must be cultivated, like plants in a garden. Otherwise they wither and die."

Ianni smiled. He kissed Leyla's hand and promised to return in an hour or two.

Leyla motioned to Oran to sit, then turned back toward her guest. "I hear the concert was a great success. I do wish I could have attended. I have admired your playing for years."

"I was pleased with the concert," said Mrs. Dimitriadis,

"especially since the radio recorded it for broadcast. But I must confess I was apprehensive. Not from the program I had scheduled, and not from stage fright, for I don't normally suffer from stage fright. I was apprehensive because I was in Istanbul. I grew up in Smyrna...in Izmir, I suppose I should say. In 1922, I escaped to Greece. In all these years I have never returned."

"Istanbul has changed so much."

"I can barely recognize it. When I left, Istanbul was still ruled by sultans."

Leyla Hanim smiled. "Ancient history!"

Gul brought in a tray with a tea service, and plates of hazelnut cookies, savory biscuits, and slices of the cake she had baked. Leyla served everyone.

"How lovely!" said Mrs. Dimitriadis

"Gul makes wonderful cakes."

"Oh, a caramel cake!" Mrs. Dimitriadis had taken a small bite, trying not to provoke a cascade of crumbs.

"A Russian cook we knew used to make this," Leyla said.

"My own father was Russian."

"But he left Russia?"

"Long before the revolution. He was unusual. He liked to wander, and he hated snow and ice."

Leyla laughed. "Well, the summers in Izmir at least are very hot!"

"You know Izmir, do you?"

"I lived there just after the First World War. My parents had died. I went to Izmir to stay with cousins."

"We were there at the same time. Perhaps we crossed each other on the street. Have you been back?"

"Not often."

"I couldn't possibly return."

"Almost nothing remains of the city we knew," said Leyla. "You would have to forget your memories and judge it afresh."

"How could I? My memories are too strong."

"I can well imagine. To see your beloved city on fire, then to make a dangerous escape to Greece..."

"I lost everything, absolutely everything. Only when I reached Athens and met my husband did I begin my slow return to life. But you already know that, it seems."

Leyla shifted in her seat and exchanged glances with Oran. "Perhaps we should have more tea. Will you take another cup?"

"Please. Do you mind if I smoke?"

"Not at all."

After serving tea and slices of cake, Leyla sat back in her chair again. "Now, tell me. You own a beautiful antique locket. As you must know..."

"I wore it at the concert," Mrs. Dimitriadis said. "I wear it each time I play. It is indeed beautiful."

"As you may know, I have a great interest in this locket."

Mrs. Dimitriadis leaned forward to take a sip of tea. "I gave it to my husband."

"It's a family heirloom," Leyla continued.

"He saved me. He took me in when I had nothing. I owed him so much."

"My ancestors owned this locket," Leyla said.

"It was stolen from him, then recovered, miraculously, from Bulgaria. We are still the rightful owners."

"Might you consent to sell it to us?" Leyla said.

Oran sat still, waiting, like Leyla Hanim, for the answer.

Mrs. Dimitriadis laughed. She took a puff on her cigarette and flicked the ashes into the ashtray.

"You must know your locket is one of a set of four, a necklace of four lockets and a gold star," Leyla said. "You must know we have recovered three, that yours is the only missing one. The necklace was the pride, the soul of my family." She felt her voice rising. "Can't you understand how much I want to complete the necklace?"

"Please!" Mrs. Dimitriadis said. "You look so tragic, I can't stand it." She reached over with a patting gesture. "Of course I understand." Her bracelets clinked and tinkled. "You must believe me, I have no wish to upset you. I wanted to come wish you well after your dreadful experience."

"I appreciate your kindness," replied Leyla. "But we have never met. I'm a stranger. Why should my recovery matter to you?"

Mrs. Dimitriadis set her teacup down on the table, peered at Leyla, and gave a little smile. "It is true, Madame Aslanoglu, that my motives in coming were not altogether selfless. I admit it. I was curious to meet you, to find out what you are like. You know much about me. It is only fair that I learn about you."

"But I know so little of your life, really."

"You have uncovered my past, haven't you? How I escaped from Smyrna with the necklace? The key event of my life! What else is there to know about me?" She took a last puff on her cigarette and crushed it out in the ashtray. "Surely you have understood the importance the locket has for me and why I can never give it up."

"Yes, I can appreciate your reasons. And who am I to insist that the emotional claim of my family is stronger than yours?" Leyla sipped at her tea, then continued. "At the very least, though, I would like to learn how you obtained the necklace. So, I'm sure, would Oran."

Mrs. Dimitriadis looked at Oran. "Indeed." She smiled at him. "You have been so quiet, not like you were in Athens. Where are all your questions?"

"I only had one," Oran said. "Leyla Hanim is asking it."

Mrs. Dimitriadis turned away from him, gave a little laugh, and opened her purse to get another cigarette.

"So if you would tell us, please," said Leyla. "We know how you dispersed the lockets: one to Enver, the restaurant owner; a second to Murat, the produce distributor in Kusadasi; a third to the boatman Yorgo, from Samos. But we have not learned how you got the necklace."

"From a dealer in Izmir," Mrs. Dimitriadis said.

"What was his name?" asked Leyla.

"Well... He was an Armenian."

"I see," said Leyla. "Had you owned the necklace a long time before you fled?"

"Several years."

"You must have been very young when you bought it. Or did your parents give it to you?"

"An uncle. My mother's brother."

"For a particular occasion?"

"To celebrate the end of the war. No...somewhat later, I think...when the Greek troops marched into Smyrna."

"March, 1919?"

"Yes."

Oran glanced at Leyla Hanım. This wasn't quite what Mr. Dimitriadis had said.

Leyla didn't notice. "You owned it for over three years," she said. "It must have been quite a blow to give it up."

"But the lockets bought me freedom. Under the circumstances, I cannot regret their loss."

Leyla tilted her head and looked away. "Every war has two faces, doesn't it?" she mused. "The capture of Izmir was a great victory for some, but for others, an overwhelming disaster." She turned back toward her guest and smiled. "Some more tea, Madame Stephanides?"

"No, thank you."

"I myself was not in Izmir when the Turkish troops marched in. I had to learn what happened from far away, from Ankara. But I almost was there..."

"Did you leave much before the fall of the city?"

"Just before the final Turkish offensive began." Leyla felt a chill up her back. She pulled at the edges of her shawl. "The company for which I worked sensed a Turkish victory. I went to

Ankara to make contacts."

"Did you cross the military lines? It must have been tremendously perilous."

"I could easily have been killed. But when you are young, and in love..."

"In love, Madame Aslanoglu?"

"I did it to demonstrate my courage to the man I loved. To my fiancé."

"Surely no Turkish gentleman would expose his fiancé to such risks! Not even in the time of war."

"My fiancé was not a Turk, Madame Stephanides. He was English."

Mrs. Dimitriadis stared at Leyla. "I beg your pardon?"

"I worked as a secretary for an English import-export firm in Izmir."

"Which firm?"

"Crossmoor and Tipton."

"It's not possible!"

"Madame Stephanides, are you not feeling well?"

"And now you'll tell me your fiancé was..."

"The owner of the business. Edward Crossmoor."

"Oh, my God." Mrs. Dimitriadis went pale. Leyla thought she was having a seizure. Alarmed, Leyla turned to Oran. But before they could get over to her, Mrs. Dimitriadis rose up in her chair and stared at Leyla.

"The poem was so childish," she said. Her voice was loud and harsh. "'Merry like swallows...'"

Leyla had no idea what was happening.

"'...in the cool zephyrs of a summer evening.' Don't you recognize the line?"

Leyla felt a sudden shock.

"'We shall live forever in love and happiness.'"

"I wrote that!"

"You sent the letter from Ankara."

"How did you know?" Leyla's heart was pounding. "How can you have seen that letter?"

Mrs. Dimitriadis spoke quickly. "The Turks had reached the city. Fire was breaking out all around us. My parents had disappeared. My whole family was gone. I couldn't stay at home. I had to flee. Edward, I thought. Edward will save me." Her voice rose. "Yes! Edward Crossmoor! The one you call your fiancé!"

"Madame Stephanides! What are you saying?"

"I was the one he loved! He was going to marry me. Believe me, I know he was!"

"Are you mad? It's impossible."

"It's true. I assure you, it's absolutely true."

"But he always told me everything," Leyla said.

"Did he now?" Mrs. Dimitriadis gave a little mocking laugh. "He was a liar." She stood up and walked over to the door that led out to the terrace. "He lied to me, and I see he lied to you."

"No!" cried Leyla. "Surely not."

"I knew that some great power was drawing me to Istanbul, to meet you, to talk with you, but I had no idea who you really were." Gripping the tall back of an armchair, she turned and looked at Leyla. "Now I understand why I'm here."

She sat down in the armchair by the terrace door, some distance from Leyla and Oran. "I'm going to tell you everything that happened on that terrible day."

Leyla watched, transfixed, her face like stone.

"I ran to Edward's house," Mrs. Dimitriadis said. "I had some worthless money, a piece of stale bread, and my pistol. That's all. I went inside, but he wasn't there. I wanted to scream and scream. What in God's name was I to do? I went into his study. The windows were closed. It was stuffy, but I dared not open the windows. I heard gunshots outside, and shouting. I was going crazy, I was so frightened. Where was he? I started to pace the room like a lunatic, back and forth, back and forth. Then I saw your letter among the papers strewn about on his desk. I pulled it out and read it. I must have cried out. For days I had been suspecting a rival, but I had no proof. Now on this horrible day I found your letter. The rival was real." She looked up at Leyla. "You."

Leyla stared, shaking her head in disbelief. "I had no idea," she said.

Mrs. Dimitriadis went on. "Job himself could not have suffered such agony. And then Edward walked in.

"'Kiki, darling!' he said.

"I screamed. I waved the letter in his face. 'You weren't going to save me,' I said. 'You wanted to throw me to the Turks. And take her!'

"He turned bright red. 'No,' he said.

"I called him a liar, a shameless liar. I cursed him! He just stood there like a statue. Why didn't he say anything? Why didn't he do something? This man had promised me marriage! I couldn't stand it. I reached into my handbag and took out my pistol."

"No!" cried Leyla. "No!"

Mrs. Dimitriadis gave her a savage look. "I pulled the trigger. Yes! I shot him."

"Edward!" Tears welled up in Leyla's eyes. "Edward."

No one spoke. Oran felt his throat go dry. He stared at the old woman across the room, but from his angle the bright sunlight directly behind her obscured her expression.

Outside, the cry of a yogurt seller filled the air.

"He fell to the floor," Mrs. Dimitriadis said. "I backed up. I must have knocked something over. I heard the sound of breaking glass. His shirt was stained with blood. What had I done? That wasn't what I'd wanted to do! I wanted him to confess! I wanted him to tell me he loved only me and to take me away." She lowered her head, then began to sob. "That's all. That's all I wanted. How could I have done it? I loved him. I didn't mean to kill him."

She opened her purse and pulled out a handkerchief. "I heard a big explosion. The house shook. It happened so close by, maybe next door or across the street. I panicked. I had to get away. But where would I go? Who would save me now? Perhaps Enver, the owner of the restaurant Edward often took me to. He had a soft spot for me. Enver would help me, especially if I could pay. But I had so little money. Edward was going to take care of that. I had put all my trust in him.

"I slipped my pistol back into my purse and turned to go, and there was the potted palm. I remembered the day Edward showed me his necklace of golden lockets. He'd kept it hidden in the flowerpot with the potted palm. The palm was in the same place it had been that day. I pushed over the pot and pulled out the plant. The crumbling soil made such a mess on the carpet. But the necklace was there. I put it in my purse. I turned to look at Edward. His eyes were wide open, his mouth, too. He was cursing me.

"His jacket was hanging on the coat rack and I covered him with it. I saw his tobacco pouch sticking out of his pocket. I took a handful of tobacco and sprinkled it over him. I don't know why. Like earth for a burial. And then..." Her voice dropped almost to a whisper. "And then I ran off."

Leyla was gazing down at her old hands folded on her lap. "The fire that swept through the foreign quarter burnt down the house, with Edward inside," she said. "But he was already dead. Shot to death. Murdered." She looked at Mrs. Dimitriadis. She felt an immense rage explode inside her. "How dare you come here to my house?" she cried. "You murderer! Thief, liar! What right have you to the locket? To any of them?"

Mrs. Dimitriadis bowed her head. "None," she said, at last. "None at all." She spoke as plainly, as bluntly as a judge at the end of a trial. "The heirs of Edward Crossmoor are the rightful owners. There is no question. Neither of Edward's poor fiancées has a right. Neither you, nor I." She opened her purse and removed the fourth and final locket. "Here, Oran Crossmoor. The 'Veil' is yours, just as I wore it last night, still attached to the ribbon of black velvet. May you and your family be blessed." She kissed it and handed it to Oran. She bit her lip to keep from crying, but when she saw the locket in Oran's palm, she began to sob.

Leyla hardly knew what to say. This horrible tragedy...so much sorrow. and yet all four lockets had come back. Do these lockets actually bring bad luck rather than good fortune? she wondered. Or do they simply bring our imperfect human nature into focus?

"I know this has caused you much pain," Leyla said when Mrs. Dimitriadis had composed herself.

"I have never confessed this to anyone," said Mrs. Dimitriadis. "I have lived a lifetime of lies."

"The anonymous letter my grandfather received," Oran said. "You wrote it, didn't you?"

"I thought I was out of my mind," she said, "but I had to take a step. Somehow I knew I would be here today, to ask your forgiveness. Please, Madame Aslanoglu. Can you forgive me?"

"It is for God to forgive, not me," Leyla said.

"Did you love him, Madame Aslanoglu?"

"It happened so long ago. I think so. But I married someone else."

"I did, too. But it wasn't the same, was it?"

"My husband was a wonderful man."

"You were lucky. But I had my career. That was my life. Now that, too, has ended."

"What do you mean?" said Leyla.

"You played beautifully," Oran said.

"How can I play without my locket? No, don't look distressed. I knew I would retire. I just didn't know when, or how."

Mrs. Dimitriadis was looking at her so sadly, with such

anguish. "In Smyrna so long ago," Leyla said, "in your place, I might well have done as you did, if, all in one day, I lost my family, my city, and my love."

"You are a saint."

"What an odd thing to say!" Leyla said.

"It is, isn't it?"

The gilt clock on the buffet chimed the hour.

"Ah!" The chimes made Mrs. Dimitriadis jump. "What time is it? Can it be noon already?" She checked her watch. "Have I been here this long? Where is my son? He should have come by now. My daughter-and-law and her relatives are expecting us for lunch." She reached for her purse. "Now, what did I do with my sunglasses?"

The doorbell rang.

"There he is." Mrs. Dimitriadis stood up.

But it wasn't Ianni Dimitriadis.

"Beril!" cried Leyla, throwing open her arms. "I had forgotten all about you."

Mrs. Dimitriadis stepped forward. She had put on a scarf and dark glasses. "Ah, your niece. How nice you look, dear. But I must be off. Can I get a taxi, Madame Aslanoglu?"

"Gul will find you a taxi," said Leyla.

"I'll walk down with you," said Oran.

Mrs. Dimitriadis looked at him with surprise. Then she smiled. She turned to Leyla. "God gives us such strange destinies. Sometimes it takes an entire lifetime to accept them."

As soon as Oran and Mrs. Dimitriadis had left, Leyla gestured toward the coffee table.

"The fourth locket?" said Beril. "I don't believe it. That's wonderful!"

"The price was high," Leyla said as she sat down.

Beril looked puzzled.

"She confessed to murder," Leyla said. "She killed Edward Crossmoor. No one ever knew."

"What? What do you mean?"

"She took the lockets from Edward's house and made her escape. The house burned down in the big fire. I always thought Edward had been trapped inside, burned to death, but now I know he had no chance to flee. But that's not all, Beril." Leyla clasped her hands together. "She was engaged to marry him, just as I was. At least we each thought we were. On the day the Turkish army entered Izmir, when her world was falling apart, she discovered she had a rival – me. She shot Edward. She killed him."

Beril threw her arms around her great-aunt. "Oh, Aunt Leyla, I'm so sorry."

"I was furious when she confessed. I was outraged that she should tell us. What right had she to inflict such sordid details on us? What was the murderer of my fiancé doing in my house? But Edward deceived us both, not only her, but me. And I had no idea."

"That's no excuse for murder," said Beril.

"What seemed straightforward – my view of Edward and his death – is no longer so simple," Leyla said. "It's not so easy to judge...to condemn. Sixty years ago, and it seems like yesterday."

"Aren't you going to call the police?"

"We've had the trial," Leyla said. "She declared her guilt. By confessing to us, and by giving Oran, Edward's descendant, the last of the lockets, she has surely atoned for her crime."

"The locket is Oran's, then?"

"I suppose so."

Beril reached out and touched her aunt's hand. "You will ask him for it, won't you?"

"We'll see. First, I'm going to take a long nap. Help me up, dear." She reached for her cane and then gave Beril a kiss. "Now...where's Gul?" She walked away from the coffee table, leaving the locket lying there.

The door opened.

"Oran!" said Beril.

Oran stopped. He looked from Beril to Leyla and back again. "What's wrong? You look so serious. We've got all four lockets."

"Not we," said Leyla. "You."

"Aunt Leyla is exhausted," said Beril.

"Did Madame Stephanides get off?" Leyla asked.

"The taxi was waiting," Oran said. "She sends you her deepest respects."

"That was kind of her," Leyla said. "I'd like to talk to you later, Oran. And I'll want to write your grandfather. Frederick Crossmoor and I...it's high time we met, even if now we can do so only by letter. But first I must rest." She smiled. "I never did tell you my favorite street corners in Istanbul, did I? I shall, I promise." She made her way slowly out of the room, heading for the rear of the apartment.

Beril looked at Oran. "You shouldn't just leave the locket sitting there, should you?"

Oran smiled. "I don't suppose I should." He went over and picked it up.

"What are you going to do with your lockets?" asked Beril.

"It depends," said Oran.

"On what?"

"I've been thinking... Why don't we go outside?" He put an arm around Beril's waist and guided her out onto the balcony.

From the terrace they could hear a tambourine. Beril stepped forward and leaned over the railing.

"Look, a dancing bear! And look at the little boy!"

Down in the alley below, a brown bear with a loose shaggy coat, wearing a muzzle, held on a leash by a gypsy, stood on its hind legs and moved around in crude dance motions while a second man sang and played the tambourine. A little boy in a scuffed shirt and patched trousers was wiggling back and forth, imitating the bear. A group of children had gathered around and were laughing and clapping.

"How did you persuade Mrs. Dimitriadis to give up the locket?" asked Beril.

"She persuaded herself."

"What will she wear at concerts?"

"She said she won't play anymore."

"That's a shame."

"She asked me, just as she was getting into the taxi, if I thought she would now find peace."

"What did you say?"

"'I'm sure you will.'"

The gypsy stopped singing and the bear dropped down on all fours. The boy bowed low and, like the men, looked up at the balconies and held out his hand.

"Do you have something to give them?" Beril said.

Oran threw down a coin. The gypsies waved back and smiled. When they had collected what they could, they gave the boy a pat and strolled on with the bear ambling behind. The boy started to follow, but his mother stepped out and gave him a scolding.

"Poor little boy," said Beril. "His adventures are over."

"Come on, let's go to lunch," said Oran.

Beril put her hands on her hips. "I'm not coming until I find out your plans."

"So you can start a new campaign to get the lockets?" Oran laughed. "You're a devil. But here's what I'm going to do. I'm going to stay on in Istanbul, make peace with a certain older woman, and chase after a certain younger woman. What do you think of that?"

Beril was smiling now. "And the lockets?"

"Happiness has its price. Even my grandfather would agree." Oran took her hand and brought it to his lips. "As for myself, I think I'm ready to pay."

**TOP HAT
BOOKS**

Historical fiction that lives.

We publish fiction that captures the contrasts, the achievements, the optimism and the radicalism of ordinary and extraordinary times across the world.

We're open to all time periods and we strive to go beyond the narrow, foggy slums of Victorian London. Where are the tales of the people of fifteenth century Australasia? The stories of eighth century India? The voices from Africa, Arabia, cities and forests, deserts and towns? Our books thrill, excite, delight and inspire.

The genres will be broad but clear. Whether we're publishing romance, thrillers, crime, or something else entirely, the unifying themes are timescale and enthusiasm. These books will be a celebration of the chaotic power of the human spirit in difficult times. The reader, when they finish, will snap the book closed with a satisfied smile.